BEST BRITISH HORROR 2015

JOHNNY MAINS is a British Fantasy Award winning editor. His critically acclaimed anthologies include *Back From The Dead: The Legacy of the Pan Book of Horror Stories*, *Bite-Size Horror*, *The Screaming Book of Horror*, *The Burning Circus*, *Best British Horror 2014* and *Dead Funny* (co-edited with Robin Ince).

Also by Johnny Mains

BEST BRITISH
HORROR 2015

SERIES EDITED BY
Johnny Mains

SALT

CROMER

PUBLISHED BY SALT

12 Norwich Road, Cromer, Norfolk NR27 0AX United Kingdom

Introduction and selection © Johnny Mains, 2015

The right of Johnny Mains to be identified as the editor of
this work has been asserted by him in accordance with Section
77 of the Copyright, Designs and Patents Act 1988.

Printed in Great Britain by Clays Ltd, St Ives plc

Typeset in Sabon 10/13

ISBN 978 1 78463 028 7 paperback

1 3 5 7 9 8 6 4 2

CONTENTS

CREDITS

'Quarry Hogs' by Jane Jakeman was originally published in *Supernatural Tales 27*

'Random Flight' by Rosalie Parker was originally published in *Terror Tales of Yorkshire*

'Shaddertown' by Conrad Williams was originally published in *Shadows and Tall Trees #6*

'Learning the Language' by John Llewellyn Probert was originally published in *Terror Tales of Wales*

'A Spider Remember' by Sara Pascoe was originally published in *Dead Funny: Horror Stories by Comedians*

'Eastmouth' by Alison Moore was originally published in *The Spectral Book of Horror Stories*

'Reunion' by Rebecca Lloyd was originally published in *Mercy and Other Stories*

'The Third Time' by Helen Grant was originally published in *The Ghost and Scholars Book of Shadows #2*

'Drowning in Air' by Andrew Hook was originally published in *Strange Tales IV*

'Alistair' by Mark Samuels was originally published in *Written In Darkness*

'In The Year of Omens' by Helen Marshall was originally published in *Fearful Symmetries*

'Apple Pie and Sulphur' by Christopher Harman was originally published in *Shadows and Tall Trees# 6*

'On Ilkley Moor' by Alison Littlewood was originally published in *Terror Tales of Yorkshire*

'The Broken and the Unmade' by Steven J. Dines was originally published in *Black Static* #39

'Only Bleeding' by Gary McMahon was originally published in *Horror Uncut*

'The Night Porter' by R.B. Russell was originally published in *Shadows and Tall Trees* #6

'Something Sinister in Sunlight' by Lisa Tuttle was originally published in *The Spectral Book of Horror Stories*

'Private Ambulance' by Simon Kurt Unsworth was originally published in *Noir*

'The Rising Tide' by Priya Sharma was originally published in *Terror Tales of Yorkshire*

'The Slista' by Stephen Laws was originally published in *The Spectral Book of Horror Stories*

'Dog' by Reece Shearsmith was originally published in *Dead Funny: Horror Stories by Comedians*

'Under the Pylon' by Graham Joyce was originally published in *Darklands* 2 (1992) and has been reprinted with kind permission from The Estate of Graham Joyce.

JOHNNY MAINS

INTRODUCTION

I WOULD LIKE TO begin by thanking everyone who bought and supported the debut volume of *Best British Horror*. On release it remained at the #1 position in the Amazon Kindle charts (horror anthologies section) for well over two months and was also #1 in the print charts (same category) as well. I'm also extremely flattered with the response it's received from reviewers, bloggers and *you*, the fans. It makes all the hard work involved putting one of these books together well worth it and shows that British horror is *Alive, Alive!* To see the book on the shelves of Waterstones and other booksellers is yet another triumph for the genre.

So, now onto this volume, the 'difficult second album' so to speak.

The selection of tales for this year's volume have again taken me by surprise, and I've chosen stories which I think build on the foundations set in the first book. Again, I've 'discovered' authors such as Sara Pascoe, Jane Jakeman, Priya Sharma, Helen Grant, Reece Shearsmith and Christopher Harman and I cannot wait to read more of their work. I've also chosen a story by the up-and-coming Steven J Dines. His work is very special indeed and I hope you think so too.

There is also a strong showing from authors who are established within the field and it is an honour to showcase the very best work from Conrad Williams, Helen Marshall, Alison Moore and Lisa Tuttle.

Before I close, 2014 saw more devastating blows to the genre with the death of the much-loved Graham Joyce, and the editor, and my friend Michel Parry. Even though their impressive legacies will satisfy generations to come, I'd rather they were both still here. This book is dedicated to them both.

March 2015

BEST BRITISH HORROR 2015

JANE JAKEMAN

QUARRY HOGS

I SEE THE BALLATCHEY *family in my mind's eye, like small puppets hanging from the frame of time. Here are moments from that puppet-show.*

"Joseph," said Catherine, with that way she had of tipping her pale face to one side when she wanted to say something serious, "Joseph, I think we should buy the house at Fremington."

Joseph Ballatchey stared at his wife across the breakfast table. Perhaps he should give her some consideration, he thought. She did look very white, and was hunched forward over the expanse of mahogany. After each baby she seemed to stoop more and more.

So he did not, as he might have done, tell her that her opinion was of little concern to him, saying instead to their ten-year old son, who sat between them, "Sit up straight, boy!"

Tom Ballatchey stopped wriggling and sat as still as if he were scarcely breathing.

"It's the air, Joseph," she said. "Up there, on the hillside, it's so much purer. Here in the town, in the street, there are all the runnels and drains and the . . . well, the . . . effluvia. Doctor Anderson says that might have been the cause."

She looked at her husband's unresponsive face. Catherine was possessed of a certain determination. She was not as weak-willed as might have been thought from her frail appearance.

"So if we were to move, and as you mentioned the house might go for a good price, I thought . . ."

Joseph Ballatchey looked at his wife and only child. Only surviving child. Two others lay buried in the crowded city churchyard two streets away, each pink and howling bundle having waved its fists about for a few months, then slackened and faded till at last the tiny coffin was born out to its resting-place.

Perhaps she was right. The town was low-lying, the air damp and marshy. Besides, old Lockyard's house at Fremington could indeed be got cheap, and maybe Catherine could breed healthily there.

He looked at his son with some contempt, seeing the nervous small face. Yes, he should have other heirs: the Fremington house would be a kind of investment in family, as it were.

"I'll consider it," he said. "You can get down, boy," and Tom almost knocked over his chair in his anxiety to get away.

It was not difficult to secure the new house. In fact, Joseph Ballatchey was owed such an amount by the young Mr. Lockyard as the former man knew could never be repaid. The Ballatcheys owned a goldsmith's business which had been started by Joseph's parents, and their shop not only sold small tempting articles of gold and silver but could supply much larger orders to the gentry; desirable items such as walnut canteens of chased knives and forks, Turkish carpets, sets of fine bone china. When young Lockyard had inherited the manor belonging to his grandfather he had run up bill after bill, and the young man was positively grateful for Ballatchey's modest offer. He was willing to throw in many of the contents, such as the oriental rugs and the French lacquer tables which the shopkeeper had supplied in the first place.

Ballatchey and his man of business looked through the deeds in the room at the back of the shop. The manor of Fremington lay half way up the hill just outside the town, next to a small church and came with a wide spread of land, which Ballatchey traced out on the map sewn into the documents.

Here is the moment, a crucial scene, perhaps, when Joseph stretched across the table, following the blue-marked land boundaries with the extended forefinger of his delicate goldsmith's hand.

"It's a good estate", said the solicitor, as if he sensed some enquiry hovering in Ballatchey's mind. "A gentleman's estate. The living of the church is in your gift, of course. The one drawback might be the stone quarry."
Ballatchey looked at him across the map and the solicitor added, "No, it's not marked there. The quarry's not on the manor land, and it's on the other side of the hill, not likely to trouble you at all. You won't even see it. It's just a trifle –"
"A trifle what?"
"Oh, er, noisy and so forth. But that won't disturb the manor – not at all." The man added quickly, seeing his fee might drop out, "He's willing to settle very low."
So they removed to Fremington, Catherine Ballatchey commenting even as the carriage loaded with all their boxes and baggage toiled up the hillside between banks of yellow gorse, "Oh, Joseph, can you not smell the breeze? We shall do so well up here, will we not, Tom?"
"I expect so, mother," said Tom. But his voice was very quiet.
Joseph made it his first concern to patrol the boundaries of his estate, which he performed on horseback, for the grounds stretched for a considerable distance. They were walled in with drystone courses which required repair here and there, Joseph making notes as he observed a collapsed section here, a fallen post there. As well as the carriage driveway which led up to the house and was closed by two splendid wrought iron gates, there were two odd gaps in the wall. They were on opposite sides of his parkland, one facing

the hillside to the north of the house, the other down the slope to the south, near the church.

Joseph was certain they had not been indicated on the plan of the estate. It would be easy enough to close them up, he thought, mentally calculating the extent of the work required. There were posts about the same distance apart and it was an odd one: about five feet, he estimated. Not wide enough for a cart or carriage, unnecessarily wide for a horse or a man on foot. Peering uphill out of the northern gap, he thought he could trace a faint track in the ground, nearly swallowed up in the grass, leading across towards that inexplicable break in the wall on the other side, as if there were some sort of path between the two gaps.

He made a note in his pocketbook, but when he rode on other details intervened and he forgot to order the necessary work to be carried out.

A few days after they had settled in, and Catherine had arranged the little gilt chairs and tables to her liking and Joseph had ensured that his tantalus was locked, there arose the important question of church. It was decided that they would worship conveniently in the small church close to the Manor, where a curate came on Sundays to cater for the few persons in the hillside district. For special occasions such as Easter and Christmas the family would attend their previous place of worship.

On their first attendance, they remarked how convenient it was to have the place so close at hand. Henderson, the curate, a raw young man with a pimply neck chafed by his collar, seemed quite aware of their status in the locality.

The only thing that marred this placid experience was the presence at the back of the church of a small crowd, all standing, for there were only a few pews, the chief of which was occupied by the Ballatcheys themselves. These persons at the back were roughly dressed, as the Ballatcheys noticed when they discreetly turned around, distracted by the cries of small children and chattering of adults emanating from the group. The men particularly looked incongruous as they stood through the hymns, their trousers tied below their knees with string, their faces exhibiting a curious roughened pallor. *As if they had lived all their lives in a flour-bag,* thought young Tom. The children were barefoot.

Afterwards as the Ballatcheys left, the young clergyman stood at the door to greet them. "Who were those people?" asked Joseph, indicating the small gaggle making their way out of the church-yard along a narrow path between uneven tombstones. The first of them, a tall man with a red cravat and a loose checked shirt, had shouldered past the Ballatcheys and merely nodded to them, a half-courtesy which Joseph found almost more troubling than a direct insult, which would at least have enabled its recipient to take some action. As it was, Joseph felt his anger frustrated.

"Ah, I beg you sir, take no notice," said the curate, evidently observing Joseph's frown. "That was Truscott from the quarry and the quarry-workers know no better. But they need not bother you. They live at the quarry and have no church there, so they come here. It is the nearest place of worship for them. We must be grate-ful that some of them attend at all."

"I suppose we must allow it," said Catherine later. "Did you notice the awful trousers that young curate was wearing – almost threadbare!"

"It must be a very poor living," said Joseph.

Joseph rode over the hill soon after that. He wanted to see this quarry for himself. Most of the buildings in the town had been con-structed out of the local silvery-grey local stone, said to be hard-wearing and good building, but he had never seen the place from whence it was hewed, nor thought about the operations involved, so different was his own trade from this rough and ready handling of stubborn masses of rock. It was also his intention to get some notion of whether the gaps in the walls around his grounds could be repaired by stone and workmen from the quarry, which would be an economic procedure.

As he came over the brow of the hill he identified the place by the cloud of dust hanging over it before he even saw the great white scar made in the green hillside, the earth taken out as if by a giant scoop. As he got nearer he saw irregular curves and holes, uneven in places, some grey and others grown over like bites taken out of the ground over the centuries. The place, he supposed, had been worked for several hundred years. These sights he could identify and place within his idea of an old quarry, but he was taken by surprise at the shacks – one could not call them houses, though they were mostly built out of untidy heaps of stone with odd planks here and there – that had arisen in some of the older scoops. When he was closer he could see paths and tracks leading among these pits, in a higgledy-piggledy sort of way, as if made by feet trudging along them over the years in all the directions that would lead them most quickly to their goals – to other hovels and to clean rock-faces where men were toiling away, the tapping of their picks echoing sharp and harsh within the bowl of the quarry. He had not realised this: that these people would not only work in the quarry but live here within it, in the pits made by quarrying, like animals burrowing into forms and lairs. But it made sense to live next to their work, he supposed, to have their own hewed-out hamlet, as it were.

Here in the story of the Ballatcheys, with Joseph at the edge of the quarry, is another of those points that seem to reverberate into the future, as if time stood still, itself recognising the significance of what was taking place, though at that moment those puppets, the actual participants, have no particular understanding of the momentous results of their simple actions.

An aged woman had emerged at the opening of a hovel. One could hardly call it a doorway, for there was merely an old sack hung over it. She had a bright red skirt – quite unsuitable for an old woman, thought Joseph with disgust – and a red cape around her shoulders, with white hair straggling down over it. A small group of children were around her, some hanging on the skirt, others further inside the hut, their faces peering out of the darkness within. All seemed to be staring upwards at Joseph astride his glossy horse.

Joseph was not an imaginative man, fortunately for him, but there was something in the face of the old woman that made him shiver. It was as if he had a presentiment, not merely of malevolence but of death itself.

"She looks sick," he thought, "She cannot be long for this world."

But though he was correct in one of these particulars, he was sadly mistaken in the other.

As he gazed around the depths below him he identified Truscott, the man who had pushed past him on the previous Sunday. He looked up and observed Joseph, then detached himself from a knot of men struggling with a great block of stone on a rough timber frame and came clambering up.

Joseph gave him a curt nod.

"You're the new squire at Fremington?"

No 'Sir', Joseph noted, and boldly spoken.

"Yes, I am." Although, strictly speaking, he was not: the Lock-yards had been the hereditary lords of the manor. The awareness of his slight social inferiority made Joseph even sharper in his tone. But Truscott spoke first.

"What may we do for you? I can fetch you a pint of ale if you have a thirst on you."

That at least was some civility, but the idea of taking a drink from the hands of this dusty fellow – why, even his hair seemed stiff and white as if it were on a plaster statue – was repellent and Joseph merely shook his head. He abandoned the idea of enquiring about repairs to his walls.

Behind the man a group of children had assembled. One of them pointed a finger at the man on horseback.

"Quarry-hogs! Us quarry-hogs!" they called out and strangely it seemed to deride Joseph, not themselves. He turned Amal's head abruptly and made for home, where he instructed Tom never to walk over the brow of the hill. The shouts of *'Us quarry-*

hogs' seemed to follow him for some way but he did not turn his head.

Tom did go for walks in other directions, though, and Catherine spent some time in her garden, pruning and training the roses that had run riot since young Lockyard had taken over the house. Soon both of them began to have some colour in their cheeks. Joseph, though he had to ride down to the town on business three or four days a week, began to enjoy riding up into the fresher air of the hillside: one could definitely sense it, he decided, noticing that the smoke and fog of the town were left behind at a certain point in his journey home. There seemed to need whatsoever to worry about the people of the quarry, hidden over the other side of the hill. They came to church on Sundays and stood at the back as before, but the curate had perhaps had a word with them, for now they waited and let the Ballatcheys leave the church first. Some of the boys even made bows at the family passed them – mock bows, Joseph suspected, but there seemed no way he could object.

"I trust the quarry people are causing no problems," said the curate a few weeks after Joseph's ride to the other side of the hill. Joseph wondered if he had heard about the encounter. "No, we never see them," he answered. The curate gave a nervous laugh. "Good, good," he said. "They mean no harm, the 'quarry-hogs' as they call themselves.

"We see nothing of them outside of church," said Joseph and turned away.

Some time after this that Joseph and his father were obliged to attend a mayoral banquet where they were representing the worthy goldsmiths of the town, and Joseph hoped to make his interest known on this occasion that he might one day stand for the office of mayor. This would require lengthy discussion, and he had warned Catherine that he would be obliged to go early into the town and might not return till the following morning.

Catherine was rather fearful, the house being isolated on the hillside, and on this occasion slept with a large brass bell beside her bed with which she intended to summon the dubious assistance of Marcorn the butler if there should be any intrusion. The wind got up and seemed to howl through the hours of darkness

Though Catherine lay awake for most of the slowly passing hours, she felt better when a fine morning dawned, and went down to the dining-room where Marcorn was standing near the side-board. The room had long windows which gave onto the park and the pearly light poured in as if the storm of the previous night had cleared the air.

However, she was not pleased by what she found, or rather failed to find, in the dining-room.

"Breakfast not laid out, Marcorn?" she asked sharply, for the usual silver dishes of boiled and poached eggs, toast and sliced meats, were not laid out ready on the sideboard.

"Madam, I thought you might prefer to have breakfast today in the morning-room," said the old man. He seemed to be staring out of the window as he spoke and Catherine was further annoyed at his inattention.

`Just because Mr. Ballatchey is not here?" she said. "Master Thomas and I expect to breakfast in the dining-room as normal. Bring the dishes in to us here." And she sat down in her usual place at the long mahogany table, gazing out across the grounds.

I am puzzled by Catherine Ballatchey. I picture her sitting stiff-backed in her chair, waiting to be served, confidently expecting the empty stretch on the table before her to be duly filled by her servant. Impossible not to feel some sadness for her, because of the dead infants down in the town churchyard and also because of what is to come.

Yet on the other side of the balance there is her determined awareness of the Ballatcheys' social position, of their chairs, pic-ture-frames, lawns, their ownership. Nothing in Catherine Bal-latchey would bend or yield in that, certainly nothing would make her forget her own standing. One might forgive her for this, since it was the aspect of her which her husband most valued and which perhaps made him desist from cruelties, for he had never been able to shake off some ingrained deference to her blue-blooded descent. Yet her coldness extended to all, from her servants to her son.

The thought creeps in: was what happened to the Ballatchey family partly a result of their own internal separations, a dissonance that meant that they could not stand united against what was to come?

But there was Catherine, as yet unaware, sitting at the dining-table, tapping the wood with a forefinger as she waited. Tom's light footsteps were heard on the stairs and he joined her a few minutes later. "Marcorn thinks we should eat in the morning-room because your father is not here," she said. "Quite unsuitable."

Tom made no comment as he slipped into place beside her. "Besides, it's pleasant to have a view when we are seated at table," she added. "We should see nothing from the morning-room."

Marcorn was bearing trays of breakfast dishes through the dining-room doors and set them down on the sideboard. His back was turned to the windows when he heard an exclamation from his mistress. "Good heavens, what on earth is that?"

Catherine Ballatchey was staring out into the grounds. Young Tom stood up and pushed his chair back as if he were preparing to slip away.

A small group of people seemed to be making its way across the lawn in front of the dining-room. The morning mists rose from the ground so that Catherine could not see their feet and they appeared to be gliding over the grass by some insubstantial means. From this distance they seemed almost like ants following a track unseen by human eyes. Ants who bore something in their midst, a stick or a dead creature, perhaps.

Yet even from a distance Catherine could not help but recognise that shape. There is something quite timelessly unmistakable and distinctive about it – there is no other object created by man and none in nature which possesses that peculiar outline. Nothing else is borne along with that quite distinctive movement, concerted yet clumsy, of men unaccustomed to carrying such a burden.

She stood up suddenly. "Marcorn, what are they doing there? Why are they carrying that . . . thing?"

"Madam, they are taking it to the churchyard."

Catherine was holding on to the back of her chair, supporting herself on the rail.

"Churchyard. Yes. But why there, across our lawn?"

The old man walked across and stared out to where the little procession had traipsed across the Ballatchey parkland. He seemed to watch it out of sight. There was a long silence in the room, complete and still, as if no-one even breathed.

Then Marcorn turned back into the room. "Shall I serve breakfast now, madam?"

"I don't think I could eat. Perhaps just some coffee and a milk roll. Master Tom will have what he usually takes – yes, Tom, you must. Marcorn, what was that extraordinary apparition?"

"The Quarry people, madam."

"But they walked straight across the park!"

"They were going to the church. They have always taken that route at these times. It shortens the distance they must carry the . . ."

"Coffin." Tom's young voice dropped the word into the gap.

"Exactly so, Master Tom."

"But surely they cannot be allowed to tramp over our grounds, Marcorn! And for such a beastly purpose."

"They must bury their dead somewhere, madam, and there is no church at the quarry. Ours is the nearest, and if they had to carry the . . . coffin around the estate instead of across the grounds, it would add a good mile to their journey."

Catherine's voice was sharp and tinny. "Well, it will be stopped, I am sure. Mr. Ballatchey will not countenance it. You may send my coffee to my room, Marcorn, I do not wish to stay here at the moment."

She left without looking at Tom, who desisted from any pretence of eating and shortly afterwards followed his mother upstairs.

Joseph returned two hours later, having breakfasted well en route at the Three Pigeons.

"Carrying a coffin? Across our land, you say!"

"Yes, Joseph. The sight was most distressing, not at all the sort of thing one wishes to see from one's dining-table. I don't find it tolerable."

"Neither do I, and we'll have no more of it. Marcorn, what can you tell me about this abominable practice?"

Marcorn seemed to hunch over as he said in a quiet voice, "It is a very old custom, sir. There is no church of their own at the quarry–"

"No, for they are a most dissolute bunch of villains, godless and lawless, as I understand."

"That is what people in the town say about them, sir. But the fact is they have always carried their dead through the ground of this house. It saves them a very considerable walk of a mile or more."

"By what right do they claim to do this?"

Marcorn seemed to become hoarse, as if his throat was closing up. "No right, sir. Just old custom." Then, as if to anticipate an objection, he added, "Old Mr. Lockyard never objected, nor the young master neither."

This mitigation had no effect. In fact, it seemed to make Ballatchey even angrier. "Then they were fools, both of them!" he cried, "and it's no wonder the young idiot lost his inheritance. Well, I am the master here now."

Marcorn looked across at his mistress, but the set mouth and cold eye which he encountered told him there would be no weakness there either. On this front, at any rate, master and mistress were at one.

It was easily dealt with, thought Ballatchey later. There was one small unpleasantness to be overcome, however. He had to get a mason from the town and it was from this man that he learned that the only cheap stone in the district would come from the hill-side quarry.

"Get it from somewhere else then. Never mind it costs dear, I'll still have it done," he said, surveying one of the two gaps in his boundary wall; those gaps which, he now realised, would just exactly admit the passage of a coffin borne on stout shoulders. In through this one in front of him, then the traverse of his property – *his* property! – and then out through that one opposite and thence into the churchyard.

The mason standing next to the master of the estate rubbed his gritty beard. This job would mean good money for him, charging for fetching stone as well as building work. But he knew something about the quarry people.

"They'll not like it, sir," he said, tentatively.

The reaction showed him what he might expect if he opposed Joseph Ballatchey. "Then if you don't care to do it you can get off my land! Damn it, I'm the master here. Do the frogs like it if you fill in their pond, sir, do the frogs like it, and shall I care? Will you go ahead with the work, or will you get back where you came from?"

Both the stone and the workmen were fetched from out of the county. The work took a day and Joseph paid handsomely for it, eyeing the raw new stone inserts into the old wall with satisfaction and even giving the bottom course a tentative and entirely useless kick with the toe of his boot. The result was a satisfactorily solid thud.

But at dusk the sound of hammering echoed across the grounds and Joseph looked out of the dining-room window to see flaming torches and figures moving in clouds of dust, their arms rising and falling as they drove pick-axes and heavy hammers into the new stonework. They had a leader, a man who stood back from time to time and directed the work, then moving them across the park to the other side in order to demolish the second infill.

Joseph thought he could make out the burly figure of Truscott. Joseph was a prudent man: he did not approach the group. He became filled with rage, but it was a cold anger, the anger of right-eous ownership.

His solicitor supported him. "Appalling! No, certainly not, they have no right of way there. You may do as you please with regard to walling in your own property. We can have them taken up if they attempt anything further. Rebuild your wall, sir, for the law will stand by you."

"Should I not apply to the owner of the quarry to restrain his men?"

"Bless you sir, there is no owner – or rather, they hold the ground themselves and have done for generations. It is what makes them so bold, you see. They say they know no master."

"Well, I shall show them they have one, at least in so far as regards the path through my land!"

The gap in the wall was made good, the debris cleared up and for the next few weeks Joseph daily regarded his parkland enclosure with satisfaction, a pleasure that was perhaps even greater at the thought that he had overcome the impudence of the quarry work-ers. He enjoyed beating down resistance even at some extra cost to himself. But one bright and clear autumn day he looked out of the dining-room window as he lit a mid-morning cigar and almost spat it out in expostulation. "Good God, those devils are there again!"

And there indeed was a small gang of ragged workers, attack-ing his precious wall with picks. They did not stop as Joseph ran towards them across the grass, his indoor shoes slipping and sliding on the wet lawn. The strong shoulders of the quarrymen heaved and struck, heaved and struck, and seemed in a few minutes to have all the infill stones lying in heaps either side of the gate.

Joseph was almost beside himself with anger, but not so foolish as to launch an attack on Truscott, who now stood out from the group and barred his way, staring most impudently as if daring him to a challenge.

Joseph rose to it. "Get out of my grounds, you dirty wretched creature!" he shouted.

But behind Truscott he could now see another small group, this time carrying a long burden between them and moving slowly towards the gap. To his shock, he recognised a thin figure dressed in a surplice leading the way. It was the young curate.

"Henderson! What on earth are you doing here? Don't tell me you countenance such goings-on!"

The man was plainly a bundle of nerves, yet he stood his ground in the face of Joseph's wrath. "Sir, this is a special burial. If I may explain –"

"There's no explanation for a breach of the law, sir, nor for an educated man such as yourself to encourage these outrageous activities!"

"This is the funeral of old Mrs. Truscott – that man's grandmother. She was a very old woman, and a leader of sorts, in her way, of their tribe, if we may so call it."

"I do so call it, Henderson. Savages they are, nothing more, nothing less."

"But we must extend the merciful rites of the church, if we may, sir, surely even to savages."

"Get out of my way – and you won't have your living long, there'll be no more of this nonsense, I can promise you that!"

As the curate stepped aside, Joseph could see that over a pinewood coffin of the cheapest kind (his mind registered the quality without conscious thought) was thrown a ragged red shawl. Where had he seen such a thing?

In the quarry, round the shoulders of that filthy old crone. The picture was clear in his mind for a moment.

"I don't give damn who it is – keep that rubbish off my land!" And, finally provoked sufficiently to take the risk, Joseph Ballatchey stepped into the breach.

He was almost instantly hurled aside as Truscott gave him an almighty push that sent him flying.

Bruised and furious, Joseph was forced to watch the little procession make its way through that gap in the wall, its progress marked by the red flare of the shawl on top of the coffin, then across his beloved park towards the other side. Here there was a pause, and he could see the bright silvery gleam of the quarrymen's picks flashing as they attacked the new obstacle that blocked their exit. Then the coffin bobbed forward through the gap in the direction of the church.

A few days later Joseph found that his fine pair of terriers, Bobbin and Tray, upon whom the family had relied to give warning of any approach to the house, had disappeared from their kennel. "Gypsies, sir, I daresay," said Marcorn. "I heard they was in the district."

"I paid a fortune for those dogs," said Joseph. "I'll put notices up in the town. I'll even offer a reward."

He did, but though every lamp-post in the town bore notices describing the animals and offering three guineas, no less, for their return unharmed, nothing was heard of Bobbin and Tray.

"Don't you miss the dogs, Tom?" said his father. "Never mind, we'll get another brace in the spring and we'll take them out ratting."

Tom Ballatchey did not mourn for the missing dogs, though he was generally fond of animals, because they had seemed always to be snapping, their sharp white teeth on show, and he did not like to see Bobbin or Tray emerging from a hole in the ground shaking a bleeding furry bundle in its jaws. He did not, of course, mention these feelings to his father.

But then all went quiet and Joseph had his wall rebuilt again across the offending gaps. Catherine began to make some preparations for Christmas, when they would dine with the larger Ballatchey family in the town. She therefore had a new gown made, in a bright yellow figured brocade which she ordered from London.

"Does it not look just the thing, Joseph?" she asked as she swept up and down the drawing-room before her spouse.

"You look very fine, my dear," he said. It was an unusual kindness on his part to say so. Joseph did not grudge her the cost of the gown, for he considered that Catherine, as the wife of a considerable figure in society, should dress accordingly, but he could not help thinking that the colour went very ill with her complexion, which, though it had seemed to become plump and rosy after their arrival at the new house, seemed now sunk down into a waxy pallor which made a ghastly contrast with the gaiety of her dress.

It is at this point that again I see the family suspended in time as it were for a few moments, before the horrors which over took them began – that is, of course, if they had not actually begun with the disappearance of Bobbin and Tray.

Catherine and Joseph, she like a cut-out in her stiff brocade, were looking out over the parkland as winter descends and mists creeps down the hillside and across the land, contemptuous of walls, on an evening close to Christmas. Tom had been sent to his bed and they had not yet summoned Marcorn to draw the curtains across the wide windows when Catherine started up in her chair.

"What can that be outside?" she said.

Joseph looked out for himself. There, showing through the mists, were faint glimmers of light on the far side of the lawn. They moved slowly, now appearing as pin-points, now glowing and flickering. With a mixture of rage and reluctant belief, Joseph understood them as the lights of lanterns moving across his grounds. And from time to time the mists parted and showed a long, dark shape borne among the lights "Damn it!" said Joseph. "What is that thing? How did they get in? I'll teach them to come on to my land ever again!"

He pushed back his chair and made for the door. Catherine called out, "No, no, don't go out there!" but he took no notice. Dashing into the hall, he took up his shotgun and loaded it hastily.

Then he ran out, straight across to the tormenting lanterns. It was a procession, no doubt about that, and what was more, a funeral procession.

He was still so full of anger he had no moment of fear, but then something, a long black rectangle, seemed to slant slowly up, above the dark centre of the apparition, and a terror gripped him as he realised what was happening.

The lid of the coffin (he had now to acknowledge to himself what the rising shape actually constituted) was opening.

At this moment Joseph might have prayed for absolute darkness, but instead nature seemed to inflict a further cruelty: the mists seemed to clear and a shaft of moonlight showed him clearly that there was something emerging, rising up out of the coffin, so that a shape appeared to be riding along borne in triumph above the bearers. A head, that of an old, old man or woman, impossible to tell, bone with little flesh upon it, a draggle of white hair, a mouth wide in a scream of triumph.

Joseph Ballatchey turned to run, but the creature leaped out of its coffin and launched itself upon his back. Catherine, kneeling on her fine Turkish carpet, with her hands over her eyes, heard the screams and the discharge of the gun.

The verdict was accidental death, there being no witnesses. Mr. Ballatchey had gone out in pursuit of intruders, must have tripped or stumbled and his loaded shotgun had discharged into his face, inflicting sufficient injury to kill the deceased. The Coroner offered his condolences to the widow in these tragic circumstances. Of the intruders there was no trace; it was conjectured they had both entered and escape by climbing over the wall that surrounded Mr. Ballatchey's land, there being no gap which could possibly admit of entrance. Or exit, added the Coroner under his breath, but there was no need for detail. No need, either, to mention some long scratches on the deceased's neck.

"For God's sake, don't speak so," Ballatchey Senior had said when Catherine tried to tell him of the nocturnal procession she had witnessed and which had suddenly disappeared like smoke after Joseph had fallen. "They'll think you're mad."

She had kept her silence.

It was a dreary Christmas, spent mainly at the home of the older members of the family in the town. They did their best for Tom, giving him a hobby-horse, for which he was far too old, and an astrolabe, for which he was far too young. He was almost glad when his mother decided they should return home, telling herself that she must have suffered merely a fearful dream of the circumstances surrounding her husband's death, that the coroner's verdict was the thing to believe. There were some compensations, after all: a fire in the drawing-room whenever she wished, Amal sold so that she had a sweet-mouthed pony, a proper lady's ride. Catherine began to settle into the routine of a comfortable widow.

But at the beginning of February, when the frost lay thick on the hillside, the butler came to her to break some serious domestic news.

"You, Marcroft, you won't go, surely?" she said. The maids had not delayed precipitate departures to inform her themselves.

"Madam," he said uneasily. "There is more. Someone has stolen the pony from the stables, during the night, I think. Will you let me speak honestly? I am very fearful for you – indeed, for anyone in this house now. There is something you could do – the weather is so hard, and it is a long way round from the quarry to the graveyard. Send for the masons and have the gaps in the wall re-opened. Let the quarry people use the coffin route again."

"When my husband died to keep them out!" exclaimed Catherine. "Never!"

The next day she caught Marcroft with his bags packed, standing in the entrance. "You're leaving." It was an accusation rather than a question.

He bowed his head.

"The carter will come to collect me soon, madam," he said. "Will you not come down to the town with me?"

It was probably Catherine's last chance of safety. Now I see her, a tiny figure telescoped by time, looking out of the hallway in a fearful moment of decision.

For a moment, she caught herself considering the possibility of leaving. To be among friends and relatives, not to have to look out into the misty parkland night after night – yes, how attractive the town, dirty as it was, seemed to her! But two things decided her to stay. One was her natural courage or stubbornness, call it what you will. The other was less powerful, ignoble in its very pride in nobility, but nevertheless had its influence: outrage at the suggestion that she, with a family tree showing aristocratic descent, should make an appearance riding in an open cart beside a servant.

"Thank you, Marcroft, I shall remain here," she said haughtily.

But as the butler turned to the door, sighing as he did so, she did think of her child. Some maternal feelings now overcame her cold nature and she called out, "Wait, you may take Master Tom. Take him to my father-in-law."

"Fetch him now," said Marcroft, almost as if he were giving her the order, but she did not object, and called the boy down.

"We must go straight away" said Marcroft. "It will be getting dark soon."

She waved brightly enough as the carter drove off with the small figure of her son sitting next to that of Marcroft but turned back into the house with a horrid feeling of expectancy – though of what, she could not tell.

She foraged in the kitchen – the first time she had ever been reduced to such a pass – and took up a plate of cold cuts to the dining-room. Here she ate a very little, and sat with the untouched remainder of the food before her, looking out of the window as darkness fell across the park.

She almost expected the bobbing lights in the distance when they appeared out of a clump of trees. She did not stop to wonder how they had made their way through the wall for she had a kind of inner resignation so that it seemed a question not even worth the asking: it did not occur to her to wonder that she had not heard the sound of picks and hammers which had resounded up to the house on the previous occasions when the coffin path had been forced open for a quarry funeral.

But all the same, she had expected them to move straight across her lawns to the other side of the grounds, where they could depart by the – not the gap, that was no longer there – but by the place where the gap had been. That was what she expected, or rather hoped for in some part of her mind that was quite irrationally looking for an ending to the shaking fear that possessed her. The transubstantiation of stone and mortar into thin air was something that no longer seemed impossible or unreal to her: she felt that, as in dreams, horrors might break through any material barrier, yet, as in dreams, so they might depart.

So Catherine watched faint lights as they came closer, till she could make out the long shape carried among them. They were now beginning to cross in front of the house on that same route that had offended her so much when she had first witnessed it. She could not tear herself away from the window but waited for the moment when the path of the coffin-bearers would take them to the other side of the grounds and they would at last disappear out of sight.

They seemed very close now – she could make out more of the shape they were carrying, and suddenly they swung towards the house, and instead of treading their own ancient pathway they turned towards her, the lights flaming as they came, approaching the house along her own driveway.

I find that I don't want to look at what Catherine Ballatchey saw next. But, like her, I am obliged to do so.

Now, though she had fallen to her knees in terror because her legs were shaking so much, she could still see the coffin, and suddenly she began to let out a series of screams. There seemed to be a figure on the top of the coffin, a seated creature draped in a cloth of some sort and pointing towards the house almost as if it were directing the path of the bearers.

Catherine managed to drag herself upright and fled into the hall with thoughts of escape. But now she could hear the sound of the feet, she was almost sure she could hear a faint screeching and yelling, and then there came a massive crash as the coffin, used like a battering-ram, burst through the doors which flung open and disgorged the funeral procession into the house. Riding on top of it was the shape of an old woman wrapped in a tattered red shawl which covered her shoulders and head, but not her face where the eyes were black sockets with malicious gleams in their depths and the cheeks and lips were mere smiling shreds of flesh. The coffin now seemed to almost fly towards Catherine.

From its height, the figure leapt down on top of her. Seized in its skeletal arms, she was overwhelmed by the stinking flesh that stopped up her mouth and nostrils.

In the course of time Tom Ballatchey returned from school and university and prepared to enter into an orphan's inheritance. Fremington Manor had long been shut up, but it was a solidly built house and could be put into good order. Tom, who had inherited the pragmatic nature of his father, set about it. There was one departure, however, from Joseph's arrangements. He ordered the coffin path to be re-opened and a high wall to be built along it for the whole of its length, so that it could not be seen from the house. Though his grandfather complained bitterly about these instructions, as in his view they reduced the value of the estate, Tom remained adamant.

My last glimpse of Tom is as he twists and turns in his lonely bed in the grand room on the first floor. Poor boy, throughout his life he will be troubled by nightmares.

Author's note: the above story is based on historical fact: in 1804 a rich landowner, Joseph Locke, tried to prevent the people of Headington Quarry in Oxford from carrying coffins across his land to save them the long walk to the church. In the ensuing quarrels, walls were built and knocked down and several local men imprisoned. Finally, the "coffin route" was walled off from Locke's grounds: parts of it still exist today. "Quarry Hogs' was what the children of Headington Quarry really called themselves in their song.

ROSALIE PARKER

RANDOM FLIGHT

Dusk was falling as Patrick slowed the car and pulled into a lay-by. Scots pines swayed in the strengthening wind. He had heard on the radio that a storm was blowing in.

"A close shave," he said out loud, laughing now. "You've still got it, Patrick." He shivered as the car cooled in the chill of the evening. "Better get a move on. 'Time's winged chariot', and all that."

Patrick, dark and good-looking, had celebrated his fortieth birthday a few days before with Annika, a bubbly, bulimic girl, in a Greek restaurant in Leeds. They drank two bottles of champagne and made quite an exhibition of themselves, which none of the other customers seemed to mind. It was the kind of place that provided cheap white china plates for you to smash, for the authentic Greek experience. Annika paid the bill and they rolled out onto the street and back to her flat. She had asked him to move in with her and, after a few days of playing hard to get, that's what he intended to do. But just when everything seemed to be going to plan, her ex husband (who still felt the need to hang around) visited Patrick's rented flat and threatened him with the police, with the result that Patrick had been forced to leave Leeds in a hurry, with little time to think of where to go and what to do next. It was a shame, because as well as being a genuinely nice, intelligent girl (when not throwing up in the bathroom), Annika was an easy touch, always good for a meal out or a trip to the races. They'd had a great time together, without, so far as he was aware, any real commitment on either side.

He'd been working the holiday scam on her and she was falling for it, and he knew she had the money – he'd found her building society book in a drawer in her bedroom. How that thug of an ex-husband of hers had got wind of it and somehow guessed that Patrick would not book the trip to the Seychelles but take Annika's cash and run, he couldn't guess. Perhaps it was just bad luck that she had told the ex about the holiday and that he turned out to be so suspicious and untrusting a person.

So here he was, heading north, somewhere in the Dales on a main road that seemed as twisty and windy as most minor roads further south. Patrick was a city boy, originally from Sheffield, and this was an area unfamiliar to him, but it seemed as good a place as any in which to lie low for a few days, in case Annika's ex made good on his threat.

Night had fallen and he decided to stop at the next town. After another few miles through the steadily increasing rain he drove into Skelton, a village with three pubs ranged around a cobbled square. It would have to do. Patrick chose *The Black Horse* because although the biggest, it was not the best kept pub, and would most likely be cheaper than *The Swan* or *The King's Head*. Money, or the lack of it, would soon become a concern. He parked the Alfa on the cobbles outside the pub, collected his brown leather holdall from the boot, lifted the latch and went inside.

The bar was warm, old-fashioned and comfortable, encased in panelled oak, a worn Axminster on the floor. The place seemed full of local farmers and horsey types: there were very few women, and those that were there looked like stable girls, drinking pints – not the right sort for his purposes. Tomorrow he would have to find somewhere more likely.

He struck up a conversation with a wiry little farmer called Bill, from whom he learned that Skelton was a race horse training centre. Bill was, naturally, curious about what he was doing in the village and Patrick gave him the story he'd come up with while unpacking his holdall in the large bedroom above the bar. He straightened his back.

"I'm on leave. I'm a Major in the Yorkshire Regiment. Major Hartley. We've just returned from a tour of Afghanistan. We're being sent back out to Iraq in a few weeks. Thought I'd see some more of my own county – get to know the Dales a bit better."

'Aye, well," said Bill, "they say this is God's Country. I certainly wouldn't live anywhere else."

"Glad to hear it," returned Patrick. "It sure as hell beats the desert."

"I suppose it does. Did you see much in the way of action while you were out there?"

Patrick rubbed the stubble on his chin. "As a matter of fact we did. Had a fire-fight with some insurgents the second week we were there. Two of our lads bought it, but we took out a few more of them. It's a dirty business . . ."

Bill frowned. "Local lads were they? I don't remember . . ."

"It's not always reported on the news. Hush, hush, you know. We recruit from all over these days. But they would've been based at Catterick."

Bill said he'd have to get back to his farm, as he had a cow about to calf. Rain lashed against the mullioned windows. Patrick bought the farmer a double malt whisky and made him earn it by mining him for local knowledge. Bill, impressed and slightly intimidated by the tall, well-spoken soldier, and made loquacious by the warm, complex whisky, was very forthcoming.

The next day, a wet and windy Tuesday, saw Patrick recceing the market square of Gribley, the town closest to Skelton. After some deliberation he picked a large, smart-looking coffee shop, choosing a table from which he could see and be seen from both the door and most of the seating area. On the short drive to the town he had been struck by the quaintness of the landscape: with its quiet roads, dry-stone field walls and substantial stone houses it could still be the 1950s or '60s. He had seen several large flocks of crows – or rooks. Their random peregrinations around the sky made him feel faintly uneasy. In fact the whole place spooked him a little – after what had happened in Leeds he was, he realised, a bit jumpy – outside his comfort zone.

The best way to blow away the cobwebs, he knew from previous experience, was to get down to work. It was still early and he had bought and drunk three cups of coffee before the first likely target came through the door. She was, he guessed, in her early thirties, dressed in good clothes and jewellery, about five feet five, a brunette and nice looking, although wearing a lot of makeup. There was something needy about her – she wanted to be looked at. He looked – she smiled. She picked a table on the other side of the room and Patrick ignored her for a while, then, on his way back from the gents, close to her table, his handkerchief dropped from his pocket. The oldest trick in the book. She picked it up.

"Excuse me!" She had the local Dales accent. "Excuse me! You've dropped your handkerchief."

Their fingers touched as he took it from her. He looked into her eyes.

"Thank you. I'm always losing them."

And before you knew it he was sitting at her table, drinking decaffeinated coffee and listening to her life story – separated – husband with another woman but supporting her financially – a couple of young kids at school – still living in the marital home in a nearby village. Out it tumbled, once he'd spun her the Major Hartley yarn, without him having to put in much effort at all. Her name was Rachel Morton and she was vivacious and a wee bit desperate, with that all too obvious neediness about her that might, he thought, lead to trouble later on.

He asked if he could see her again and they arranged to meet the following evening at an Italian restaurant across the square. He spent the afternoon in the cafes of Fairlees, a small market town about ten miles west of Gribley. Luck was against him, however.

The following lunchtime he bumped into Flick in a pub in Fairlees. Flick was around fifty, he thought, divorced and smart and the owner of a high-end dress shop in the town. He told her that he was ex-army, now working as a researcher for a film production company. He was in the Dales finding locations for their next feature film. As it was a contemporary drama, she might be able to help provide the costumes. They spent the afternoon in bed in her flat, and it was only with some difficulty that Patrick managed to leave in time to meet Rachel at the restaurant in Gribley.

Rachel was late because her babysitter had forgotten to come. She had had to telephone the girl and promise to pay her an extra ten pounds.

"It's impossible to find anyone reliable," she complained. "These teenagers are no good, and Guy is too selfish to help out. He'll only have the kids at weekends." She stroked Patrick's arm. "Perhaps next time you'd better come to mine."

The date progressed well. He presented her with a single red rose – he did it ironically and she liked it – and managed to borrow fifty pounds, extracted as a test of his skill. She spent most of the meal complaining about Guy, her estranged husband, who, he learnt, worked for an investment bank. At the end of the meal Patrick kissed Rachel chastely on the cheek and she invited him to dinner at her house on the following Friday. He got the impression that she would be ringing her husband to tell him about her new boyfriend as soon as he had left.

He spent the next few afternoons with Flick, who had been led to believe that Patrick would be going back home to London in two weeks' time. She invited him to stay at her flat until then. Patrick wasn't entirely sure that it was a good idea, but the financial imperative overrode all else. He settled up at *The Black Bull* and moved himself in.

He found Flick intelligent, undemanding and good company, but he had yet to find the chink in her armour, the vulnerable spot that would lead him to her money. How much money that would turn out to be was difficult to say. Her flat was small but stylish in a minimalist, contemporary way, and her shop very obviously made her a good living. He was sure there was more money somewhere – he could smell it.

Rachel's house was another thing entirely. It was large, detached and cluttered with knick-knacks and ornaments, scented candles and children's toys. Rachel, it seemed, was a compulsive purchaser – shopping her main hobby. When Patrick arrived, her children, Chloe (five) and Jake (three) were still up. After some initial shyness, they clambered all over him, singing nursery rhymes and spouting made-up nonsense. He didn't dislike children; he was indifferent to them, but these two seemed to accept him as a friend. He made a great deal of fuss of them, which appeared to gratify Rachel. She finally put them to bed and served up a rather good casserole and a bottle of wine. Patrick went through the pretence of drinking only one glass, although they both knew that he would be staying the night. (He had told Flick he was working and staying at a hotel in Bradford). Later, in bed, Rachel cried a little, then pulled herself together, and they had an enjoyable time.

Three days later, over lunch, he told Rachel about how he had been diagnosed with Post-Traumatic Stress Disorder and needed to buy himself out of the army, and how his savings were tied up for the next few months. He didn't even have to ask her directly – she offered to lend him £20,000 there and then, more than enough for him to replace the Alfa and have some left over for expenses. That afternoon she took a cheque made out to him from her building society. He couldn't believe it had been that easy.

Driving back to Flick's, after paying the cheque into his bank account, Patrick was again distracted by the odious flocks of crows. There was something about the regimented unpredictability of their flight that got under his skin. He was trying to think of how to get at Flick's money. £20,000 was all well and good, but it wouldn't last forever. He was sure he would be able to extract more from Rachel, but Flick was the bigger challenge. A number of crows broke away from the main flock and swooped low over the road. Patrick flinched and the car swerved. He swore.

"Get a grip, for God's sake!"

He stopped at the tiny village shop and bought a bottle of whisky. The shopkeeper did not bother to hide his curiosity.

"Are you on holiday here?" he enquired. "I've seen you around. Renting a cottage?"

"Just passing through," answered Patrick, pocketing his change. "Visiting a friend."

It seems you couldn't even buy a bottle of whisky without being interrogated. The place was so small that he stood out, that was the problem. He was getting himself noticed, and that was not a good thing at all.

Flick was in the bath. She called out to him:

"Help yourself to some wine. There's a bottle open in the kitchen."

He gulped down a glassful, poured out another, then let himself into the bathroom. Flick was engulfed in a mound of bubbles.

"You look tired Patrick. Are you all right?"

"I'm more than all right. I've had some good news. A little investment of mine has paid off."

She splashed around in the foam. "Oh, goodie! Are we going out for dinner?"

"We are. But I've been thinking, Flick. You could invest too. It would be well worth your while. I could . . ."

Flick laughed. "Why on earth would I want to do that? The shop's my investment." She sat up, her breasts bobbing invitingly on the choppy bath water. "Go on, out with you. Watch the telly for a bit or read the paper or something while I get ready."

Later, in the Thai restaurant in Fairlees, he tried a different tack.

"Did *you* not want any children, Flick, or was it your ex?"

"We couldn't have any. It was before the days of test tubes and stuff."

"I have a son. Not many people know. He's called Ivan. His

mother and I had a brief relationship in the '90s. He's eighteen and at university in Liverpool. He's quite ill, as a matter of fact. Needs an operation. He's on a waiting list. You know what the Health Service is like. He's really sick. If I could find the money I'd pay for him to go private."

"What about this investment of yours? Wouldn't that pay for it?"

"Oh, well . . . no. That's nowhere near enough. Flick, where would you go if you needed to raise some cash?"

Flick was looking thoughtful.

"I don't know, Patrick. I've never borrowed any money. I had a job and saved like crazy, and I built the shop up from scratch. Do you have any other family you could ask?"

Patrick was silent for a while.

"No. No family to speak of. You couldn't help, could you Flick? I'd pay you back."

She laid down her fork.

"Oh, Patrick. I don't know. How much are we talking about?"

He took a deep breath: "Thirty grand."

"I don't have that sort of money! Leave it with me, though."

And with that she changed the subject.

The next morning Flick left early on a buying trip to Leeds. Patrick, at a loose end and restless, found an ordnance survey map on Flick's kitchen dresser and went out for a walk. He headed north, through fields, up a steep hill and onto moorland, using the map to guide him. A keen easterly wind was blowing. He found himself striding out along the rough track, perfectly at home in the unaccustomed solitude. The view was stunning, a patchwork of fields, walls and villages, with the heather-clad fells beyond. The better part of him wanted to keep on walking and never go back down there again.

Patrick had a date with Rachel in the coffee shop – "their" coffee shop, she had said on the phone – in Gribley. He parked his new

Alfa (not brand new, but only a year old) outside. He had bought it from a second-hand dealer in Darlington. The part-exchange deal he had negotiated was not particularly advantageous, but he still had a few thousands to tide him over.

It was obvious that something was wrong. Rachel wouldn't look him in the eye.

"What's up? You can tell your Uncle Patrick."

"Shut up."

"Hey, come on! What've *I* done?"

Rachel burst into hot, angry tears.

"Who is she, that old tart you were with in the Thai in Fairlees? I saw you!"

Patrick laughed easily. "She's no-one. Just someone I had a bit of business with. Come on. Don't upset yourself."

He tried to stroke her hand but she pulled it away.

"I know you've got someone else. It's happened to me before, remember."

"I don't need anyone else. I've got you."

"I'm such a fool. I know nothing about you."

"We're good together, aren't we?"

"That's . . . not enough. Not now . . . Look Patrick, I'm not playing any games. I want my money back."

Patrick swallowed hard. "Oh . . . I might need a little . . ."

"I want my money back this week. I should never have lent it to you. Give it back and we'll talk."

Patrick stroked her hand. "I'll see what I can do. It may take longer . . ."

Rachel finally looked him in the eye.

"I'm pregnant Patrick. It's yours. I don't know what to do about it. I don't expect anything from you."

The colour drained from Patrick's face.

"I'm leaving now," she said. "Call me when you've got my money and we'll talk."

Patrick checked that Flick's car was not in its space then let himself into the flat. He packed his holdall (he could do it very quickly), left the key she had given him on the kitchen table and drove straight to Rachel's.

He didn't know if Rachel was inside or not but she wasn't answering the door. He pressed the bell a few more times. It was difficult to work out how he felt about her – Patrick was not often given to introspection. He didn't even know if he believed her about the pregnancy – could she know that quickly? And he thought he'd been careful. After his initial desire to see her and talk her into letting him keep the money, his instincts were telling him not to take any chances: to leave now and get as far away as possible.

He backed the Alfa down the drive. Abruptly, he felt the car lift and then drop back down, as if he had driven over a road-hump or some kind of obstruction. In the rear view mirror he could see a light-coloured bundle lying on the tarmac behind him. It looked about the size of a child. Perched at one end was a shaggy, ink-black crow, pecking where the eyes would be. It *was* a child, he could see now, a child wrapped in some kind of shawl or blanket. One of Rachel's children? What the hell was it doing, lying on the drive? He hadn't seen it. And where was Rachel?

The crow raised its head and cawed. Patrick felt sick. He could see something wet, gelatinous, coating the curved tip of its beak. The bird fixed him with its shiny eye, then returned to its pecking.

Patrick reversed the car round hard. The Alpha screeched off along the village road. Pulling his phone from his jacket he dialled 999 and requested an ambulance. The car rocked from side to side as overhead the crows wheeled and swooped, the flock tracking the progress of the Alfa. There was nothing random about the movement of the flock as it shepherded the car and it's occupant out of the village, out of the dale, onto the motorway and away.

CONRAD WILLIAMS

SHADDERTOWN

Does he like to hear her talk about Manchester in the days when she was young, and fit enough to do what young girls did? He seems to. Sometimes, when she talks, she drifts away a little. It's as if she's transported herself back to the Pendulum or the Twisted Wheel or all-dayers at the Merry-go-Round. Back then her lungs were pinker, more elastic. She could suck deep the air that carried the oxygen to send her careering around those sprung dance floors like something electrified. "They called me 'Place'," she tells him, "because I was all over it." Her name, though, her real name, is Peggy. Billy calls her Peg.

Now she finds it hard to get out of her chair. Walking from one room to another brings on a panic that threatens to fill her up completely. Her mouth is constantly open. Her shoulders are hunched from years of fighting for breath. There are some good days, but mostly bad.

Peggy doesn't see Billy as often as she'd like. She won't drive because lorries induce panic attacks when they overtake her (50, inside lane). She won't go on the trains or the buses because she doesn't want to suffer an incident; she doesn't want to die going blue in the face while a bunch of strangers stare down at her. But she loves Billy as if she had given birth to him. His mother, Jill, isn't around much (a young woman, still got it, and wants to enjoy it while she can . . . party, work do, weekend away . . . you don't mind, do you? You wouldn't begrudge me, would you? I mean . . . let's be frank, we don't know how many more opportunities Billy will have to . . . well, I don't need to spell it out, do I?) and leans on Peggy a lot to provide childcare. She doesn't need to say the things she does, but she says them anyway, as if that will persuade her to spend more time with her grandson. She doesn't seem to hear when Peggy tells her she'd be happy to spend all day with him, every day with him. It's no hardship.

Except, it is. George, Peggy's husband, died three years ago. She's had to have a bed made in her living room now, so perilous are the stairs for her. She shuttles between the tiny kitchen and the living room, to all intents and purposes a ground floor flat while the upstairs gathers dust. Terry, her son-in-law, installed a tiny cubicle shower in the far corner of the kitchen, under the stairs, spending most of his time swearing and sweating and eyeing her violently as if to say *I wouldn't have to be here if only you'd do what your name suggests*. She has to sit down in order to use the shower. Not because she runs out of puff but because she'll bang her head on the rose if she doesn't. When Billy comes to stay, as he has done today (girls' afternoon in Liverpool, shopping and cocktails and then a nightclub . . . I'll try not be late to pick him up tomorrow) he has the bed; she goes to sleep in her armchair, the armchair George claimed for his own. She can still smell the oil from his scalp on the headrest.

Each time Billy comes to stay she's momentarily broadsided by the look of him. He seems different. Bigger, more energetic. Sometimes she gets this funny feeling that it's not the same boy. Sometimes he's surly or rude. Sometimes he's a little reserved. Sometimes he marches straight into the kitchen and helps himself to what's in the biscuit barrel. He can never sit still, even when they watch morning cartoons together after breakfast. She gets tired and breathy just watching him fidget. He's like his dad in that respect.

Or maybe his dad just doesn't like being here. Terry's always first out of the door when it's decided they'll leave, car keys jangling from his finger. Claustrophobia, he says. He doesn't like being crammed into a tiny living room with so many people. It doesn't stop him getting in a small plane on his annual jaunt to Magaluf with his golf pals, though, does it?

"What do you want to do, Billy? I've got a jigsaw puzzle somewhere. Or there's these colouring books you left last time."

"I've been inside so long, Peg. I want to go out."

"Don't your mum and dad take you out?"

A shake of the head. He's always got the pilchard lip on him. He used to laugh a lot when he was a baby.

"What did you do yesterday?"

"Mum and Dad stayed in bed because they had overhangs."

"Who got your breakfast?"

"Me. I can get my own breakfast."

"But Billy, you're only six. How do you reach the bowls? Do you never have a cooked breakfast?"

"I had lollipops."

She feels anger move through her but it's strangely languorous, like the torpor that comes when she puts a sleeping pill under her tongue. She no longer gets a proper rage on her as she used to. It's far too taxing.

How does Jill allow herself to be like this? Peggy never treated her like this when Jill was Billy's age. She wasn't brought up to be so . . . unmotherly. We had fresh fruit and vegetables always. Peggy never opened a tin that contained anything that came out of the ground. Jill was out rain or shine. She had scabs on her knees up until she was a tween. A right tomboy, she was.

He wants to go out.

"Okay," Peggy says. "Okay."

"Where are we going, Peg?" Billy asks, once they've struggled on board the bus. A man stands up to allow her to sit and she's momentarily put out by that; he must be ten years her senior, but she sits anyway, and Billy stands in front of her, his left nostril encrusted with pale green gunk, every button on his coat missing.

"We're going to the Land of Far Beyond," she says. "Or is it Upside-downville? Or is it Shaddertown? I forget."

"Oh, Peg," he admonishes, but he's smiling. Being here on the bus, with its peculiar smell of diesel and damp and worsted coats reminds her of trips out with Jill, over twenty years ago. Condensation on the windows. Every bump and gear change felt through the bones of your arse. They went ice-skating in Altrincham. Afterwards they'd drink hot chocolate and compare bruises. Peggy's lung capacity hovers around the twenty per cent mark now. She might be able to get one ice skate on but that would be enough to finish her off for the afternoon. When it comes, it feels as though there are fingers, too thin and hard to be real, gripping her shoulders and bending her backwards. It's how she imagines it must have been for Christ on the cross. Hyperexpansion of the chest muscles and lungs. An inability to expand. The shallowing of air. Should have stayed in and watched *Balamory*. Should have had an easy day. Teach him how to play Old Maid. Get him to read to her. *Owl Babies. We're Going on a Bear Hunt*. Sometimes she dreams of being chased, something clawing at her from the darkness, something trying to grab hold of her and get the job done properly. She tries to sand down the edges of her fear with hopes that it might be George reaching out for her, but how could it be, when the hands are tipped with such ghastly, denuded fingers?

The bus stops outside the library and they get off. What breath she can muster churns from her mouth in a frantic grey torrent, as if it is aghast at what it has experienced inside her lungs. Each breath she takes feels shallower than the one before.

"Right, come on," she says, and she likes the way Billy's ears prick up. She's got her voice on. The voice that must not be disobeyed. She'll try to be full of vim and verve for him. For her Billy. She won't show him her grey, failing side though it seems to be winning these days. *Death, coming up on the rails.*

Where did that come from? She suffocates the thought before it can bloom in her mind.

She smoked for fifty years, every single day. Never less than twenty cigarettes between rising and retiring. She started when she was twelve years old. When she couldn't cadge money for fags or pinch them out of Mum's handbag, she'd roll brown paper into tight tubes and smoke that. She liked the way Marlene Dietrich looked when she smoked. Peg copied the hairstyle, and did her make-up the same. The cupid bow lips. Smoky eye shadow. George used to call her Lili, after the famous song. He might even sing it to her if he'd had one too many pale ales.

My love for you renews my might
I'm warm again, my pack is light
It's you, Lili Marlene
It's you, Lili Marlene.

All trampled over by crow's feet now. Here I stand at the milestone of my days. And she doesn't wear lippy anymore because it bleeds into these smoker's lines around her mouth.

Fifty years of purse and drag. The French inhale. Oh, yes, very sexy. Brown lungs, gummy with tar. The oral habit. The daily sound of the death rattle in a woman clinging on.

She doesn't bother suggesting it any more, an afternoon with her daughter and Billy, and Terry if he has to, maybe to the park for ice cream and playground rides, or a bus into town for lunch and the pictures. "What's the point in us all being here?" Jill asks. "It defeats the object."

Peggy won't challenge or cajole. She's tired and, yes, afraid of Jill's reaction. The bared teeth and the spittle; the implication that this is her job, her duty. Billy had been staying with Peggy and George when he took his first wobbly steps across the lounge. Jill had been funny with her for weeks after that, as if she'd been cheated of something she could have shared with her Instagram friends and her Facebookers and her Twitter followers. *OMFG!!! Billy took his 1st steps 2day!!! Totes amazeballs!!! LOL!!! #bigboy #yummymummy #awesomesauce*

They have to pause as they walk south-west to the edge of St Peter's Square. They have to pause again before crossing the road to the entrance of the Midland hotel. It's a journey she wouldn't have thought twice about when she was young. A journey coped with in seconds. Once she walked from Glossop to Bolton after she missed a night bus home. It took her eight hours. They got off this bus quarter of an hour ago.

"Are you all right, Peg?" Billy asks. The line has gone from his forehead, what she calls, in private, his Terry line.

"I'm dandy," she says. "I'm right as rain." For some reason, she thinks of her own grandma, Agnes, many, many years dead. Peggy used to sit on her knee, staring up at her bewrinkled, bewhiskered face and ask her how old she was.

"I'm as old as my tongue and a little older than my teeth," she would say. Peggy never understood where this crypticism came from, this bizarre compulsion to not answer the question directly. It's an age thing, she thinks. It's a way to keep the mind chugging along.

Jill likes dumping Billy on her because she knows they won't go outside. She probably thinks they're in now, watching TV, eating chocolate, playing cars. Well buttocks, bums and arse to you, my love. Jill's argument now is stranger danger. "Our Maddy. Poor Jamie. I won't say goodbye to Billy as he's led away on some blurry CCTV footage while you huff and puff to keep up. We're not the only ones who keep our kids inside. We're not bad parents."

You're not parents. But she has to bite her lip. She has to nod. This is nowadays, isn't it? Because back when Peggy was young you could leave your front door open and not expect to be raped by some itinerant stranger. It was all fields back then. It was pop in and out and latch-key kids. Pedophilia wasn't invented until 1966, was it?

The guide at the entrance to the Midland Hotel has a face as long as Leung's takeaway menu. Peggy and Billy stand on the damp pavement while he consults his clipboard. There's nothing clipped to it. He notices this and drops his arm, displays a pained expression, or is it a cheated expression? Peggy doesn't know him well enough to gauge. She doesn't know him at all, although he reminds her of a bus conductor who used to collect fares on buses she took when she was at school. He spoke in deliberate Spoonerisms. *Pears fleas*, he'd say, his fingerless gloved fingers poised above the ticket machine dial. *Yank thue. Stext nop, Saguley Banatorium.*

"Name?"

"Meggy . . . Peggy McGill. And Billy McGill."

"Peggy short for?"

"No. Peggy McGill."

"No. Is Peggy an abbreviation?"

"No, lad. It's a name."

He consults his clipboard. He straightens his arm.

"Well, it doesn't matter. We're not oversubscribed. How old is your son?"

"I don't have a son. I have a daughter. She's twenty-six going on five."

"It's just that some of this tour will be me talking about things and it might go over his head. Nazis and that."

"It'll go over mine as well, then. I wouldn't worry."

Soon there's a group of half a dozen standing in the damp, wearing variously disappointed faces.

"I'm Clive," says the guide, consulting his clipboard. "I'll be showing you around the forgotten chambers of Mancunium today. I hope you brought stout shoes and a torch."

Peggy stares at her flats. At least Billy is wearing his boots.

"Have you got a torch on you?" she asks. "Don't boys carry things like that around with them all the time?"

"I've got a light on my bike," Billy says.

"Never mind, look. Everyone else has got one. We'll stick close."

The guide talks for a while about the hotel, how it would have been Hitler's north-west nexus of operations had the Nazis successfully invaded Britain. German bomber pilots were expressly forbidden to release their payloads anywhere near the hotel for fear of damaging it. The guide's voice is the endless gritting cycle of a cement mixer. Billy fidgets. The cold is clinging to the ends of Peggy's fingers like a needy child. What has all this talk of architecture and Nazi plans, and Rolls meeting Royce, and the Beatles being thrown out because they didn't adhere to the dress code . . . what has all this got to do with the tour? Underground Manchester. As Jill might say, *this is not doin wot it sez on the tin dot co dot uk LOL!!!*

Eventually it's time to move off. It's a little way to the entrance to the tunnels, explains the guard, reminding them that they have signed waivers that abrogates the tour company from all responsibility should someone be mown down by any vehicle, including a bicycle. Somebody says something about litigious culture. Someone else says something about the nanny state. Billy, in a too-loud voice, tells Peggy that this morning he did a poo that looked like Uncle Derek's moustache.

Soon Peggy has become the back marker. Maybe they should just peel off to a café for hot chocolate. She'll get Billy a comic. He'll be happy with that. He's only six after all. What was she thinking, bringing him here? But the talk of tunnels and torches has excited him. *Do you think we'll see any rats? Do you think we'll find the goblin king?*

Peggy looks at the thin face of the guide and bites her tongue on *Look no further*. She has to concentrate on her breathing, so she smiles and winks instead. She can feel the tubes in her lungs winking too. Once, when she was young, she could drink in litres of air. She'd do it to tease George, who liked it when her chest expanded. *Look at you*, he'd say. *All fulla love.*

Dark spots crowd the edge of her vision, as if they've already started along one of the tunnels.

They've stopped again. They're on James Street standing in front of an unassuming brick building with large wooden gates and a tower. The guide tells them, through his mouthfuls of cement, how this building was the entrance to the main tunnel of Manchester Guardian, an underground telephone exchange built in 1954 when the Cold War gripped the world. The tunnel would have been able to withstand the blast of a twenty kiloton atomic bomb, preserving communications links even if the city had been razed. There was enough food to keep people going for six weeks. The toilets had restful scenery painted on the walls. The guard laughs. "Of course," he says, "by the time the tunnel was ready, the Soviets had developed much larger bombs that would have obliterated the place. Waste of money if you ask me."

The guide eyes Peggy's shoulders, bowing like the spine of a pitched tent in high winds. She's waiting to be taken to one side, the dropped voice, the reiteration of point twelve on the terms and conditions, people with health problems such as high blood pressure and heart defects should be aware that there are a number of stairs to be negotiated during the course of this tour. When it comes she maintains eye contact and tells him she's fine. "We're nearly there," the guide says.

"I'll look after you, Peg," Billy says. In the past Billy has made monsters from clay to scare her bad cough. She has a drawer filled with them. They are drying out now, crumbling golems, but she refuses to throw any of them away.

"Then I've nothing to fear," she says.

The entrance to the tunnels is through an office at the rear of a busy department store. They descend well-lit steps covered with linoleum, bypassing two office workers texting feverishly. To each other, Peggy imagines. At the bottom is a heavy, padlocked door. The guide pulls out a single bronze key from his pocket. Brandishing it like Neville Chamberlain with his piece of paper, he unlocks the door. The sound of the tumblers turning sends echoes into the space beyond. Peggy thinks: leave now. Take Billy to the football museum instead. Take Billy to the helter-skelter in Spinningfields. Take Billy away.

But people are jostling for position, and she feels herself being herded through the doorway by those behind her, and she reaches for Billy's hand and he squeezes it and everything will be fine.

The temperature drops the moment they pass through into

the gloom. The guide is ahead of them and he's saying something about how they were going to install a simple lift but it's logistics, you know, but she can't properly hear and it doesn't really matter because she's here for fun with Billy and it will all go over his head and her head. Soon there's no light and people start flicking on their torches. Some of them are poor, cheap affairs, casting not enough light to illumine the low ceiling above them. Peggy gets closer to a couple huddled together who are carrying a large, powerful rubber-cased torch that seems bright enough to find its way between the cracks in the brickwork and surprise people up on the surface.

It's dank down here; the cold has a raw, weirdly elderly touch to it. It's ill-tempered. Impatient. It's like being prodded, an old aunt wearing too much make-up pinching your arm before declaring there's not enough meat on you to last till lunchtime. Billy's hand is warm inside hers. Her left foot disappears into a puddle and she almost loses her shoe. The cold judders along her leg like in the cartoon she watched with Billy where Bugs Bunny, or Daffy Duck, or whatever cartoon animal it was hits a petrified tree with an axe. If the cold reaches her heart she's sure she'll stop moving and shatter into a million pieces. The thought makes her want to laugh more than anything else though. Silly old carrot, she thinks. Just think of the bath and the rum-laced hot chocolate you'll enjoy later.

She used to laugh a lot. God, George could pull a giggle from her, and often when she was determined to be angry with him about something. But he was one of those people it was impossible to remain annoyed with. Now if she so much as chuckles or titters or snorts it can bring on a fit of coughing that convinces her she might die. She no longer watches the funny shows she likes on TV. She tries to avoid spending time with the girls who know how to tickle her: Penny or Jenny or Flo.

The guide is at the front. His voice comes to her in strange swells and beats, like the rhythm of the sea on the shore. He's saying something about the Manchester and Salford Junction

canal. He's saying something about a shelter from the German
bombings. There are steps coated with slime, and pieces of rubble
lying around where the brickwork has started to fail. Great arched
ceilings stippled with stalactites. Some day they will cease to take
people down here because of the risk. The doors will be sealed off
and whatever is left down here will be trapped for good. *Watch
yourself here!* Part of a wall has collapsed into one of the arterial
corridors, partially blocking it.

Shards of graffiti are picked out by the lunatic splashes of light.
She can't make out the names, or the deeds, or the insults. Scraps
of old warnings from the war remain. The guide reads out a few:
No insobriety. No rowdiness. No unseemly conduct. In a corner of
this particular . . . what do you call it? Chamber? Cellar? Crypt?
(no, let's not do that . . . let's not give ourself a reason to be fearful)
there's a dummy slumped over its knees, dressed in a red-checked
flannel shirt and black jeans. Its head looks to be made from poly-
styrene. People giggle and point. It looks punched in, crumbling.
It reminds her of George, how she found him that morning after
breakfast when he'd gone upstairs to get dressed. It was as if death
had upset him so much that he had the time to sit down against the
foot of the bed and cry into his chest about it. But think of George
thirty years younger at the Twisted Wheel, dressed to the nines in
blazer and brogues while she was always at sixes and sevens over
what to wear. His hair scraped back with the ubiquitous back-
pocket comb. The Oxford trousers and sports vests. The smell of
sweat and Brut. The amphetamines; the jaw grinding. Juicy Fruit
and Doublemint. He moved so hard and fast on the dance floor
she was scared sometimes that he might break. The heat and the
smoke in that place grew so thick that it condensed on the ceiling
and returned as a light yellow rain.

They move deeper into the Manchester underground and her
mind sinks with it. She remembers how slim she was back then,
and how taut the muscles in her calves from all the dancing. George
could almost enclose the span of her waist with one outstretched
hand. Where did they get their energy from? The calories they

must have burned off! And afterwards, in George's little Hillman Imp, they'd drive up to Saddleworth with the windows open and they'd be smoking and singing rare-soul classics and they'd make love in the moors for a while, or in the car if it was too cold, and back to George's parents' house in Longsight as the sun came up, just in time for bacon and eggs with George's old man before he went off to the bleach factory.

All those days of twists and shimmies. The miles covered more or less on the spot. All that energy spent. The endless cigarettes. And throughout it this was down here: coldness and damp and coursing water. *The Land of Far Beyond. Upside-Downville.*

The guide's voice slaps against the damp brick and falls at his feet. He's saying something about how dark it really is down here. He invites everyone, for thirty seconds, to switch off their torches and to put their hands in front of their faces. *You won't be able to see a thing.* In the split second between this palsied light and the utter black that follows, Billy tugs his fingers free of Peggy's hand.

"No, Billy," she snaps, but then the delighted yelps of alarm get in the way of her warning and all she can think, as she swings around, trying to catch hold of Billy's arm, is: *This is what it is like for George every single day.*

She shuffles forward a little, blindly groping (just as we used to, George, out on those wild, black moors, remember?) but she succeeds only in bumping against a figure that recoils at her touch. The feel of her (must have been a her, too thin an arm to be male) is waxy under her fingers, but maybe that's because she's so cold, and anyway, people these days wear strange waterproof fabrics and . . .

"Billy!"

She hasn't shouted like that for a long time, maybe not since Jill was a teenager. Billy doesn't answer. People are still laughing about the dark. It's a darkness she has never known. It seems so deep as to be beyond understanding. Even in her own bed, when her eyes are shut, the colour is not nearly so extreme. The guide says: *this is what it must be like to be profoundly blind.* He says: *it is literally blacker than the grave.* In the absence of light, his voice seems different, as if it is wetter. She doesn't understand how the light can alter the acoustics of a place. Maybe it can't – of course it can't – so then it must be her own rising panic that is adding juice to his words.

"Turn the lights back on!" she caws, but the effort of shrieking his name has deflated her. *Kippers in a smokehouse*, Jill used to sing, cryptically, to the tune of "Mirror in the Bathroom" and it's only in recent years Peggy's realised she must be referring to the lungs in her chest. She thinks of the tar marbling them, like bitumen she used to tease from the road on hot summer days. She decided she wouldn't follow George into the earth. When she goes she'll face the flames. She imagines the crematorium workers who would have to shovel her out, their faces when they see those two smouldering lumps, tacky with crude fuel, burning on long after the rest of her is dust.

It's been much longer than thirty seconds; minutes, it feels like, before the torches spring back to life in a contagious relay. They seem much brighter than before, even the cheapest model causing her to avert her gaze. She hunts for his tiny shadow, the little cowlicks of bed hair. She claws her way towards the guide, but already he is off through the archway – *Mind your head! Mind your head!* – and everyone pushes forward to see what lies ahead. No queuing down here in the dark. No manners in the Mancunian shafts. The light is shrinking from the chamber

we don't abide that shine in shaddertown

and she spins, spiked with adrenaline, ready to lash out at the owner of the grinning little voice that hissed at her. But there are only the etiolated shadows of the departing, jerking and frisking against the walls.

"Wait," she calls out, but she barely hears herself. Billy must be in the middle of that scrum of people. She has to believe that. If he were here, in this darkening room, he would call out for her. He's always calling her. *Keep up Peg! Peg, can I have a biscuit? Peg, where are my toy cars?* He'd call out to her, if he were able. Did he fall? She peers into the gloom but she can't see any figures, other than that damn stupid dummy. Maybe he's hiding, playing a daft game. She hasn't the puff to admit defeat. *I give up. I give up. Ally Ally in come free.*

She staggers from the chamber and one of her shoes skips off her foot as easily as if it had been snatched away. She crouches and pats the earth around her, but she feels only soil and brick dust. Forget it. Billy needs me. I need Billy. She leaves the chamber and she's slowing down because the light has dwindled to such an extent that only a dim graininess remains. The hubbub of excited voices has gone and now she can hear the rumble and squeal of her chest, her breath coming in shallow plosives. She's straining so hard to hear beyond that for Billy that her ears might bleed. She can imagine Jill with her arms folded across her chest. She can imagine triumph in her face, more so than any grief, and her heart is pierced with double the guilt.

Perhaps they've found Billy and he's all in a tizz, blubbing, they can't get any sense out of him so they take him up to safety. She has to find out. Maybe someone will realise she's not come up after them and they'll come to help. She'll make damn sure that cement-mouthed chocolate teapot of a guide loses his job, that's a given.

Peggy makes her way through the archway and along the corridor, tensing herself for obstacles she might trip over. Her one shoe carves sharp *skrit-skrit* noises into the walls. Peg-leg. Ha, George would have loved that.

She's almost at the end of this corridor – she can smell the canal, and feel cool air coming from what must be some sort of junction up ahead . . . that surely means she's close to the steps where they descended, doesn't it? – when she hears another grating in the rubble behind her. She turns, hoping it might be Billy, but instead she sees a pall of smoke funnel through the archway she's just vacated. It's lit palely within, a soft, mellow light, the colour of burnt amber. It shifts constantly, contracting and expanding as if powered by some internal engine, though it might just be the ebb and flow of air through all of these tunnels. Some trick of light and shade. A weird internal example of marsh gas. Billy, maybe, acting the goat. He had a torch all along and now he's playing tricks on Nana.

She draws in breath and the pall swings towards her. She speaks and as his name trickles out of her, the pall contracts. What is this? Is this consciousness shrinking? Is she about to faint? She mustn't, for Billy's sake. The moan might have come from her, it, or the tunnels but it doesn't matter. She rounds the corner and there are the stone steps, muddy and wet and subtly gleaming, like barely-set mortar.

Fear is at her heels, but also the awful feeling that she might be making a mistake and leaving Billy behind in the dark. She turns and sees the pall rounding the corner as if it was on a thread attached to her shambling feet. And she thinks: *every toxic inhalation*.

She's right to go up. She can report Billy missing if he's not with the rest of the touring party. Within ten minutes there will be a search party down here.

o you wish . . . you think you can climb these steps in ten minutes o my o you!

But it's her only choice. Billy will be found, but only if she gets out of here. She plants her shod foot on the first riser (thirty steps, just shallow ones, not as steep as those at home, but three times as many . . . come on old girl, you can do it . . . you used to glide up the steps at the Oasis as if they weren't there, and then dance all evening to Blue Dice or The Gordons or The Needles) and begins the long haul to daylight.

She counts each step and she does not look back. *Four, five, six* . . . she sucks at air that has turned intractable. It sits, niggardly and hot in her chest, as if her lungs were strangers to their job. She tries to imagine George up ahead, reaching out to her from the dance floor, the light catching in the oil in his hair and the rings on his fingers, the polished buckle on his high-waisted trousers. He looks lean and wolfish and sizzling with nervous energy. Young again. Christ, what she'd give.

Come on Peg, come on my Lili, let's give it some rice.

Eight, nine, ten . . . But there's something rising behind her too. Something within that bronze fug of smoke, she thinks, that is not so pleased to see her progress. She imagines a Billy trapped down here for decades, a Billy that is fish-grey, his eyes pale from the lack of sunlight, his skin mucoid and failing, touched by iridescent green flashes. She imagines that happy, chubby boy emaciated from hunger, lost in the maze, trying to find his nana. Clawing at the air for her.

My love for you renews my might
I'm warm again, my pack is light

By the time she gets to thirty steps, to forty, to fifty (*out now? I should be out by now?*) her legs are moving more quickly, and – miracle! – her chest seems less congested. She feels her ribs expand beyond any point they've achieved in fifteen years and the light is thickening around her, so bright, so playful she feels she might be able to reach out and touch it, cradle it in her hands like molten gold. Now, though, she smells the stale stink of old smoke in her wake, as if it's trying to catch up after all these years away. Her lungs ache in recognition. She might be able to summon enough breath, should that snatching grey claw ever manage to land on her shoulder, to power a scream.

JOHN LLEWELLYN PROBERT

LEARNING THE LANGUAGE

My name is Richard Lewis Morgan. I am Welsh. And there is something horribly wrong with me.

Right now, I'm about two thirds of the way up Skirrid Fawr, or the Holy Mountain as it's known to many of the residents of the nearby town of Abergavenny. My girlfriend Natasha is just a little bit ahead of me – she's already out from under the tree cover and making her way across the long, bare, open summit of the mountain to the white stone marker at the end. I've taken this opportunity to take a breather and go over as much of all of what's happened as I can remember. My mother always told me if something is bothering you a lot, then you should think about it, say it out loud even. Things always seem more manageable if you say them out loud

Natasha will not be coming back down the mountain.

Actually, writing that has made what I have to do a little easier. The knife in my pocket is made of stainless steel and I've owned it since I was a boy. I'm the only one to have ever used it, except for the time Reverend Watkins borrowed it once to get the hymn book cupboard open in Llantryso Church. It's the only thing I have that my father gave me. Apart from my destiny, of course.

Some people call this place the Holy Mountain because when Christ was crucified God struck it in his anger, cracking the mountain in two. You can still see the fissure today, overgrown with brambles and ferns and dotted with sheep who don't mind venturing into what some presumably believe is a divine rift. Why God should have aimed his wrath at Wales rather than at Jerusalem, or Rome, no-one has ever been able to explain to me. It's also claimed that once, when the Devil strode across Wales, his foot came to rest on this place and thus broke off a fragment of the rock. I like that story better, but then I would. While I have never seen much evidence of God at work in this country, I know that this is a land of ancient power and even more ancient beings. My mother and father knew it, too. After all, that was how I came to learn of them in the first place.

If I move on a little I can just see Natasha ahead of me, her white jacket bobbing along the mountain top. She'll be at the marker in a bit. It was put there many years ago by the Welsh National Trust. It's what they call a triangulation or 'trig' point, to allow you to orientate yourself with other mountains in the area. Far fewer people know that it is no coincidence these triangulation points are where they are; that they are markers of the deep seated power of each mountain; that a sacrifice to the spirit of a mountain must be made at the site of the marker. In blood.

She's nearly there, and there's no-one else around. I didn't expect there to be this early on a Tuesday morning.

Time to get moving, I think.

I have already mentioned going to church in my childhood and you might therefore be forgiven for thinking that my family were Christians. Until I reached a certain age I had assumed that myself. We went every Sunday, my mother, my father, and I.

I should have suspected something was wrong when I learned

that my school-friends' church attendances differed from my own in one significant way. They always went to the same one, whereas my parents did their best to attend a different church every Sunday. There were so many in the area around Abergavenny that it easily took us several months to get round them all. Each Sunday the routine would be the same. Father would tell us where we were going and mother would pack a small picnic if we were going to be driving for more than an hour. We were always the first to arrive and my parents would spend the time before the service making a careful examination of the graves before securing themselves a seat at the back just prior to the service beginning. Father would be jotting things down in a small black notebook right up to the point where the vicar took his place at the front, and again afterwards before leaving the building. Each vicar, and each congregation, was always very welcoming towards my parents, presumably because they always told them they were thinking of moving to the area, and that it was important to them to see what the local church was like. If I asked if we were really moving house once we were in the car afterwards, my mother would give me a look, and ask me if I really wanted to leave that lovely house of ours?

Seeing as I've brought it up, this is as good a time as any to describe 'that lovely house of ours'. Accessed via a tiny country lane on the outskirts of town, the house where I grew up was the Victorian vicarage to the now derelict and desanctified church that adjoined it. I loved that old house, even though the sun never quite seemed to reach it, even though we often needed to have the electric lights on throughout the day, and even though for much of the year it was so cold there that I would wake to a crust of ice coating the inside of my bedroom window. It was my childhood home and I regarded it with the same affection that my parents did.

I was fortunate, I suppose, in having parents who did not need to go out to work. We were by no means well off, but I always had reasonable clothes to go to school in, and my considerable academic achievements at such a young age had already served to ostracise me from my peers. Unfashionable clothing had merely served to cement my reputation as 'odd' – something I was quite happy to encourage.

Thus it was that I was out of the house more than my parents were. My father spent most of the daylight hours in his study, a vast book-lined room in which he would lock himself for hours engrossed in whichever volume he had taken down from the woodworm-ridden shelves.

One day, my father chanced to leave his study door open and I, being a curious child who had never been told to stay out of it, found myself examining the heavy tome he himself must have been reading before being called to the telephone. I could read at least as well as any boy my age, and it was with a mixture of confusion and fascination that I tried to read the peculiar combinations of consonants, the arrangements of vowels and letters into words that were as unpronounceable as they were unreadable.

I was in the process of turning the page when I became aware of a presence behind me. My father had returned. He did not seem unhappy with my gentle handling of the page, and so I asked him.

"Is this Welsh?"

He appeared to ponder my question for a moment before replying.

"It is," he said. "But a more ancient and darker Welsh than most who now call this land home would be aware ever existed."

"Can you read it?"

A smile. "Some," my father said. "And just a little more every day."

"Is it what you're looking for in the churches?"

The smile broadened but no answer was forthcoming. "I think your mother is looking for you," he said. "You'd better go to her."

My mother hadn't been looking for me at all, and when I returned to my father's study the door was once again locked.

I never learned to speak modern Welsh. My parents were among the many residents of the country who were unable to converse in their native tongue and so it was never an issue in our household.

The dark Welsh, however, the ancient and almost forgotten language my father had shown me in what turned out to be a quite unique volume, was another matter altogether. My education began one morning over breakfast, with my father scribbling a few letters on the back of the envelope that had housed yet another final demand for the electricity bill.

He passed the creased paper over to me. "How do you think that should sound?" he asked.

I frowned. To me it just looked like a random collection of letters that didn't belong together. But I did my best, producing something that made me sound as if I could use a powerful decongestant.

"Try again," said my father, "but try making the sound in your throat, rather than your nose."

I did as I was told.

"That's better." My father was obviously pleased, and my mother flashed me an encouraging smile as she cleared the plates away.

By the end of the week I had mastered a number of new 'words' and was able to move onto my first guttural and awkwardly pronounced sentence. I remember that Saturday afternoon well, as I was made to repeat the five words over and over until I could recite the sequence of noises perfectly, and without the aid of the volume from which my father had transcribed them.

"Good," he said, eventually satisfied. "Now when we go to church tomorrow, I want you to say those words under your breath once the vicar steps into the pulpit. Very quietly, mind. No-one else must hear them. Not even your mother and me. Do you understand?"

I nodded. "Why?"

His response made no sense to me at the time. "Because the ones we want to get in touch with need to be called in the right way," he said. "They won't listen to us, but they might listen to you."

"Who are they?" I wanted to know. "Are they friends?"

"We hope they will be," said my mother, resting proud hands on my shoulders. "We hope they will be very good friends indeed."

"But how will they be able to hear if I'm so quiet?"

I could see my father had to suppress a chuckle at this. "Because they have very special ears," he replied. "Ears that can only hear certain special words."

"Are they Welsh?"

Both my parents nodded in a way that suggested pride in their child who had taken a great leap forward.

"They are," said my father. "The purest Welsh there is. From the times when England did not even exist, not as anyone knows it now."

"Is Wales older than England, then?" My parents were in a revelatory mood and my twelve year old self was keen to exploit it.

My father seemed to be considering something for a moment and then, prompted by a nod from my mother, he spoke again.

"Wales is not just older than England, my son," he said. "There are some who believe it to be the place where life first sprang from on this planet. To be born Welsh is to be born not just privileged, but to be born into an ancestry that leads back to a time before man, before the mammals that led to the development of man."

"Before dinosaurs?"

My mother nodded. "Failed experiments of those who first came here," she said. "They cast them out to other parts of the world, where they eventually died and gave rise to fossil fragments – the only evidence of their passing."

A bit like the chat your parents try to have with you about the birds and the bees, this was all rather hard to believe.

"We did about dinosaurs in school," I said. My parents nodded. "And evolution." They nodded again. "And the Bible." Here they frowned and shook their heads.

"Throughout millennia people have tried to come up with explanations for who we are, where we came from, and where we might go after this life," my father said. "None of it is true. The truth is in the volumes in my study, and I have so much yet to decipher, so much that I need help understanding."

"You can help us," my mother explained. "You are able to say the words, and you are just young enough that your voice should be in the right frequency to reach them."

"But why in a church?" I wanted to know.

"People feel they are closer to God in a church," said my father. "In Wales, they are closer to the ancient beings that slumber beneath the Earth. It is easier for Them to hear you in such places."

"And the gravestones?" My parents exchanged looks. "You're always looking for what's written on them," I said.

"It is not what's written on them that's important," my mother said, "but the way in which they have been arranged. These, too, are markers of the receptivity of one of the Ancients to our communications."

"And we believe we have found the one where we may best be heard." My father's eyes were glittering with triumph, even though he had received little in the way of confirmation that he was on the right track.

"And we're going to go there?" I asked.

"We are," said my father.

"On Sunday," said my mother.

"Tomorrow," they both said together.

You may be wondering why I was sat in St Peter's Church in the tiny parish of Llanwenarth Citra the next day. You may be wondering why I had not refused point blank to be involved in something that sounded at best ridiculous and at worst frankly dangerous. But I was twelve, I was shunned by school friends and had no-one other than my parents to talk to. When you are that age and that alone, it's very difficult not to go along with what you've been told to do.

So there I was, sitting at the back of this small church, in between parents who were convinced that when I made some strange noises something fantastic and unworldly was going to occur. Quite what it was they hadn't told me, and now I wonder if they had actually thought that far.

The congregation ceased its sullen rendition of How Great Thou Art and the packed congregation resumed their seats, as did we. Father had pointed out before the service began that with us present the congregation made up an odd number, which seemed to be of great significance to his mind. Now, as the vicar ascended the steps to the pulpit, my father prodded me, as if I needed reminding of my task.

Even at the last minute I hesitated, wondering if it might perhaps be better to face the wrath of my parents than whatever I might call forth from the depths of the planet.

But in the end, I did as I was told.

At first, nothing happened. The vicar, an elderly man with a few wisps of white hair crowning his otherwise gleaming bald head, continued to address his rather meagre flock with alternating words of condemnation and reassurance, the people before him nodding in agreement as he poured loathing on those whom he claimed were responsible for the general state of moral decay in the country.

Everyone assumed the rumble we heard was due to an encroaching electrical storm.

When the building began to rattle I imagine some must have thought they were to be witness to the first earthquake in Wales in a millennium. Perhaps others thought the wrath of God was about to be visited upon them.

Which, in a way, it was.

People only began to panic when the red fog descended.

It cloaked the building rapidly, covering the windows and turning the feeble daylight an unearthly shade of scarlet.

"Fear not, my brethren," said the priest in the most fearful voice I had ever heard. "If we are to be judged, let us not be afraid, for our hearts are pure and minds are –"

We never got to find out what the vicar thought our minds might be like, because at that point the stained glass exploded inward, and the red mist that had coalesced on its surface began to drip into the building, running down the white walls, pooling on the floor tiles and spreading towards the frightened crowd, who even now were retreating to the centre aisle in a bid to escape the creeping miasmic horror.

All eyes turned to the pulpit and widened in horror. The vicar, struck by numerous shards of splintered glass, was now slumped over his pulpit, his body a rainbow of glittering colours, the predominant of which was red.

My parents stood, horrified by what I, and by turns they, seemed to have caused. They turned for the door, only to find that others were already ahead of them. The middle aged robust-looking lady who opened the door found herself faced with more of the red fog, which billowed in and, like superheated acid, dissolved her flesh from her bones as it made contact.

"Send it back!" My father was squeezing my shoulder so hard it hurt. "Send it back now!"

"I don't know how!" I sobbed through tears. "You didn't teach me any other words."

"Backwards," said my mother. "Say them backwards."

"It was hard enough saying them forwards," said my father, his normal reserve gone. "How is he possibly going to be able to reverse the words of summoning?"

Personally I had no idea, but I was going to try. Amidst all the screaming and the stampeding, the desperation and the panic, I climbed onto a pew and tried hard to remember the final word my father had taught me. Then I reversed the letters.

I spoke the first word.

Nothing. Just the same screaming and madness and encroaching red death.

Never mind, there were four more words to go.

Carefully and methodically, I remembered each one, turned it around, and spoke it, using the same guttural whisper my father had showed me.

As the last croaking syllable left my lips, something happened, although it was not what I was expecting.

The world turned white.

At first I thought I had been blinded. Then, as my eyes began to adjust, I realised that I, and everything around me, was covered with ash. Tiny fragments of it floated through the air, coming to rest on the motionless bodies of those around me.

Including those of my parents.

I jumped down from the pew, stirring up a fine cloud of white powder as I did so, and waded through more of the stuff to where my parents' bodies were lying. I reached out to touch my mother's ash-coated face, and the flesh beneath crumbled into yet more of the dust that surrounded me. I grabbed at her hand and it turned to nothing beneath my fingertips.

My father's body was the same, as was the body of everyone else in the church. A slight breeze blew through the broken windows, and reduced the shapes that still resembled human forms to powder. I took faltering steps towards the door, and made my way out into a world that I quickly realised was not my own at all.

The sky was not just the wrong colour – a strange admixture of red and gold peppered with orange pinpricks that I assumed must be stars, although a few of the large ones were obviously planets – it was the wrong shade as well, as if the sun that gave this realm light was much further away than the sun is from our earth.

The church was still there, standing behind me against this darkly glittering backdrop, and the graveyard was there, too. Now, however, the teetering stone markers resembled rotted teeth in the mouth of some vast and cankered beast, and I wondered if the leathery substance on which I was standing might be its tongue.

I took a step forward and the world shook, the ground yielding a little beneath me, as if perhaps I was walking on flesh rather than earth. A sound midway between an ambulance siren and a creature screaming in distress seared my ears, and I put my hands up to cover them.

But that was not the worst.

As I looked up to the heavens, at that vista so unnatural and so alien, the sky itself parted, splitting open lengthways, and an eye vaster than the entirety of creation regarded me with curiosity.

I could feel it probing my mind, filling it with knowledge, with experience beyond my years, as if it was preparing me for something. I suddenly felt older, much older.

I realised with terror a little later on that it was not just my mind it had changed.

"We thought we'd lost you, too."

The nurse had a lovely Welsh accent. The doctor with her was English and I instantly disliked him. Both of them looked at me as if I was lucky to be alive, and when I glanced down to see most of my body covered in bandages I could see why. I would have asked them what had happened but it took several days before I was on a sufficiently low dose of morphine to let me form sentences.

In a word, Llanwenarth Church had exploded. The ongoing investigation had postulated a leaking gas main (didn't they always?) but nothing had been proven. The building had been destroyed and nearly everyone attending church that Sunday morning had been killed.

Everyone, that is, except me.

And even I was not who everyone thought I was.

I had mumbled my date of birth to both nurses and doctors to be rewarded with sympathetic looks and reassuring words.

"I'm sure you'll remember who you really are soon," one especially pretty nurse had said when I had insisted I'd been born just over twelve years ago.

"My dear fellow . . ." the consultant had given me a stern look on his ward round a few days later, ". . . you seem to be an intelligent young chap so I'll be blunt with you. Who knows, it may serve to jolt you back into reality. However old you may think you are, by my reckoning you are at least twenty five, if not older than that. I'm sure your real date of birth will come back to you in good time, as will your real name and where you come from." He flipped through the case notes. "As for your address, our computer system has no record of a house being there. Nevertheless, I'm sure once you're up and about and out of here everything will start to come back."

"Up and about?" I croaked in a voice much deeper than the one that had quoted those unwieldy words in the church days – or was it years? – ago.

The consultant nodded. "Beneath those bandages is a whole collection of minor cuts and abrasions. A couple of your wounds needed suturing and there's a nasty burn on your right arm, which is why you were on the morphine, but that's healing nicely. There's really nothing to stop you from getting out of that bed and seeing if you can remember how to walk. In fact I insist on it."

I was wheeled from my bed to the Physiotherapy Department two floors down by a bored-looking porter who stopped to converse with one of the young female domestic staff. It turned out he was still very sorry about going off with someone else at the nightclub last Saturday and that if only she would give him another chance he would prove how faithful he could be.

This conversation was intended to be conducted out of my earshot, but somehow I seemed to have developed an extremely acute sense of hearing. More peculiar than this, however, was my realisation about halfway through what they were saying, that they had been talking in Welsh, a language that up until that moment had always been a complete mystery to me.

The porter returned, red-faced, and continued to push me towards the lifts. On the wall next to the push buttons was a list of all the floors and what was located on them, in English and Welsh.

I could understand both languages perfectly.

I was still shaking as I was wheeled into the Physiotherapy Department. The physiotherapist was stern, but I probably needed it. She thought my lack of coordination was because of shock which, in a way, it was. But it wasn't the result of physical trauma that caused me to totter and wobble along the walking bars, rather it was the shock of having discovered my new ability, as well as having to adapt to a body that was now several inches taller, hairier, and considerably better developed than the puny twelve year old one I seemed to have been relieved of by my experiences. It didn't take me long to get used to it, however, and before long I was considered physically fit for discharge.

The psychiatrist, however, wasn't so sure, and, after a month of counselling in an attempt to recover what she called my "lost years" I was eternally grateful to her for arranging my discharge to a halfway house close to the hospital. It was somewhere I could "mentally get back on my feet again" rather than being left to fend for myself, something that would inevitably have led me to living a hand-to-mouth existence on the streets of Abergavenny. Fortunately I did not have to remain within the confines of the building, and so, one sunny day shortly after I had arrived there, I made my way to where my parents' house should have been.

It was a walk of about two miles, and took me straight through Abergavenny town. As I walked, I noticed two very strange things. The road signs, all in Welsh as well as English, were now perfectly readable in both languages.

But the Welsh communicated something entirely different to me.

As I read the words, as I took in their meaning, I realised I was interpreting them as the Dark Welsh my father had introduced me to at my home in that increasingly distant never-land of the youth I seemed to have lost. The words spoke of a rising, of a return, of the sacrifices that must be made and of the locations at which they needed to take place. And most important of all they stressed the very special quality the victims had to possess. Not virgins like in the horror films, or babies like in the black magic novels my mother used to consume. Oh no, the sacrificial victims needed to bring about a reawakening of the Ancient Ones of this land only needed to possess one quality.

They had to be English.

Why have the Welsh always despised the English so? Harboured a hatred of that nation that always went beyond the friendly rivalry of a rugby match or simple neighbourly competition? Even when I was a child in school the teacher would make unpleasant jokes about the English, and the children who claimed that nationality would squirm in their seats, embarrassed and not understanding why they should come in for such vilification.

The Welsh have always hated the English, and now, perhaps for the first time in millennia, I had been shown the reason why.

You need to be made to hate something before you can be made to kill it. And if that hatred is ingrained over generations it just makes it all the easier to carry out your task when the powers that put that hatred there in the first place tell you it is finally time for them to return. The Welsh people were created by this land. Clad in the mud and dirt of the ancients, they rose full-formed from the hills and the rivers and the valleys. Fashioned by its elements and rooted in its history, the Welsh have always been here, and always will be. The English are from everywhere and nowhere. Nomads and vagabonds, they have dared to call a land their own that they really have very little claim to. At least, not in the way the Welsh can claim their heritage.

So let it be the English who suffer so that our land might truly live.

By the time I arrived at the site of my parents' house I was not surprised to find no trace of it. It wasn't needed anymore. For all I know it had never existed. The crumbled remains of the desanctified church were still there, although now something told me that were I to trace my steps back to Llanwenarth I would find ruins that were very similar.

It does not take much to disorientate a man and I, it seemed, had become the plaything, or perhaps more accurately, the Messiah, of the Ancient Gods of Wales. I walked back through the town, trying to ignore the road signs, trying to ignore the whispering voices in my head that were insisting, in the Dark Welsh of the ancients, that the first victim needed to be soon, that English blood needed to be spilled on the sacred Welsh soil of a nearby mountain to begin the cataclysmic chain of events that would change this land, and the world, forever.

As I stumbled back into the halfway house, my fingers pressed to my temples to try and shut out that infernal whispering, I almost cried out, screaming at the creatures in my head to stop, that there was no-one I could offer them, that there was no-one I knew who I could convince to come with me to their dread place of sacrifice.

There was a girl sitting in the front room, flicking through a magazine.

She had the weary, vaguely tarnished look of someone who has seen too much at too young an age. A bit like myself, actually. She looked up as I entered and gave me her best attempt at a smile.

"Hello," she said in an accent that sent a vortex of hot blood swirling through my veins. "I'm Natasha."

There isn't much left to say. Here I am, four days later, close to the Place of Sacrifice. Writing all this down has helped, I think, although I've just gone over it all again and I realise I'm finding it more and more difficult to determine how much of what I've written actually happened and how much is me trying to remember what happened and getting it wrong. There might be lots of things wrong, I think, but I also think I know how to make them right.

Natasha's reached the marker now. How white it looks, gleaming in the morning sunlight.

The Welsh sunlight.

The sunlight of my fathers, and their fathers, and of those who live beneath the mountain.

The English shall not have it, none of them.

Natasha will be the first. The first in a long line of glorious sacrifices to the spirits of this holy land on which only the Welsh are fit to tread.

Natasha will be the first, and then I shall look for others.

And if you are English, I will be looking for you.

SARA PASCOE

A SPIDER REMEMBER

I THINK WE LOVED each other. It's difficult to remember what he was like before. At least I know what's happening to me, which makes it less scary.

Or much worse.

I *said* I loved him, out loud, to his face. And to other people. I like to get intense with my partners, analytical late nights drinking and listening to great music. I have a record player, which puts some people off me. Especially the neighbours. I felt very close to him for that first year. I was thinking about getting a tattoo of his name, I'd never done that for a boyfriend before, except once.

He was very tall, so people always commented and made the same jokes and he had to repeat the same passive aggressive responses. I got neck pains when we kissed standing up. An achy echo of him remaining for hours after a lovely date. He was laid down at the end, so it would have been easier to kiss him. But I didn't. He was no longer him.

Even after a year, we were still learning about each other's minds and behaviours. Despite the jazz-underscored introspective conversations at my flat, I didn't even know he was scared of spiders until he woke up that night: "It's on my face, it's ON my FACE!"

I'm sitting here now wondering why the government are covering this up. If I'd had any idea of the danger . . . but then I guess
no one would ever go to sleep at all. Die from that instead. That's
what happens: seven days and then you're gone. And psychosis
from the third day, so there *are* similarities.

"You're dreaming," I had told him. And not politely. I hated
him for waking me up.

He was moving around stupidly. "I can feel it, it's on my face."

"It's just a bloody dream."

"IT'S A SPIDER."

He swam his lengthy limbs and I went back to sleep.

In the morning he showed me it. Dead. He'd held it in his hand
all night to prove that I should have been more sympathetic. Which
pissed me off.

"It's still just an insect."

He was being so childish. "It was running over my face."

"You're lucky you don't live in Africa or something, or the
jungle."

"I choose not to live there, because I hate spiders."

"You can't choose where you're born."

"I would have moved."

It wasn't an enjoyable row. There was no relief afterwards from
having purged a poison, found new equanimity. It was petty and I
wasn't going to apologise for not helping him kill an arachnid in
the night. He needed to grow up about it. He sulked for the afternoon; I wish he'd leave. We watched TV to avoid talking. I made
an excuse about an early morning to ensure I went to bed alone.
When we caught each other's eye we pretended to smile.

Dinner that weekend was planned. I had a feeling he was planning to break up with me, the arrangements seemed so formal, and
we hadn't "made up" properly. Our phone calls had been lists of
what we had done, no laughter. I should have apologised, I look
back now and wish I'd been nicer, but I didn't know.

In the restaurant I thought he seemed thinner in his face and
a bit pale. Fragile. This is definitely it, I thought, despising him in

preparation. We ate in virtual silence, my contempt for him oppressed me. He slumped with his head in his hands when offered a dessert menu.

He was so rude to the waiter. "No. I can't. Can you go away? I have to tell her something."

The poor guy left. Another poor guy looked at me.

"Kate . . ."

I made my face ready to say, "That's fine, babe. That's what I want too, to just be friends or . . ."

"I can still see him."

"Who?" I looked around for the waiter.

"The spider I killed."

"What spider that you killed?"

"The one who lived in your house."

I was relieved. Stupidly laughing. I must have loved him, I could breathe again, hysterically happy. His face folded into itself as he cried.

"I'm sorry, babe, I thought you were going to break up with me." I spoke softly and tried to reach him across the table. "I'm not making fun of you."

"It runs about my eyes."

It was difficult to hear him, he was telling himself more than me.

"I can see it, around the edges, and then straight across my . . ."

I watched him cry and realised he was mad.

I took him home with me that night, feeling responsible and not wanting to be. I lied positively, about a doctor helping him. I was thinking anti-hallucinatory drugs, he imagined some arachnid-killing eyewash. He left in the night and I didn't wake up. I hoped he would be okay but didn't know what I could do.

I could've phoned him or believed him but I didn't.

Four days later he found his way back somehow. Maybe a taxi had dropped him because he didn't seem sure where he was. Banging on the door woke me up, the last restful night I'll ever have. He dribbled words, dropping them separately and widely apart. A doctor. No one believed. Worse now. Many many. So lots. Prison. The hospital.

"Do you want me to take you?"

I needed to call someone, I couldn't deal with this on my own.

He shook his head and walked in circles around the room. Less and less control of his limbs as I watched him. His words became noises. I rang for an ambulance, gave them all the details. "It's a psychotic attack, he thinks he has spiders in his eyes."

His hands swiped at his eyes as he swirled about the room. I was reminded of zombies. A body living with no one left living in it. The doorbell squawked as he fell flat on his face. I heard his nose break, and I saw the back of his head.

His hair was moving.

Screaming, I ran to the door, tried to get out as the paramedics pushed their way in. They were wrapped in plastic, now I know why. There was a woman in a suit, she caught my arm, held me back.

"They're in his hair, they're in his hair," I tried to explain to her.

She shushed me angrily and pulled me into the front room, we stood near my record player. Next to the sofa. Where I'd used to chat and drink and live.

They were wrapping him in clear plastic sheeting and I could still see the red rim under his hair. The edge of the nest, as they streamed out, hundreds of spiders swarming from his skull. Small, tiny, harmless spiders.

"It doesn't usually get as far advanced as this. It's a bad case. I'm sorry about your friend," the woman said, not sounding sorry.

"It's disgusting," I said. I should have been sick or something, done something human. Instead I just stood there as she gave instructions to the crew. Tests. Incineration. Lies about cause of death to relatives.

Outside there was an ambulance and a smaller unmarked van. I got in the back without asking any questions. I couldn't talk, everything was shut off. I thought about calling a lawyer, or someone from work. I thought I saw a spider.

Only natural, after all that had just happened. Of course I itched a bit. My skin prickled and crawled, I kept imagining I could feel tiny legs running over my body. They had lived in the mind of someone I loved.

We drove for hours. My feet and legs fell asleep and I couldn't feel them. And after a couple of peripheral jolts, I saw it properly. It ran straight across. Across the world, all I could see of it. The biggest thing and the nearest thing and it was already inside me.

And now I try not to panic. I sit in a contained cell asking them to kill me. But they won't, they don't understand enough yet, they need to study how it happens. The effects. They aren't even kind, because I'm revolting to them. And so the spiders dance, more of them every hour, I watch them and they are all the world. And every person who knows what I am going through is dead already. And I know how he felt. And it's too late to console him.

I wish I believed in heaven.

ALISON MOORE

EASTMOUTH

Sonia stands on the slabs of the promenade, looking out across the pebbly beach. It is like so many of the seaside resorts from her childhood. She remembers one whose tarred pebbles left their sticky blackness on her bare feet and legs and the seat of her swimsuit. She had to be scrubbed red raw in the bath at the B&B. Her hands are wrapped around the railings, whose old paint is flaking off. When she lets go, her palms will smell of rust.

The visibility is poor. She can't see land beyond Eastmouth.

"I've missed the sound of the gulls," says Peter, watching them circling overhead.

He says this, thinks Sonia, as if he has not heard them for years, but during the time they've been at university, he got the train home most weekends. Sonia does not think she would have missed the gulls. She is used to the Midlands and to city life.

She lets go of the railings and they walk on down the promenade. Sonia, in a thin, brightly coloured jacket, has dressed for warmer weather. Shivering, she huddles into herself. "Let's get you home," says Peter. For the last half hour of their journey, while the train was pulling in and all the way from the station he's been saying things like that: "We're almost home," and, "Won't it be

70

nice to be home?" as if this were her home too. Their suitcases, pulled on wheels behind them, are noisy on the crooked slabs. "They'll know we're here," says Peter.

"Who will?" asks Sonia.

"Everyone," says Peter.

Sonia, looking around, sees a lone figure in the bay window of a retirement home, and a woman in a transparent mac sitting on a bench in a shelter. Peter nods at the woman as they pass.

"It's quiet," says Sonia.

"It's quiet most of the year," says Peter.

He points out a modernist, pre-war building just ahead of them. "I've always loved coming to see the shows," he says. "My all-time favourite act is Cannon and Ball." Reaching this seafront pavilion, they stop to look at the posters. "Look," says Peter, "Cannon and Ball." He is beaming, cheerful when he says, "Nothing changes."

Peter lets them into the house with a key that he wears on a chain around his neck. His mother comes into the hallway with her arms wide open, saying to Sonia as much as to Peter, "You're home!" Taking Sonia's jacket, looking at its bright colours, she says to Sonia, "Blue and green should never be seen!" and then she puts the jacket away.

As they sit down to dinner, Peter's mother says, "Sonia, what were you planning to do with your summer?"

"I've applied for a job up north," says Sonia. "I had the interview yesterday, and I think it went well. I should hear tomorrow whether or not I've got it. I gave them this number – Peter said that was all right. If I get the job, I'll save up for a while and then I want to go to Las Vegas." She mentions pictures she's seen of the place, all the lights.

"If you like that sort of thing," says Peter's father, "you should take an evening stroll along our prom. You'll see it all lit up." He chews his food for a while before saying, "It's a lot hotter there, though. It wouldn't suit me. We stick to England, the south coast."

A gust rattles the window and Sonia turns to see the wind stripping the last of the leaves from a potted shrub in the back yard.

"Look," says Peter's father, "the sun's coming out for you," and he nods towards a patch of sunlight the colour of weak urine on a whitewashed, breeze-block wall.

Peter's mother opens the wine and says to Sonia, "You'll be needing this." Sonia supposes she is referring to their long train journey, or perhaps the cold weather; it isn't clear.

"It's nice to have you home," says Peter's mother, later, when they are clearing the table.

"I think Peter's glad to be home," says Sonia.

"And what about you?"

"I don't live here," says Sonia. She is surprised that Peter's mother does not know this.

"You didn't grow up here," agrees Peter's mother. Opening the back door, she throws the scraps into the yard and the seagulls appear out of nowhere, descending instantly, filling the yard with their shrieks. "Our home is your home," she says, as she closes the door, "but I do remember what it's like to be young and independent. There are lots of empty flats around here and they always need people at the pavilion. The place is crying out for young blood."

"I wasn't planning on staying long," says Sonia.

Peter's mother nods. She looks around the kitchen and says, "Well, I think that will do. I'll go and change the sheets on your bed."

Their bags are side by side in the corner of Peter's bedroom. Hers has a sticker on the side saying I Las Vegas, even though she has never been there. His has a label giving his name – Peter Webster – and his home address, his parents' address, so that it can't get lost.

They go to bed early but Sonia lies awake in the darkness, in between the cold wall and Peter, who is fast asleep. She finally drops off in the early hours before being woken at dawn by what she thinks is the sound of babies crying, but it is only the gulls. She finds the noise depressing.

~

Sonia, in the bathroom, doing up the belt of her jeans, can hear Peter's mother talking on the phone at the bottom of the stairs. "No," she is saying, "I don't want it. I've changed my mind. Please don't call here again." Sonia checks her face in the mirror before coming out, finding Peter's mother on the landing now, outside the bathroom door. "All right, dear?" says Peter's mother. "Come down to breakfast. I've made pancakes with syrup, just like they have in America!"

Sonia stays in all day. At the end of the afternoon, at ten to five, she phones the company she had hoped would call to offer her a job. She speaks to a receptionist who says, "Please hold." Then she speaks to a secretary who tells her that the job has been offered to someone else. The secretary sounds impatient and terminates the conversation as soon as she can. Sonia redials – she has some questions to ask – but no one picks up; they've all gone home.

When Sonia goes up to bed that night, she finds that the sticker on her bag has been doctored with a permanent marker. 'Las' has been neatly changed to 'East' but 'Vegas' required a heavier hand, a thicker line. *I Eastmouth*.

The following day is Saturday. After breakfast, Sonia watches the dead-eyed gulls gathering on the wall of the yard. They grab at the scraps Peter's mother puts out, and if the door is not kept closed they will come inside, wanting the cat food, taking more than they have been given.

"I think I'll go for a walk," says Sonia.

"I'll come with you," says Peter, beginning to get to his feet.

"I'd rather go on my own," says Sonia. Mr and Mrs Webster stop what they are doing and look at her. They watch her as she leaves the room.

She puts on her shoes and looks for her jacket but she can't find it. She asks Peter's mother if she's seen it and Peter's mother says, "I'm washing it. Wear mine." She takes down a heavy beige coat and helps Sonia into it. "Yours was too thin anyway," says Peter's mother. "You'll need something warmer now you're here."

Sonia walks a mile along the promenade before coming to a stop, leaning on the railings and looking out to sea, watching a yellow helicopter that is circling in the distance. As a child, she used to wave to rescue helicopters even though she knew they weren't really looking for her; she just did it for fun or for practice. She raises her hands now and waves, scissoring her arms above her head, like semaphore, as if she were someone in a high-vis jacket on a runway, although she does not know semaphore; she does not know how to say 'stop'. The helicopter turns away and leaves.

"Sonia."

She turns around and finds Peter's parents standing behind her.

"We thought we'd walk with you," says Peter's mother. "What a good idea, a little leg stretch."

They walk along with her, nodding to the woman in the transparent mac as they pass the shelter.

When they reach the end of the promenade, Peter's father says, "We should turn back," and as they walk Sonia home again they tell her about the evening's entertainment: a show at the pavilion and dinner at the Grand.

"I've booked you a table," says Peter's father. "It's a fine place. It's where I proposed to Peter's mother. We go there every year for our anniversary."

"Have the seafood platter," says Peter's mother.

Peter, wearing one of his father's ties, walks Sonia along the blustery promenade. The seafront is all lit up with lightbulbs strung between the lampposts. "See?" says Peter. "Who needs Las Vegas?" At the pavilion, they see an Elvis. Sonia finds him disappointing. When the show is over, they go on to the Grand.

They are greeted as 'Mr and Mrs Webster' and Sonia opens her mouth to correct the misapprehension but they are already being led through the restaurant towards their table in the corner, and in the end she says nothing.

When the waiter comes to take their order, Sonia asks for a pasta dish.

"Are you not going to have the seafood platter?" asks Peter.

"I don't think so," says Sonia.

Peter looks concerned. He orders his own meal without looking at the menu.

Sonia, looking around at the decor, says to Peter, "I doubt they've changed a thing since your parents first came here."

Peter touches the flock wallpaper and says, "That's a nice thought."

The waiter returns to light their candle and pour the wine. They raise their glasses, touching the thin rims together. Sonia brings hers close to her mouth but barely wets her lips before putting it down again.

"All right?" says Peter.

Sonia nods. She has not yet told him about the test she did in his parents' bathroom, about the white plastic stick with the little window in the middle, the vertical line that proved the test was working, and the sky-blue, sea-blue flat line that made her think of a distant horizon seen through an aeroplane window. She has not told him that when she came out of the bathroom with the plastic stick still in her hand, Peter's mother was standing there, and that when, after breakfast, she looked for the stick, it had been moved.

The waiter returns with their meals. Peter, smiling down at the food on his plate, picking up his fork, begins to talk to Sonia about the possibility of a management position at the pavilion. His dad, he says, can pull a few strings.

The waiter is coming back already. He is going to ask them if everything is all right, and Sonia is going to say yes even though she has barely had a taste yet. Peter is holding his fork out across the table towards Sonia, offering her a piece of something whose fishy smell reminds her of the stony beach, the tarry pebbles, and the gulls that will wake her at dawn.

She sees, in the molten wax around the wick of the candle, an insect. Sonia picks up her fork, aiming the handle into this hot moat. She is an air-sea rescue unit arriving on the scene to lift the insect to safety. Carefully, she places the insect on a serviette to recover, as if it has only been floating in a sticky drink.

"I think that one's had it," says Peter, and Sonia looks at it and thinks he might be right.

Peter, who had the whole bottle of wine to himself, is still sleeping the next morning when Sonia gets up, puts on the beige coat and lets herself out of the house. She walks down the promenade again, away from Peter's parents' house, heading in the direction she and Peter came from when they arrived here. She goes as far as the end of the promenade, where she stops to watch the gulls, and then she goes further, climbing up above the town until she is standing a hundred metres above sea level in the wind. She is still in East-mouth, though. She cannot see across to the next town. When she looks at her watch, she realises that she has been gone for a while now. As she makes her way down from the cliffs, she hears the toll-ing of a bell; it is coming from the church that stands on top of one of the hills that surround the otherwise flat town.

On the promenade, all the shelters are empty. All the bay windows of all the retirement homes are empty. She realises that it's Sunday and wonders if everyone's at church. Peter's parents might be there, and perhaps even Peter.

She veers slightly away from the promenade now. It is the start of the summer and ought to be warmer, but it is windy and cold and she is glad of Peter's mother's coat. She has her purse in the pocket. She heads down a side street that brings her out at the train station, which is overlooked by the church.

Alone on the platform, she stands in front of the train time-table. She looks at her watch, although pointlessly, as it turns out, because when she consults the timetable she finds that no trains run on Sundays. She wanders to the edge of the platform and looks along the tracks in the direction she would go to get home, and then in the opposite direction. Is there really nothing at all on a Sunday, she wonders; does nothing even pass through?

She is still there when she notices that the woman in the transparent mac is now standing at one end of the platform. She is talking on a mobile phone but she is looking at Sonia and so Sonia nods at her. She doesn't know whether she has been recognised. The woman, putting away the phone, approaches. When she is within touching distance, she says, "You're the Websters' girl."

"No," says Sonia, preparing to introduce herself, whilst at the same time noticing the locals coming down the hill, coming from church. The service is over. It seems as if the whole town is heading towards them, like an army in beige and lilac.

"Yes," says the woman. "You are. You're the Websters' girl."

The crowd is nearing the foot of the hill; they are close now and one by one they look at the woman in the transparent mac and they nod.

REBECCA LLOYD

THE REUNION

I STILL HAD MY own key, a heavy, ornate iron object Charles had pressed into my hand on the day I left home. I'd carried it with me through several moves over the years, unable to bring myself to return it to him.

I hadn't been back to Shuttered House for a long while, I tried not to go there, and my parents, Charles and Isobel, didn't encourage it. We stayed in touch by phone, but they'd never done anything about the droning noise on the line, and it was sometimes so loud that even shouting didn't help. 'It's like everything else in this house,' Isobel said once, 'not working. But you know your father.' I didn't think I did know Charles, or even Isobel, but to have told them so would have caused terrible hurt, and then, as they'd always done, they'd have blamed each other and began another of their protracted and savage wars.

I'd forgotten about the peculiar claustrophobic smell that lingered in the house, and as I walked into the marbled entrance hall and took off my backpack, it was so powerful it made me gasp. It was a finer odour than that of wet leaves on a forest floor, yet of the same nature. It was as if the very foundations of the house, the stone and oak it was made from, exuded it. I suspected the smell was in large part responsible for the atmosphere, it kept you conscious always of the age and history of the place. Even if Charles had allowed heating in Shuttered House, I don't think it would've made much difference except in the very smallest of the rooms.

I'd decided, as I drove up through the avenue of yew trees that I'd try to find Isobel first, because Charles would be less offended to be the one discovered second. There were countless ways in which I could offend my parents; some so subtle they were beyond comprehension. I had a couple of days in which to reacquaint myself with their eccentricities and odd behaviour.

The drawing room door was open and I could see right through to the fields from the great leaded windows. I didn't sense Isobel was in there. I suspected, as it was a cold morning, I'd find her in the extra kitchen tucked behind the ballroom and close to what remained of the old vegetable garden. I took my backpack with me in case Charles appeared from nowhere to haul the thing off with him to hide in one of the bedrooms. The kinds of bargains I'd have to strike with him to get it back were outlandish, in the past they'd included removing yew berries off the driveway because he hated the transparent slime they contained. 'Rude black tongues as well. Considering removing the lot of them and planting hornbeams instead,' he said.

Isobel was in the small kitchen wearing a silk dress with a flounce at the back of it. She had all the gas rings lit on the stove and was warming her hands. Her hair had grown long and she'd scooped one side of it up into a diamante hair slide. She looked frozen, she had a purple feather boa wound twice around her thin neck and hanging to her thighs. "Fairy," she whispered, "I'm so glad you've come, you've no idea what he's been up to lately."

"Isobel, it's freezing in here." She came towards me in her silver dancing shoes and watched me unpack my bag on the table. "I've got you some really pretty long sleeved vests."

"Have you said hello to him yet?"

"I came straight to find you first. He told me you'd fallen on the Grand Staircase a while ago."

She shrugged. "Not all the way, just to the midsection."

"I saw the carpet as I came in, it's completely shot. There isn't a single step you can walk on safely now. If you don't do something about it soon, one of you'll end up in hospital."

"I did order a new stair carpet from Barringtons ten years ago, but they might not have kept it for me, I'm embarrassed to ask them. Anyway, it doesn't affect Charles; he uses one of the other staircases."

"It does affect him, Isobel. He was in tears on the phone. I think you falling really shook him." I handed her the vests and watched her face while she inspected them. "You did fall because of the rips in the carpet didn't you?"

"I caught my heel in one of them and fell backwards. He said it was my fault for drinking too much. I told him I was going to leave him, and he just laughed."

"Laughed at you?"

"Yes, at the idea that I could ever leave him. He tilted his head back and roared."

"On the phone he sounded really frightened. That's when he asked me to come down." I went to take her hands, but she moved away from me slightly.

"There's something he wants to talk to you about, and you mustn't laugh at him when he does."

"So, where d'you think he'll be now?"

She glanced at my backpack. "Hard to say, Fairy. He'll have seen your car, and then come in through the front to look for your bag. Lurking in the Damask Room, I expect. He bought himself a television set and put it in there. I'm not allowed to watch it."

"So nothing much has changed between you two, then?"

She rubbed her hands together and blew on them. 'No. We had a terrible fight shortly after he got the thing.'

"Oh, Isobel, why didn't you phone me?"

She shrugged. "The phone."

"What was it about this time?"

"The usual business; heating. I thought he might've come round to the idea. It was as if he'd suddenly realised we were in the twenty-first century and decided to embrace it when he got the TV. So I mentioned the poisonous words central heating to him one night. He threw something at me down the whole length of the table." She'd put two of the vests on over her dress and wound the boa around her neck a couple more times.

"Do you want me to talk to him about it?"

She smiled. "No point. He'll never change his mind about Shuttered House, but he's got another plan. You should go and find him now, Fairy. He'll be annoyed if he thinks you've spent too much time alone with me."

Charles was in the Damask Room as Isobel had thought, but he was hiding. I tried the five great oak chests in turn, the Japanese screen and the German wardrobe, and found him finally behind the curtains. "Found you!" I sang out, and hugged him. What hair he had left had turned silver. He still had his pigtail, a long thin plait that looked like the tail of an ancient rat.

"Fairy!" he said, as if my arrival at Shuttered House was a complete surprise. "You've seen her, I suppose?"

"She's in the little kitchen. It's terribly cold in there."

He stared at me as if I'd suddenly addressed him in a made-up language. "I've got a television," he said, pointing across the room towards the vast fireplace. "Second hand, but the picture is pretty good from time to time."

"What was it that you wanted to talk to me about, Charles?"

He looked hurt. "Why, aren't you staying?"

"Yes you know I am. Overnight."

"Who said you could stay as long as that?"

"You did on the phone. You asked me to come down to discuss an idea you had."

"Of course I did. That's the answer to your question, then."

"That's the answer to my question?"

"Yes, Fairy. Don't repeat me; it's a very annoying habit. There's plenty of time to talk."

Despite everything I'd said about the Sucking Room, it was the one they'd chosen for me. We were at dinner when I found out. My chair was positioned exactly halfway between them down the long oak table in the smallest of the three dining rooms; Charles had found his tape measure, and while Isobel made dinner, he'd located the exact midpoint and manoeuvred my chair into position. I was wearing my coat. "There are no mice in that room," he told me. "It was the second valet's room, nice and snug."

I looked down at my lap and wished to God I'd never come to Shuttered House. At night in the Sucking Room, it was pitch black and it didn't seem to matter if you kept the window curtains and the heavy brocade bed curtains open, it was always as dark and silent as the deepest cave. "Well in that case, you won't be seeing me much before lunchtime," I shouted over to Charles. "You've got no idea have you, how long it takes to get out of that room in the morning?"

"You're just being silly, Fairy. Isn't she, dearest?"

It was so silent in the Sucking Room that you could hear the workings of your own inner ear, a high-pitched hum absent in the presence of any other sound, even the most distant one. "Have you ever even been in that room Charles?"

"I might've done once."

"I put some magazines in there for you, Fairy," Isobel called to me. "We were thinking of you. It has that little bathroom and toilet where the big baroque built-in gargoyle wardrobe used to be. We didn't want you roaming the house at night trying to find a bathroom if you needed one."

I realised I was frightened. The last time I'd visited, I'd slept in that room. It was one of the smallest rooms in the house, just to the left of the top of the Grand Staircase. My most rational thought about it had it simply as somewhere intensely claustrophobic, but in my most panicky thinking, it tried to keep you in there, and it made you forget things so you'd have to go back and search about in the damp and heavy drapery for whatever it had spitefully concealed from you.

"Roaming about," Charles echoed. "Roaming about in Shuttered House isn't to be entirely encouraged. Isobel and I don't do it."

I picked up the dinner card beside my plate as if I hadn't heard him, and read what Isobel had written there – cream of veal and barley soup, roast loin of lamb with mint sauce, mashed parsnips, baked potatoes, orange marmalade pudding, cheese and biscuits. I suspected we might get soup and a baked potato; Isobel's dinner cards were merely what she'd liked to have made if she'd been able to. I noticed her handwriting had become shaky.

"It's probably warmer in the valet's room than anywhere else in the house," Isobel said, "certainly warmer than the Orchid Suite."

"It's going to be a cold winter, apparently," I said, taking my cue from her. I didn't look at Charles; I kept my head down while Isobel ladled soup into three bowls at her end of the table. "Going to freeze for weeks, apparently."

Charles drummed his fingers on the arms of his chair. "Important to keep on the move then, isn't it? I suppose that's a bit difficult in a narrow boat. Boring anyway only being able to walk up and down, surely?"

"I don't have to walk up and down to keep warm. It's as warm as toast in there," I told him.

"Is that a fact, now?"

"Absolutely. Small space, wood burning stove. A wood burning stove is a fantastic thing."

"Where d'you get the wood from?"

"I buy it from the garage, and sometimes find bits when I go walking. I'm never cold in the winter."

"A wood burning stove, how interesting, Fairy,"Isobel said clearly, as she came towards me slowly down the length of the table with my soup. "To be never cold in the winter, how wonderful."

"Wouldn't do for here of course," Charles remarked, in his special voice that tells the rest of the world to be silent.

Isobel couldn't help herself – "nothing would do for Shuttered House, would it though, Charles? Any kind of comfort at all would destroy its bloody integrity."

"Correct, dearest. That central heating lark means you have to drill great big holes through ceilings and floors. Can you imagine the amount of piping that'd be needed if I did decide to rape Shuttered House in that way? And, if nothing else, that's the way mice get through and leave their little droppings all over the furniture. Then they chew things up to make their nests. You do know, don't you that some of the hangings and tapestries here are fifteenth century?"

"This place is dangerous, Dad," I muttered without thinking. There was a hair in my soup like a water snake in a grey swamp, and I was trying to hook it out with my fork. Isobel had reached my father's place at the head of the table as I spoke, and as I looked up, she was standing by his side, staring at me. Charles's face was flushed and I couldn't tell if he was angry with me or shocked at my sudden lapse into intimacy.

"Of course it's dangerous, Fairy. Why do you think I love it?" he shouted.

My parents hadn't invited anyone else to Shuttered House for ten years. At one time, they'd held dinner parties in the west drawing room, particularly in the summer when the guests could wander outside through the french windows and onto the Rose Bower Walk. "But I couldn't do everything by myself," Isobel told me once. "Your father was so hopeless. When you have people to dinner, you need someone else to do the serving, and help people to drinks. He was always hopelessly drunk before the guests arrived."

I'd already left home then, yet I went back from time to time because despite certain things about Shuttered House and my parents that made my stomach twist into sour knots, there was no other place like it, no other place as strange.

It would take Isobel a couple of hours to dress for the dinner parties. She liked chiffon and trailing things, overlarge pearls and absurd shoes with bows and clasps and exaggerated heels. Her hair was elaborate, swept up away from her face, and coiled, bundled and teased in tricky ways, like our once topiaried hedges. She was in the habit of waiting until she'd supposed the guests were assembled in the drawing room, before appearing at the door as if just passing through and exclaiming joyfully at the unexpected presence of them all.

There were only ever three couples who came to these edgy events, the Grants, the Epsom-Cordings and the Murrays. Mrs. Grant always brought along some soup, or a dessert, in the knowledge, I believed, that Isobel was incapable of producing an edible meal. The Epsom-Cordings brought a few bottles of cheap wine, but made sure they had their own expensive one between them at the table. The Grants made jokes that filled in the long silences and diverted the attention of the other guests from Charles and Isobel. For in truth, these dinner parties were an arena in which my parents played out different aspects of their anguished relationship with each other, and the guests were merely props. More peculiar still was the fact that my parents changed roles when they had company. My mother bullied Charles relentlessly in front of the guests, and he dithered and beamed, and flapped about with coats and seating arrangements and aperitifs.

Even in those days, the issue of heating was constantly causing rows between them. "If I did anything to this house, it would need planning. Your mother and I would have to go away. No use doing small bits and pieces, it would be like a patchwork quilt then. We'd need to do everything together at the same time. Could take years. Can't possibly leave Shuttered House for that long."

They spent a lot of time in the upper kitchen then, there was a huge hole in the ceiling where clumps of plaster had fallen away to expose the old grey wooden slats beneath. They had a gigantic purple abstract painting on the wall, partly hidden by the fridge. The sink was small and useless and the bench adjoining it crammed with jars, bottles and gadgetry. There was no room to put anything down. A terrible soiled curtain hung beneath the sink on a piece of string and half hid a slew of sad things like dishcloths and scrubbing brushes. They did have a washing machine, but it didn't work. Although the kitchen was enormous and with a high ceiling, it'd become small and shabby as the number of cardboard boxes full of Charles's newspapers increased around the edges of the room.

I followed Charles out of the house through the servants' door at around eleven o'clock. I felt zombie-like and suffocated after my night in the Sucking Room. I'd considered leaving the door open as I arrived at the top of the Grand Staircase the night before in the hope that the room's effect would be weakened. Then it occurred to me that if I did so, my sleeping body would be exposed to the great corridor with its uneven floor, endless locked rooms, and the inexplicable whispering sound; I'd closed myself in for the night and tried to quell my revulsion.

I walked behind my father through the remains of the Rose Bower and into the topiaried garden. At the fountain he stopped, and turned around. "Well, Fairy, it's so good to see you. You've been living on that narrow boat for a while now, haven't you?"

"About eight years, Charles."

"It's a funny way of living; I don't suppose it would suit everybody."

"Perhaps not."

"Life of a vagabond, eh?"

"Of course it's not. I work like everyone else. It's just a choice."

"You could travel about if you wanted to though, couldn't you?"

"Yes. I take the boat out quite a lot, especially in the summer." He was picking clumps of moss off the rim of the fountain. "Not by myself though," I added.

"Oh. I thought you liked being alone and single."

"Of course I do, but I couldn't handle the boat alone when I'm taking it out. I take a friend with me to deal with the locks."

"I've been thinking that Isobel and I should give it a go."

I laughed, and quite loudly. It was, I thought, the beginning of some elaborate joke. "Yes. You could divide the boat off into two halves. You could live in the bow and Mother could be tucked away down the stern end."

He lifted his hand to silence me. "I'm in earnest, Fairy. I'm not sure how much longer your mother and I can go on with things in Shuttered House. I found her when she fell, you know, but it was merely by chance I was in that section of the house. She could have been there all night long. First time she'd let me touch her for ages."

"What are you saying – that you want to sell the house?"

"No need to whisper, Fairy. I've already discussed it with Isobel, and the house can't hear us."

I had a vision of Isobel in her silver shoes standing helplessly with the windlass next to a pair of vast lock gates. "What on earth did she say?"

"She asked if it'd be warm."

"And?"

He shrugged. "You told us both at dinner last night. Warm you said, warm all winter."

I moved away from him and turned to look back at the house. The light fell in such a way that all the windows were inky black and the grey of the house itself, darker. I'd noticed a striking crack in the drawing room wall up by the ceiling, earlier. It wasn't there when I'd last visited. The pinkish heraldic wallpaper had been sucked into it and turned grey. It was like the grinning mouth of an oafish boy. "This is ridiculous Charles; you'd hate leaving Shuttered House. Are you serious?"

"I think so. I don't know what else to do."

"It'd be like amputating a limb wouldn't it?"

"I've no idea, but the house is draining all our energy now."

"A gangrenous limb."

"Would you mind awfully if I did sell up?"

I drew in a breath. "I hate Shuttered House, every crumbling brick and twist of it, every damp room, dark corner and ripped curtain."

"There's no need to be quite so dramatic about it, Fairy. Looking after the house has been my life's work; it's hurting to hear you speak like that about it. I love the house, it's my soul."

"Look what it's done to you, Dad, and to Isobel. Do you think you could ever have got away with the way you both carry on if you'd been living in a semi somewhere?"

"What on *earth* are you talking about, carry on? I wish you wouldn't call me Dad, it's so infantile."

"Isobel's clothes, for one thing."

Charles laughed, and taking me by the arm, guided me through the twisted old topiary and back towards the house. "I absolutely agree with you, Fairy. Your mother chooses to be frozen all the time rather than give up her fancy stuff. But you can't blame Shuttered House for her strange behaviour, surely; it's plain vanity isn't it?"

"Where are you taking me?"

"I'm just going to show you where I spend most of my time these days."

Charles led me through a series of low ceilinged corridors in the depths of the house to a basement room with some natural light in it. He found me a chair, one of the ones I thought they'd thrown away when I was twelve. The others in the set of six were side by side along one wall with their grey-flecked stuffing bulging from the arms. 'What are these horrible things doing in here?' I asked.

Charles laughed. "Like revisiting your childhood, eh? I thought you'd be surprised."

"And this," I said, "isn't it Isobel's Japanese carving knife she lost years ago?"

"That's correct, Fairy. I chipped the blade and didn't dare tell her." He laughed. "It was after one of our dinner parties. I persuaded her that the Epsom-Cording woman had stolen it."

"Why, Dad, why do you do these things?"

He frowned. "Isobel has always been impulsive, Fairy; it was one of the things that first attracted me to her when we were young, and of course she was a great beauty. But you do expect a person to calm down eventually and act sensibly."

"What are you talking about?"

"She was forever throwing things away without consulting me. She got rid of all my boxes of newspapers one year from the old kitchen. I decided after that it was better to drag things down here when she put them out for collection, rather than challenge her about it."

I stared at him. "Has anything ever been thrown away from Shuttered House?"

"Only normal rubbish. I've rescued everything else; you really don't know when something is going to come in handy. Most of it's in the three rooms next to this one. They're getting pretty full now."

"It must be like trying to empty the ocean with a teaspoon for Isobel."

"Your mother wouldn't dream of coming down to the basement rooms, she doesn't like the way they smell. So she'll never know, and what she doesn't know won't harm her. Look, Fairy, whatever you may think, I love Isobel dearly. She thinks if she throws things away, you know – tries to change things in the house, it'll bring us together again. So I'm not going to stop her doing that, am I?" I studied my father as he stood before me; he had on a particularly ornate waistcoat, purple silk with embroidered edges. He was wearing a fez. "I want your mother to be happy, Fairy."

"How do you imagine you're going to live on a narrow boat, when you can't bear to throw anything away?" I spoke calmly and slowly. "I think you're quite insane, Charles."

He sat down slowly, opposite me. "That's the whole point, Fairy. If we did live in a boat, I wouldn't be able to rescue things and preserve them. I want to get out of the habit."

"But surely Isobel won't agree to leave Shuttered House. Where would she keep all her silly clothes and idiot shoes?"

"You're wrong, Fairy. We've talked about it a lot. She'd do anything to be warmer. I want me and your mother to become friends again." He looked down at his hands. "Husband and wife, even."

"Save your marriage?"

He nodded, and then burst into tears and hid his face with his big hands. I bit my lip and wondered if I should touch him or not. "Hey, Dad," I said gently, "I didn't realise things were that bad."

I arrived at the Orchid Suite before lunch. Isobel had left the doors open for me. She was brushing her hair at her ornate bow-legged dressing table. "What did he say?" she asked.

"That you're thinking of moving onto a narrow boat and getting rid of the house. Is that right?"

Her hands looked frail and mauve-coloured. "It's what *he* wants, Fairy. He threatened to leave me here alone. He said he'd always wanted a life of freedom, like a gypsy man. He said I could go or stay, it was up to me."

"He'll get over it. It's just one of those moments, isn't it?"

She shook her head. "I don't think so; he's been talking about it ever since I fell."

I felt nauseous, and spoke to her flatly. "Why did you need me to come here then, if it'd all been decided beforehand?"

"Don't be silly, Fairy. You're our daughter."

The trees along the canal had begun to lose their leaves, and the slightest breeze fluttered them onto the water where they came together in patches and drifts of vivid colour. Eventually there were so many of them floating downstream that the canal began to look like a never-ending curtain.

It wasn't particularly cold and I sat out most evenings on the rear deck and watched the fading light turn the rusty brown of the water dull. Small fish came to the surface in great numbers and made tiny bubbles and ripples along the far bank. Except for the soft chinking of blackbirds disturbed, it was silent along that stretch, and I was glad to be back home.

Isobel had known about Charles all along. "I'm forever throwing things out, Fairy, and he just takes them back out of the trash and hides them somewhere in the house."

"Really?" I'd watched her combing her hair, and couldn't imagine her anywhere else but Shuttered House. "Life on a narrow boat is very physical, Isobel. There's a lot of jumping on and off and tying ropes, and you'd have to deal with locks and sometimes the lock paddles aren't kept greased and they're hard to wind."

"It's what your father wants, though. So I'll have to get used to it."

"But why don't you just move somewhere smaller?"

Isobel laughed. "It wouldn't be dangerous enough for Charles."

"There's not much in it for you, Mum."

"Can you walk around in a tee-shirt in the winter on your boat?"

"I could, yes. But life on the canal is just as much about being outside."

I wondered how long it'd take my parents to give up the idea. I was pleased they were thinking about their fractured relationship, although in truth, I couldn't remember a time when there had ever been harmony between them, and each time I'd witnessed their fights, and sometimes been the object of them, I'd grown more despairing of the two of them.

I heard from my parents again in October, they'd bought a forty-foot cruiser stern narrow boat on the canal about thirty miles from my winter moorings. It took me a while to believe it. "Where are you?" Charles barked, "we'll come and see you. What a life eh? I wish I'd known sooner." I stared at my mobile as if it had bitten me.

They came noisily and fast in the late afternoon, causing a great muddy backwash along the banks. A wedge of ducks took off at the sound of the boat's horn. "Fairy," Charles shouted, as if surprised to find me waiting on the bank.

I couldn't see Isobel, and for a moment, I wondered if he'd left her behind. I didn't speak until I'd helped him moor up; nothing gracious came to mind. "I don't know what to say, Charles."

He beamed at me. "Welcome aboard The Reunion, Fairy."

"You did it then," I said stupidly.

Isobel was in the dinette, and her face was radiant. I squinted at her for a moment. "Are you all right, Isobel?"

She had her fur coat on and some leather gloves.

"Let's have some tea, you can make it can't you, Fairy? Your mother hasn't got her sea legs yet," Charles said.

"I can hear you, Charles, you're only a couple of inches away from me," I said, as I filled the kettle.

They'd put Shuttered House on the market, but they'd been warned that it could take a very long time indeed to sell, if at all. "I was hurt by that remark," Charles said. "Rather spiteful, I thought."

"Do you miss the house, Isobel?" I asked her gently.

She shook her head and nodded at the same time, and I couldn't read her expression, she seemed enthralled and child-like. "This boat's got central heating," she said.

They stayed for a week, moored up behind me. Isobel hardly came out, but Charles seemed to be everywhere, mopping the roof, checking the mooring ropes, and poking at the engine. I went for walks with him and felt both irritated and protective at the same time. I was confident that when the novelty of the experience had worn off, they'd return to Shuttered House and take the straggly old dump off the market. "What's the plan now?" I asked him.

"We'll move on, I think, Fairy. There are about seventy miles to explore, aren't there?"

I nodded. "There's a flight of locks further downstream. Do you want me to come down with you and help get you through?"

"Heavens, no. Your mother has to get used to the mechanics of the thing. She'll manage. I can't get her into deck shoes, but she bought herself some Italian cowboy boots and a pair of rather fetching leather trousers with fringes down the sides."

I laughed. We were walking back along the towpath towards the boats. "But there are a lot of bridges as well and some of them are very low."

He shrugged and beamed at me. "You know what Fairy? Isobel and I haven't, well you probably know this, shared a bed together for years. We're getting used to it again, and I must say it's a pleasure to have a warm body up next to yours on a cold night."

I'd never seen my father so buoyant and I could do nothing but smile at him.

They left as noisily as they came. I didn't help them cast off, Charles was determined that Isobel should learn how to crew. I could hardly bear to watch her struggling with the ropes; her face was white and rigid. They promised they'd keep in touch whenever possible, and I hoped that when they reached the locks there'd be people around to help them. For the next two weeks, I tried to keep them out of my thoughts. The weather had turned rough with capricious cold winds and constant bouts of rain, and I couldn't imagine Isobel jumping on and off the bank and dealing with ropes and knots.

Charles phoned me. They were moored up a few miles past the last locks. "No, of course she couldn't manage. She can't make head nor tail of the windlass, and we had a real drama at the drawbridge." I'd forgotten about the drawbridge on the bend before the winding point. "She got the thing up all right, then refused to go back and crank it back down. There was a line of cars waiting to cross. I forced her to do it eventually. She's hopeless at practical things, Fairy. If we have to moor up with stakes she can scarcely lift the hammer."

"Do you want me to come down with a couple of friends?"

"Look, what's the point? We have to do this by ourselves. Your mother's always had crazy ideas, and this narrow boat business is the maddest of all."

I didn't say anything for a moment. "Dad?"

"Yes?"

"I didn't realise you weren't keen on the idea. I thought this was all about saving your marriage."

"Of course I'm keen on it Fairy. I'm keen on anything your

mother dreams up to make things better between us."

"It was her idea?"

"Of course it was."

"She told me it was yours."

"No, no. How could that be? You know how I feel about Shuttered House. Isobel thinks that if she lives like you, she'll become as independent as you; she admires you dreadfully, you know."

"Really?"

"And however hopeless she is, she's dealing with the space business much better than me. I'll admit I'm finding it tough, like being in a sardine tin."

"You're missing Shuttered House."

I try to remember the last hurried conversation I had with my father, but only small fragments of it return. "She hides inside every time a bridge appears and when we get there she shouts head! head! It's so annoying, Fairy."

They'd made it as far as the Wash and at that point, there was nothing to do but turn back and retrace their steps. I like to believe that they managed to work a few things out and undo some of the tight ice-frozen knots in their marriage finally. I went down to the Wash myself and pulled into the last safe mooring place after Straddling Lock. You can see the ocean from there stretching away to the horizon. "We've worked things out, Fairy," my father had shouted down the phone. "We're all right now. We're going on the big adventure."

"What big adventure, Dad?"

"Out, out, where do you think?"

"How's Mum?"

"She's very happy now. I told her that once we get out there won't be any jumping on or off. No mooring, nothing. We'll just keep on going."

The line was bad and I couldn't quite get his drift. "Speak slowly, Charles. Where are you?"

"At the end. We're at the end."

"You've reached the Wash?"

"It's beautiful out here. You can see for miles. It's the space you see, Fairy. Your mother and I need the space again. I'm phoning to tell you that we love you."

"Wait Dad!"

'Wait who, Fairy?'

"Wait, Charles. When are you coming back? I'll make dinner, get some good wine." Even as I spoke, stumbling over my words, I knew.

"Got to go, my love. Got to go."

No remains of The Reunion, or my parents, were ever recovered. They'd ploughed straight out into the wide cold sea. They'd been seen once by some fishermen, the boat was slewing badly in the monstrous waves, and it must have been taking in water by the bucket load. When I think about them now, I imagine them together on the rear deck, Charles is steering and Isobel is just behind his shoulder with the palm of her hand on his back, her hair free and her face eager, and the sea as calm as a mill pond, as calm as a canal on a summer's morning.

HELEN GRANT

THE THIRD TIME

"**I**'M SORRY, STEPHEN," said the dying man. He lay propped on a pile of snowy-white pillows. His gnarled and liver-spotted hands grasped feebly at the metal bed rails, as though he would lift himself upright one last time and speak as man to man, and yet he lacked even that power. He could do little more than turn his drawn face towards the figure silhouetted in the golden square of window.

"Sorry, Uncle Toby?" said his nephew, turning from his contemplation of the gravel drive and gardens below. His own sleek cabriolet was parked down there, its scarlet bodywork gleaming in the evening sunshine. The sight gave him little pleasure; things weren't going as well as he'd expected lately and the repayments were difficult to meet.

"What have you got to be sorry for?" Stephen asked. He spoke lightly, but his brows drew together almost imperceptibly. *I hope he hasn't changed his will*, he said to himself.

"It will be troublesome to you," said the old man hoarsely.

"What will, uncle?" Stephen went over to the bed, although he stopped short of patting the arthritic old hand that trembled on the bed rail. He was afraid of overdoing it, of assuming a familiarity that they had never really had. Uncle Toby might think he was simply after the money. Was he? Stephen didn't even want to ask himself that question.

"Dealing with – the heirs."

The heirs? God in heaven – he has *changed his will.*

Stephen struggled not to allow his dismay to show on his face.

The old man's eyes, faded blue, were on him. "You needn't worry," he said. "I've still left most of it to you."

Stephen flushed, more from annoyance than out of embarrassment. It was appalling to think that the old man had seen through him as easily as that. However, he simply said, "That is very kind of you, uncle," in his mildest tone.

"Never mind," said his uncle impatiently, his head moving restlessly on the pillow. "Listen, Stephen. I never meant to ask you to do this. I intended that the matter should be settled before the estate came to you. But . . ." He exhaled heavily. "It has been too much for me. You must do it. And – I am sorry."

"What must I do, Uncle Toby?"

"You must pay them the money back."

"Who . . . ?"

The palsied hand sketched protests in the air. "Stop asking questions and let me speak, Stephen. I'm very tired." Two long stertorous breaths followed and then the old man began again. "The estate is nearly as it was in my grandfather's time. That's something to be proud of – mostly. The wood had already been grubbed up by then, but it's not difficult to know where it was. The lane that leads up from the bottom of the gardens is still called Betton Wood. It's just open land now, Stephen, with nothing particular to recommend it. You won't miss it when you come into the estate."

"You've *sold* it?" Stephen couldn't keep the dismay out of his voice – but there was worse to come.

"Yes, and you must give the money to the heirs."

"What heirs?" Stephen had forgotten his uncle's injunction to stop asking questions.

"The ones it belongs to. *Should* belong to. It took me a long time to find them. A lifetime, in fact. My grandfather tried, because the matter troubled him too, but he never managed it. Things have changed now, though, since so many records have been computerised."

"Digitised, you mean."

"Whatever you say. The fact remains, you can get at things now that it would have been very laborious to find when I was your age. And so at last I tracked them down – the descendants. They live in Australia, in a place with an absolutely extraordinary name which escapes me at this moment. You'll find it in the papers, though . . ."

"But Uncle Toby," began Stephen, with a perplexed look on his face, "do you mean to say you've sold part of the estate and you really intend the money to go to these people in Australia? Are they relatives of ours? I thought . . ." he gathered his courage and pressed on. "I thought there was only me and Aunt Judith?

"And – and anyway, if the family hasn't heard from them since before your grandfather's time, I don't think you're *obliged* to them in any way. Although," he added hastily, "it is, of course, your right to do as you please with the estate."

"Hum," said his uncle. "No, they are not relatives. In fact we have no connection with them at all, other than through our ownership of Betton Court and the attached lands. No, Stephen, before you ask me any more questions, I want you to go to my study and bring me the papers that are in the top drawer on the right-hand side of my desk. They are not difficult to find; they are in a brown manila folder marked *Betton Wood*."

As the door closed after his nephew, the old man remarked under his breath, "Even such a blockhead as you should be able to find them." He waited, relaxing into the pillows and closing his eyes, as though his head ached.

Stephen Philipson made his way along the passage to the study. The passage was oak-panelled and windowless, and therefore rather gloomy even on bright days. Now, with the sun sinking to its rest, it was downright dingy. He looked ahead to the turn of the corridor and saw someone flit about the corner. Most certainly it was one of the nursing staff who attended his uncle; who else would it be? And yet in the dim light the figure was rather indistinct. Stephen could have sworn that its attire was rather more bohemian than one would have expected from a person in uniform. He shrugged to himself. The personal grooming of his uncle's nursing staff was not a matter of great importance. He had forgotten about it almost as soon as he entered the study.

Toby Philipson's study was one of the most attractive rooms in the house. It had a great bay window overlooking the grounds. The fine old beech trees threw long shadows at this time of day. The room itself was done out in dark wood, with the soft furnishings in faded shades of green and crimson. There was a library elsewhere in the house, but there were bookshelves here too, filled with their owner's favourite volumes. There was a big Turkish rug and a large desk near the window with a very old-fashioned black telephone standing on it; and placed close to the hearth were several high-backed Chesterfield armchairs, the leather worn and shiny with age. Altogether it was a very comfortable room in a bachelor-ish sort of way.

Stephen found it appealing but also to a certain extent intimidating; he couldn't imagine himself as the master of such as place as this. It had everything he hadn't had in his own life to date: easy, comfortable, luxury; an air of gentility. He, Stephen, had a lifestyle that was fine enough seen from the outside, but that had been won by dreary graft and politicking. Worse, his position was as insecure as that of the King's favourite at a mediaeval court. It was hard to imagine himself in Toby Philipson's shoes, and impossible to stop himself from wanting it.

He went over to the desk and opened the top right-hand drawer. Sure enough, there was the manila folder, with *Betton Wood* written on it in his uncle's firm handwriting.

On the way back, with the folder under his arm, he noticed again how very dark the passage was. The lamps were illuminated but the light that they shed was sallow and insufficient to penetrate the gloom. Stephen saw that they flickered, too, which was worrying; if the electrics were faulty it would cost a fortune to get the place rewired. His suspicions were confirmed by a sudden and curious sensation that something less distinct than an echo, some current of energy as fleet and inaudible as a bat squeak, had passed through him invisibly and vanished. The tiny hairs on the backs of his hands were standing up as though through static. He wondered if it were possible that electricity was actually being discharged into the air from some faulty connection. Could such a thing even happen? He wasn't sure, but it wasn't an encouraging sign. Something like that had to be dangerous, and that meant electrician's bills.

At any rate the fault was intermittent. The lights stopped flickering and became constant, and noticeably brighter.

When he opened the door and went back into his uncle's room his expression of concern swiftly turned to one of actual alarm. He saw at once that the old man was in an extreme of agony, his aged body clenched as rigidly as a fist, the eyes upturned to show the whites.

"Uncle Toby?"

The old man did not reply. Stephen, panicking, looked futilely for a buzzer or bell with which to summon the nurse; finding none, he turned to the door, intending to shout for help. Then he heard a gasp, and turning back he saw that the seizure had passed. His uncle lay on the pillows panting and coughing as though he had been revived from near-drowning. His face was a very alarming colour, so grey that the skin had an almost bluish cast.

"Uncle Toby?" Stephen went to the bedside. "Where's the bell? Let me ring for the nurse."

"No," croaked his uncle.

"But you're ill, you need . . ."

"No," said the old man emphatically. He took a heaving, shuddering breath. "I'm used to it, Stephen. The nurse can't do anything for me anyway. It will finish me soon, and that will be an end to it." The blue eyes moved restlessly, their gaze seeking out the manila folder. "Sit down – not there, here by me. Haul that chair over. Now, open the file."

Stephen did so, and found that the topmost document – there was a small sheaf of them inside – was a letter from a firm of solicitors, clearly representing Toby Philipson. It was addressed to someone whose name Stephen did not recognise, in a place called Wonglepong, Queensland. The word COPY was stamped upon it.

Stephen looked for the date and discovered that the letter had been sent some seven months before. He skim-read the contents with a sinking feeling; his uncle had sold the land all right, and he had offered outright to make a gift of the proceeds to this person or persons, if they would make themselves known to his lawyers. Inevitably they would have accepted; who wouldn't? He bit his lip, drawing his brows together in a frown.

"These are the people?" he said aloud, fingering the corner of the letter. "In Wonglepong?"

"Yes," said his uncle, and the word was almost a sigh.

"What did they say?" asked Stephen, steeling himself for the reply.

"Nothing," said the old man. "They've never replied."

Maybe they never got the letter, thought Stephen. It was hard to think of another reason why someone would ignore such an offer. Aloud, he said, "Well, I think you've done as much as anyone could do, uncle. I should just . . ."

"No, no," said the old man, almost in a passion. "Don't tell me to forget it. This is very important, Stephen. They *must* have the money, do you hear me?"

"But why?"

"Look at the other documents." A trembling forefinger stabbed at the air. "Look, look."

Stephen did so, rather reluctantly. After a few minutes, he said, "I can't follow this, Uncle Toby. What is this – Old English?"

"Hardly," said his uncle tiredly. "I'll explain it to you, if I must. It relates to a trial – you must at least be able to see that? Well then. A long time ago, before there were Philipsons at Betton Court, there was a family named Bryan. The husband died and the wife married again, becoming Lady Theodosia Ivie, and it is her trial that is described in those pages. She was proved to have committed perjury and forgery. In fact she was a thorough . . ." The old man paused, and it seemed to Stephen that he was listening, somewhat apprehensively. "Well, don't let us indulge in name-calling. At any rate, the case went against her, but this was not the first time she had been mixed up in something of the kind. When she was still Theodosia Bryan of Betton Court, she is said to have appropriated some land that belonged to two children who had no one to represent them. And you know, Stephen, what the Bible says about those who do such things." The old man's eyes were unblinking. "I see that you don't know. It says, *accursed be he who removes his neighbour's landmark*. Or she, as the case may be."

"Really?" said Stephen.

"Yes, really. The land, of course, was the area that used to be Betton Wood, and the children, or at any rate the children's descendants, are these people in – Wonglepong. The land belongs by rights to them, and since it is hardly to be imagined that they will travel some ten thousand miles to claim it, I sold it, and intend to pay the money to them. I cannot do it before I die. I've no time left – no energy. *You* must do it, Stephen. I want you to have this folder. Take it with you when you go back to London. You'll need to start work on it as soon as possible. Tonight . . . tomorrow."

His nephew was bemused. "But Uncle Toby – this business with the wood and the landmark, it must have been ages ago."

"Centuries," said his uncle.

"Well, won't it seem strange that we are trying to pay them back after all this time? Perhaps that's why they haven't replied. They think it's a joke or a hoax, maybe an attempt to get something out of them, like these spam messages you get."

"Spam messages? No, don't try to explain. It doesn't matter what they think, as long as they accept the money."

"But Uncle . . ."

"Stephen, don't you see? It's not them we're doing it for! It's *us*!" The old man reared up off the pillows in his excitement, batting away the hand that his nephew extended in a tentative gesture of restraint. "Oh, it won't do me any good now. I'm finished. But *you* – it has to be done for *you* – and for *her*."

"Her?" Did he mean Aunt Judith? It took Stephen several moments to realise what the old man meant. "You mean Lady whatever-her-name-is? She's been dead for God knows how long, Uncle Toby. She isn't going to care either way."

"But she *will*, Stephen! And so will you if you don't make sure that money is paid over. You'll hear her, Stephen!" The liver-spotted hand grasped at the younger man's sleeve, and it was all that Stephen could do not to recoil. "You'll hear her every evening when the sun goes down. Once – twice – it goes through your head – you can have no idea of it. The things she can make you see! Every evening . . ."

"Calm down, Uncle Toby. That's not possible . . ."

"Damn fool!" exploded the old man. "Why do you young people have to be so bloody *rational*? You think I don't know what's possible? I've heard her myself – tonight. She'll be back again before sun-up, but I won't know when. That's the agony of it, Stephen! You know you'll hear it the second time, and it plays on your nerves all the while, and when it happens it's *worse* than you think it's going to be! She's out now, Stephen. Before it was the land – she was tied to it – but now it's the money, and where is the money? It's numbers on a piece of paper, and they belong to me, so she follows *me*, Stephen! Aaahhh . . ."

The old man fell back on the pillows, his mouth a taut square of agony, his eyes tight shut.

"Uncle Toby," said his nephew, trying to sound firmer than he felt, "this is no good. We have to call your nurse." Now at last he saw the buzzer on its white cord, half hidden between the pillows; he pulled it out and pressed it several times, urgently.

Before long the sound of hurrying feet could be heard coming down the passage. Stephen, still leaning doubtfully over the bed, would have drawn back, but before the footsteps reached the room, his uncle's eyes opened again. The gnarled hand grasped at his wrist.

"When I hear her the third time in one night," whispered the old man with a dreadful effort; "then I'll be dead."

His eyes closed again and the grip on Stephen's wrist relaxed. For one moment Stephen thought that this time the end had really come, but then the wrinkled mouth dropped slackly open and the sound of laboured breathing proved that the old man still lived.

Nevertheless, Stephen was deeply shocked. When the nurse came into the room, a compact bustling figure in white, he was quite unable to speak to her. He simply stood back, and watched as she bent over his uncle, speaking soothingly, expertly taking his pulse.

After a few minutes she glanced at him and said, "I'm very sorry, Mr Philipson, but it might be better if . . ." She hesitated, but Stephen had taken the hint.

He nodded self-consciously. "I understand. Goodbye, Uncle Toby."

Reluctantly, he picked up the manila folder marked *Betton Wood*. As he left the room he asked himself whether there hadn't been something a little off in the woman's manner. She had spoken politely enough and her expression was blandly neutral, but he thought there had been a look in her eyes – some slight taint of resentment. Did everyone think he was a sponger, a carrion crow circling the corpse before it was even cool? He flushed to think of it.

Stephen hurried down the stairs. He couldn't wait to get outside, into the fresh air. He'd blow away a few cobwebs on the drive home – it was only a pity he'd be making most of the trip in darkness now.

As he crunched his way across the gravel to the car, he glanced back at the house. Was it his imagination, or did the lights visible in the front windows flicker momentarily? He shook his head resignedly.

He had almost made it home when they called him on his mobile to tell him that his uncle had died.

Stephen took the following day, a Monday, off work – more on administrative than compassionate grounds. A death in the family was a very painful thing, he thought: the red tape was aggravating, and worse, there would be a lot of expense. The big one, of course, was inheritance tax – that was quite hefty enough to make him consider anew whether he was going to want to hold onto the Court. It wasn't close enough to London to be really convenient and it would cost a fortune to run. It could probably be rented out at an outrageously advantageous price to a Russian or Saudi businessman, but that would mean supervising a colossal amount of work beforehand – starting with the faulty electrics. Everything seemed to mean money upfront – money, and paperwork.

It wasn't until late in the afternoon that he picked up the manila folder marked *Betton Wood* again. It had lain all day neglected on the coffee table in his sitting-room. Now he sat down on the couch and looked at it sceptically.

A neighbour's landmark, indeed.

Stephen was not sure whether to laugh or groan about it. The whole idea was crazy – trying to repay a misdemeanour – an *alleged* misdemeanour – that was hundreds of years old. It was pure good luck that the unknown people in Wonglepong, Queensland, had either failed to receive the letter or decided not to believe in it. Why should they have the money, anyway? They had no real connection with Betton Court. The cash could be far better employed in helping to pay off the death duties.

The moment *that* thought occurred to him the folder acquired a glamour of interest that it had hitherto lacked. He put down the glass of whisky he had been nursing and reached for it.

How much . . . ?

As his fingertips touched it, Stephen felt a startling and unpleasant sensation. A single note, sharp and resonant as the sound of a wet finger tracing the rim of a wine glass, rang through his head. It rose to a shrill peak and then abruptly it was gone, but Stephen had the impression that it had simply vanished into a register too high for his ears to hear; for seconds afterwards he seemed to feel a subtle vibration within his skull, and there was a metallic taste in his mouth, as though he had bitten on tinfoil.

Tinnitus, he thought, dropping the folder on the table and pressing his hands to his ears, and then, *No, migraine, a bloody awful migraine.*

Everything was grey – dead – even the flame-coloured sunset visible through the plate glass window had faded to sepia, blending into a city skyline that appeared to be crumbling into decay.

Stephen grimaced, squeezing his eyes tight shut, and when he opened them the effect had entirely vanished. Everything was normal. The apartment had returned to its own colours. The sinking sun flared orange over the London rooftops. Each detail was sharp and distinct, without trace of weathering or dilapidation.

He pressed a hand to his mouth, feeling faintly nauseous.

Migraine aura, he said to himself. He cleared his throat, and then he said it aloud.

"Migraine aura." He looked at the sheaf of papers spilling across the table-top and said, "I don't think I'll do any work on that tonight."

His words were absorbed into a silence that was as deadening as a layer of snow. He poured himself another measure, a more generous one this time, and as he did so his hands were trembling.

The following morning, Stephen awoke with a throbbing headache that confirmed his self-diagnosis of migraine aura. Or perhaps, he thought doubtfully, as he staggered into the living room and saw the severely depleted bottle of whisky standing on the coffee table like a reproach, it was down to overindulgence. The mere sight of the tumbler with a residue of whisky in it made his stomach lurch alarmingly. He went into the kitchen and took three aspirin with a large glass of water. Then he rang the office and told them he'd be late in.

"Food poisoning," he said, and even he himself could tell that he sounded too rough to be disbelieved.

After that he went back to bed and slept for the rest of the morning. The sun was high in the sky when he woke, feeling relaxed and well rested. The headache had gone.

Stephen showered, shaved and dressed carefully in a dark suit, double-cuffed shirt with gold links and a woven silk tie in peacock colours. As luck would have it, he had an out-of-town meeting with a client that afternoon, so there was no need to go into the office at all now. Instead he had a very pleasant drive – he was travelling against the flow of traffic both ways, and on the return journey he put down the soft-top and enjoyed the late afternoon sunshine. He turned off the motorway before he was back in the city, and had a light dinner at a country pub, limiting himself to a single beer – he didn't want to lose his licence. By the time he reached home, the sun was setting behind him.

Stephen drove into the quiet street that ran behind the block where he lived. It was a rather sharp turn into the entrance to the underground car park where he had a space; he always took great care, not wanting a scratch or scuff on the car's gleaming scarlet bodywork. As he turned the wheel, there was a sudden appalling sensation like a detonation within his head. The sound was so shrill and loud that it was like a physical pain, a steel spike driven savagely through his skull. It was followed by a second report as the wing of the red cabriolet hit the wall and crumpled into an ugly tangle of metal, but Stephen didn't hear that at all. He slumped behind the wheel, the whites of his eyes showing through half-closed lids, his hands jittering in his lap as though he were having some kind of fit.

The world reformed slowly around him. He became conscious first of voices, one male, one female.

"Are you all right, mate?" said the male voice. The speaker sounded as though he was about the same age as Stephen, also from London, but not by any means as well-off.

The woman was old – you could tell that at once from the fussy, disapproving tone. "I suppose he's drunk. Drink driving. Disgusting."

Stephen opened his eyes and saw two things like scarecrows leaning over the sides of the car towards him – thin, faded, swathed in the tattered rags of clothing. Then his focus sharpened and he saw them for what they really were: lidless, lipless creatures, more bone than flesh, hung about with the last rotting remains of garments that did not conceal the horribly sunken chests, ribs showing like stripes. He screamed hoarsely.

"Get off me – get off me – get off!"

The car had stalled but he fumbled hysterically for the keys.

The old woman and the window cleaner who had hurried over when they saw Stephen's car hit the wall saw what was about to happen and both stepped back smartly. The engine roared into life.

Stephen backed the car up a couple of metres, aimed it at the garage entrance and shot inside with a squeal of tyres. On the way in he managed to scrape the car against one of the concrete pillars and as the old woman and the window cleaner gazed after him open-mouthed they distinctly heard the crash as the front of the car hit the wall at the end of the parking space.

They looked at each other, the old woman a little pink with indignation, the window cleaner barely suppressing a grin.

"Tosser," said the window cleaner.

"Well I never!" said the old woman, although it was unclear whether she was aiming this remark at Stephen for crashing the car, or the window cleaner for his language.

Inside the flat, Stephen finished off the bottle of whisky, pouring each generous measure with hands that shook as badly as his aged uncle's had.

What the hell just happened to me? he thought feverishly.

Toby Philipson's words floated unbidden through his mind. *You'll hear her every evening when the sun goes down . . . The things she can make you see!*

No, he said to himself, shaking his head as though to rid himself of biting insects. *No. It's ridiculous.*

All the same, he found himself eyeing the folder on the coffee table and the fan of documents that had spilled from it, with a kind of wary repulsion, as though it were a somnolent rattlesnake. He was reluctant even to touch those papers. Besides, he knew perfectly well what they contained. A transcript of a trial so far beyond living memory that it might never have happened, and a letter addressed to some people in Wonglepong with whom he had not the slightest connection.

Power of suggestion, he said to himself. *Uncle Toby spooked me with his stories of shrieking ghosts and landmarks, that's all.* He put up a hand and rubbed distractedly at his brow. *Or it was that migraine I had yesterday. You can get all sorts of weird effects with those.*

That made sense – far more sense, anyway, than the idea that some seventeenth century noblewoman with an ancient wrong to right was haunting his cranium with her screams. Still, Stephen winced at the idea of it happening a second time before sun-up.

That's the agony of it, Stephen! his uncle had said. *You know you'll hear it the second time, and it plays on your nerves all the while, and when it happens it's worse than you think it's going to be!*

He felt a wave of sympathy for the old man. He must have been off his rocker, but whatever he thought he'd been experiencing, well, if it was anything like what had just happened to Stephen, it was a wonder the old fellow had lasted as long as he had. He must have been a very tough old bird.

Stephen brought himself up sharply. *This is rubbish. Uncle Toby was older than God and very sick, and I just had a migraine. Anything else is just madness.*

With more sang-froid than he felt, he reached over and picked up the sheaf of papers, tapped them neatly on the table-top to line them all up, and slid them back into the folder. He'd file them to-morrow – under *waste paper*, possibly. Or perhaps he'd just take the folder down to the courtyard below and set light to it. Either way it would make little difference. Either those people in Queensland would wake up and write demanding their money, or else they'd forget the whole thing. No input was required from Stephen.

He went to bed with a bellyful of whisky and awoke in the morning with a sour taste in his mouth, but no trace of a headache. He was able to leave for work as usual, and since he was heading directly to the office, not out to a client, he took the train. Without seeing the damage to the red cabriolet, he could almost forget the incident had ever happened.

As the working day progressed, Stephen became aware of a growing restlessness. It was early autumn, and the days were still fairly long, but he found himself peculiarly conscious of the sun's slow progression down the sky. As the shadows began to lengthen and the sunshine slanting through the plate glass windows of his office acquired the gilded tints of early evening, he began to fidget. He had a meeting scheduled at the end of the day. Normally this would not have bothered him – in this line of work you didn't expect to clock out on the stroke of five – but now he found himself wondering whether it would happen again. The screaming sound in his brain. The visions of decay. Stephen couldn't imagine coping with that during a business meeting, with half a dozen other people sitting around him. The ones at his level – they were always snapping at each other's heels, looking at a way to get ahead. If they noticed him turning green because of noises in his head, they'd be the first to take advantage with false sympathy and suggestions of gardening leave. And as for the boss, Nicholas Fenn, dubbed "Old Nick" behind his back, his disapproval would roughly equate to the pollice verso given to defeated gladiators.

Stephen began to perspire, tugging irritably at the collar of his shirt, as though the air were too thick to breathe. He tried to calculate how long the meeting would last at worst – to remember exactly when he had heard the thing on the two previous nights. Of course, the sunset was a minute or two earlier each day . . . Then Old Nick's secretary Delia looked in and told him the meeting had been put back forty-five minutes; as the door closed behind her an actual whine escaped Stephen's throat.

There was nothing for it, though. To dodge the meeting would be as bad as making an exhibition of himself. He'd have to grit his teeth and get on with it, and hope Old Nick managed to limit his seemingly limitless monologues for once.

The meeting began. The sun was very low in the sky; already it had dropped behind the buildings on the west side of the street. With all the lights on and the smell of freshly-brewed filter coffee on the air, the meeting room was cheerful enough, and yet Stephen found himself having to suppress the impulse to keep glancing out of the window at the evening sky.

He was overwhelmed with the dreadful conviction that if *it* happened, it would be before the meeting ended. He managed to keep his part of the discussion going, but under the polished table-top his left hand was curled into a fist, the nails digging into the palm of his hand.

Then it happened. He felt it approaching, like a crackle of static. When it came, it was worse than anything he had experienced yet. The sound erupted inside his head, brutal as an electric shock, loud as a klaxon, drilling into his brain as though it wanted to bore tunnels through the very tissue like some kind of auditory Creutzfeldt-Jakob Disease.

Stephen was rigid with agony; if he had been standing he would have fallen. By happy chance he was seated and all the attention was elsewhere; Old Nick was holding forth again.

As the shrieking died away he knew what to expect. All heads were turned away from him, towards Nicholas Fenn, so he was spared the sight of their dead faces, but he could see Old Nick's all right. It was hardly human, the decomposing flesh the ripe colour of bruises, gelatinous, nearly liquefied in places. When Nick spoke, the rotting substance of the face parted and Stephen could see the yellow teeth and the ligaments moving within it. Below the soft flaccid rot of the neck the Savile Row suit, expensive shirt and silk tie were spotted with mossy-looking mould.

Then it passed. Nicholas Fenn was simply Old Nick again – florid, self-important, aggressive, but very much alive. The Savile Row suit was impeccable. The subordinates who hung on every word like sycophantic courtiers toadying to a Tudor monarch were themselves once more.

Stephen unclenched his fists and relaxed his shoulders. With the return of normality came a sudden and unexpected thrill of triumph. He'd known what was coming – had faced it – had survived it without giving anything away to those around him.

I've won, he thought.

Now that the cri du jour (as he ironically dubbed it) was behind him, and no harm had come of it, Stephen relaxed. He didn't have the car with him, so instead of driving home after the meeting, he went to an expensive bar near the office with a couple of the others. He didn't really consider them friends; they'd stab him in the back given an opportunity, and he might quite probably do the same to them. Still, they were acceptable drinking companions, so long as you didn't have enough to do or say anything indiscreet. After a while, that seemed a possibility, so Stephen moved on to another bar, further away from his place of work.

There he met a girl. She was diminutive and very blonde with brown roots, and wore a clinging dress that seemed to be made of bronze scales. She had a very slight accent; Stephen couldn't tell what the accent was and didn't ask.

When they got back to his flat she seemed impressed, wandering around with a glass of wine in her hand, admiring the furnishings and the view of the London skyline that was costing Stephen so very dearly. After a while he took the wine glass gently from her hand and kissed her. A little later they went into his bedroom and he discovered that the body under the bronze scales was just as gorgeous as he had imagined.

The scream when it came was like a thunderclap. Stephen had

forgotten the thing that he had apparently inherited along with the Betton Wood issue; he expected nothing anyway given that he had heard it at sundown, and now his defences were down entirely. If the first one had been like a grenade going off, this one was a bomb. Something seemed to give way inside his head; he could feel the force of it exploding out in all directions like blast damage. His ears rang and *my God* they hurt; he thought for a split second he could feel the eardrums straining outwards, bursting with the pressure of the explosion in his cranium.

His head lolled; he looked down and he saw himself and the girl, their bodies entwined as closely as two human beings could be, but he saw them as they would be after six months underground. Between bones that showed through the ruined remains of flesh, worms writhed, fat and white. The girl's face was a lunar landscape, dead and grey, with craters where the eyes should have been.

Stephen didn't make a sound. His eyes rolled up into his head. When he came round, the girl had wriggled her way out from under him and was standing by the bed wearing not very much at all and screaming into the telephone in a language he didn't understand. The operator must have worked out what she wanted though, because not much later the paramedics arrived.

"It wasn't a heart attack," Stephen insisted. Then he saw the way they were looking at him and touched his face. His fingers came away bloody; his nose had been bleeding.

The next morning, Stephen telephoned Toby Philipson's solicitor, Alasdair Weston. He phoned from his office, with the door tight shut. Even if he hadn't had a private call to make, he would have wanted to shut the others out; they were talking about him, he knew it. He looked like death warmed up, he knew that too. In the cold light of day, with the buzz of human activity just outside his door, he couldn't quite believe in the disembodied shrieking that went with Betton Wood.

Power of suggestion – and stress-induced migraine, he said to himself. Still, whatever it was, he couldn't face much more of it. These people in Wonglepong had to be made to take their money, whether they wanted it or not. He'd tell Weston's to write to them again immediately.

But Alasdair Weston said, "We *have* written to them, Mr Philipson. We've written four times altogether. Your uncle was very firm on the need to contact them."

"There's only one letter in the folder," said Stephen.

"I apologise for that," said the solicitor with the smooth ease of someone who is used to handing out expressions of regret as easily as Monopoly money. "But we have copies of the others on file here."

"And they've never replied?" asked Stephen.

"No." The older man hesitated. "I am sure your uncle had his reasons for wishing to – ah – reimburse these other parties. However, given the extreme length of time since the original dispute, and the failure of the persons in question to respond, I think we might reasonably let the matter rest there, Mr Philipson."

"No!" shouted Stephen into the telephone. Then he forced himself to lower his voice. "No. Look, it's very important to me to see my uncle's wishes carried out – and as soon as possible."

"Mr Philipson . . ."

"Don't 'Mr Philipson' me. It's absolutely vital that this is done. It can't wait." Stephen realised that he was perspiring; he blotted his forehead with his handkerchief. "Look, can't you find someone in Queensland who'll go out there and speak to these people in person? Just find a lawyer in the state who'll send someone. I'll pay out of the estate, if that's what you're worried about."

"Well, Mr Philipson – it's an unusual request. I can't guarantee that the costs will be low if we attempt such a thing . . ."

"I don't care," Stephen told him wildly. "Just do it."

After he had put the phone down, he put his head in his hands.

Uncle Toby, Uncle Toby, he said to himself. *Why did you have to let it out? You could have fenced off the land and left it to scream to itself. Why did you have to bloody let it out?*

Then he said aloud, "This is insanity. I must be having a break-
down or something."

Something pressing on the brain. Perhaps that was it. Stephen
wondered whether a tumour, even a benign one, could cause symp-
toms like this – phantom sounds, hallucinations. At any rate it
made more sense than the explanation involving ancient land dis-
putes. He'd have a word with the doctor. In the meantime . . . he
glanced out of the window at the bright morning sky. Hours to go.
Nothing to worry about – yet.

It was hopeless to think that Alasdair Weston would get back to
him that same day, especially with the time difference between
London and Queensland. Stephen still clung to the hope that the
whole thing might be traced back to migraine or some other physical cause, but all the same he took care not to be travelling at sundown. Feeling frankly foolish, he went home to his flat, took off
his jacket and tie, and lay down on the bed to wait.

As the last of the sun flamed down behind the city skyline, the
dreadful shriek thrilled through his brain. His body clenched as
though in the grip of a seizure. He kept his eyes squeezed tight shut
until after it had passed; there was nothing he wanted to see whilst
that appalling influence lay over his eyes.

Afterwards he was damp with sweat that cooled rapidly and
unpleasantly on his skin. Stephen poured himself a measure of
brandy and his hands trembled. He tried not to think about a
second cry. It hadn't happened the first couple of times; maybe it
wouldn't happen tonight. He had some more brandies, thinking
that he might slug himself into a sleep so deep that nothing would
wake him.

It didn't work, though. At a little after 2 a.m. that scream bored
through his head. It was impossible to sleep through; it was like
being trepanned. Stephen rolled over onto his back, his hands
jammed to his ears. As the agony died away, his head lolled off the
side of the bed and there in the mirror on the front of his wardrobe he saw his own face reflected upside down, dead and grey. He

lacked the energy to move, even to put his hands before his eyes. Slack with horror, he gazed at himself, and then he saw it. In the reflected room, behind his own decaying body on the bed, he saw the half-open door that led to the dark hallway, and in that dim slice of the space beyond the door he saw a movement. Through the gap something insubstantial, barely glimpsed, reached for him. Suddenly and irrationally he thought of the figure he had seen ahead of him in the passage at Betton Court, the afternoon his uncle had sent him to find the folder in his study. Not a nurse then, no, but . . .

Her. I'm seeing her.

Then the moment had passed. There was nothing there. His gaze slid to his own face and it was no longer that of a corpse but of a very shocked live person. Stephen rolled onto his stomach and vomited helplessly onto the carpet beside the bed.

Days passed, in which Stephen Philipson grew more nervous and more haggard and so grey in the face that he began to resemble his dead self. He was barely sleeping – the first dreadful shriek came punctually each evening at sundown, but the second one was unpredictable. Once it came so close on the heels of the first that he thought his brain or his eardrums had finally given way; the next night he lay wide-eyed and restless waiting for it to visit him, watching the fluorescent hands of the alarm clock creeping round and round, and it did not come until the grey tints of pre-dawn were creeping like mould up the early morning sky. Most of all he was terribly afraid that he would see that figure again, and more clearly.

The thing had him now; he *believed*. It was not anything he could tell anyone else – he knew that; they would think he was mad – but all the same he knew that it was true. It was not migraine or stress or too much whisky that dogged him. He had to get rid of the money Toby Philipson had received for Betton Wood, and soon. He didn't have the old man's astonishing inner resources; the fear was killing him. If – *she* – came to him in person and uttered the third scream, he was convinced it would be the end of him.

He telephoned Alasdair Weston each day, aware that he was beginning to sound distinctly unhinged in his desperation to offload the money.

Then one morning, Weston, whose voice had sounded increasingly weary each time he had spoken to Stephen, suddenly sounded brisk instead. He said, "We have some news for you at last, Mr Philipson. We had a local law firm in Queensland send someone out to the address in Wonglepong . . ."

"And . . . ? Did they say yes?"

"And, I was going to say, it appears that the parties are both deceased – one of them recently, the other several years ago."

"What?!" Stephen's knuckles were white on the telephone receiver. "They're dead?"

"Both of them."

"Well, what about children? Did they have any family?"

"No," said Alasdair Weston. "They weren't a married couple. They were brother and sister, apparently. It was the sister who died just recently; the brother went, as I say, several years ago."

Stephen had to suppress the urge to start screaming into the telephone. *This cannot be happening,* he said to himself. He controlled himself with a supreme effort but he could not stop himself from shaking.

"Look, who did they leave their money to?" he asked. "They must have heirs."

"Apparently not," said Alasdair Weston. "The agent who went out there took care to ask around, as I emphasised the importance of settling the matter. It seems the brother left what he had to the sister, and when she died she had no one she wanted to leave anything to."

"Well, what will happen to their estate?"

"I suppose in due course it will pass to the State."

"That's no good," said Stephen raggedly.

"It does at any rate settle the matter as regards the money from the sale of Betton Wood," said the lawyer primly. "We can most definitely allow the matter to rest there, without reproaching ourselves. Everything was done that could be done. You simply cannot pass the money on."

"But I . . ." Stephen faltered. *But I must.* It was no use saying that to the old lawyer. The man saw nothing in the matter but a rather trivial piece of business. In an irrational flash of anger, Stephen wished he could pass the whole sorry mess onto the older man – let him see how professionally urbane *he* could be if he hadn't slept properly for a week because something was screeching inside his head powerfully enough to make his nose bleed! Let him try to apply the bloody law to *that!*

It came to him then. Perhaps that was the answer. Apply the law to the problem.

He said, slowly, "Mr Weston – Alasdair – the money that Uncle Toby got from the sale of the wood – can I refuse that part of the bequest? I mean, it was willed to me, wasn't it, so that I could see that it went to the correct people? And as it can't go to them, and I can't do what my uncle wanted, can I just refuse to take the money? After all, the will hasn't been through probate yet."

There was a short silence at the other end of the line, which Stephen correctly interpreted as disapproval. Then the old lawyer said, "Yes, you may refuse it. However, unfortunately it is not possible under English law to refuse only part of a bequest. You may refuse the whole inheritance – but not one part of it only. This would mean . . ."

But he didn't need to spell it out to Stephen. It would mean refusing everything Uncle Toby had left him. It would mean no Betton Court – no gentleman's life in the country – no injection of either property or actual cash to prop up his faltering finances. He would still struggle to meet the repayments on the scarlet cabriolet and the London flat, with the threat of losing them forever hanging over his head. He would still have to kowtow to Old Nick, trying to elbow the other aspirants aside. In short, the long awaited change for the better would never, ever come.

He was sick, physically sick with the need to rid himself of the nightly hauntings, and yet this other alternative was so ghastly that Stephen hesitated. He said, "And if I did – refuse the whole inheritance – where would it go?"

He knew the answer before the lawyer set it out for him, ringfencing it carefully with legal language and delicate provisos. As long as Uncle Toby had not made any other specifications about where the estate should go – and they both knew he hadn't, although the lawyer said he had to check – the whole lot would go to his Aunt Judith.

"I'll call you back," he croaked into the phone, and hung up.

The door of his office was still closed but there was a slender glass section at the side of it and now he saw that someone – it was Delia, damn it – was peering in at him with an expression of concern. Stephen made himself smile dismissively at her, although the expression felt as though it had been tacked to his face with nails. When she had gone, he put his head in his hands.

Aunt Judith.

She'd accept the inheritance – he knew that for certain. There was absolutely no love lost between her and Stephen, just as there had been no love lost between her and Toby Philipson or indeed any other human being Stephen could think of. She'd done nothing to ingratiate herself with his uncle during his lifetime – nothing to make him remember her in his will – and Stephen didn't imagine she'd dally with any other fine feelings such as guilt if she took the money.

She was a grim-looking woman with a wrinkled, heavy-featured face and iron-grey hair cut in an unsuitably girlish bob, caught back at one side with a hair slide. In a family circle as small as theirs, you would have thought that she might have taken an interest in her nephew, but in fact she took no notice of him at all.

She'd refused to come down for the funeral, pleading lack of funds. If she'd ignored Stephen before the contents of the will were known, she probably actively resented him now for inheriting the whole lot. No; he didn't think she'd turn the bequest down.

Whether he should lose the horror that accompanied it upon her was another question entirely, but he couldn't debate it for very long. The dread that stole over him as the sun crept down the sky was appalling; the need to escape it overwhelmed all other considerations. And this was only the autumn! How would it be when the days shortened, and then winter came? He might have sixteen hours a day expecting the torture to descend upon him at any instant. And how long could he continue to work after night fell? He might endure one meeting with Old Nick and the others without giving his anguish away, but he couldn't do it day after day after day. Everything would fall apart.

He meant to leave it until the following day before he called Alasdair Weston back, but in the end he phoned the old lawyer that same afternoon, before he left the office.

Stephen gave his instructions, overriding the older man's protestations that he should consider the matter a little longer – postpone the decision a day or two. The ghost of his old, unharried self suffered a pang of regret as he gave away the country house, the land, the investments, the money – the things that he had yearned and waited for, for so long. He felt them drop away from him, as though someone had hacked off a limb with a sword. But he also felt a great sense of relief, as though it were an amputation rather than an attack. At that moment the prospect of a full night's sleep, silent and untroubled, was the sweetest thing he could possibly imagine.

He made some excuse and left the office a little earlier than usual, so that he could pack up the folder marked *Betton Wood* and send it off to his aunt care of the lawyers that very evening. The sooner it was off his hands, the happier he would be. Indeed, rather than entrust it to the languorous vagaries of the post, Stephen ordered a courier and had the folder biked over to Alasdair Weston. Then he mixed himself a very strong drink and stood by the window of his flat, admiring the sunset over the city. It seemed to him as he looked at the streaks of flaming orange tinting the clouds over London, that something was invisibly and subtly streaming away from him, something as silent and dangerous as radioactive fallout borne on the wind. He wondered whether his Aunt Judith would hear the thing that very evening. Had she had the news yet? Indeed, would that make any difference? At any rate, he had washed his hands of the affair. Let the apparition try its mettle against his aunt; it might find it had met its match at last.

The next day Stephen awoke feeling wonderfully refreshed. Over the days that followed, he occasionally felt a pang of regret for the life he might have had if he had kept the inheritance. It was impossible not to feel slightly aggrieved at Toby Philipson's actions; it would have been quite tolerable to inherit an estate with a single corner that had to be avoided, instead of a heap of banknotes and a shrieking ghost. All the same, the relief he now felt was so great that it was positively invigorating. He threw himself into his work with gusto, swiftly regaining the ground he had lost during his "difficult spell". Old Nick praised him so enthusiastically at a group meeting that Stephen began to think that earning his own fortune might be more rewarding than being handed one by a relative. He stopped worrying about the car and the flat, and simply enjoyed them.

He was half expecting a telephone call from his Aunt Judith, either questioning or accusatory, but it never came. He had one short conversation with Alasdair Weston, regarding the formal refusal of the bequest, but that was all. He had the impression that the old lawyer thought that he was unbalanced. Well, let him think what he liked; Stephen was free, and that was all that mattered.

Autumn deepened, and the nights began to draw in. Sometimes it was twilight, or actually dark, by the time Stephen got home to his flat. He was always unmolested; the sunset had ceased to be a cause of dread to him. In the second half of November, the Christmas lights went up in the streets and it was positively pleasurable to walk about after dark, looking up at the coloured bulbs that winked against the night sky like a string of bright jewels laid out on a velvet cloth. The shop windows were lit up with glittering displays, and work began to dissolve into a round of social events – corporate entertaining for the company's clients, and rather less formal parties for the employees.

It was after one of these events, shortly before Christmas, that Stephen found himself once again in the bar where he had met the girl that time. The afternoon was well advanced and he and his colleagues were in a state of slightly unstable camaraderie, fuelled by a rather expensive sparkling wine. He looked around the bar, which was crowded, and remembered the girl – her long blonde hair, the dress made of overlapping bronze scales. It was shame he hadn't taken her number, he thought, though perhaps she wouldn't have wanted to see him again anyway after the fiasco last time. All the same, he found himself scanning the packed room, looking for her, just in case.

There was a large gilt-edged mirror behind the long bar with its line of gleaming pumps. As he turned his head, something caught Stephen's eye in the reflection. It was curious that something should snag his attention in that heaving mass of humanity, and yet it did. He saw – or thought he saw – someone very slender or perhaps actually bone-thin, swathed about somehow in garments that were incongruously untidy-looking in comparison to all the sharply tailored suits and sleekly fitted dresses. This person – if it was a person, and not a shadow half-seen and misinterpreted by a weary brain – seemed to turn or twist away, so that the ragged ends of sleeves or perhaps a cape briefly skimmed the air.

The next instant there shrilled through Stephen's brain an appallingly familiar and piercing note, so loudly that it might have been a gunshot to the head. He lurched and plunged into the crowd, pressing his hands to his ears. Crimson blood leaked from one nostril. The sound seemed to go on and on, a terrible screaming ricochet inside his cranium. Glass crunched slickly under his shoe; he had dropped his wine. On all sides people – *dead* people, he saw with horror – were pushing at him, telling him angrily to shut the fuck up, what was matter with him? He must have screamed himself, but everything was drowned out by the screech inside his own skull, and when it died away his hearing was dulled as though he were deep underwater.

Disorientated, agonised, stumbling like an animal at the shambles, Stephen managed to find his way out of the bar and into the street. There he leaned against a wall, wiped his mouth with a shaking hand that left a smear of blood on the upper lip, and tried to calm himself.

It's back.

That was obvious, at any rate. Stephen thought too that it was worse, so far as he could judge when the baseline was one of intolerable agony. It had intensified. Hitherto, he had read in that dreadful shriek pure force of will. Now he thought it sounded angry – angry with *him*.

He had escaped it once, by passing it off onto his Aunt Judith; now, somehow, it had returned to him and it had fallen upon him like a beast that has been baulked of its prey once already. How could this be? He could barely think straight with the memory of it still boring through his head.

It took him a while to flag down a taxi. No doubt the drivers saw him standing on the kerb so unsteadily with blood on his face, and decided it was more trouble than it was worth to pick him up. *Drunk and aggressive*, they'd be thinking. *In one fight already.*

At last, though, one of them did stop for him, and Stephen ordered the driver to take him all the way home. He wasn't risking the underground like this; if he heard that thing again as he wove his way along the platform he'd probably fall under the first train that came along. As the car pulled away from the kerb he got out his mobile phone with palsied hands and dialled Alasdair Weston's number. It took him three attempts to manage it; his fingers wouldn't do what he wanted them to, and he kept calling the wrong numbers.

When he did get through, he got a recorded message. The practice was closed until the day after Boxing Day. What was this now? The twenty-first. Stephen sank back on the seat with a groan of horror.

At the block where he lived, he paid off the cab driver and staggered inside. He didn't bother trying to call Weston's again. It was obvious what had happened. His Aunt Judith had died. Either she had died intestate, and the estate had reverted to him as her only living relative, or else – more probably, he thought – she had forseen this and left it to him on purpose. That would be like her.

You passed it to her first, his conscience reminded him. Stephen grimaced. It would almost be funny if it weren't so appalling.

Somehow he made it upstairs and into the flat, where he fell to his knees on the carpet and pressed his hands to his face.

God in heaven, what am I going to do?

He couldn't endure six days of hearing it – perhaps even seeing it – again. He couldn't imagine how Aunt Judith had stood it that long. She must have been made of iron. And why hadn't he seen this coming – that the inheritance would revert to him if she died? Stephen supposed he could refuse it again, but he could do nothing formally until Weston's re-opened.

Something moved within close earshot – he heard a light pattering sound, soft as rain, within the apartment.

Stephen waited for the cry – waited, and waited. Nothing. The terror of what he could not see was worse than the fear of seeing what he dreaded; after a little while he opened his eyes, but found that he was alone. Wind rattled at the window; perhaps it really had been rain he had heard.

He got up and went to the kitchen, moving like an old man. There was no whisky in the cupboard – he'd never got round to replacing the bottle he'd finished – but he found the brandy and poured himself a generous quantity. As the liquid blazed a warming trail down his throat, he tried to raise his spirits by planning what he would do about the inheritance. His own face, reflected in the smoked glass of the kitchen cabinet, looked about a hundred years old.

I'll find Alasdair Weston's home number – even if I have to go round to their offices and break the door down to get it. And then I'll phone him – no, I'll go over there, and I'll insist he takes my instructions to refuse the bequest again. The State can have the bloody money, and the land, and Betton Court.

Then he looked at the kitchen clock and thought, *How long till morning? Oh God – how long?*

It was the winter solstice, he remembered. The longest night of the year.

Behind him, something rustled – the sound of cloth moving against cloth – and in the corner of the reflection in the smoked glass something flickered. The brandy was halfway to his mouth when Stephen heard it again – the angry scream like a bomb going off in his brain. The brandy glass fell from his hand and smashed unheeded on the tiles. The world turned grey and dusty, webbed with the extrusion of spiders. He glanced down at his hands and saw the dull gleam of ivory-coloured bone breaking through the remnants of flesh. His reflection was a pulpy thing of rank decay, the head wagging loosely at him.

She was in the room with him now. He sensed it even before he saw the ragged ends of draperies from the corner of his eye.

Stephen couldn't look at her. He squeezed shut the eyes from which tears of terror oozed, hot as blood. It hardly mattered; he could *feel* her, close by; he had an acute physical sense of her exact location in relation to himself. Her two eyes blazed at him; the jaws and teeth gaped as though the scream that they had uttered were still streaming out of the withered throat.

He stood transfixed, for what seemed like an eternity, and then he was aware at last that she had gone. He opened his eyes and found himself standing in a pool of brandy, from which the glittering shards of broken glass protruded like fangs. He didn't bother to clear up. He took a new glass and the bottle and went into the living room.

There, he opened the curtains and looked at the night sky. There was a dull tinge, a sickly mixture of grey and yellow, over the London skyline, but Stephen knew better than to think that that was the sun's faint light. It was the glow of artificial lights, all over the city, warding off the dark of the year's longest night.

He sat on the sofa and poured himself another brandy. His hands shook so much that a large quantity spilled onto the carpet. It didn't matter. Nothing mattered, except waiting for the sun to rise – and that was hours away.

The clock in the kitchen ticked quietly, the hands stealing around the dial with agonising slowness. *Twice,* he thought. That was something to hold on to. The thing had visited him twice already that night. Then he remembered what Uncle Toby had whispered to him, clutching at his arm. *When I hear her the third time in one night . . . then I'll be dead.*

No, Stephen said to himself. *It's never happened more than twice.* He took a great mouthful of the brandy and swallowed, feeling it burn all the way down. *It's not going to happen tonight either. I just have to get to the morning and then I can get rid of this whole thing.*

He sat, cradling the brandy, for a long time. The lights over the city barely changed; shop window displays were illuminated long after the doors had been locked, and the street lamps were on all night. Once, blue lights were briefly visible, accompanied by a siren that now sounded harmless.

In the small hours, the sounds from the streets below diminished. Still Stephen sat with set face, watching the sky and waiting for it to be morning.

At a little past four a.m. he felt it coming, as subtle as a sigh in another dimension, sweeping towards him on invisible wings. He lifted his right hand, still holding the glass with the left, and he could see the tiny hairs standing up on the back of it.

If he had not been so exhausted, Stephen would have wept. *Not a third time. I can't take it – it's not fair . . .*

The sound hit him like a tsunami, engulfing him, harsh and metallic like some great sheet of iron giving way. It expanded, shrilling up the register, reaching and passing a pitch of sharp agony. Abruptly Stephen's eardrums ruptured. The pain spiked into his tortured brain but made no difference to the sound: he was hearing it with more than his physical ears. It was worse than anything he had heard before; it was like a white-hot branding iron pressed into the deepest part of his head. The brandy glass fell from his hand and his bladder muscles let go. His eyes rolled up into his head; his body bucked and twitched on the couch, as though he were being electrocuted.

At last something else burst. Stephen seemed to pass through a clinging and filmy barrier, the agonising sound in his head fading as he did so. He knew what had happened, even before he looked down and saw his own lifeless body sprawled on the couch.

How could he see, when his consciousness was no longer behind those eyes that stared so fixedly? Stephen discovered that he still had a body, of sorts; he could put out his own hands and see them before him, though he thought that he would be invisible to other people. The living ones. He turned his hands over, studying both sides, and if he had still possessed the facility to feel bodily sensations, he would have been nauseous. He could *see* the corruption that would come, the shutting-down of all activity in the cells. As the body that now lay on the couch decomposed and degraded, so would this ethereal Stephen follow it into rotting ugliness.

He had a sense of the wrongness of this. This was not supposed to be how it ended. There was something – somewhere – else that tugged at him, insistent as a fish hook in his insubstantial flesh. And yet he could not answer the call. Something held him here.

He became aware then that he was not alone in the room. *She* was there, once more at the corner of his vision as though waiting to scream once more into his appalled ears. He didn't have to look directly at her to know what she was: a thing older and fouler to look at than himself, the mouldering rags of clothing indistinguishable from the strips of flesh that hung about her, the memory of hair on the brown dome of the skull like a sketch on ancient parchment. The teeth, of which too much showed.

She wasn't screaming any more. Stephen sensed rather than heard the question – although it was nothing as properly formed as a real question, more of a formless but insistent probing, as repulsive as the touch of a toad. It was the blindly questing remainder of a very old obligation to set things right, and he had nothing to give it.

The Bryans had sold Betton Court; it had passed squarely to the purchasers, and from them to the Philipsons. Toby Philipson had had only two living relatives. When he died, he had passed the estate with its eldritch burden to Stephen, and Stephen had passed it to his Aunt Judith. Aunt Judith had died, and Stephen was therefore the very last of his line. There was no one to pass it to.

If he had thought to make a will and left the estate to someone else – anyone – Alasdair Weston, Old Nick, it didn't matter whom – might he have escaped? But it was too late.

Stephen looked at his own corpse lolling on the couch. He willed himself very hard to go back inside the body. If he could have just ten minutes – just five – just *two* minutes of life, he might change things. He could write a last will and testament. Even if it weren't witnessed, surely it would stand up in court with nobody to challenge it? He strained with every non-existent fibre of himself; he clawed at his own body with hands that passed uselessly through the dead flesh. But there was no going back.

He didn't need to tell the thing beside him what had happened. She sensed it. There was nowhere for her to go, nobody else for her to torment and beseech. There was only Stephen, and she would not let him go – not ever. She attacked him with a storm of screaming, and after a while Stephen began to scream too, noiselessly and endlessly.

ANDREW HOOK

DROWNING IN AIR

IT WAS THE photograph of a gas mask wedding that first brought Aiko Van Der Berg to the volcanic island of Miyake-jima.

The ghostly skull-like circles of the masks adorning the hidden faces of the wedding party in their sepia drenched formal clothing, added mystery to what might otherwise be a familiar family shot: the white-dressed bride clinging to the arm of her brown-suited husband; guests in rain macs with hoods over their heads; the repetition of figures scuffed at the edges of the picture as though they had been partially erased.

Perhaps most significantly, the masks imparted anonymity to the bride and groom on what otherwise would have been *their* day. The occasion was lost to them. The masks held sway.

Aiko had been fascinated. Additionally, he had respiratory problems. Maybe this was also why the picture had appealed.

He had boarded the overnight ferry at ten-thirty the previous evening, leaving from the Takeshiba Sanbashi Pier near Hamamatsuch, Tokyo. It had been a clear day: pale blue skies opalescent, as though signalling new beginnings. As night descended, a blanket of cloud had shrouded the city, raising the temperature. He felt stifled in his tiny cabin on the ferry, declined the offer of a meal with a fellow traveller, and had spent an uncomfortable night rolling from side to side with the swell of the sea. Instead of rocking him asleep, it reminded him he was alive and didn't afford much of a slip into unconsciousness.

Aiko was in Japan on holiday. His Dutch company had willingly granted him extended leave following the exacerbation of his health problems. He wanted to see the land of his mother's birth. She had married his Dutch father shortly after the war. Aiko meant *love child* in Japanese. A Dutch boy's name as well as a Japanese girl's name. Aiko had sometimes been uncomfortable about the indistinction in gender, but mostly he had been proud of his foreign origins. Other than some high school teasing he had avoided bullying, unlike another boy he had known who had been beaten to death.

Perhaps it was the sea air, or the movement of the waves, but on the journey Aiko's memories pitched and rolled, fantasy and reality jumbled like two dice in a shaker. When he was awoken after a desultory two hour's sleep shortly after five a.m. he dressed semi-comatose, going through the motions of being awake without actually *being* awake. Come the time to stand on deck and view the island appearing out of the night the dream canopy still had yet to lift. He saw himself as others might see him whilst watching a film: a figure on deck with suitcase in hand, fifty-two years old, thinning white hair, a paunch which moved ahead of him wherever he went. Indistinctive features. Just another man amongst the many men who lived in the world. Not a bad man. But a man all the same.

The remainder of the passengers were Japanese. It wasn't quite yet the tourist season. On the shore he could see families waiting, hugging themselves for warmth in the cold morning light. None of them wore gas masks, but each of them carried one. He could see them dangling from straps in their hands, or slung over shoulders, or peeking out of day sacks, like disembodied alien heads or cyberpunk Halloween masks.

It was because of the high sulphuric gas volume that the residents of the island were required to carry gas masks with them at all times. The volcanic Mount Oyama being the culprit. Aiko stood on deck and breathed deeply. There was little trace of anything untoward in the air, only the familiar sulphur smell of bad eggs drifting onwards over the waves.

Seeing the early morning crowds he was reminded of a second photograph he had found whilst researching the island. A party of boy scouts, their numbers stretching back into the horizon, each traditionally dressed but wearing those masks which appeared white in the contrast of the monochrome image, tubing snaking from their mouthpieces like corrugated snakes or the trunks of deformed elephants. Upon observing the photo Aiko realised it was the human face which defined humanity. Without it – without expression – the race was reduced to nothingness.

One of the Japanese on shore was holding a cardboard sign. The name *Aiko Van Der Berg* had been written on it in black ink. As he disembarked from the ferry he made his way over to the sign holder: a man in his late-thirties. The man waited until Aiko reached him and identified himself, even though he must have been aware that Aiko was the person he was waiting for because he had been the only European to make the trip.

Aiko's Japanese was rudimentary, the man's Dutch and English non-existent. They acknowledged each other and exchanged simple pleasantries, before Aiko was beckoned into a waiting vehicle and driven to the hotel where he intended to spend the following week.

Even from the short journey Aiko could see that the volcanic island was a mixture of hard rock punctuated by areas of extremely vibrant and varied flora. The juxtaposition of life and death intrigued him. Without the volcano, the richness of the soil would not be so great. Yet with the volcano the prescience of possible evacuation and death would always be present. Whilst only a handful of people had died through eruptions and lava flow since the 1940s, the island had been evacuated completely during 2000, with residents only allowed to return permanently five years later.

Aiko's room at the hotel was perfunctory and clean. Although the sun was now sapping the final vestiges of night from the sky, he lay flat on the bed in his clothes and sank into a sleep which was as alien as his surroundings.

A tightening in his chest woke him. The dream dissipated as smoke, leaving no more than a vague sensation rather than a memory. Sulphur smells lingered like olfactory residues of cooked breakfasts. He felt around in his jacket pocket for his inhaler and took a blast, easing his air passage. Sitting up, he realised he could see the volcano through the hotel window. Naturally, it was immobile, but even so he had the intimation that it might move closer towards him, belching fumes directly into his lungs.

His respiratory problems had lain beneath the surface until cycling to work in high wind one cold February morning had forced what seemed to be a never-ending stream of damp air into his mouth. He had pulled up at the side of the cycleway and waited as other cyclists flew past, their battle with the wind less tempestuous than his. Struggling through a morning's work with a wheeze louder than the antiquated heating system he had excused himself early and visited the medical centre. It was there he was prescribed the inhaler, and the palpable association of breathing with life had begun for him.

In the hotel room he undressed, showered, and put on clean clothes. Then he made his way into the dining area for a simple breakfast.

The daughter of the owner sat one table away; school books spread out in front of her with fallen leaves.

She looked sixteen. Wore a sailor suit and had a red ribbon in her jet black hair. Plain shoes and white knee length socks adorned her feet and legs. She glanced up, smiled the smile of someone who has made an effort to smile, and then put her head back down amongst the books. Not to study, but as if to sleep, with one eye half-opened in his direction.

Hanging over the back of her chair was a gas mask.

The man who had driven Aiko to the hotel presented him with a menu. Then he nodded over to the girl, who feigned reluctance and came to stand by Aiko's table. They exchanged a few words in Japanese which Aiko didn't understand. It was then that the girl spoke.

"My father says I am to show you around the island. That is, if you want me to."

Her English was falteringly perfect, accented with distorted vowels, but refreshingly uncomplicated.

"The question is," said Aiko, "do you want to?"

She nodded slowly. He wasn't sure she had understood the slyness in his question, or whether the presence of her father meant that she couldn't refuse. Whatever might be, he would allow her to accompany him today and then she could do whatever she pleased. It was a Saturday and there was no school and he imagined she had over a hundred things better to do than show an aging Dutchman around an island which he could easily discover himself.

She held out a hand, her nails bitten to the quick. "My name is also Aiko," she said. And for a moment Aiko felt himself part of a circle which was now complete.

She let him eat in peace, gathered up her school books, and shovelled them into a backpack covered with anime stickers and smiley faces. Then she left the dining area with a quick promise to return. Aiko noticed she had left the gas mask on the corner of her chair.

He swiftly finished his meal, drank some coffee. Then stood and walked over to where she had sat and lifted up the mask. It was rudimentary in design, mass-produced. The large glass eye-holes reflected his face. The breathing apparatus looked simple. He presumed there was a filter within the extended mouthpiece. It struck him that he didn't know exactly how a gas mask worked. It was too small for him, although the temptation to place it over his head was intense. He almost wanted there to be some kind of volcanic eruption, so he could put it to the test. Yet strangely he wasn't sure if he wanted the mask to succeed or fail.

Returning it to the chair he realised he had been holding his breath. He exhaled. Inhaled. Exhaled again.

Behind him there was a cough, and he turned to find the hotel owner standing stiffly. In his hand he held a mask suitable for Aiko to wear. He nodded at it. Smiled disconcertingly, like an air hostess demonstrating safety procedures with the wan hope that they would never need to use them. Aiko bowed and thanked him, took the mask in his hands, realised how heavy it was in comparison to the girl's, and then he returned to his room, cleaned his teeth, and packed his camera and a few other items into his day pack.

In the lobby of the hotel, Aiko was waiting.

"There isn't much to see," she said.

Aiko shrugged. "Show me what you can."

She nodded. "Do you have your mask?"

"It's in the bag."

"You won't need it." She almost laughed. "But they make us carry them. It's such a pain."

He smiled at her youth. Imagined what she might be like twenty, thirty, forty years hence. Imagined how she might die. For her, death was an eternity away, a slight smudge on a distant horizon. For Aiko himself it was leering into his face, gripping him by the shoulders, forcing him to look directly into its maw.

It was a cloudier day than the previous one in Tokyo. The sun backlit clouds, gave them fabled silver linings.

Miyake-jima was no more than a large village. Aiko wandered with her hands behind her back. He wondered if she were avoiding the gazes of her friends. They occasionally passed small groups of girls who exchanged a few words with her then giggled. But Aiko realised that she must frequently show guests around the island and was reluctantly used to her position. Yet despite that presumed experience not even an uneasy camaraderie drifted between them, which he was sure he was as much to blame for as she was.

In actuality, it was disconcerting to be in the presence of someone so young. Aiko hadn't married. He had no children. The budding sexuality of Aiko which was tethered to the surface of her skin unnerved him. Once, he found himself reaching for his inhaler before realising he didn't need it.

Around mid-day he offered to buy her lunch at a small noodle bar. They ate *kitsune soba* quietly, the taste reminded Aiko of his Japanese mother. He had grown up with Japanese food, and it comforted him with the knowledge that she was once around.

Maybe it was then – in that first mouthful – that suddenly he took stock of who and where he was. The week he had spent in Tokyo had been disorientating yet familiar: a large city, lights, the harbour, shopfronts, skyscrapers, these were indigenous now to modern life, regardless of location. But here: in a relatively small village on a small island Aiko felt himself placed in the universe as succinctly as if a large hand had manoeuvred him in some other-worldly game of chess.

By mid-afternoon, the female Aiko was kicking her heels against the pavement and Aiko had to conclude there was nothing more for her to show him.

"You can go if you want," he said, when he saw her looking fondly towards a group of her friends who were chatting silently behind their hands. Then, so as not to be offensive: "Please. I would like it if you joined them. I found our time together to be most useful."

She nodded. The girl and the woman fought inside her. "There is a *taiko* performance this evening. My father asked me to invite you."

Aiko knew of *taiko*. The island was famous for its traditional performances, known as *kamitsuki kiyari taiko*. They were drum performances. Myth had it that the sun goddess hid herself in a cave until she was tempted out by an erotic dance performed by a shaman-like deity, Ame no Uzume, who stamped her feet on a wooden tub. After hearing the dance the sun goddess was persuaded out of the cave and light returned to the world.

Aiko had some taiko performances on CD, and once his mother had taken him to a show in Amsterdam when an ensemble led by the famous Daihachi Oguchi had visited the Netherlands.

He thanked Aiko again, and watched her join her friends. A butterfly returned to the wild.

~

Truth be told, Aiko realised there was little on Miyake-jima to interest him. He decided to curtail his week to just one or two more days. He would tell the hotel owner the following day, not wanting him to think that Aiko had been slack in showing him the sights of the island.

Instead, back in his hotel room he showered again, then pulled the gas mask over his head and lay face upwards on the bed, looking at thin black cracks in the white ceiling plaster through the tinted glass of the mask.

When he had visited the medical centre following the windy bicycle incident he had described the sensation of being unable to breathe as drowning in air. His doctor had nodded, explained that he meant suffocation rather than drowning, because drowning referred only to water whilst suffocation implied a lack of air.

Aiko had nodded and kept his opinions to himself. He knew what he meant. It wasn't insufficient air, but too much.

His breathing was laboured. Although he hadn't considered it prior to wearing the mask he now reached his hand down his torso and held his penis. It refused to stiffen. He tried to think of something to enliven it, and refused to think of Aiko; repeatedly. Eventually he gave up. The inside of the mask was hot and he couldn't have fitted it correctly because the lens became dappled with condensation. Even so, he kept it on, and whilst in one moment he was awake the next he was asleep.

Again, he woke with a tightening sensation in his chest. Aiko opened his eyes and jolted. Someone wearing a gas mask was holding him down. He jerked his body against the bed but couldn't move. The figure was naked and he recognised the body. Searching behind the eye sockets in the mask he glimpsed himself. He immediately relaxed. He had experienced sleep paralysis before and knew what he should do. He had to regulate his breathing; by controlling his breathing he could control his fear.

Then he remembered he was wearing the gas mask and the pain in his chest intensified. He couldn't concentrate on regulated breathing. The knowledge he was awake and unable to do anything intensified his fear. The figure in the mask kept him pressed to the bed. He could feel a layer of sweat between his back and the sheet. He tried to breathe – realised he had been breathing. Clenching and unclenching his fists began to dissipate the sensation. Finally, the figure over him faded away in a burst of volcanic ash and he wrenched the mask off his head. Sitting up, he breathed deeply, stutteringly. He reached for his inhaler and took two blasts. Perched on the side of the bed, he held his head in his hands. The small bedside clock showed it was six in the early evening. The sun was being consumed by the night.

He stood and looked back at the wet stains on the bed. They were outlined by a thin layer of dust.

If Aiko's father noticed Aiko had slipped her hand into Aiko's then he made no acknowledgement.

They sat in the auditorium as the lights were dimmed and the curtains opened revealing the stage set with drums; their skins as taut as that on Aiko's chest.

Aiko started breathing again.

Aiko leant across and whispered into his ear: "During the Miyake festival in July they play the taiko from eleven in the morning until eight at night, leading the mikoshi shrines around the town."

Aiko nodded. A peculiar sensation gripped his stomach at Aiko's proximity. He released her hand from his grip.

The drums began. They pounded a beat which bore into Aiko's chest.

Aiko realised he had left his inhaler back at the hotel.

Earlier that evening, he had wiped sweat from the inside of the gas mask. He wondered what other guests had worn it. Who they might have been. How important or unimportant. He realised that there was a line of importance which stretched from youth until old age. That the youth believed unequivocally in their importance and the old realised with increasing fear the nature of their unimportance.

He wondered how important he was right at that moment.

With the death of his parents. With no wife or children. With business colleagues who respected him but with whom he didn't socialise. With these certainties he realised his importance was minimal.

Importance for him equated to impotence.

In the auditorium he glanced at Aiko, but even she had lost interest. He decided not to dwell about her hand in his. Wondered if – in fact – it had actually happened.

It was of no importance.

The drums continued.

Not only did their beat repeat throughout the performance, but they followed an historical journey that had begun over two and a half thousand years previous. Aiko felt enraptured by time. He could imagine the shaman teasing the sun goddess out of the cave. He wondered if an erupting volcano and the resulting lava flow would mimic the flow of light from the sun; yet knew in reality what would descend would only be blackness.

Should the volcano erupt, and sulphuric fumes enter the auditorium through the air vents, his inhaler would no longer be sufficient.

Aiko had left the gas mask back at the hotel.

Aiko was wearing the mask.

Each beat of the drum danced ash from its surface back into the air.

Aiko turned his head. Aiko turned hers. The eye-holes of her mask regarded him blankly.

Aiko stood. The entirety of the audience were masked. He gripped the back of the seat in front, and a head turned to watch him. Aiko could hear breath passing in and out of the tube, in and out of lungs.

He clutched his chest. He could hear his own breath.

He saw Aiko leaning over him, her mouth parted in a stifling kiss.

Aiko stood on the deck of the ferry, watched the shoreline of Miyake-jima recede as the boat headed towards Tokyo. Mount Oyama dominated the background, pumping gas into the atmosphere. It was only a slight eruption, but no doubt had contributed to Aiko's attack.

Thankfully Aiko had been schooled in cardiopulmonary resuscitation.

Aiko waved goodbye from the shoreline. Standing next to Aiko's father. Aiko waved back until both men were no more than heads on sticks. Night enclosing them in a fist, obliterating their traces as might volcanic ash, before distance took them completely.

Overnight, amid desultory sleep, Aiko's memories rolled and pitched; reality and fantasy jumbled like two dice in a shaker.

The journey had begun. No mask required. Aiko wondered if Amsterdam would be exactly like her mother had told her.

MARK SAMUELS

ALISTAIR

GRYME HOUSE HAD stood for centuries, having been built in 1706 as an out-of-town home for a wealthy merchant. At that time Highgate was still a country village beyond London proper, when the metropolis was surrounded entirely by open fields with a swathe of woods off to the west.

The house stood behind an outward-bulging brick wall that was thick with green moss and which was tall enough to obscure all but the top floor and roof when viewed from the street.

The garden that lay between the wall and the house was overrun by weeds and brambles, being long neglected during the time that the elder Grymes had occupied the place. They had little time or inclination to keep the grounds in order and had let unchecked nature take dominion. Only the path from the rusted trellis gateway to the entrance portico was free of undergrowth. Covering it was an ivy-wreathed wrought iron passageway.

The ivy allowed no other plant to encroach into its territory, inexorably strangling any such intruder with its sinewy vines.

One might easily imagine that it was not just simple neglect that caused Gryme House to be half-hidden away, but that a deliberate concession to good taste had been made.

The sight of the house had long ceased to be picturesque, for, unlike its close companions, it did not possess the same aura of antiquity. The impression formed was instead of some growth that had sprung up from deep within the earth.

It was rotten and festering, projecting from the thorny undergrowth in the manner of a colossal fungus. External buttresses held up one side of the house from collapse and the roof sagged visibly. Plaster flaked away from beneath the eaves of the top floor, revealing a yellowish tinge like jaundiced skin.

James Thorpe's wife, Amelia, had inherited Gryme House from her parents. They had died last year, and he felt guilty that his relationship with his in-laws had been so distant, even though he had never liked them. He suspected that Amelia also had tried to keep them apart, though he had little evidence of this, only her vague indifference when it came to making a visit.

The house in Highgate had solved almost all of James and Amelia's financial problems in one fell swoop. Now they needed to pay no rent and thus their disposable income, given London prices, leapt. What with the arrival of Alistair four years ago, their previous flat had been cramped, and now the child had the run of a three-storey house, albeit a decaying house sorely in need of major renovation.

Amelia's parents, the elder Grymes, had been in their forties when she'd been born, and by the time James came to know them, thirty years later, they were elderly recluses who scarcely ventured out of the house. Consequently, the building had fallen further into acute decay, despite its being on genteel South Grove in a prime location in Highgate, backing onto the disused and picturesque cemetery with its woodland-like ambience.

Much to James's surprise, Amelia had scarcely wanted to change anything in the house after they'd moved in. She was content, even glad, to retain all the furnishings and fittings that she recalled from her childhood; the antique furniture, the heavy drapes, and the curios scattered inside cabinets and closets throughout the rooms.

Gryme House had been in her family for generations, and, being the only offspring of her parents, Amelia displayed enthusiasm at the prospect of entering into her birthright and passing it on to Alistair in turn. She would shepherd the boy around the rooms, explaining to him where each object came from, and how old it was, and how one day it would belong to him as it now belonged to her. This sometimes made James feel like an adjunct to the two of them, integrated as they both were into the soul of the house through generations.

The only part of the building that had undergone any significant change had been the room on the second floor that James had turned into a study.

It had formerly been a spare bedroom, used whenever the old Grymes had received visitors, which had been not at all except for those rare occasions in the past when he and Amelia had stayed over.

He'd kept the wall panelling and introduced several bookshelves in which to store his collection, added a bureau to store those papers he needed close at hand and a laptop computer so he could work on the biographies that formed his main writing income.

He'd turned away from fiction in his mid-thirties, not being able to generate enough sales to get out of the mid-lists, and realising that it would only be by chance that he'd ever strike it lucky in that field and produce a bestseller. His agent had suggested the change in direction and, although James found the transition easy enough, the fact that it had not been made of his own free will but was forced on him by commercial considerations continued to rankle. Instead of producing a body of original work himself he was instead writing about the lives of dead writers who'd succeeded, where he'd failed, in establishing at least a literary cult reputation.

His book *Thomas De Quincey: Heaven and Hell in a Jar*, received cordial critical notices and his next two, *Anna Kavan: A Soul in Ice* and *Stanislaus, Count Stenbock: A Peacock Life*, were hailed as masterpieces of definitive re-evaluation. They'd brought in more money than James had earned before whilst trying to make a living as an author, although it was still not enough to enable him to feel that he was comfortably off and, for all his hard work, all he ever seemed to manage was to keep the family's collective head above water financially. Other writers that he knew who had stuck with fiction were forced to pen either erotica or to ghost-write celebrity memoirs in order to bring in a decent income, but this was not a route that he could consider without coming to the conclusion that it represented a fate much worse than his own.

He further explained away to himself his having decided to take such work after the birth of his son when, he claimed, his self-centred ambition to be recognised as a serious novelist stood between him and providing the very best that he could for his own family. But the birth of Alistair had not given James the emotional connection that made this plausible.

When he held the child in his arms in the hospital, after the birth, he'd expected an overwhelming rush of pride, a sense of genetic continuity that was primal in its force, but although he'd been relieved when the pregnancy was over and all was well, he hadn't experienced that new sense of living totally for his offspring that he'd been told would follow.

It had been different for Amelia. The bond between her and Alistair had been immediate and of a depth that he found startling. James had scrupulously avoided exhibiting any feeling of jealousy, and had settled into the role of attentive father without qualms, but at the centre of his relationship with the boy was a psychological gap that he could not, try as he might, fill.

He couldn't help thinking that it was the consciousness of this gap that made him acquiesce when Amelia's parents died, and she suggested that they move into the old house instead of putting it on the market and using the proceeds to find a place of their own. He'd hoped that, by entering fully into that side of his wife's life, in the place where she'd grown up, he might somehow become absorbed more deeply into the older ancestral familial dynamic that existed between her and their son.

But all he had done was to turn himself into even more of an outsider. The memories Gryme House contained were alien to him and his study had increasingly become a refuge as well as a place of work. It was the one space in the building in which he felt completely at ease.

Sometimes he'd sit up there late into the night, pretending to work, but actually drinking himself into a semi-stupor, until an hour when he was sure Amelia would be asleep and his crawling into their bed wouldn't wake her.

Occasionally, on his way downstairs, he would run into Alistair prowling around in the darkness, playing some silent game of his own devising. Nothing was said between them and the boy would scamper back to his room at James's approach, the subject not raised in front of Amelia the next morning. James wondered if he cut a terrifying figure in the shadows, a father in the guise of a drunken giant, his aspect altered horribly after the midnight hour. If that were so, it had become their secret. At least this much they had in common; both were night people. If only Alistair didn't look so much like his grandfather, Ezekiel Grymes.

Alistair often had screaming fits in the night. He could only be comforted by the presence of Amelia, and would cry out even louder when James tried to stand in for her. For a while he tried to overcome Alistair's disdain for his attempts, but the result was invariably that the child's agitation became alarming, to the point where James became worried that the neighbours might think Alistair was being abused. He'd suggested that Alistair might have some undiagnosed medical condition, but his fears were dismissed by Amelia whose ability to calm James down took a matter of minutes and was sometimes almost instantaneous.

When he asked her what she did to make the boy tranquil again she explained that it required nothing more than soothing words and a mother's embrace. Again, James was conscious of the gulf that existed between them.

On one occasion, after having failed in his attempts to soothe Alistair, once Amelia arrived to take care of him, and while James waited outside the bedroom, he'd been forced to leave by the child's discomfort at his presence.

He heard Amelia whispering something to James in a strange language that he could not understand and which sounded like no language he had heard generally spoken before. The words were delivered in a guttural, throaty way that varied in intonation and tone, as if inflexion played a key part in its structure.

He was reminded of the time when, during a visit here to Gryme House during the time it was occupied by Amelia's parents, he'd overheard an argument between the ancient couple that had switched, as their fury mounted, from English into the same bizarre and outlandish dialect.

It consisted of many consonants and few vowels, but was delivered not in human accents but in a manner more like the growling of a dog.

Close by Gryme House the hillside necropolis of Highgate broods over London from one of the city's highest points. The vast cemetery is in two parts, divided by the treacherously steep thoroughfare of Swains Lane, between the older West section and the newer East section. Most of those with an interest in the Eastern area are drawn by the fact that Karl Marx is buried there, his grave marked by a grotesque and enormous concrete bust.

The Western area, on the other hand, has tended to attract a different type of devotee: nocturnal seekers after the weird, the horrible and the fantastic. For them the region is a wonderland of charnel glamour. Since the 1970s, when vandalism, rumours of ghouls, and satanic rituals were rife, it has been closed to the public, except for guided tours.

The high walls surrounding it do not deter these devotees. Nor do the gates that are always locked. The lure of the Victorian

Gothic world within draws them back time and again; they make obeisance to its riot of crumbling mausoleums, tombs and headstones and its wild woodland landscape, as surely as any worshipper in a church.

But, unbeknownst to those who frolicked above ground, deep in the depths of the hillside, other beings frolicked. Their world was one of darkness, their territory a series of warrens that opened out into the bottom of graves, mouldering vaults and musty catacombs. For centuries they had fed on what was put into the earth in coffins, sucking the marrow from bones even after the flesh had rotted away. Their cackles and giggles were muffled by the weight of soil above their heads, and no echoes resounded around the cramped tunnels through which they scurried.

Of late, their numbers had dwindled, and some of the more inquisitive of the underground beings had ventured all the way to the surface in the middle of night, sniffing the air and gazing wide-eyed with awe at the sight of the moon in the sky. The lunar-light was a glittering pinprick of silver in their dead-black eyes.

Alistair looked down at the cemetery from the window of his bedroom on the first floor. The full moon allowed him to see almost everything that was taking place there. He watched as the strange dogs emerged from mausoleums, or pushed aside gravestones from below. It was much more exciting than any of the DVDs that father and mother allowed him to watch, although some cartoons were almost as good.

It was late and he'd awoken in the middle of the night, which he did on a regular basis now, but he was careful to try and not disturb his parents, who were probably asleep. He'd slip out of bed, clad in his Scooby Doo pyjamas, and relished the freedom he'd gained since they taken away his cot with its barred sides.

Once he'd moved a stool in front of the window, it was easy to climb up onto the sill, stretch out along its length and look down over the grounds of the cemetery. Sometimes, at night, Alistair would see foxes, even badgers, but of late he'd not seen as many and when they did appear they were often snatched away by the strange dogs.

The game the dogs were playing seemed to have ended.

Alistair yawned.

He was thirsty but it was a long way down all the stairs to the kitchen. He remembered that there was half a chocolate milkshake in the fridge; he'd not drunk it all when father had taken him to McDonald's and he'd brought it back home.

He still had trouble with the stairs and found going down them scarier than climbing up. Perhaps that was because of the tumble he'd taken, when mother and father were afraid he'd broken his wrist.

And it would mean going down the stairs in the dark, past two floors, past his parent's bedroom. The thought of the darkness didn't scare him at all though and he could never understand why anyone would fear what was such a wonderful place to hide.

Alistair climbed backwards off the window sill and then jumped lightly from the stool to the carpeted floor.

He opened his bedroom door as quietly as he was able and then padded down the corridor until he came to the stairs. He could see pretty well in the dark, much better than people realised, so that was no problem, but the sheer scale of the dizzying descent he would have to make made his stomach flutter.

He'd have to tightly grip the rails of the banister as he took the steps one at a time so as not to fall over in the dark.

The house was old, incredibly old, and seemed to have a life of its own. It groaned and creaked in the night as if shifting in its sleep. Alistair believed that it was probably the oldest house in the world, but he knew its sore points.

He knew which steps groaned and which floorboards creaked when they were trodden on and he adjusted his footfalls accordingly.

It seemed to take forever, and at the half-way stage he'd almost turned back when the Grandfather clock had loomed large and struck the hour of three just as he passed it.

Once the chimes had died out and the low thudding of the pendulum could be heard again, it seemed again that the house had turned in its sleep, spluttered and then was snoring once more.

Alistair pressed on until he came to the ground floor. He ran his fingers across the bottom of the coats hung up in the hallway, enjoying the feel of his mother's faux-fur. He had an urge to pick up one of the umbrellas in the elephant's foot stand, and flourish it about, as if it were a rapier and he was Peter Pan, but thought better of it.

A rectangle of moonlight streaming in from the end of the hall lit up the black and white tiles of the kitchen floor. The tiles were cold underfoot after the warmth of the carpet covering the stairs and the corridors, and Alistair felt the shock of the chill in the soles of his feet. He pottered over to the refrigerator, a huge white 50's retro model, and stood on tiptoe in order to reach the handle. He tugged at it and pulled it back, squinting as the inside light turned on and it exhaled an icy breath.

There, on the middle door shelf, next to a bottle of iced tea, was his milkshake carton. He took it down and slurped through the straw, looking around at the contents of the fridge as he swallowed the chocolaty drink.

There were all sorts of foodstuffs and drinks in there that he'd never tried. In the middle shelf was a joint of lamb that had been left overnight to defrost after being stored in the freezer compartment. It lay in a dish and, peering more closely, Alistair saw that a pool of red liquid had collected around its base.

He put down his milkshake on the floor and dipped his fingers into the dish, turning his fingertips red. He then began licking them clean. After that, he carefully took the lamb and dish out of the refrigerator, laid it on the tiled floor and then used his straw to drink up the rest of the redness, which he found much more delicious than milkshake.

From outside he heard the howling rising again from the graves in the cemetery, and scampered into the garden.

He would climb the separating wall and see his grandparents, and his grandpa who was his real Papa.

They probably had a special treat for him.

They had promised one day that they would take his substitute Papa away for good when he was a big boy.

Perhaps it would be tonight.

HELEN MARSHALL

IN THE YEAR OF OMENS

That was the year of omens – the year the coroner cut open the body of the girl who had thrown herself from the bridge, and discovered a bullfrog living in her right lung. The doctor, it was said by the people who told those sorts of stories (and there were many of them), let the girl's mother take the thing home in her purse – its skin wet and gleaming, its eyes like glittering gallstones – and when she set it in her daughter's bedroom it croaked out the saddest, sweetest song you ever heard in the voice of the dead girl.

Leah loved to listen to these stories. She was fourteen and almost pretty. She liked dancing and horses, sentimental poetry, certain shades of pink lipstick, and Hector Alvarez, which was no surprise at all, because *everyone* liked Hector Alvarez.

"Tell me what happened to the girl," Leah would say to her mum, slicing potatoes at the kitchen counter while her mother switched on the oven. Leah was careful always to jam the knifepoint in first so that the potatoes would break open as easily as apples. Her dad had taught her that before he had died. Everything he did was sacred now.

"No," her mum would say.

"But you know what happened to her?"

"I know what happened, Leah."

"Then why won't you tell me?"

And Leah would feel the slight weight of her mother's frame like a ghost behind her. Sometimes her mum would touch the back of her neck, just rest a hand there, or on her shoulder. Sometimes, she would check the potatoes. Leah had a white scar on her thumb where she'd sliced badly once.

"You shouldn't have to hear those things. Those things aren't for you, okay?"

"But mum –"

"Mum," Milo would mumble from his highchair. "Mum mum mum mum."

"Here, lovely girl, fetch me the rosemary and thyme. Oh, and the salt. Enough about that other thing, okay? Enough about it. Your brother is getting hungry."

And Leah would put down the knife, and would turn from the thin, round slices of potatoes. She would kiss her brother on the scalp where his hair stuck up in fine, whitish strands. Smell the sweet baby scent of him. "Shh, monkey-face, just a little bit longer. Mum's coming soon." Then Milo would let out a sharp, breathy giggle, and maybe Leah would giggle too, or maybe she wouldn't.

Her mum wouldn't speak of the things that were happening, but Leah knew – of course Leah knew.

First it was the girl. That's how they always spoke of her.

"Did you hear about *the girl*?"

"Which girl?"

"*The girl*. The one who jumped."

And then it wasn't just *the girl* anymore. It was Joanna Sinclair who always made red velvet cupcakes for the school bake sale. She had found her name written in the gossamer threads of a spider web. It was Oscar Nunez from the end of the block whose tongue shrivelled up in his mouth. It was Yasmine with the black eyeliner who liked to smoke pot sometimes when she babysat Leah.

"Maybe it'll be, I dunno, just this one perfect note. Like a piano," Yasmine had murmured before it happened, pupils big enough to swallow the violet-circled iris of her eyes. "Or a harp. Or a, what's it, a zither. I heard one of those once. It was gorgeous."

"You think so?" Leah asked. She watched the smoke curl around the white edge of her nostrils like incense. There were only four years between them, but those four years seemed a magnificent chasm. Across it lay wisdom and secret truths. Across it lay the Hectors of the world, unattainable if you were only fourteen years old. Everything worthwhile lay across that chasm.

"Maybe. Maybe that's what it will be for me. Maybe I'll just hear that one note forever, going on and on and on, calling me to paradise."

It hadn't been that. The omens weren't what you hoped for. They weren't what you thought they would be. But you *knew* when it was yours. That's what people said. You could recognize it. You always *knew*.

When Hector found her – (they were dating, of course Hector would only date someone as pretty and wise as Yasmine, Leah thought) – the skin had split at her elbows and chin, peeled back like fragile paper to reveal something bony and iridescent like the inside of an oyster shell.

Leah hadn't been allowed to go to the funeral.

Her mum had told her Yasmine had gone to college, she couldn't babysit anymore, Leah would have to take care of Milo herself. But Leah was friends with Hector's sister, Inez, and *she* knew better.

"It was like there was something inside her," Inez whispered as they both gripped the tiled edge of the pool during the Thursday swim practice, Inez's feet kicking lazily in hazy, blue-gray arcs. Inez had the same look as her brother, the same widely spaced eyes, skin the same dusty copper as a penny. Her hair clung thick, black and slickly to her forehead where it spilled out of the swimming cap.

"What kind of thing was it?" The water was cold. Leah hated swimming, but her mum made her do it anyway.

"God, I mean, I dunno. Hector won't tell me. Just that . . . he didn't think it would be like that. He thought she'd be beautiful on the inside, you know? He thought it would be something else."

Leah had liked Yasmine – (even though she had always liked Hector more, liked it when Yasmine brought him over and the two of them huddled on the deck while Leah pretended not to watch, the flame of the lighter a third eye between them). Leah had wanted it to be a zither for her. Something sweet and strange and wondrous.

"I thought so too," Leah whispered, but Inez had already taken off in a perfect backstroke toward the deep end.

It was why her mum never talked about it. The omens weren't always beautiful things.

There had always been signs in the world. Every action left its trace somewhere. There were clues. There were giveaways. The future whispered to you before you even got there, and the past, well, the past was a chatterbox, it would tell you everything if you let it.

The signs Leah knew best were the signs of brokenness. The sling her mum had worn after the accident that made it impossible for her to carry Milo. The twinging muscle in her jaw that popped and flexed when she moved the wrong way. It had made things difficult for a while. The pain made her mum sharp and prickly. The medication made her dozy. Sometimes she'd nod off at the table, and Leah would have to clear up the dishes herself, and then tend to Milo if he was making a fuss.

And there was the dream.

There had always been signs in the world.

But, now. Now it was different, and the differences both scared and thrilled Leah.

"Mum," she would whisper. "Please tell me, Mum."

"I can't, sweetie," her mum would whisper in a strained, half-conscious voice. Leah could see the signs of pain now. The way her mum's lids fluttered. The lilt in her voice from the medication. "I just don't know. Oh, darling, why? Why? I'm scared. I don't know what's happening to the world."

But Leah wasn't scared.

~

A month later Leah found something in the trash: one of her mother's sheer black stockings. Inside it was the runt-body of a newborn kitten wrapped in a wrinkled dryer sheet.

"Oh, pretty baby," she cooed.

Leah turned the lifeless little lump over. She moved it gently, carefully from palm to palm. It had the kind of boneless weight that Milo had when he slept. She could do anything to him then, anything at all, and he wouldn't wake up.

One wilted paw flopped between her pinkie and ring finger. The head lolled. And there – on the belly, there it was – the silver scales of a fish. They flaked away against the calluses on her palm, decorated the thin white line of her scar.

Leah felt a strange, liquid warmth shiver its way across her belly as she held the kitten. It was not hers, she knew it was not hers. Was it her mum who had found the thing? Her mum. Of course it was her mum.

"Oh," she said. "My little thing. I'm sorry for what's been done to you."

She knew she ought to be afraid then, but she wasn't. She loved the little kitten. It was gorgeous – just exactly the sort of omen that Yasmine ought to have had.

If only it had been alive . . .

Leah didn't know what her own omen would be. She hoped like Yasmine had that it would be something beautiful. She hoped when she saw it she would know it most certainly as her own special thing. And she knew she would not discard it like the poor drowned kitten – fur fine and whitish around the thick membrane of the eyelids. Not for all the world. Not even if it scared her.

She placed the kitten in an old music box her dad had brought back from Montreal. There was a crystal ballerina, but it was broken and didn't spin properly. Still, when she opened the lid, the tinny notes of "La Vie en Rose" chimed out slow and stately. The body of the kitten fit nicely against the faded velvet inside of it.

The box felt so light it might have been empty.

Now it was October – just after the last of the September heat had begun to fade off like a cooling cooking pan. Inez and Leah were carving pumpkins together. This was the last year they were allowed to go trick or treating, and even so, they were only allowed to go as long as they took Milo with them. (Milo was going to dress as a little white rabbit. Her mum had already bought the costume.)

They were out on the porch, sucking in the last of the sunlight, their pumpkins squat on old newspapers empty of the stories that Leah really wanted to read.

Carving pumpkins was trickier than cutting potatoes. You had to do it with a very sharp, very small knife. It wasn't about pressure so much. It was about persistence – taking things slow, feeling your way through it so you didn't screw up. Inez was better at that. It wasn't the cutting that Leah liked anyway. She liked the way it felt to shove her hands inside the pumpkin and bring out its long, stringy guts. Pumpkins had a smell: rich and earthy, but sweet too, like underwear if you didn't change it every day.

"It's happening to me," Inez whispered to her. She wasn't looking at Leah, she was staring intensely at the jagged crook of eye she was trying to get right. Taking it slow. Inez liked to get everything just right.

"What's happening?" Leah said.

Inez still didn't look at her, she was looking at the eye of the jack-o'-lantern-to-be, her brow scrunched as she concentrated. But her hand was trembling.

"What's happening?"

Cutting line met cutting line. The piece popped through with a faint sucking sound.

"You know, Leah. What's been happening to . . . to everyone. What happened to Yasmine." Her voice quavered. Inez was still staring at the pumpkin. She started to cut again.

"Tell me," Leah said. And then, more quietly, she said, "please."

"I don't want to."

Plop went another eye. The pumpkin looked angry. Or scared. The expressions sometimes looked the same on pumpkins.

"Then why did you even bring it up?" Leah could feel something quivering inside her as she watched Inez saw into the flesh of the thing.

"I just wanted to – I don't even know. But don't tell Hector, okay? He'd be worried about me."

Leah snuck a look at Hector who was raking leaves in the yard. She liked watching Hector work. She liked to think that maybe if the sun was warm enough (as it was today – more of a September sun than an October sun, really) then maybe, just maybe, he would take his shirt off.

"It's okay to tell me, Inez. Promise. I won't tell anyone. Just tell me so *someone* out there knows."

Inez was quiet. And then she said in a small, tight voice, "Okay."

She put down the knife. The mouth was only half done. Just the teeth. But they were the trickiest part to do properly. Then, carefully, gently, Inez undid the top three buttons of her blouse. She swept away the long, black curls of hair that hid her neck and collarbone.

"It's here. Do you see?"

Leah looked. At first she thought it was a mild discoloration, the sort of blemish you got if you sat on your hands for too long and the folds of your clothes imprinted themselves into the skin. But it wasn't that at all. There was a pattern to it, like the jack-o'-lantern, the shapes weren't meaningless. They were a face. They were the shadow of a face – eyes wide open. Staring.

"Did you tell Hector?"

"I'm telling you.

"God, Inez –"

But Inez turned white and shushed her. "Don't say that!" Inez squealed. "Don't say his name like that. We don't know! Maybe it is, I mean, do you think, maybe He . . . I mean, oh, Jesus, I don't know, Leah!" Her mouth froze in a little "oh" of horror. There were tears running down her cheeks, forming little eddies around a single, pasty splatter of pumpkin guts.

"It's okay, Inez. It's okay." And Leah put her arm around Inez. "You'll be okay," she whispered. "You'll be okay."

And they rocked together. So close. Close enough that Leah could feel her cheek pressing against Inez's neck. Just above the mark. So close she could imagine it whispering to her. There was something beautiful about it all. Something beautiful about the mark pressed against her, the wind making a rustling sound of the newspapers, Hector in the yard, and the long strings of pumpkin guts lined up like glyphs drying in the last of the summer light.

"It's okay," Leah told her, but even as they rocked together, their bodies so close Leah could feel the hot, hardpan length of her girlish muscles tense and relax in turns, she knew there was a chasm splitting between them, a great divide.

"Shush," she said. "Pretty baby," she said because sometimes that quieted Milo down. Inez wasn't listening. She was holding on. So hard it hurt.

Inez was dead the next day.

Leah was allowed to attend the funeral. It was the first funeral she'd been allowed to go to since her dad's.

The funeral had a closed casket (of course, it had to) but Leah wanted to see anyway. She pressed her fingers against the dark, glossy wood of the coffin, leaving a trail of smudged fingerprints that stood out like boot marks in fresh snow. She wanted to see what had happened to that face with the gaping eyes. She wanted to know who that face had belonged to. No one would tell her. From her mum, it was still nothing but, "Shush up, Leah."

And Hector was there.

Hector was wearing a suit. Leah wondered if it was the same suit that he had worn to Yasmine's funeral, and if he'd looked just as good wearing it then as he did now. A suit did something to a man.

Leah was wearing a black dress. Not a little black dress. She didn't have a little black dress – she and Inez had decided they would wait until their breasts came in before they got little black dresses. But Inez had never got her breasts.

The funeral was nice. There were lots of gorgeous white flowers: roses and lilies and stuff, which looked strange because everyone was wearing black. And everyone said nice things about Inez – how she'd been on the swim team, how she'd always got good grades. But there was something tired about all the nice things they said, as if they'd worn out those expressions already. "She was my best friend," Leah said into the microphone. She had been nervous about speaking in front of a crowd, but by the time her turn actually came she was mostly just tired too. She tried to find Hector in the audience. His seat was empty. "We grew up together. I always thought she was like my sister."

Leah found him outside, afterward. He was sitting on the stairs of the back entrance to the church, a plastic cup in one hand. The suit looked a little crumpled but it still looked good. At nineteen he was about a foot taller than most of the boys she knew. They were like little mole-rats compared to him.

Her mother was still inside making small talk with the reverend. All the talk anyone made was small these days.

"Hey," she said.

He looked up. "Hey."

It was strange, at that moment, to see Inez's eyes looking out from her brother's face now that she was dead. It didn't look like the same face. Leah didn't know if she should go or not.

Her black dress rustled around her as she folded herself onto the stair beside him.

"Shouldn't you be back in there?"

Hector put the plastic cup to his lips and took a swig of whatever was inside. She could almost imagine it passing through him. She was fascinated by the way his throat muscles moved as he swallowed, the tiny triangle he had missed with his razor. Wordlessly, he handed the cup to her. Leah took a tentative sniff. Whatever it was, it was strong. It burned the inside of her nostrils.

"I don't know," Hector said. "Probably. Probably you should too."

"What are you doing out here?"

Hector didn't say anything to that. He simply stared at the shiny dark surface of his dress shoes – like the coffin – scuffing the right with the left. The sun made bright hotplates of the parking lot puddles. Leah took a drink. The alcohol felt good inside her stomach. It felt warm and melting inside her. She liked being here next to Hector. The edge of her dress was almost touching his leg, spilling off her knees like a black cloud, but he didn't move. They stayed just like that. It was like being in a dream. Not *the* dream. A nice dream.

"I miss her, Leah. I can't stop it . . . you look a bit like her, you know? I mean, you don't look anything like her really, but still," he stumbled, searching out the right words. "But."

"Yeah," she said.

"I'm glad you're here."

She took a larger swallow. Her head felt light. She felt happy. She knew she shouldn't feel happy but she felt happy anyway. Did Hector feel happy? She couldn't tell. She hadn't looked at enough boys to tell exactly what they looked like when they looked happy.

Suddenly, she was leaning toward him. Their hands were touching, fingers sliding against each other, and she was kissing him.

"Leah," he said, and she liked the way he said her name, but she didn't like the way he was shaking his head. She tried again, but this time he jerked his head away from her. "No, Leah. I can't, you're . . . you're just a kid."

The happy feeling evaporated. Leah looked away.

"Please, Hector," she said. "There's something . . ." She paused. Tried to look at him and not look at him at the same time. "It's not just Inez, okay? It's me too." She was lying. She didn't know why she was lying about it, except that she *wished* it was true. She wished it was her too. She wished Inez hadn't found something first.

He shook his head again, but there was a glint in his eyes. Something that hadn't been there before. It made him look the way that Inez's mark had with its wide, hollow eyes. Like there could be anything in them. Anything at all.

"I've found something. On my skin. We were like sisters, you know. Really. Do you want to see it?"

"No," he said. His eyes were wide. Inez's eyes had looked like that, too, hadn't they? They both had such pretty eyes. Eyes seeded with gold and copper and bronze.

"Please," she said. "Would you kiss me? I want to know what it's like. Before."

"No," he whispered again, but he did anyway. Carefully. He tasted sweet and sharp. Like pumpkin. He tasted the way the way a summer night tastes in your mouth, heavy and wet, wanting rain but not yet ready to let in October. The kiss lingered on her lips.

Leah wondered if this was what love felt like. She wondered if Yasmine had felt like this, if Hector had made her feel like this, and if she did, how could she ever have left him?

She didn't ask for another kiss.

The world was changing around them all now, subtly, quietly at first, but it was changing. It was a time for omens. The world felt like an open threshold waiting for Leah to step through. But she couldn't. She couldn't yet.

The day after the funeral Leah cut her hair and dyed it black. She wore it in dark, heavy ringlets just as Inez had. She took a magic marker to the space just below the collar of her shirt, the place Inez had showed her, and she drew a face with large eyes. With a hungry mouth.

She looked at forums. They all had different sorts of advice for her.

If you say your name backwards three times and spit . . .

If you sleep in a graveyard by a headstone with your birthday . . .

If you cut yourself this way . . .

Those were the things you could do to stop it, they said. Those were the things you could do to pass it on to someone else.

But nothing told her what she wanted.

For Milo, it started slowly. When Leah tried to feed him, sometimes he would spit out the food. Sometimes he would slam his chubby little hands into the tray again and again and again until a splatter of pureed squash covered them both. He would stare into the empty space and burble like a trout.

"C'mon, baby," Leah whispered to him. "You gotta eat something. Please, monkey-face. Just for me? Just a bite?"

But he got thinner and thinner and thinner. His skin flaked off against Leah's shirt in bright, silver-shiny patches when she held him. Her mum stopped looking at him. When she turned in his direction her eyes passed over him as if there was a space cut out of the world where he had been before, the way strangers didn't look at each other on the subway.

"Mum," Leah said, "what's happening to him?"

"Nothing, darling. He'll quiet soon." And it was like the dream. She couldn't move. No one could hear what she was saying.

"Mum," Leah said. "He's crying for you. Can you just hold him for a bit? My arms are getting tired and he just won't quit. He wants you, mum."

"No, darling," her mum would say. Just that. And then she would lock herself in her room, and Leah would rock the baby back and forth, gently, gently, and whisper things in his ear.

"Mummy loves you," she would say to him, "c'mon, pretty baby, c'mon and smile for me. Oh, Milo. Please, Milo."

Sometimes it seemed that he weighed nothing at all, he was getting so light. Like she was carrying around a bundle of sticks, not her baby brother. His fingers poked her through her shirt, hard and sharp. The noises he made, they weren't the noises that she knew. It was a rasping sort of cough, something like a choke, and it made her scared but she was all alone. It was only her and Milo. She clung tightly to him.

"Pretty baby," she murmured as she carried him upstairs. "Pretty, little monkey-face."

It was only when she showed him the little kitten she had tucked away in her music box that he began to quiet. He touched it cautiously, fingers curving like hooks. The fur had shed into the box. It was patchy in some places, and the skin beneath was sleek and silvery and gorgeous. When Milo's fingers brushed against it he let out a shrieking giggle.

It was the first happy sound he had made in weeks.

What were the signs of love? Were they as easy to mark out as any other sort of sign? Were they a hitch in the breath? The way that suddenly any sort of touch – the feel of your hand running over the thin cotton fibres of your sheets – was enough to make you blush? Leah thought of Hector Alvarez. She thought about the kiss, and the way he had tasted, the slight pressure of his lips, the way her bottom lip folded into his mouth, just a little, just a very little bit, like origami.

Leah checked her body every morning. Her wrists. Her neck. She used a mirror to sight out her spine, the small of her back, the back of her thighs.

Nothing. Never any change.

The stars were dancing – tra lee, tra la – and the air was heavy with the fragrant smell of pot. They passed the joint between them carelessly. First it hung in his lips. Then it touched hers.

"What are you afraid of?" Leah asked Hector.

"What do you mean, what am I afraid of?"

Leah liked the way he looked in moonlight. She liked the way she looked too. Her breasts had come in. They pushed comfortably against the whispering silk of her black dress. They were small breasts, like apples. Crabapple breasts. She hoped they weren't finished growing.

She was fifteen today.

Tonight the moon hung pregnant and fat above them, striations of clouds lit up with touches of silver and chalk-white. It had taken them a while to find the right place. A gravestone with two dates carved beneath it. His and hers. (Even though she knew it wouldn't work. Even though she knew it wouldn't do what she wanted.)

The earth made a fat mound beneath them, the dirt fresh. Moist. She had been afraid to settle down on it, afraid that it wouldn't hold her. Being in a graveyard was different now – it felt like the earth might be moving beneath you, like there might be something moving around underneath, below the sod and the six feet that came after it. Dying wasn't what it used to be.

"I mean," she said, "what scares you? This?" She touched his hand. Took the joint from him.

"No," he said.

"Me neither." The smoke hung above them. A veil. Gauzy. There were clouds above the smoke. They could have been anything in the moonlight. They could have just been clouds. "Then what?"

"I was afraid for a while," Hector said at last, "that they were happy." He was wearing his funeral suit. Even with grave dirt on it, it still made him look good. "I was afraid because they were happy when they left. That's what scared me. Yasmine was smiling when I found her. There was a look on her face . . ." He paused, took a breath. "Inez too. They knew something. It was like they figured something out. You know what I mean?"

"No," she said. *Yes*, she thought.

Her mother had been cutting potatoes this morning. Normally Leah cut them. She cut them the way her dad had taught her, but today it was her mother who was cutting them, and when the potato split open – there it was, a tiny finger, curled into the white flesh, with her dad's wedding ring lodged just behind the knuckle. Her mum's face had gone white and pinched, and she dropped the knife, her fingers instinctively touching the white strip of flesh where her own wedding ring used to sit.

"Oh, god," she whispered.

"Mum," Leah said. "It's okay, Mum. It'll be okay."

But all she could think was, "It should have been me."

Because it was happening to all of them now. All of them except for her. When Leah walked down the street, all she could imagine were the little black dresses she would wear to their funerals. The shade of lipstick she would pick out for them. Her closet was full of black dresses.

"I've never felt that way about anything. Felt so perfectly sure about it that I'd let it take me over. I'd give myself up to it."

"I have," she said. But Hector wasn't listening to her.

"But then," he said, "I heard it."

"What?"

"Whatever Yasmine was waiting for. That long perfect note. That sound like Heaven coming."

"When?"

"Last night." His eyes were all pupils. When had they got that way? Had they always been like that? The joint was just a stub now between her lips, a bit of pulp. She flicked it away.

"Please don't go away, Hector," she said.

"I can't help it," he said. "You'll see soon. You'll know what I mean. But I'm not scared, Leah. I'm not scared at all."

"I know," she said. She remembered the way Milo had been with the kitten. He had known it was his. Even though it was monstrous, its chest caved in, the little ear bent like a folded page. It was his. She wanted that, God, how she wanted that.

And now Hector was taking her hand, and he was pressing it against his chest. She could feel something growing out of his ribcage: the hooked, hard knobs pushing through the skin like antlers. He sighed when she touched it, and smiled like he had never smiled at her before.

"I didn't understand when Yasmine told me," he said. "I couldn't understand. But you – you, Leah, you understand, don't you? You don't need to be scared, Leah," he said. "You can be happy with me."

And when he kissed her, the length of his body drawn up beside her, she felt the shape of something cruel and mysterious hidden beneath the black wool of his suit.

That night Leah had the dream – they were on the road together, all four of them.

"Listen, George," her mother was saying. (What she said next was always different, Leah had never been able to remember what it actually was, what she'd said that had made him turn, shifted his attention for that split second.)

Leah was in the back, and Milo – Milo who hadn't been born when her father was alive – was strapped in to his child's seat next to her.

"Listen, George," her mother was saying, and that was part of it. Her mother was trying to tell him something, but he couldn't hear her probably. So he turned. He missed it – what was coming, the slight curve in the road, but it was winter, and the roads were icy and it was enough, just enough.

"Is this it?" Leah asked. But her mum wasn't listening. She was tapping on the window. She was trying to show him something she had spotted.

Leah knew what came next. In all the other dreams what came next was the squeal of tires, the world breaking apart underneath her, and her trying to grab onto Milo, trying to keep him safe. (Even though he wasn't there, she would think in the morning, he hadn't even been born yet!)

That's how the dream was supposed to go.

"Listen, George," her mother was saying.

The car kept moving. The tires kept spinning, whispering against the asphalt.

"Is this what it is for me?" Leah tried to ask her mother, but her mother was still pointing out the window. "Is this my sign?"

And it wasn't just Milo in the car. It was Inez, too. It was Oscar Nunez with his shrivelled-up tongue, and Joanna Sinclair, and Yasmine with her black eyeliner, her eyes like cat's eyes. And it was Hector, he was there, he was holding Yasmine's hand, and he was kissing her gently on the neck, peeling back her skin to kiss the hard, oyster-grey thing that was growing inside of her.

"Leah can't come with us," her mother was saying. "Just let her off here, would you, George? Just let her off."

"No," Leah tried to tell her mum. "No, this is where I am supposed to be. This is supposed to be *it*."

And then Leah was standing in a doorway, not in the car at all, and it was a different dream. She was standing in a doorway that was not a doorway because there was nothing on the other side. Just an infinite space, an uncrossable chasm. It was dark, but dark like she had never seen darkness before, so thick it almost choked her. And there was something moving in the darkness. Something was coming . . . because that's what omens were, weren't they? They meant something was coming.

And everyone had left her behind.

When Leah woke up the house was dark. Shadows clustered around her bed. She couldn't hear Milo. She couldn't hear her mother. What she could hear, from outside, was the sound of someone screaming. She wanted to scream along with it, oh, she wanted to be part of that, to let her voice ring out in that one perfect note. . . .

But she couldn't.

Leah turned on the light. She took out the mirror. And she began to search (again – again and again and again, it made no difference, did it? it never made a difference).

She ran her fingers over and over the flawless, pale expanse of her body (flawless except for the white scar on her thumb where she'd sliced it open chopping potatoes).

Her wrists. Her neck. Her spine. Her crabapple breasts.

But there was still nothing there.

She was still perfect.

She was still whole. Untouched and alone.

CHRISTOPHER HARMAN

APPLE PIE AND SULPHUR

T HE GREYHOUND BUS wheezed to a stop, its doors hissed open and the driver said, "Only seats for two more."

"It's all right," Malcolm said, usually the spokesman in these situations. "Karl doesn't mind standing." He grinned at Karl.

"Yeah, thanks mate," Gareth said, in his uninflected voice, swinging his rucksack off his scrawny shoulders and preparing to board.

"Sorry lads," the driver said, not looking all that sorry. "There's no standing in the aisle allowed. Not safe on these roads. Go over the limit of thirty-nine and my job's on the line."

Karl was too tired to smirk at the rhyme and the jobsworth who was pretending not to have noticed it himself. Passengers watched from presumably every seat but two.

"Could one of us *sit* in the aisle?" Malcolm said. He smiled, teeth clenched.

"Nope," said the driver, looking ahead, mentally filing his fingernails.

Each waited for one of the others to volunteer to tramp alone the three miles to the village on the hard, winding, up-and-down blacktop. A lot to expect after five hours of the horseshoe of hills, then the knee-capping descent down Wetherlam – all under the late summer sun.

The driver revved the engine to indicate his reserves of patience weren't unlimited, then, as the three conferred, the doors whispered that a decision had been made for them and the bus moved off.

"When's the next?" Karl asked, aching, hot. A disappointing end to the last of their roughly tri-annual hikes, the final get-to-gether before Malcolm and Gareth relocated to the east and south coasts. He'd enjoyed today, though he'd never liked the walking as much as the views from the tops, the spread of hills like the backs of faceless beasts with muzzles buried in lakes, rivers and forests. Before the sun had burned it away, mist strands were like sheep's wool snagged on coarse pelts of woodland, stuck to glue-like yellow blobs of gorse.

"An hour – and that one might be full too. The Tilberth-waite Country Fair is on today." Leaf shadows dappled Malcolm's bald crown and owlish face as he examined the Ordnance Survey map. Karl and Gareth watched the bus disappear, along with what had been the prospect of a beer or two in Connerstone, then the Stagecoach service's uninterrupted hundred mile run to Manchester.

Karl said, "I can hear it, the fair." A faint voice over a Tannoy system, commentating, cajoling.

"Don't think so, Karl," Malcolm said, making one ear bigger with his cupped hand. "It's two or three miles away."

Sheep shearing, wrestling, dog races, stalls selling everything from jam to woolens held little appeal for Karl, nor stifling shuf-fling crowds.

No longer audible, the festive noise must have been blown elsewhere.

Gareth pushed his glasses up the bridge of his sweat-shiny nose and lifted his slim-line camera to frame a stile in the stone wall. An arrow sign pointed to Guards Wood. Malcolm said it was the start of a longer route to the village which would be kinder to their feet, and offer more shade. He looked at them for agreement and they nodded, having no better suggestion. While Gareth immortalized the partially rotted stile, Malcolm edged his barrel-like torso through the gap. Karl and Gareth followed.

A path went by a thin band of ash and birch. Karl guessed it was Guards Wood which glowered, a green-flecked massive wall of lumpy tar three or four tilted, misshapen fields away. The dark cloud directly above could have been the woods' blackness reflected against the blue sky.

"That might get us before the finishing line," Malcolm said, relish at the challenge in his energetic stride along the ash path. His map was stretched between his hands; it was more necessary here than it had been up in the hills, where there had been one clearly indicated route. Sheep watched them approach, their faces stupidly noble, before prancing away under bouncing burdens of ragged wool.

A gate overgrown with weeds was the first indication of a dilapidated property; it was enclosed by a chaotic hedge with upright slates, the size of encyclopedias, running along its base. Gareth snapped at them with his camera. A crooked tree grew through a partially collapsed roof. There was a crumbling barn and a grassed-over yard. A farm once, so long out of use it no longer stank.

"They've all got stars engraved on them," Karl said, peering down at the slates.

"Pentagrams," Gareth said, blasé, as if you saw them all the time.

"What, to keep demons out?" Karl said. "These broken ones where they got in? Actually, the sheep do look sort of devilish."

"Now chaps," Malcolm said, "we'd better get a hurry on. The only evil here is that dratted black cloud."

Karl thought Guards Wood could run it a close second; it looked dense, airless.

They paused at a tree with gnarled twisting branches hung with shriveled bulbs, unlikely to mature into eatable apples. There were several opened bottles hanging from strings. "Shooting practice?"

Karl wondered aloud. His heart pumped as it never had on the steepest slopes.

"None are broken," Gareth said. "Looks like the old method to catch wandering demons."

"Dear-y me, Gareth," Malcolm said; he'd no time for such nonsense.

Darkened by foliage, a thick branch high up looped in a graceful extended S laid on its side. It didn't seem to belong. Karl sucked in a breath as it shifted position. No, *he* had. Warm air hissed through leaves.

They walked on. In the ten minutes since the road, Karl hadn't spied one other walker. He reflected that dedicated hikers kept to the hills. This was landscape you glanced at as you drove by it. It looked abandoned, sheep its custodians, masticating grass and watching with disdain as the three of them passed.

Five more minutes elapsed and the wood was a towering wave about to break. Malcolm stopped, eyed his map as he might a willful child in one of his classes, and complained at the scale being too small. A horsefly landed on it, mistaking it for the world. He batted it away and wiped at his gleaming forehead with his handkerchief. Being honoured with a name must mean the wood was of a size and character to deserve one. Karl couldn't think of anything in its favour other than the shade it would offer.

"Ready?" Malcolm said, as if the brief stoppage had been primarily to give his companions a rest.

The path rose to a sagging stone wall. Malcolm went first, striding over the broken remains of a kissing gate.

No diminution of the heat. Karl felt they'd entered innumerable stuffy rooms, defined not by walls but by the pillars of the trees, furnishings a matter of masses of brambles and other unidentifiable greenery. Maybe they should have avoided the wood, the way the birds had. Sunlight falling into distant glades and rides darkened the heavy cover elsewhere. The mix of trees suggested it was an old wood. That was the extent of Karl's arboreal knowledge and it was confirmed not long after. Gareth stalked forward, camera poised, towards a collapsed wooden frame the size of a TV screen. Under cracked glass, words, some not eaten by insects or dampened to illegibility.

". . . birch, oak and ash, natural to . . . kingdom. Ecosystem thrives . . . maintenance of a continuous canopy . . ."

Karl thought the choking underbrush wouldn't be as continuous if, as he suspected, woodland overseers weren't as scarce as the birds. He'd no sense of how far they'd penetrated the wood – and there were no longer sightings of sunlit glades. Close, heavy air pressed. Pattering on leaves began slowly like hesitant applause.

"I think the trees have told the black cloud we're here," Malcolm said, shrugging off his rucksack and pulling out his waterproof. Gareth and Karl did the same.

They walked like beggars, heads bowed as the air filled with rain and the swishing of their waterproofs. They stepped carefully over roots intersecting the path like prominent veins on a wet hide.

Karl couldn't be bothered remonstrating with Gareth, who was close enough behind to be kicking lightly at his heels. The hissing of millions of leaves sieving the rain focused into unintelligible whispered words directly behind his ear. Gareth hadn't been previously given to japes and Karl was about to suggest he shouldn't start now. Then he noticed his friend walking stolidly several yards ahead.

Karl flung himself around. Puddles had formed on the empty path. The rain hissed and crackled like fire. His own flapping wet trouser legs had kicked at his ankles.

"Sun's back," Malcolm called out.

Some distance ahead a glade overflowed with buttery light. Karl's limbs un-stiffened. Abruptly, the rain stopped but for sporadic fingertip taps on his hood.

Moments later they stepped into a wide break lined with gorse. There was a litter of rocks and stones from a glacier that could have passed just yesterday. An empty wedge to the right in the trees revealed a pin-prick flash of a distant windscreen, a section of the lake like a bent nail, a flank of the mountain whose summit they'd reached in time for sandwiches and the midday news on Karl's headphones.

They walked down the ride until it was clear the right-hand path Malcolm said to look out for had been grown over, or broke away from a different glade entirely. But here was another path heading off to the left just short of where the ride ended in dense foliage.

"Can't see it on the map but it's got to lead to somewhere," Malcolm said.

"Paths *always* lead somewhere," Karl complained, stopping, rebellion inside him. "Let's go back and look for the path on the map."

"The map's not reliable here," Malcolm said. Karl felt the same about the wood. The trees looked too dense to even let a path through but Malcolm and Gareth were heading into them.

Karl followed and after a moment turf was light and springy underfoot and there were cushions of moss. "Had this place in mind all along," Malcolm said, his grin signaling how untrue that was.

Like a faulty TV picture, the whitewash flickering between the dark tree trunks. At their feet, a winding series of stepping stones, flush with the grass. They ended at a short length of fence into which was set a low gate with a sign across it, *Journeys End Refreshments*. "Should be an apostrophe before or after the 's' in 'journeys', but I'm prepared to forgive on this occasion," Malcolm said.

"I've some water left if you want some," Karl said. "Let's just get back. I want beer, not tea." Hidden here, the house's saving grace was not being made of gingerbread.

"Keep hold of your water, Karl," Malcolm said, lifting the latch with a sharp snap.

Karl went through last, the latch raining a rusty powder onto his fingers.

The whitewashed cottage was at the end of a long narrow

lawn. Around the door was a trellis of faded red roses. There were windows at each side and two upstairs – all with closed shutters apart from the one to the right of the door. Murk behind the large single pane of glass.

They dropped their rucksacks by a lone round table halfway down the garden by the wall. "I'll parley with the natives," Malcolm said, anticipation in his face at what a delight this was certain to be.

"Sure there are any?" Gareth said to Malcolm's back. The closed shutters and dark window gave Karl hope but then a face appeared in a gap in the doorway, and he noticed a shape, vaguely visible in the window.

A hefty someone. More likely a female, to judge from the profusion of banana-sized and sharp-pointed crescents of yellowish hair around the solid base of the dark block of the head. Working at a sink or worktop?

A few words were exchanged and Malcolm called back, "Apple pies and tea do for you?" Gareth said "yeah" and Karl raised his thumb, rather than his voice and affront the stillness of the trees. Malcolm had gone to the un-shuttered window where he stooped to a book on the ledge. He wrote into it then was strolling back to the table.

He asked Gareth how many photos he'd taken. Gareth checked, said "thirteen".

"Lucky for some. A good day, don't you think, Karl?"

"Not bad," Karl said. The trees had twisted it out of shape, the house stopped it dead.

Malcolm said, "I envy you, still having hills on your doorstep when we're gone."

A hundred miles was no "doorstep" – and walking alone held no appeal, even if he'd known how to read maps. That's why he'd joined the Hill Billies. Malcolm and Gareth had joined separately at the same time. A disparate trio of physiques and personalities bound together from the first day in a loose camaraderie. The Hill Billies group had folded four walks later. Karl had a vague notion the three of them had infected it in some mysterious fashion, thus ensuring its demise.

He couldn't feel the breeze carrying the sounds of the country fair down corridors between the hills and over the dense carpet of woodland. Many voices, with one amplified and surging over the rest.

Karl said, "Hear that – ?"

"Stand by your beds, gentlemen," Malcolm interrupted, smoothing the altar-white tablecloth.

Tall and very slim, the young woman carried a loaded tray and approached with quick small steps of her tiny feet. The close-fitting maroon garment she wore down to her calves had a sheen in which darker shades billowed like smoke.

She placed the tray on the table; the pies had strikingly golden crusts and pillows of clotted cream. Karl tried to catch her eye, just to see if he could. She had large wide-apart eyes. Supposed to be an attractive feature, weren't they? He'd beg to differ. Malcolm said, fulsomely, "Thank you. You've saved our lives." Her lengthy thin-lipped smile encouraged him to go on.

"How's business? You're quite hidden away." He could ask questions like that.

"Coming to an end," she said, her voice sibilant, how the trees would talk if there were a breath of air. "We're going home. We aren't from around here."

"No?" Malcolm said. Still smiling, and as if she hadn't heard his invitation to expand, she turned and went back to the cottage.

"See her teeth? Like a baby's milk teeth," Karl said, pushing at his apple pie with his spoon.

"Except for the incisors – they were a grownup's." Gareth was observant without ever being obviously so.

"Arms too small," Karl said. "Perfectly proportioned, just . . . too small."

"Oh, we are pernickety today." Malcolm lifted a hideous china teapot. "Shall I be Mother?" he said, as always proceeding to be.

They drank and ate.

"Eggy. Too much egg," Gareth said. Karl agreed – the strong flavour of egg yolk in the pastry battled with apple. "You fussy eaters," Malcolm chided, smiling under his cream moustache.

He and Gareth finished theirs first. Malcolm lifted his cup. "To new beginnings." His declaration rebounded off the trees like not-quite-articulated responses. Karl and Gareth echoed it in re-strained murmurs then all three silently contemplated Gareth's im-minent departure to a life as a notably youthful mature student in and around Falmouth Art College, Malcolm's recent appointment to a deputy headship at a Grimsby primary school. Karl was closer to a sacking than promotion at North West Energy's call centre after losing his cool again and hanging up on an irate customer last week. A tally of two strikes; a third and he'd be out.

"It's a word I use sparingly, but 'heavenly' just about sums up this place." Malcolm leaned forward; a self-satisfied little gust of laughter. "These establishments –" Low-voiced – this was for their ears only. "They're uniquely English. There's usually an attractive young girl at front of house. Mother is formidable, matronly, has a farmer's wife build, keeps to the kitchen." They glanced to the window in which the shadowy bulk was motionless, as if watch-ing them back. Malcolm went on, "Dad's even more in the back-ground. He does the books, the DIY. Always mysteriously busy. Probably early-retired from some significantly more demanding professional occupation." Malcolm sat back. He was fond of making affectionately astute observations and was pleased with this one.

"Not surprised they're packing up," Gareth said. "Can't be much passing trade." Other people's financial situations always interested him where nothing much else about them did. Despite a handful of exhibitions and positive reviews, photography wasn't proving lucrative. He scraped a living from part-time jobs. He got out his camera, a small neat basic model he prided himself on finding wholly satisfactory for finding the strange in the ordinary.

Malcolm patted the solid mass of his stomach. "That was lovely. Simple and comforting." With a slight frown, he smacked his lips around a lingering aftertaste. Karl pushed aside his plate, a third of the pie uneaten. Neither of the others offered to finish it off. Malcolm got up. "I'll go and pay."

He walked across the grass. Standing before the cottage, he pressed both hands to his stomach, frowned, then pushed at the door and stepped inside.

A listlessness came over Karl with the lynchpin of Malcolm gone. "Come *on*," he said, impatient after three minutes or so.

"He could get a Trappist monk gabbing." A skill Gareth didn't have and probably didn't envy. He got up and walked to the cottage door. He adjusted a function on his camera and photographed the slab of the doorstep, then stooped to the book on the window ledge. He wrote into it then tipped his head as if he'd heard a sound from the doorway. He went to it and stepped inside.

Karl listened. No voices, no birdsong, no brush of tree foliage. The treetops waved to such a slight degree it could just as well have been the blood pumping through his eye sockets. He felt observed, and not from the trees, though he had a peculiar sense of them "facing" the garden and cottage. Not from the window either; dense gloom within.

He stood before the window a moment later. Nobody inside. A bare plaster back wall; no sink or cupboards as far as he could tell.

It was an open foolscap-sized book on the window-ledge. On facing pages row upon row of signatures with attached comments all written in a brownish red ink. A visitors' book. Gareth Shuttleby's was the last name, written in a tiny pinched hand, with, typically, nothing else added. On the preceding line, "Malcolm Goodey" in a controlled flourish that would have looked more fitting on a legal document. A fulsome comment next to it: "Excellent: a Heavenly enclave." One empty line left to fill at the bottom of the right-hand page. Karl took up the pen: it was cold between finger and thumb, a smooth texture like polished bone. The silence was acute; the trees, like an audience bound in shadow, made for a sense of intense expectation – he couldn't think what else might.

Writing his name would feel like giving too much of himself.

He felt a new-found appreciation of his anonymity answering calls at North-West Energy. There, he was nameless – he liked things that way. No, he'd keep "Karl Crier" to himself. He couldn't help thinking Malcolm and Gareth should have been equally reticent. He very much wanted to leave but first he had to find out what they were finding so compelling in the house. Malcolm might be deep in conversation but surely not Gareth.

He pushed at the door and stepped inside

– and down.

Shock, at the unexpected drop of a foot or so. An odour of leaf mould and mildew. Dirt underfoot and the remains of rotted floor-boards, beneath the layer of dead leaves. There was a landing – and no way up to it with the wooden stairs below, collapsed and rotten, strangled by some parasitic weed. "Hello? Anyone?" he said, his voice tight. Why hadn't either of them cried out when they stepped into this place? Karl just wanted to cry. Nobody had lived here in years, yet the girl had brought out food – he could taste it now and felt queasy.

Rough stone walls exuded coldness and damp. His boots pushing through leaves, he peered into the gloom at the back of the house. A florid tongue of leafy branches thrust down through a window to feed on weeds, rubbish and glass shards.

Discoloured chunks of white ceramic, mingled in rotted leaves on the floor, were the only indication that the room at the front may once have been a kitchen. Lighter than elsewhere, the space was harder to endure. Stepping backwards his foot squelched something soft. He looked down and his stomach rolled at the half-embedded worm wriggling in the decayed apple.

Stepping back outside, he saw that the visitors' book was no longer on the window ledge. Were the staff and Malcolm and Gareth enjoying a joke at his expense as they hid not far off in the trees? In the gloom of the house he could have missed some other doorway – but nothing would persuade him to venture back inside.

"Yeah, very funny," Karl called out, nodding as if it were. "You can come out now." He thought someone was about to when he glimpsed movement.

Sunlight outside deepened the gloom in the kitchen, occupied again. The more he stared, the less he wanted the two shapes with the girl to be more clearly delineated. Alone out here, he refused to believe the human-sized pepperpot had a crescent of horns around a black muzzle with nostrils you could fit fists in. It and the girl were in the shelter and deep shade of a fleshy black canopy, like a warped mattress. In the pillar-box thick stalk that supported it were several dark pits like empty eye sockets.

The girl held a book before her. Karl could only think it was the visitor's book. His limbs felt calcified. How long before perusal of the book was transferred to him? Twisting, he felt rooted in the lawn before a supreme effort freed him. He ran, grabbed his rucksack and then the gate's latch snickered drily and puffed rust onto his hand as he pushed.

A random fleeing until the woods expelled him. More unknown paths dipped in and out of further misted islands of woodland, rose and fell on meadows and pastures ruckled like mouldy green bed linen. An arrowhead of geese honked laughter in and out of low cloud. Sheep fled from him on stick legs, matted fleeces leaping.

He was able to triangulate from the positions of the mountains a tortuous way to the village. A chill, a faint fuzzy patina of grey on tree and hill, as if summer had shifted into autumn in under an hour.

Connerstone offered little relief. Damp grey stone, grubby whitewash, faded stucco. Rumbling cars glided in slow lines. Voices bloomed and diminished on the crowded paths outside a mini-gallery, the gingerbread shop, *Souvenirs and Gifts,* cafes and pubs. He sensed lassitude – people filling the time before departure. Grey light washed colours from their clothing.

At a convulsion in his stomach, Karl tasted apples and foul eggs. The girl had been real but those companions must have been distorted reflections from the garden and the trees. Going inside to demand an explanation he would have found that out for certain –

and the whereabouts of his friends. His phone would clear up the latter mystery.

Malcolm's recorded voice introduced and instructed like a deliberate delaying tactic before Karl could say, his voice clipped, "It's me. I'm in the village. Are *you*? Ring me back." From Gareth's number a ringtone like a robotic cough.

There was just over an hour before the Stagecoach service was due to leave the terminal. He'd kill time until then. He wandered, as much in the roadside gutters as on the paths.

He was returning along the main street when there was the unhealthy rattle of an engine and a bus began to draw past him. Karl looked up at the passengers. They were still, listless, like prisoners, each pair in their tiny shared cell. Despite the state of the bus – a drab grey, dented, rust patched – their clothing suggested they were tourists or day- trippers rather than users of a regular local service.

Gareth, in the middle of the back row, was neither. Karl stumbled, recovered, looked again. *Gareth?* Lacking any livery, the bus clearly wasn't part of the Stagecoach fleet they were booked onto in less than an hour's time. So what was Gareth doing onboard?

Karl kept pace, leaping, waving, shouting. Gareth stared forward, oblivious, his expression even more closed-off than usual. People on the path went about their business with bovine intent, Karl's antics of no interest. The bus picked up speed. Some obstruction up ahead had been cleared, but then, short of that, it took a squeaking left-turn into a side road.

Entering a moment later, Karl could see no sign of it though he heard the diminishing rattle of an engine from trees bordering the village.

Karl went and sat in the Yewdale Arms. A grey cast to the light in the window. Wood panelling was dull, as if sandpaper had been applied to it. He barely touched his Guinness. It couldn't have been Gareth on the bus. That would make no sense. Behind glass and the reflected street, just someone *like* him.

Later, when he arrived at the bus terminal, the Stagecoach vehicle was ready to go and nearly full. None of the passengers were Malcolm and Gareth. He could have taken his seat but the puzzle would have gnawed at him all the way home. Waiting outside the coach, he rehearsed to himself the diatribe he'd aim at the pair should they appear in the next moment. At a loss when they failed to, and as the coach slowly pulled away, he tried their mobile phone numbers again. No replies. He left the terminal and wandered again, bewildered.

There was a corner building with books on three floors. He browsed in the local section. In slim stapled volumes no references to Guards Wood; the origin of its name was lost in the hills, or knowledge of it buried in Connerstone Church graveyard. Guarding against what?

On the uppermost floor he looked over the roofs of the village to the upland approach to the fells. A dense fur of woodland draped over an incline must be a near edge of Guards Wood. Were Malcolm and Gareth still up there?

A dull silver mass edged into his eye corner and Karl gasped. The bus had shuddered to a halt on the opposite side of the road below. He was certain this was the same dilapidated vehicle as earlier.

With the passenger door at the front on the far side, it was hard to tell if anyone alighted or got on. No bus-sign or shelter, no line of traffic to hold it up. That it had stopped directly opposite him expressly to display Malcolm in the rearmost window seat was nonsense, though coincidence seemed even less likely. Karl's heart vaguely complained as he ran down three flights of compressed stairs and out onto the path.

He stared across the road, and was struck that nobody stared back at his agitated presence – least of all Malcolm. Karl looked down at his own body in an involuntary check that he was fully present. For a moment he was unsure if it was Malcolm in the back seat, such was the unfamiliar set of his face. He and all his fellow passengers could have been victims of some terrible and inescapable fate. Pictured in a bracingly honest coach holiday brochure they couldn't have been any more motionless.

Karl now knew for certain this was the same bus he'd seen on the main street. And that was definitely Gareth on the far side of Malcolm, still in the middle seat and facing down the central aisle. It was better that they were here. He could forget about Guards Wood now.

He ran, preparing to knock on Malcolm's window – and the bus moved off. He yelled and waved frantically with both hands, saw the staring unyielding square page of the driver's face in the side mirror. He sprinted after the bus until it took a turn into a tiny estate of grey-pink rendered rented houses. Its trundling speed in the confining streets was sufficient for it to elude Karl. It had exited at some point, for Karl knew he'd covered every yard.

He sat on a bench by a deserted tiny playground with his head in his hands. If this was a practical joke, to all appearances it was affording Malcolm and Gareth no pleasure. He returned to the bookshop. The manager didn't look up from his examination of a till receipt and when he finally acknowledged Karl's presence he'd evidently forgotten him hurtling by earlier like a book thief. He hadn't heard of *Journeys End Refreshments* though he knew Guards Wood.

"Everyone does. If you've any sense you go round it."

"Me and my friends went through," Karl said, an ache in his chest like grief.

"Still there are they?"

"No. I've seen them on a bus. It was outside just now. Didn't you see it? Grey. Looks a wreck."

"Yes. Better the bus than the woods," he said, oozing complacency. "You should have joined them."

"They should be joining *me*. It wasn't the bus they were supposed to be on. I've seen it twice now. Couldn't get their attention. We had seats booked on the Stagecoach run to Manchester."

It no longer felt like any consolation, the three of them safely out of Guards Wood. Karl slipped out into the street. Voices and traffic sounded like they were from radios turned down low. If he was slumped in a chair outside Journeys End, replete with apple pie, when was he going to stop haunting this washed-out Conner-stone and wake up?

Later, he walked between darker shadings of slate and stone. Hints of evening in touches of chill air from side roads. Cloud like the thick-ribbed drab sand of a seabed. In an alleyway between shops he got out his phone. The same gratingly breezy recording of Malcolm's voice. Gareth's repetitive coughing ringtone was like something dying.

He booked into the Beaumont Hotel. That evening, in the bar he sat at a table and drank mineral water. Coming down from alcohol would exacerbate the ache of abandonment that rippled wider than the sundering from his friends.

A large shaggy dog, an unidentifiable cross-breed, wandered, accepting crisps and peanuts before retiring behind the counter. A sudden odour of cider or raw apple broke into Karl's fascination with the flames in the wood burner. A waft of rotten eggs had him standing. Deep snorts and porcine squeals under the counter. A sinuous movement of a shiny reddish brown embedded itself into a group of voluble young women. Whispering laughter was like a vapour around their harder chuckles. It dispersed as he stood before the group; none of them was the girl from Journeys End. It took a moment for them to notice him staring. He returned to his seat and gave it up soon after. Nobody else appeared to notice the sulphurous smell which the dry heat of the wood-burner intensi-fied until it was more than he could stand.

The streets were as empty as the paths and glades of Guards Wood, and as silent – until he heard the rattle of the engine. It drew him through the village and had faded to nothing by the time he was in sight of the car park, a crossword puzzle layout demar-cated by wilting flowers in stone troughs, low walls and head-high shrubs.

The bus was in a corner. Approaching warily he saw that the grey wasn't paint, but the absence of it. He was reminded of fa-vourite toy cars, taken from the toy box so often they began to lose their lead paint and reveal the matte metal beneath. Deep scratches in the bodywork. Rust wounds. Lifting his gaze he saw threads of bright orange where cracks in the glass caught the sodium light.

A double shock seeing the seated figures in the dark interior, hearing the engine cough suddenly like a diseased thing. He staggered back as, moaning through its length, the bus moved off. Karl followed until it was heading through the exit and withdrawing like a bloodless tongue into the stone jaws of the village.

Visible through the rear window, four heads on the back row, five if that right-hand corner seat had been filled. Later maybe, the passengers' dispersal to hotels and bed-and-breakfasts – though their continued presence was making them seem as integral to the functioning of the bus as the sick engine.

The crowd awoke him. A vast crowd, an ocean of voices dragooned by an overwhelming voice soaring and swooping above them. It couldn't be the country fair again, not at this late hour, and in any case the sounds weren't entering via the leaded panes of the window.

He got out of bed, opened his door a few inches. Nothing audible from downstairs, other than a sound that soon he identified as a lazy flap of turned pages.

In the soft illumination of night-lights he went down the stairs. The multitudes, gone now, could have emanated from a TV or radio.

The visitors' book was on a walnut occasional table. Cold air laid a page finally to rest and stiffened Karl's limbs.

On facing pages, names. The latest entry had Gareth's precise tiny signature. The preceding name was Malcolm's.

Were they in this hotel? A coincidence – or they had discovered he was staying here. They must have booked in late – any earlier he would have seen them in the bar, unless they'd chosen to hide in their rooms. Speculating on how their reunion with him might proceed, he drew a blank, couldn't in fact envisage any kind of reunion. Again no comment by Gareth's neat inscription. Malcolm had written "Heavenly enclave" rather than come up with something new for the Beaumont. Similarly, there was a single space waiting to be filled at the bottom of the right-hand page. The ink was the same reddish brown as in the book at Journeys End. There was even an identical make of pen, fawn, shiny, like a long slender bone of a bird.

Karl flipped over the book; the front cover had a reddish brown encrustation like the scab over a healing wound. He pressed his splayed fingers into it, wanted to press it out of existence. He stepped away from it. "Heavenly enclave" flattered Journeys End, the visitors' book for which was before him now. In the morning, oh yes, in the morning, he'd slam the book down onto the reception desk and demand an explanation and –

A footfall at the end of the passageway to the staff quarters, a shadow poised in the doorway. Karl said, "What's this doing here?"

Placing a finger on the last two names in the visitors' book, the paper felt smoother. He looked down – it was cleaner, newer – and he didn't recognize the names. There was a column for dates in the left-hand margin. There was a blue biro chained to a blotting pad.

The manager said nothing; he wasn't even present.

After breakfast, a crackling like fire after Karl had keyed in his friends' mobile phone numbers. Later that morning his phone battery was dead, and his charger was in his flat in Manchester. He could be there himself by evening if he caught today's Stagecoach run.

At midday he left the hotel and drank in a coffee shop and watched pedestrians and vehicles. He browsed unthinkingly in souvenir shops and outdoor clothing emporia. He was in dread and hope of seeing the grey bus. If, bizarrely, Malcolm and Gareth were still onboard he'd find some way to get on. He'd confront them, shake them out of whatever stupor held them. He wouldn't be taking that empty back seat, he'd be ensuring two more would be vacant.

Mid-afternoon he sat on the churchyard wall. Unshaven and in the clothes he had climbed mountains and slept in, he was as note-worthy as a lamppost to the apathetic crowds on the path.

A sustained snort from the open back doors of a butcher's van shocked him. A hiss of airbrakes had him covering both ears and retreating into the church. His gaze skittered over the visitors' book in the porch and he entered the nave where he sat on the back pew.

In a side chapel as dark as the bole in a tree, a bank of candles in transparent votive holders cast a lurid red light, rendering the priest's face demonic.

Cries from the street, masses of them. An amplified voice barged and blundered. Karl shook his head; a country fair can't have in-stantly manifested itself in the graveyard. He didn't believe in it even when the priest said, "Now that's a glorious din." His eyes retained a faint redness when he turned to face Karl. "Hell is other people, it's been said. That's true enough." A toothless smile, if it was a smile. "You can't escape it."

Filling the long slits of the side pockets in his soutane, his hands must have been enormous. He was bringing the darkness of the chapel out with him. Karl didn't want to hear whatever else the man intended to say and left.

Outside he listened. Only village sounds, muted as if heard through thick canvas. The fair must have been a recorded event, blasted out of the open window of a vehicle going by.

The graffiti-decorated porta-cabin was indicative of how the police viewed the general run of tourists' issues in the village. What would they make of this one? Inside there was a tiny TV screen over the desk: Karl couldn't tell from the tiny busy figures if he was seeing the streets outside or the exterior of some obscure daytime drama. It held the apple-chinned officer's attention until Karl re-peated himself in a raised voice, and even then he looked to the window first as if Karl had called from outside.

Karl omitted details that would demolish his chance of a fair hearing. The officer dragged his pen across the incident book opened out on the counter. He began asking questions; where was

Karl from, did he have a job, did he live alone? "I don't think I can help you here. Looks like your . . . *friends* are alive and well. Not sure you're in good shape though. You look like death warmed-up. Take my advice and take yourself back home – wherever that is." A place the officer appeared to have little faith in.

The village was like floating debris on a sluggish stream. Shutters came down on the front window of the greengrocer's. Battered suitcases were being loaded into the open wound in the side of a coach.

In the Yewdale Arms Karl sat at a table close to the bar, drank scotch and placed his ticket on the table before him. Seat thirty-nine. Would the company accept it for today's service? At home, at work, he would let the mystery resolve itself.

The priest entered and Karl felt a curdling sensation in his stomach, a taste of apple and bad eggs. Sitting opposite him, the priest crossed his black-trousered legs, entwining them down to his coal-black shoes. He nodded at the coach ticket. "Thirty-nine – you're the last. They aren't going anywhere without you. You must accept the inevitable."

"They?" Karl's back prickled with cold, his front baked as if the priest exuded heat.

"'They' are a delightful family – but homesick." Dreamy reminiscence on the priest's face. "They've been stuck here for ages and can't return until they've met their quota of names – thirty-nine to be exact. Thirty-nine is a number replete with diabolical significance." He snickered. "Sadly for them, thirty-eight isn't."

"Names?" Karl pocketed the ticket. If the coach left at 4:50pm, same as yesterday, he'd be away from this lunacy.

"Yes, obviously you haven't signed the book. They aren't happy about that. That's the payment they required for that sumptuous repast."

Karl wanted to swing with his fist at the delta of throbbing red veins in the priest's temple. In the soutane's side pockets, an outline of abnormally long fingers. The man's stomach rumbled like magma. A taste of apples and foul eggs crumpled Karl's face.

"Go to Hell," Karl said. His frown felt half way down his face.

The priest's sigh seemed to issue not just from his crooked mouth. "I wish." On one side his gleaming forehead drooped like wax to his cheek as airbrakes screamed. Karl got up, quivering.

In the tall window, just under the curtain rail and in the plain glass over the lower half of frosting, a band of faces blurred, stilled.

Malcolm's and Gareth's gazes passed through Karl as unheeding of him as subatomic particles.

Bubbling pitch behind him. He turned to see the opening to the Gents door narrowing under the bent arm of the self-closing device. A hot layered and meaty stink made him gag. He rushed out, swallowed air in the street, felt nauseous. No bus in sight but it didn't matter, as he knew Gareth and Malcolm were no longer aboard.

There was a bottleneck of tourists at the entrance to a side road. Motionless forms beyond a ferment of people entering and exiting some establishment a little way down with a "Closing Down Sale" sandwich board notice outside. He crossed over, keeping his gaze steady. Two people; Gareth and Malcolm, he firmly believed until the sinuous slenderness of one couldn't possibly be Gareth nor the obesity of the other Malcolm.

Though the pair had gone by the time he'd made his way through the crowd, Karl sensed they'd found a better spot from which to observe him.

On the corner, the butcher's shop; in its window a pig's head with tiny eyes stared glassily at him from a bed of lettuce leaves and apple halves. Then his attention was drawn to a narrow maroon pennant, rippling off its pole and tumbling down the other side of the petrol garage's shallow pitched roof.

At the terminal shortly before 4:50 the driver told him the coach was full and that his ticket was for yesterday. The coach slid away. An official said there were no more services to anywhere before tomorrow. Karl returned to the Beaumont and booked another night. He tried not to be upset by anything other than what this was costing him financially.

He could hear guests packing, prior to departure in the morning. With frequent pig-like squeals of door hinges, the hotel was a sty.

He watched TV for four hours before hisses and grunts underlying the actors' voices had him switching off. He made no other preparations for sleep other than to close his eyes and wait for the last door to squeal savagely on its hinges.

Later, out of the darkness, came the turn of a page. He stared at a slight swaying of the curtains for minutes before leaving his bed and parting them down the middle.

At the dead centre of the deep window ledge was the Journeys End visitors' book. He closed his eyes, willed it not to be there, and looked again.

Thirty-eight names, and a space opposite number thirty-nine. There was the pen, a slender piece of bone carved to a point. He'd tear the book to pieces-throw them into the stream. His fingers were curved like talons when he heard the voice.

"Greetings this fine night."

The words shook through him. A male voice, not loud but like a mountain speaking. Karl looked into the deep-set window in which the grotesques were reflected.

Deep snorts and squeals from the porcine thing loosened the flesh on his bones. Next to it, a twisted flourish, a cartilaginous shiny length in shades of reddish bronze emitted harsh whispers, like escaping gas. They were both in the protective shadow cast by a great fleshy dark cap that extended some way past the walls and ceiling it rendered insubstantial. Holes in the massive thick trunk watched him intently. He thought one of them had spoken.

This was the window of Journeys End again, except that he and they occupied the same side of the glass. Tight as a family. Inseparable.

"We fed you well." Like gravity speaking.

"Yes. De-delicious." His voice was the last toothpaste squeezed from a tube.

"You must sign our visitor's book." In the monumentally deep and reasonable tone a planetary pressure to comply.

"I prefer not to put my name to things," Karl managed to say.

"Your name is important to us."

Karl let out a bitter, tremulous spurt of laughter. In the glass, the scatter of holes that observed him would have been light-years deep if light had been conceivably involved. Seen directly, not reflected, he thought he'd be gone into them, never to emerge. They didn't want that – what they wanted was what was happening, his fingers grasping the pen.

Hissing in his head. Snorts and grunts rooting hungrily in his guts.

"You want to be with your friends, don't you?" The voice – from the floor of the universe. "Come with us."

"Where?" he said, though the question seemed spoken through him.

"*Home.*" A triumvirate of yearning inhuman voices sent the curtains billowing. He felt a void the depth of his skin away.

"Whose home? I'm happy here, thank you."

With the lie, resistance began to drain through his right hand and into the bone pen which was moving into position over the empty space on the page.

As the nib drove home, he obstructed it with his free left hand.

White hot pain awoke him to daylight. Grey-blue light around the edges of the closed curtains. Voices; doors opening and closing. Vehicles were moaning on the main street.

A small painless black wound in the back of his hand. There was no pen on the window ledge to have caused it. No book either.

In the dining room he couldn't eat breakfast. Afterwards, at the reception desk, the manager finally noticed him and Karl asked for his bill.

The manager had chicken skin. His upper lip was bowed in a smile but not the lower.

"I'll pay by cheque."

"If you tear out the slip, I'll stamp it for you."

The manager stamped the hotel name and passed the slip back to Karl.

The pen had scratched Karl's unruly signature when he noticed its bony hue. He dropped it and it clattered hollowly onto the desk. The scratching had scored through the cheque to the scabrous book beneath which the manager deftly pulled away. Speechless, Karl pointed with his wavering pierced hand in a tempest in which the manager's ears flapped and his long fingers rippled like thin pennants.

The hotel leaned four ways in turn. Doors banged open and shut, open and shut. Easy chair cushions plumped and flattened like lungs. The floorboards rippled like conflicting currents in water. Stair risers rose and fell like wreckage on rough waters. Pictures floated as far out from the walls as cords attaching them to hooks would allow. Horseshoes clip-clopped randomly over rough plaster walls. Insane celebration, everywhere.

The halves of the front door opened and shut like heart valves. On an out-swing he darted through onto the path and looked up at the swinging Hotel Beaumont sign. The building was alive and he was too close. He backed, and it came from his left before he'd time to think about evading it. A violent impact; a thought struggled in his head, died.

The earth shook beneath him; a dry heat. Through the bars of his eyelashes a column of figures approached, some slipping out of sight to either side, some would be in touching distance soon. He shrank back and down.

"Call off the search," a familiar voice said.

He opened his eyes. Malcolm and Gareth hauled their rucksacks up into the overhead rack. Malcolm looked at his ticket, then at the tiny brass stud on the back of the seat next to Karl's. "You don't mind me taking thirty-eight, do you Gareth?" Malcolm said, plumping himself down. *And I'm in thirty-nine as stipulated on my ticket here in my hand. All seats taken. We're ready to go.* Karl's mouth twitched towards a smile.

"So, Karl, where the heck did you get to?"

A new note to the engine and the crocodile skin of grey tarmac became grey silk as the coach glided out of the station and turned onto the main street. Connerstone sharply delineated after the fuzzy imposter in which everything had been like a watercolour left out in the sun.

"Speak to me, Karl," Malcolm said, joining thumbs and tips of middle fingers to make a big circle.

"Journeys End," Karl said.

Malcolm looked at him as if trying to work out several conundrums at once. "They certainly do." Gareth and Malcolm looked at each other, then Gareth aimed his camera at Karl. The lens brought to mind the vague pit of a dark tree bole.

"Not now, Gareth," Malcolm said. "Are you alright, Karl?"

Karl thought about that. "Not sure."

"Okay." Staring at the headrest before him, Malcolm formulated a response. "There was a deluge in Guards Wood. Next thing we look around and you'd gone. We spent ages calling out, wandering. Thought you must have headed to the village. When we got here we walked up and down the main street, had a drink in the Yewdale then came here and here you were, out like a light in the corner. So, a happy ending."

Try telling your face that, Karl thought. He watched Malcolm and Gareth as intently as they watched him. No hint of a struggle to contain mirth or gaiety. It's all me, Karl thought, and wasn't he glad about that? Walking at the rear he could have slipped on a wet root, hit his head and knocked himself out. Meanwhile Malcolm and Gareth could have walked on, oblivious. What if some instinct for self-preservation embedded in a state deeper than sleep had subsequently guided him to the village and the coach in time for the return trip to Manchester?

No sinister fracturing of reality. He was here, now, thinking rational thoughts, in the company of his friends and heading home. This was the best outcome after the trio of monstrosities, the priest, the hotel manager; they'd stirred to life in his unconscious, representations of his dread of the future, his only friends gone to distant places, his unsatisfactory job in that wet miserable city.

Now he could let his friends go, bring a better attitude to his job, appreciate wet glum Manchester.

The miked stone-dry voice of the driver came over the speakers. "Good evening ladies and gents. Hope you're seated comfortably. We are finally leaving. Home again jiggety-jig."

Karl longed to get there. Gareth clicked his camera at the pattern of the rubberized flooring of the aisle.

Outside the village, the coach followed Connerstone Water to the north where the road began to wind as it rose. The declining sun painted hillsides, flashed through scatters of trees. Areas of woodland cover thickened, darkened as the sun became an indeterminate crimson low in the west. At a high elevation there was no more climbing. Ranks of mountains on all sides under an empurpled sky dusted with pink cloud and salt stars. Subsequent to a series of dips, the hills were taller; suspended between peaks the sky had insidiously become dark as graphite.

The coach increased its speed where caution might have been advisable. Karl thought the driver was keen to get home. *Me too*, he thought.

No chatter. Looking along the gap between headrests and windows Karl saw heads leaning.

"You should get some shut-eye," Malcolm advised Karl. "And get your doctor to check you out first thing in the morning."

Not long after, Malcolm was following his first piece of advice and snoring softly, puzzlement verging on anxiety in his furrowed brow. Most eyes were shut if the jerking heads, visible between the headrests, were any indication as the coach swung and dipped around the interlocking buttresses of mountainside. No moon, no stars, no lights of farms or isolated hamlets. Karl supposed the darkness was stretching the distance to the motorway.

Malcolm's body leaned against him, pressing him into the window. He noted many minute scratches. The glass was of uneven thickness, as if it had approached a liquid state in extreme temperatures and oozed, subsequently hardening again. At the bottom of the frame, where the exterior bodywork bulged out slightly, he noted a matte grey. As his heart turned over, he told himself the whole coach wouldn't be that non-colour. He pushed Malcolm back so he was snoozing upright. Gareth's head was tucked down into his narrow chest.

This must be another route bypassing by miles the approaches to Windermere, the next town. The road would level soon, the mountains step back and valleys spread wide. To be endured until then, the shrouded distances, at once vast and claustrophobic. Without stars or moon, an elusive ambient light must be lending these eminences the greater part of their massiveness, comprising as many precipitous walls as slopes.

A pull forward, the bus on a descent. A diffuse redness was intermittently visible below. It couldn't be the sunset at such a low point in the soaring encompassing terrain.

Karl envied the others sleeping. Closing his eyes, the dark spreading through him was like sleep and he didn't resist.

When he awoke, a faint red tincture glinted off some surfaces, glowed on others. Elsewhere, intense gloom monumentalized natural features to produce awesome battlements and redoubts, soaring pillars and spiked bridges. Daylight would make the mountains sane again, and hours prior to that the coach would be entering Manchester.

Malcolm's expression suggested his dream had become tragic and terrifying. Karl wondered if he should wake him. The road had leveled off. Either it was an extraordinary sunset behind and below the miles-wide dark edge ahead, or artificial lights of a size fit to illuminate a gargantuan sunken stadium.

The bus came to a stop. The engine cut out but the window glass continued to vibrate. Karl realized a gigantic voice outside was responsible. Tiny cries flocked around it. It awoke Malcolm, Gareth and the rest of the passengers. Was it the same voice he'd heard scraps of since coming down from the hills to Guards Wood? There had been the country fair at Tilberthwaite and there were, he presumed, others. Late as it was, this fair had yet to conclude. He'd get Malcolm to identify the vast hollow in the mountains on his map when they got home.

The driver spoke over the microphone in a voice that brushed like a yard broom. "When you've made your way off the vehicle, you'll be taken to the place in three groups."

Such stupendous numbers, their cries like the pipings of an asthmatic chest a continent wide. But the voice of the Master of Ceremonies dominated them all. It exclaimed unintelligibly between screeches of uncontrollable laughter. The speakers amplifying the voice Karl pictured as being as tall as buildings, and in untold numbers.

The passengers were getting out of their seats.

"You know I've never actually been to a country fair before. Wonder how long we'll have?" Malcolm's eyes bulged, the desperate calamitous dream continuing in them.

"Should be time to take a picture or two," Gareth said. Not good ones if Gareth couldn't control the wild shake of his hands holding the camera.

The doors weren't open yet. Gareth, Malcolm and Karl standing at the end of the aisle, numbers thirty-seven, thirty-eight and thirty-nine, would be the last to leave. Karl looked past his appalled reflection into the darkness. The mountains were like gigantic workings under a rock-solid sky. From precipices, immense silhouetted birds launched themselves and flapped lazily as if on hot up-draughts and appeared to be biding their time.

Conflicting rhythms; the limping beating bass note in Karl's chest, the running sensation in his head, someone on inner highways coming to convey news that would congeal his blood.

From the canopy of the fungal growth, growing from the thick stalk up against an adjacent cliff, she emerged, a rippling sheaf of molten maroon. Outside the closed door she looked along the windows, her tongue flickering out of her long-lipped smile. Karl heard her hiss, unless that had been the doors opening. "Make haste," the driver ordered in his blow-torch voice.

Intense heat entered, and there was a powerful odour of sulphur – and apples to remind them all of home.

ALISON LITTLEWOOD

ON ILKLEY MOOR

It wasn't until I turned off the main road and up towards the moors that it really struck me that this had been my home. There was that old sound, the wind billowing its way across the tops and down into the valley, a sound out of memory; but the way it buffeted the car was real enough. I reached out and turned the radio up, but in my mind it was another tune I heard, different lyrics:

Wheear 'ast tha bin since ah saw thee?

I smiled. Where indeed? I hadn't felt the need to come back here since Dad had died, and that was years ago. I had my own place now, my own job; my training was done, my school days long behind me. I'd never thought to see Inchy – Warren Hinchliffe – again. I jabbed at the radio, turning it off, and listened to the sound of the wind coming over the tops. Up there were swathes of green, patched with the lighter shades of dead grass and the darker growth of heather, the purple flowers darkened to grey under a cloudy sky. And grey paths wound through it all, leading nowhere, or so it had seemed when we were small.

I remembered what Inchy had said on the phone: *It'd be just what I need.* I had the impression that he'd been prepared for my rejection. He'd just lost his job, he said, nothing special, just helping out on a farm, but now it had ended: *I need summat to help me start ower*. And he'd waited in silence, and the old guilt had crept from his end of the line to mine.

Wheear 'ast tha bin since ah saw thee?

I'd been miles away, while he had stayed, along with the memory of what had passed between us, the thing we had done. I pushed the thought away. I'd started again long ago; the least I could do was help Inchy do the same. I dropped down the slope and saw the pub – *The Cow and Calf* – named for the giant out-crops of millstone grit that could just be seen at the edge of the moor, and I slowed, and pulled into the car park.

Inchy was propping up the bar. I recognised him at once, though he wasn't so much taller than me as I'd remembered, and he'd been working on a beer gut in the time I'd been away. He didn't smile when he saw me, didn't act surprised, didn't say "How've you been?"; he just nodded to where a pint stood at his elbow.

"I was going to have a Coke –"

"You might as well 'ave it. Get it dahn thee neck, Andy." And then, belatedly: "All right, mate?"

"Not bad." I grinned at him before taking a drink. It was cold, but more welcome than I'd expected.

He grinned back and drained what was left of his own pint. "Lad's day out, and all that. Get you out o' t' city furra bit. God's own country."

I tried not to let him see how the beer was going straight to my head. "My dad always called it that."

"Aye, well, 's changed a bit round 'ere since them days. 'S all posh folk in Ilkley now – more accountants and bankers than you can shek a stick at."

I kept quiet, taking another sip. He knew what I did for a living, didn't he? I was already wondering if this had been a good idea.

"Not locals. Not like us. Remember 'ow we'd go off looking for frogspawn an' that, in t' streams?"

I smiled. I did remember.

"They don't do that these days. Now it's all off to ballet in their fancy Land Rovers, or walking their labra-fucking-doodles. They sink a hundred quid on designer wellies, and chuck a hissy fit if they get 'em mucky. Well, we'd best go, mate."

He pulled on an army surplus jacket and nodded at my padded coat. "Cragface, eh?"

"Craghoppers." I shrugged and bent to tighten the laces on my hiking boots, only then realising how clean they were. They'd been more than a hundred quid, but they were guaranteed comfy out of the box, and I hadn't been walking in a long time. When I straightened I expected Inchy to narrow his eyes or make some comment, but he didn't; he only nodded.

"We'd best get off then," he said.

Once we got walking, it was just like the old days. Inchy had always led the way then too; he was a few months older than me but he'd always been taller, and he seemed more so now, since he was higher up the hillside. The wind barrelled off the slope, flattening the grass, and we leaned into it. The path led steadily upward past the side of the old quarry and it felt as if I was fifteen again, playing hooky from school, led astray by "that boy," as my mum used to call him. She'd even correct me if I said his nickname – Hinchy, she'd insist – but he was never called that; no one ever said their aitches, not round here, not then.

The old song started to run through my mind as we climbed higher:

On Ilkla Moor baht 'at . . .

We used to sing it for a joke and it seemed more than ever like one now, with the wind raging around us. How on earth could anyone have kept a hat on their head? The wind was cold too, chilling my ears and the nape of my neck. *Tha's bahn to catch thy deeath o' cowd*, we'd sung. I paused and pulled up my hood, holding it in place, the fabric buffeting about my head. It was loud, and at first I didn't realise that Inchy had spoken.

"Cow n' calf."

He pointed down at the quarry, towards the two huge boulders. The calf stood away on its own, the cow jutting from a longer crag. Beyond them was more moor and fields and little villages and all the long grey sky watching over it all.

"Bet you never knew t' legend," he said. "There was this giant, see. Rombald. He ran off from 'is wife – dunno what 'ed done – an' 'e stamped on them rocks and split t' calf off from t' cow. Course, it never looked like no bloody cow n' calf to me."

I laughed. "Me neither. I could never work out why they called it that."

"Aye, well." Another pause. "'E split summat up, anyroad."

I stared after him as he started to walk, seeing only his back, the dull green of his coat blending into the landscape. I wasn't sure he'd said what I thought I'd heard. I blinked the idea away. He hadn't meant anything; it was only the rocks he'd been speaking of. I shrugged and started after him, climbing higher, away from the quarry and the pub and the view behind it.

As we laughed over the old days, I started to remember them in a way I hadn't for a long time. The further I'd gone, the hazier the memories had become; now Inchy brought them back. I remembered trying to smoke a cig he'd nicked from his old man's pocket; unscrewing people's gates on Mischief Night; and coming up here, to the moor. That, most of all; and I remember the way it felt, as if anyone in the world could look up and see us and know what we were up to, and yet hidden too, as if we were a hundred miles from anything.

We fell quiet. There was only the sound of the wind and the rustle of our coats, and I started to drift, and I heard the old song once more in my mind:

Tha's been a cooartin' Mary Jane
On Ilkla Moor baht 'at . . .

I pulled a face. There were things I wanted to remember and things I didn't, and this was one of the things I didn't.

It was Inchy who'd got a girlfriend first. Of course it was; he was taller than me, and harder, and he always seemed so much older, even though the difference between us was small. And Joan was the best of them, the one all the lads fancied. It wasn't long before they started going out, and Inchy suddenly didn't have so much time for fishing or wandering or anything else.

She was pretty, Joan Chapman. Her long dark hair was never tied back and she had a pale oval face and, what all the lads thought but wouldn't say in front of Inchy, the best pair of tits in school. She had a laugh like a drain and sparkles – it sounded corny even now, but she did – she had sparkles in her eyes. She looked like she was going somewhere, but of course she never did; she hadn't gone anywhere, had never even become any older than we were then. But I hadn't had to think about that, or not too much, because by then I'd been leaving. I was wondering how far that was true of Inchy when he said, "'Ere: I wanted to do summat. For *'er*."

"You what?"

He turned and I saw that his face was white. It came as a shock to see the way he kept blinking, as if he was trying to hold something back.

He pulled something from his pocket. I stared at it. It was a candle. I didn't know what on earth he was thinking: it wasn't something I wanted to remember, and anyway, a *candle* for God's sake, just as if the wind wasn't howling over the tops like the very devil. And it was daylight, even if it was thin and mean, the clouds heavy and grey.

"I thought we could," he said. "Old time's sake. Finish it, you know? Just summat to . . ."

Start ower, I thought. I felt suddenly sick, the beer uneasy in my belly. I didn't want to agree, but I found myself saying: "All right."

"Serious?" He brightened at once and I suddenly felt as if I was the older one. I nodded and he went on, towards another grey rock, this one overhanging the hillside as if at any moment it would tumble to the valley below.

The pancake stone was balanced on a small grey outcrop, its position precarious, and yet it had stood there for years. Its name had never seemed quite right; it was flat on top but it looked to me more like an anvil, pointing out over the empty air. Ancient markings were carved into it, cup and ring formations, some almost joining so they looked like part of some larger pattern that had long since been lost.

"Here," he said.

"Inch, I'm not sure –"

The look he sent me was so hurt I didn't say anything else.

Anger I could have understood, but this, from him, was worse. He took the candle and set it into one of the cups, but it wouldn't hold. He jammed it instead into a crack in the rock and pulled a matchbox from his pocket. The wind almost took it from him. He struck a match and it blew out at once. He swore under his breath; the wind whipped the curse away.

"Ne'er mind," he said. "I brought summat else."

He fiddled in his pockets and took out a small plastic bottle. Carefully, he tipped some of the liquid it held into one of the cups. "'S what they were for, they reckon," he said. "Lighting fires."

I looked at the rock. I wasn't sure anyone knew what the patterns were for, not really, but I somehow felt there must be more to it than that.

This time he threw the match down as soon as it sparked and the liquid caught, flaring, and he jerked away from it. The flame became invisible almost at once.

"I 'eard," he said, "this place behind t' rock – Green Crag – they used t' call it land o' the dead. They did rites, an' that."

I pulled a face. I didn't know where he was getting this stuff. For all I knew, he was making it up. This trip was a mistake, I knew that now.

Tha's been a cooartin' my lass Joan . . .

I shook my head, trying to clear it. I felt my guilt stirring, rising into the air with the flame that was already dying, dead and gone like . . .

"This is wheear she did it," he said.

I whipped around to face him. "What?"

"Oppened a vein. Right 'ere. Laid 'ersel' down on t' rock, an' –"

"No. She *didn't*."

He half turned to stare at the stone, just as if he could still see the fire burning there, as if anybody could.

I took deep breaths. He had to be lying. I'd heard she'd killed herself – of course I did, everybody knew, everybody knew everything in a place like this – but I'd imagined her doing it in the bath, lying down, putting her wrist under the water before she sliced.

But I *hadn't* known, had I? Because I'd left. I'd gone away to college because I couldn't wait to turn my back on it; I hadn't *wanted* to know.

And now he'd brought me here. Inchy had brought me back.

Tha's been a cooartin' my lass Joan (baht thee trahsers on) . . .

The voice in my head had become mocking. No: accusing.

It hadn't been my fault. I'd told myself that so many times. I may have gone after her, *set my cap at her* as my mum would have put it, but it was Joan who'd decided: it was her choice. And when she realised it was a mistake, when we'd split and she tried to go back to Inchy and he wouldn't have her – that wasn't my fault either, was it? He'd been happy enough to have me back, as a friend. I'd often wondered how he could bring himself to forgive me but not her, but friendship was like that, wasn't it? It was for keeps. It was for *ever*.

Now I looked into his face and I found myself wondering who the hell he was; who he had ever been.

"I would've bought her a ring," he said, his voice distant. "If she 'adn't – I mean, I know we was young. But I would 'ave. Eventually."

I went on staring. I realised my mouth had fallen open; I closed it again. When he didn't say anything else I tried to find words, but there were none. All I could think was, *he said he didn't care*. He'd said she was just a lass and she didn't matter, not really. He'd laughed at her when she tried to win him back. He told folk she'd let anyone lift her skirt and he called her a slag, even when she cried to his face. If he hadn't told me he wasn't bothered, if I'd known –

But I looked at him now and I *did* know. Of course he couldn't forgive her. He hadn't been able to forgive her because of how deep the hurt went, and I saw now that time hadn't eased it, only weathered it, carving the grooves deeper.

When he turned, it didn't come as a surprise to see that he was crying.

"Inchy. I – I'm going back to the pub," I said, and I backed away.

"'Ang on." He looked startled.

"I didn't ask for this. Look, I said I was sorry. I *am* sorry. But this –" I raised my hands and let them fall again.

"Look, I din't mean nowt. But this is why we came, in't it? We did that to 'er, thee an' me, and it seemed right, tha's all. It's done now. I've said wha' I want to say, an' tha's it. No more, all right? It's ower."

"Is it, Inchy?"

He rubbed a hand over his eyes and he smiled. If it hadn't been for that smile, I would have turned and gone back then and there, but I didn't; I looked at him for a long time, neither of us wavering, and then I nodded and I stayed.

"Rombald's missus dropped that," Inchy said.

I looked at the odd cairn set into the wiry grass. It was made of grey stones of similar sizes, forming a low, rough circle. It reminded me of a plate with an indentation in the middle.

"Skirtful o' stones," he added. "She were runnin' after 'im, see, when 'e put 'is size nines through t' cow n' calf. And then she dropped all t' stones she were carryin' and med this circle. Dun't know 'er name. Nubody did."

I gave him a sharp look, but there didn't seem to be any hidden meaning in what he said. He seemed to have put Joan out of his mind; he'd been striding out with new energy, his cheeks reddened by the continual assault of the wind. It was me that couldn't stop thinking about her. I opened my mouth to ask why the giant's wife was running after him, but realised I didn't want to know. I had an image in my mind; me and Inchy heading off up Curly Hill on one of our expeditions, and Joan catching up with us; the look she'd had on her face when she pulled on Inchy's arm. The look on her face after he'd brushed her off. She hadn't been angry. If she'd been carrying something then, a skirtful of stones, I imagine she'd have just dropped everything too; she'd have let it all go.

I started walking, pulling my hood tighter. The wind was full in my face, chilling my eyes and my skin. It felt like little knives. I walked faster. I probably deserved it.

But Inchy had deserved it too. I felt a stab of anger. He was the one who'd let her go, wasn't he?

I was leading the way, though I hadn't asked where we were headed. I didn't suppose it mattered. I wasn't even looking at the moor, not really; I was looking into the past, and I could see Joan's face as clear as anything. It struck me now she had always been a little like the moor, half ordinary, something that was just *there*, but half wild too; her hair always flying and in knots, something unfathomable in her eyes.

I wondered if it was still there when she died.

I almost felt I could hear that lilting song again, and the words crept across the moor:

Then we shall 'ave to bury thee . . .

I shook my head, spoke without turning. "Inchy, did you hear something?"

He didn't reply.

"Inchy?"

His voice, when it came, was gruff. "Nowt but the wind. And you know what, mate? Me name's *Warren*."

I was only half listening. He was right, it *was* only the wind, but it sounded as if there were voices in it. I was sure, at some point in the past, I'd heard it called a devil wind; now I thought I knew why, only it sounded less like a devil than a host of demons crying together.

Bury thee, bury thee . . .

I shook my head. I was tired and wishing I was a hundred miles away, back in my old life – no, my *new* life – and that bloody wind just wouldn't ease up. I was allowing the past and other people's mistakes and yes, my own, to get to me. It was only then that Inchy's words sank in.

Me name's Warren . . .

I whirled around. He wasn't there.

I scanned the hillside, knowing how the dull green of his jacket would have faded into it. It wasn't any use. Inchy had gone.

Bastard.

I took a few steps back the way I had come, watching for any sign of another living being, and I saw none. Despite the wind, I felt hot all over. He'd lured me out here and then ditched me, an act of petty revenge, and why – because he'd lost his job, was jealous all over again?

I squinted into the cold air. He surely couldn't have passed out of sight so quickly. But it occurred to me that maybe he wasn't out of sight. He might be crouching in the grass, hiding in his green coat; but somehow it didn't feel like that. The place felt empty. He'd already scarpered, heading back to the warm pub and leaving me to freeze. No doubt, when I got there, I'd find he'd let my tyres down too. Well, good luck to him. He was going nowhere, someone who hadn't even had the nous to grab the girl he'd cared about and hold onto her.

The sky was heavier than ever and everything had darkened, taking on the colours of a storm. In the distance the space between earth and sky was streaked black with rain. It seemed to echo something inside of me.

I could try and blame Inchy all I liked, but the knowledge squirmed in my gut: *it was my fault*. It had always been my fault, not because I went after her, because I fancied her, but because the reason I'd gone after her was that Inchy had had her first.

He had always been taller than me. He was always tougher. He was the one who smoked without chucking his guts up, back when smoking was something cool. I pictured him in the pub, clutching his pint glass with his yellowing fingers, and I imagined the rot creeping inside him.

But I'd been the one who set out to destroy something. I was the one who'd *thought* about it, something Inchy never seemed to do, not back then. Now it seemed that had changed. I could hardly blame him.

It didn't matter. All I had to do was retrace my steps and get out of here, leave it all behind, just as I had before. I turned a full circle. All around me was purple heather, long grass bowing in the wind, and bared grey earth. It looked as if there were paths everywhere, radiating like the spokes of a wheel. My belly contracted as I re-alised I was no longer sure which way I'd come. But it should be easy, shouldn't it? All I had to do was head downhill. Except now I appeared to be standing at the summit of a crag. That couldn't be right, could it? *Everywhere* was downhill.

My mouth felt dry. I cursed Inchy for the alcohol I'd had earlier. It was confusing my mind, clouding my judgement. Still, I couldn't stay here; I'd pick a direction and get moving. I'd soon know if I was going the wrong way. Scowling at the moor, wondering if Inchy was still out there, watching, I started to walk.

As I went, the old tune became the background to my steps, the re-frain to my thoughts. I remembered us singing it, the story of comic cannibalism where the man caught his *deeath o' cowd*, was buried and eaten by worms, which were eaten by ducks, which were eaten by the people. I never knew who the 'we' in the song was supposed to be, the singers or someone else, and now I wondered.

Then t'worms'll come an eyt thee up . . .

That had seemed the funniest line of all. It wasn't so funny now.

Then we shall all 'ave etten thee. On Ilkla Moor baht 'at . . .

I stopped walking and frowned. I didn't think this could be the right way. The moor all looked the same, flat and bleak and with nothing to relieve the monotony, and across everything, that merciless scouring wind.

I remembered I should be walking away from it, the wind behind me, but it seemed to be coming from all directions; whichever way I turned it blustered and spat in my face. My cheeks were numb, all feeling long since faded. I turned and started to walk back the way I had just come. As I did, it started to rain.

I'd forgotten how bloody miserable the moor could be. Even the air seemed grey and it was hard to keep my eyes open; I squinted against the rain. It lashed my hood, drowning everything in a loud patter. Fuck this. The sooner I got off the moor the better. I tried to move quicker and my boots slid on the wet, slicked-down grass. I landed on my arse, pushed myself up, went on again. I could hardly see at all. I found I was muttering the words of the song, over and over:

Tha's bahn to catch thy death . . .

I realised what I was saying and shut my mouth. I'd be off this hill soon, then I could dry off in the pub before heading home. I've have the heater on full blast. I'd be too hot then, and I wouldn't bloody care.

It was then that I saw the light.

It hung there on the other side of the rain, a faint yellow glow, and I realised: it was *her* light, it was the pancake stone, and I was back after all. It had to be. It had somehow kept burning and soon I'd be there; I'd see all the lights of Ilkley and Ben Rhydding shining out from the valley, calling me back. I hunched myself against the rain and hurried towards it.

The light flickered in and out of existence. One moment I'd think I was getting closer and then there it was, in the distance again. I must be going in a circle. Or I was seeing things. Whatever it was, I couldn't seem to find it. And all the time the rain kept coming down and the sky was growing darker.

I tilted my head, allowing my hood to fall back and let the rain find my face. It was dead cold, and I cursed, pulling my hood back up, though it wasn't any use; the rain was inside it. I shivered and turned. The light was still there, but it was behind me now. I didn't know how I'd got turned around but I started off again, unable to tell if I was going up a rise or moving slightly downhill. The light kept moving. It bobbed and wavered, confusing my eyes. I had to reach it soon. The moor couldn't be that big. If I just kept going in a straight line, sooner or later, I had to reach its edge.

It was Inchy, it had to be. He'd hidden a lamp out here and he was taunting me with it, and I had to give it to him; he was fast. One minute it was off to the left, the next, away to my right. I'd tried to keep straight but somehow I'd found myself following anyway, being drawn this way and that. Well, enough; I wasn't playing any longer. I was cold and wet and tired.

There was a large boulder in front of me and I leaned against it, slicking water from my coat. The rain was easing off at last. I knew I couldn't stay here for long: cold was spreading from the rock, finding its way inside my skin. Still, I couldn't quite bring myself to move. I stayed while the rain reduced to a light patter and then I felt something, almost as if the rock at my back had trembled, and a moment later I heard it; a dull, hollow boom ringing out across the moor. I reached out and touched the rock, and thought I could still feel it; a faint resonance that took a while to fade.

A few seconds later, the sound came again. I froze, listening. It had to be thunder, didn't it? It could take on all sorts of odd sounds, out here. It's just that, for a moment, it had made me think of footsteps; the footsteps of a giant, echoing in my ears.

Damn Inchy. It was his stories, playing on my mind. Stones and giants, old legends that wouldn't die. The cow and calf, where were they now? And something flashed across my mind, something I'd heard long ago, that there had been a bull once too; a rock bigger than any of them that was broken up and carried off for building. No one ever seemed sure if it was true or not and it was odd to think that something so large could simply disappear, out here, and no one could even agree if it had ever existed.

Just as the rain was letting up at last, the wind was rising again. Its voice moaned across the hills, and my head began to throb with it, aching behind my eyes.

I forced myself to my feet, my wet jeans sticking to my skin, and set my face to the darkness. It wasn't the rain now, robbing everything of light; soon night would fall. I would be out here all alone, and no one would come to help.

But it wasn't entirely dark. Somewhere ahead and a little to my left was the gentle glow of a light. No: *two* lights, now.

Tha's been a cooartin' my lass Joan . . .

I must be seeing things, that was all. But it was easy, with night hailing at the edges of the world, to believe that both of them were out here with me: Inchy and Joan, walking hand in hand maybe, together again . . .

I shook my head, trying to dispel the image. It was nonsense, of course. I started walking again, pulling my coat tight around me. I'd be off this moor in no time; I would soon be warm.

Except there seemed to be no end to this place. It was as if I'd walked into some giant land that went on and on. Everywhere I looked was the moor, dark and smudged with shadows that could have been rocks, could have been anything. *The land of the dead*, he'd called it.

It was suddenly easy to imagine the way Joan might have felt when she came up here all alone. The way she would have sat down on an ancient stone, perhaps smoothing a hand over the things that were carved there. And she'd opened a vein, over those cup markings perhaps, the hollows ready to receive what she gave . . .

And what had the old gods offered in return? What had she asked for as she lay there dying – *me?*

A slow chill spread through my chest.

Then we shall 'ave to bury thee . . .

Something struck me then, something that had never made any

sense before. The last verse of the song, the very last – it was about revenge, wasn't it? Only I'd never understood why. Yes, that was it:

That's wheear we get us ooan back …

The 'we' had had their revenge because they'd eaten him, the man who'd courted the girl and caught the cold and been buried and eaten by the worms – but why *our ooan back?* The song never explained what he'd done to them.

But the song was a part of this place. No one even knew who'd written it; it had been sung down the ages. Now, with the light failing and no one in sight and nothing around for miles, it almost felt as if it had been intended for this moment. It repeated itself inside my mind, but the intonation was different:

That's wheear we get us ooan back. On Ilkla Moor baht 'at …

I shuddered. *Here*, that's where it would be. This was where Joan would come to me, to thank me properly for what I'd done. She'd come with the rain and the wind in her hair, her eyes all a-sparkle in the dark.

I let out an odd sound and started to hurry onward, stumbling in my haste. I realised I was singing as I went, and I knew it was crazy but I couldn't stop. I sang the words faster and faster, no inflection in them now at all, not thinking about what they meant or where they had come from, and I stumbled and slipped and for a time, everything was dark.

When I woke, the cold was bone-deep. I was lying on something hard and I touched it, felt the whorls and dips beneath my fingers, and I pushed myself up. My head swam. I was lying on a grey rock, partially hidden in the ground, and I must have hit my head on it because there was something dark there that looked like blood. I looked at the cups and the rings, delineated more clearly than any I had yet seen. I thought of Joan, her blood. How much had she given? Perhaps this would help. It was an offering, a libation; something. Perhaps it would be enough.

I lay back, not caring that the ground was hard. It wasn't dark any longer, I realised. It wasn't dark and the wind had fallen still, its voices silenced. I was still on the moor but now it was beautiful. The moon had risen and stars were sprinkled across the sky, sparkling like eyes, watching me. I imagined staying here forever, just looking up at them and letting everything slip away.

Then the sound came again, a long, ringing echo as of giant footsteps, and the earth shook beneath me.

I think I smiled. And I remembered a line that we used to add to the song when we were small:

On Ilkla Moor baht 'at
Wheear's that?

The words seemed to whisper in my mind now: *Wheear's that?* And I looked into the sky with its infinite stars and I realised I was no longer sure.

STEVEN J. DINES

THE BROKEN AND THE UNMADE

ONE

*T*HE GERMAN SS *arrived in December, 1943, and announced that our deportation would commence the following morning. In our schools that evening, the teachers gave us no homework.*

Mothers stayed with young children, washed them from head to toe, hung their wet clothes on barbed wire. I was fourteen and big for my age. My mother busied herself cooking the last of our food and packing a suitcase. My father, unable to look at either of us for very long, sought without success that level of drunkenness that might allow him to forget the coming morning. I went for a walk.

Everywhere, the dark, bare soil was set with Yahrzeit candles. The camp like a mirror held up to the late night sky. I wandered among those stars for hours before I finally returned to my parents.

We prayed and wept all through the night.

When will it end.

I'm so tired it is not even a question anymore.

I sit up in bed. Stretch the ache from these ancient bones. Somewhere in the gloom of the basement the boy from the train is standing, watching me. I don't have to see him to know it. Eyes open, eyes closed, he is always there, timeless as a photograph. The cap turned sideways. The yellow Star of David stitched to the left side of his coat. Pupils swollen so large by the dark it is like staring into two pits rimmed with blue fire.

I get up, slowly. Put on my dressing gown. Stamp slippered feet to announce that I am climbing the stairs and entering their world. Saul Aaronson, persona non grata.

My family are already sitting around the breakfast table. They don't bother to get me up anymore. They don't wait. They conduct breakfast as though they prefer the company of an empty chair over me.

My son, Nathaniel, is wearing the T-shirt again, the one I cannot bear to look at, but I say nothing and take my seat. The cereal bowl in front of him is almost empty and he has some splashes of milk clinging to his beard as if he hasn't quite been able to find his mouth this morning. Anger will do that, make you miss the mark when you ought to be stepping up to it.

Sitting opposite him is Aliya, my daughter-in-law: her face is spotless, beautiful, troubled. The bowl in front of her is full, but it saddens me to watch her stir the milk as if she has lost something in there that she can no longer find. At least my grandson Joshua doesn't notice any of this stuff. He's too busy playing with one of the Star Wars figures his father gave to him, in-between oblivious sips of his orange juice. Darth Vader. Right. Surely there must be better things a father can pass on to his child.

But who am I to say? I no longer have a voice in this family. I am too old and I see some fucked-up shit; Nate's words, not mine. So, no one talks to each other, and maybe that's all because of me. It is these moments that are the worst, when we become ghosts ourselves, silently haunting each other during meals I can no longer bring myself to eat. And the boy from the train, he stands behind me, close enough to feel his breath on my neck; that is, if he had any breath to give. He watches us. Watch is all he ever does: the ghost of a memory that refuses to go away.

When will it end.

On the way to the funfair, I ask for all of the windows to be down. This invites cool air into the car at something like fifty miles per hour, which in turn invites Nate to curse under his breath. But even with the windows open the entire way they feel like no more than a slit, particularly inside a vehicle containing three adults and two children. Yes, the boy from the train is here too, sitting between Joshua and I on the back seat. Not that my grandson knows this. When I tried to tell him the story of the boy a few months ago, or at least a watered down version of it, he looked at me like he didn't believe a word about either the death camps or my ghostly parasite. To a boy of twelve, even one who likes to live in his imagination, it all must seem farfetched and far off.

He sees what he wants to see. Like the rest of us, I guess.

At the funfair, I trail behind Nate and Aliya as Joshua races ahead, through the huge gate.

DREAMLAND. Where Dreams Are Free.

This is, of course, an outright lie, because everything comes with a price. Everything.

Nate walks ten feet apart from Aliya while he reheats some previous argument. There's anger in my son's bones, and I find myself staring at the ground, too ashamed to see – or hear – it seep into the rest of him.

Two large inflatable skeletons greet me at the gate. Keeping my eyes down, I walk swiftly past them and inside. I glance back to see the boy from the train loitering near the entrance before vanishing into the crowd. I wonder if I am to have a few seconds respite, but then the boy's face appears on a teenager over by the hotdog stand, and then on another, queuing for a ride, and then on every teenager's face I see, flitting from one to the next like some mask passed around.

"Three shots for a dollar!" someone yells.

I turn to see the barker at a shooting stall holding up what looks like a Luger that shoots corks. I beat a shuddering retreat.

It's happening again, I think.

The screaming children. Beeping arcades. Flashing coloured lights. It's too much.

Inflatable skeletons . . . because it's October and Halloween squats right around the corner . . . inflatable skeletons everywhere. Hollow-eyed grins of bone. And Nate . . . the T-shirt. Pink Floyd's *The Wall*: a screaming face of red on a background of blue, mouth opened impossibly wide and nothing, nothing inside it but yawning, unending darkness. And more children, screaming behind the face of the boy they wear like a mask. And that gaping, agonised mouth on the chest of my good-for-nothing son. And the boy from the train suddenly standing next to me, mouthing words I cannot hear, cannot lip read. *Why* can't *I hear you? What is your name?* I don't remember. Did he ever tell me? On the train maybe . . . or beneath the mottoed gate.

Arbeit Mecht Frei.

Screams.

Bodies.

Bodies.

Bones.

The boy –

"Take me home," I say, heart pounding inside my chest. I find my son and pull the sleeve of his T-shirt, half expecting the elongated mouth to turn and swallow my hand up to the wrist. "I have to get out of this place. *Now*."

On the car journey home everything is Aliya's fault, according to Nate.

"It was your idea to invite him along," he says.

I listen to them talk about me like I am not there in the car with them, like I am the ghost. My daughter-in-law starts to cry. She hardly makes a sound, and it occurs to me that with walls between us I probably would not hear her sob. Which makes me wonder about the silences in that big house we share . . . are they all filled with tears?

And what else? What else does he do to her?

I shut my eyes and imagine a car crash in which everyone dies. It is beautiful, both in its simplicity and its symmetry. The line ends as it was meant to end back in 1943, either on the train or as the outcome of one of the thousands of coin-toss moments inside Birkenau. But it didn't end, of course, and when I open my eyes my *farshtinkener* son still lives and breathes and drives safely under everyone's radar.

Someday, though . . . someday my crash will come.

Tuning them out, I glance sidelong at my grandson on the back seat next to the boy from the train. The boy stares at the side of my face like I have a dirty stain on my cheek. I rub at it, even though it isn't there, even though it will never come off. Meanwhile, my grandson is clutching something in his hand.

The Reichsfuhrer-SS . . .

Darth –

Himmler.

 – Vader.

"Lift the mask, son. You'll find him wearing round spectacles over a toothbrush moustache."

My grandson can only give me a vacant look.

Back at the house, I stand in the hallway and watch my son and his wife carry their fight upstairs and left, into their room. Joshua follows close behind, sliding Vader up the banister, although on the landing he turns right. He stops and flinches at the sound of a slap behind him, then quickly resumes walking toward his bedroom door with Vader – *Himmler* – flying alongside him like some angel of darkness.

I listen for another slap.

The boy from the train brushes past me to stand on the bottom-most step. He turns to face me, the weight of his stare chilling me marrow deep.

I hear no further blows.

But the silence is choking.

And the boy's stare . . . feels like sympathy, compassion. But by the time my brain is done with it, it seems to only feed my ravenous guilt, which I carry with me, down and down into the basement.

The sun betrayed us. By rising, it condemned us all. The SS carried out roll-call, at the end of which five hundred and fifty "pieces" were crammed inside ten wagons. What are we pieces of, I wondered as I listened to the doors being locked from outside.

The train did not move until evening, and then it moved slowly, with long stops on the way. Through a slit in the wall I watched our homeland disappear behind us.

The wagon was cold. Dark. Some light and air entered through a slit, but not enough; not nearly enough. We were pressed together, painfully so in most cases, and I could hear my parents' cries of discomfort from the far end. Pinned in a corner as I was, I had ho hope of reaching them.

The boy was roughly my size, perhaps a year or two older. I understood it wasn't his fault; fate had forced us together. In fact, fate had shown us a small mercy for the boy might have been heavier and crushed the life out of me before we ever arrived.

In a way, he saved my life.

Still, it was difficult to breathe. And terribly cold.

And loud.

Folk do not go quietly to their deaths, nor with dignity; blows were dealt indiscriminately in the dark.

Thirst became a real problem too.

When it snowed I collected what I could from the slit and drank the melt. I shared some with the boy. He said nothing but drank gratefully from the cup of my hand.

The journey took three days.

Three days to reach bottom.

The train stopped.

The boy and I exchanged our first word.
Farewell.

The boy is waiting for me by the foot of the bed. The shadows in the basement rally to hide him. I lie back on the covers. The springs squeal, reminding me of the brakes of the train. I don't even try to push the memories aside anymore. They're immovable as boulders anyway.

I see the officer strike the woman for taking too long to answer his question. I see the angry mark it leaves on her cheek: a Nazi flower. The woman does not allow herself to cry because she knows the officer will only plant more, entire beds of the plum-coloured blooms, all across her body.

I see the officer's jacket fall open to reveal a T-shirt underneath. A howling, bloodied face on a background of blue.

I see my grandson, lining up storm troopers outside a hijacked spaceship, Darth Himmler hovering over the captured prisoners, an angel black, capable of flight and things beyond belief.

Open my eyes.

The boy from the train is gone.

I rise cautiously from the bed, peering through the gloom. On the far side of the basement, I see a hole in the wall and light spearing through it. I cross the floor and raise my hand. A tiny sun appears on the centre of my palm. It is cold. The sun is cold.

I move my hand closer to the hole, pushing the cold light back until my hand is over the opening and the light stifled. I can hear feet shuffling behind me; many feet. Then bed springs squeal as someone's weight settles on them, squeal again as the first weight is joined by a second, then a third, a fourth, and so on until it sounds like punching brakes. I am too afraid to turn around, to discover how many others have joined me inside the wagon. And it *is* the wagon. The walls may move, the walls may vanish, but they've been here inside me for seventy years and they're not going anywhere.

The air is being used up, thinned out; it is getting harder

to breathe. A part of me knows that it must be all in my mind, because *real* ghosts do not use up air molecules but inhabit the spaces between them.

I pull my hand away from the wall. The hole and the spear of light are gone.

Panic rises in my throat.

I lift my hand, look at the place where the cold light kissed my palm, and see only darkness clinging to my skin. I turn from the wall and hurry across to the bed. The other passengers are no longer there, but I can feel the weight of their stares from all four walls.

I lift the pillow, snatch the gun from underneath.

On the other side of the bed, on the other side, the boy from the train waves his arms at me while shaking his head, just as he did when those Nazi sons-of-bitches sent his mother to huddle and weep with the old and the young, the broken and the unmade.

The boy mouths something but no sound can escape his lips. You need air in your lungs to deliver words. Otherwise, they simply slide back down your throat.

"And I don't have the imagination to give you any," I tell him. "Not kind ones. Not for me." My mind flashes to Joshua role-playing with his Star Wars figures. "Go see my grandson. They're all about that at his age. Making stuff up. I'm done talking. It's nothing but a waste of good air anyway."

I point the gun at the wall, pull the trigger.

Inside the tiny basement room it is a thunderous sound. But the hole I hoped to see materialise does not; it is little more than a pock-mark on the face of the wall. And that wall's many eyes, starved of oxygen, bloodshot from the tears of strain, continue to watch me from behind their shadow-veils. I fire another shot, another. But the brickwork is too tough and there is no light to be found.

No light to be found anywhere.

Then the door to the basement opens. Nate and Aliya appear in the doorway with the same look on their face.

At last, I think, *they've found some common ground.*

A look that communicates a simple message, loud, clear: *What have you done, Saul?*

I start to say the words, *It's what I* haven't *done*, but then I see the flower peeking at me across the shoulder of my son, the deep purple blossom on her smooth cheek. I see the necklace of Nazi flowers about her throat and realise – finally – that it has to end. The hurt. Everything.

Now.

TWO

The Germans ordered us to disembark. The platform was vast. Bright lamps struggled to hold back the night. A line of idling trucks awaited us a short walk away. As soon as our feet touched the soil, twelve men swooped upon us, an odious jury with hate in their bones and long shadows that darkened our startled faces.

They made us leave our bundles and luggage beside the train. I heard my mother call out to me in a whisper, but I was too afraid to reply.

An officer asked for her age and if she had any illnesses.

"Can I see my son?" she pleaded.

"Yes, yes, later," he replied curtly.

When she persisted, he planted a bruise on her face with the butt of his Luger. Then he pushed the barrel hard into the same cheek and asked the question again.

She answered, and he motioned toward a fast-growing group of women, children, and old men.

Someone spun me around. A blonde tower of a man held me by my collar and asked my age. His voice was polite. Was I to be murdered by courtesy? As I opened my mouth to reply, the boy from the train suddenly appeared behind the German, holding up two hands, four and three fingers respectively.

"Seven," I answered, quickly. "Su-su-seventeen."

In his courteous brain the officer flipped a coin. "Over there," he said.

Away from my mother.

Away from my father, too, whom I saw embracing her, until a sharp kick buckled his knee and put him writhing on the ground.

The boy from the train joined our group and stood beside me.

I realised that he had possibly saved my life for a second time.

"Tell me your name," I said, at once mortified that my voice seemed to echo the Germans'.

We stood and watched as the group containing my parents was led away at gunpoint.

The night swallowed them up and never gave them back.

"Saul," he whispered. "My name is Saul."

"On the trucks," a voice ordered us. "Schnell! Schnell!"

Six hours out of the hospital and my new foster parents mention the new bike they have waiting for me in the garage. It's not the smartest move ever, but I understand that Mr and Mrs Weissmann know about Grandpa Saul and what he did. Clearly, they want to be seen as good, kind people – good, kind *parents* – by giving me this two-wheeled symbol of freedom and hope.

"Once the rest of your bandages come off, Joshua, you can take it for a spin," Mr Weissmann says. "Wearing your helmet, of course."

He is not only good and kind, my new dad, but he seems pretty funny as well.

Somewhere, though, they're missing the point. I've died twice, so far – once in the ambulance and then on the surgeon's table as they attempted to prise the bullet from my brain – and while I don't know if the third time will really be the charm or not, I know I've been too long in a hospital bed with an itch I couldn't scratch to wait around for trifling things such as bandages or permission or anything else for that matter.

"Let me ride it now and I promise I won't go farther than two hundred feet from the driveway," I offer.

While Mr Weissmann relents, Mrs Weissmann stands up

from the table and walks out of the kitchen. At least there is no sobbing or, later on, bruises poorly disguised by facial product. She just seems worried, no more, no less. It's sweet and it's refreshing.

And it's one of those mid-sized mountain bikes. Silver and green. Somewhere between a BMX and an adult model. I like it because it doesn't know *what* the hell it is.

Mr Weissmann adjusts the seat height, checks the brakes four times, and ensures the helmet chinstrap is secure before he presses the button to raise the garage door.

Mrs Weismann reappears, bruise-free and dry-eyed. I feel bad that I expected anything else. She even smiles as Mr Weissmann puts an arm around her shoulders and they walk out onto the driveway to watch under a Spring sun as my tyres purr against the blacktop.

Two hundred feet come . . .

. . . and go.

I feel bad, wracked with guilt in fact, deceiving my new family like this. They are barely out of the wrapper and I am already breaking their rules. The world seems to grow a little bit darker for a moment until I glance up and see a lonely cloud stealing across the face of the sun.

"I need to know, Grandpa," I manage to say between gasping breaths. "Why – why you did it."

"Did what?" a voice startles me from behind. "Oh wait. Never mind."

I peer over my shoulder at a boy pedalling hard to keep up.

"Thomas Weissmann," he says. "Jim and Debora's kid. We missed each other back at the house. Mum said you took off on the bike, so she sent me after you. I'm supposed to bring you back in one piece."

"Tell your folks I'm sorry. Tell them . . . I had to go somewhere." To avoid any confusion, I add, "*Alone.*"

"It's cool, bro. But I got to tag along. Sorry. I promised I would."

"I'm not your bro."

"True," he says. "But for the purposes of this little trip of ours it looks like you are."

"All right, but swear on your life you won't tell them – anyone – where we're going."

"I swear. Now, care to fill me in?"

I consider trying to make a break for it but I am already snatching breaths and cramping in one leg.

"I'm going home," I tell him. "I need to know why I made it and no one else did. Why I survived . . ."

"How are you going to do that?" he asks.

For a moment I can only hear the sound of bike tyres ripping along the road. Then I realise that Thomas is waiting for an answer.

"I don't know," I tell him. "I guess I'm hoping something will come back to me."

When we reach the house I find a For Sale sign leaning on the un-cut yard. I push it facedown on the grass. I find a rock, pick it up. Break a window. Climb inside while my new brother loiters on the yard, kicking rocks, pretending not to look at the house of horrors.

Realisation dawns: this is precisely how all of my fellow students and teachers will react to me once I return to school – with hesitation and avoidance. I am condemned to carry this house on my back, forever. A snail, its shell on fire.

"Maybe you should call your folks," I say to him. "Tell them we're all right."

It took us ninety minutes to get here, the old house on the hill. Blood is spreading across the sunset sky, congealing toward night.

Thomas shakes his head. "I left my phone. Besides, they'll only ask me a bunch of dumb questions. Are you ready?"

"I think so."

I sigh along with the house's old timbers then climb the stairs to check my old room.

Somebody has hoovered the place, stripped off the bed sheets. Probably the clean-up crew. Only they've missed a spot on the wall next to my bed. There is a spatter of blood on my *Ironman 2* poster. Blood . . . red exoskeleton: easy to miss, I suppose. But the tears sting my eyes as I start to see what it all means.

Superheroes bleed.

Superheroes die.

"Everybody knows that," I say.

What they might not know is that they can also point a gun at your head and blow a piece out of your skull.

I drag a forearm across my leaking eyes.

Fuck you, Grandpa.

Thirty minutes later, I am sitting on the topmost stair of the hall staircase, looking down at Thomas standing on the bottom and looking up. In my hand, my favourite of all the Star Wars figures dad gave to me. Darth Vader. I found him under the edge of my bed. Now I turn him in my restless fingers, cold plastic refusing to warm.

"The house is empty," I declare.

"What did you expect?" Thomas's voice rises up the stairs.

"A clue, maybe. Something."

"A clue, to what?"

"I dunno. Why Grandpa Saul killed us."

"But you're not dead. You made it."

"It doesn't feel like it. It feels like a big piece of me's gone and there's a hole in its place."

"You're only what – twelve?" Thomas says. "You can come back from this. It wasn't your fault he got all twisted up."

"Maybe," I say, squeezing Vader in my hand. "Or maybe I should have known something was wrong. He freaked out when we took him to the Halloween fair. One of his flashbacks or something. He seemed much better on the ride home. But then dad was yelling at mom about all kinds of stuff, so I probably wasn't paying much attention. He saw ghosts, you know. Grandpa did."

Thomas's eyebrows climb his forehead halfway. "Ghosts? Really?"

"*One* ghost, apparently. The same one, every day. He told me about him. A boy he met on a train during the war. Y'know, the one where they put all the Jews in the gas chamber. I'm not sure I believe it."

"Which part?" Thomas asks.

"Either. I mean, how can ghosts exist? And how can anyone kill sixty million people? Without a nuclear bomb, that is. It's impossible."

"I think it was six million," Thomas says. "And all the history books say it happened. As for ghosts, well, I can't explain that, but there are books about them too."

"Maybe," I say, standing up, brushing dust from my knees. "I think Grandpa Saul saw what he wanted to see. But here I am, and I can't see anything." I glance at Vader in my hand. "Who knows, maybe it's all some kind of Jedi mind trick or something."

We laugh; but behind the laughter I can feel a sadness creeping up on me. A wave rising. Ready to fall. Break.

I want to run from it, hide, but at the same time I want to stay and search for answers. My scalp itches underneath the bandage.

I close my eyes. Breathe. Let my mind replay what I remember.

I see the front door crash open. My father and mother walk inside the house. They are arguing. Dad is winning, if volume and profanity are a means to measure such. Dad has on the Pink Floyd T-shirt he only wears because he knows Grandpa hates it. He doesn't even like their music. But he likes to poke the bear (although if Grandpa *is* a bear he's an old and sick one) because Grandpa drove Grandma away many years ago, when dad was still a boy, by playing genie and hiding in a bottle, not wanting to come out. And Mom is wearing the same long dress she wore to the fair . . .

I open my eyes. See my parents walk through Thomas. Not ghosts but living memories from that day. They walk upstairs toward me, Dad's voice growing louder with each step. I stand aside and let them pass – stupid, I know. They walk through their bedroom door, but I can hear it slam and feel the shudder run through the timber frame into the floor, into the balls of my feet.

Whoa.

"What is it?" Thomas asks from the hall downstairs. "What's wrong?"

I turn to answer, but the front door closes and standing there on the rug is Grandpa, before he took a gun and put it to work.

I'm standing behind my bedroom door, ear pressed to the whispering timber. Dad wants Grandpa out of the house and into a facility. Mom says, *Your father, Nate? Your own father?* Dad throws some curse words at her, and maybe a couple of punches to the stomach, too. Except it isn't Mom he's hitting, not in his mind; it's Grandma, for leaving him all on his own with Grandpa Saul.

I turn to Thomas sitting quietly on the bed.

"Hide underneath. It might not be safe in here."

"Why?" he asks.

I don't want to believe a bad thing can happen twice but what I'm hearing is telling me different.

"I think it's happening again," I tell him.

"You're remembering things," he says. "Replaying them in your mind. You mustn't do that. You need to move on. Come on, we should get out of here."

My head seems to shake itself. "I don't think I *can* move on."

"You have to."

I turn on him then. "You don't get it. I've lost everything."

"I know."

"I should have died – with my family."

"But you didn't."

"They might have answers. Some answers, at least. This could be my one and only chance –"

"They don't, Joshua."

"You don't know. You don't know anything."

"They're not real. I know you want them to be, but they're not. This is all you, brother. All. You."

"I don't think so. They're showing me what happened . . .

things I didn't – *don't* – know."

"Who is?" Thomas asks, spreading his arms wide. "I don't see anyone. Why *is* that?"

"They're not your ghosts," I tell him in a calm voice. "They're mine."

It is a poor choice of words and I don't have time to correct myself. On the other side of their bedroom door, my mother's cheekbone meets my father's knuckles – hard. Then I hear her gasping for air. He is choking her. I remember running across to my bed, thrusting my head under the pillow. Vader dropping to the floor. Pressing the pillow to my ears to block out that terrible, gasping sound. Now, I listen as he throttles her to within seconds of her life.

Then from the guts of the house: a gunshot.

Suddenly their door opens and the landing groans under their weight. Mom is crying. Dad tells her to quit.

Quit.

Like it is *her* bad habit.

I listen to their footsteps descend the staircase, punctuated by tears, whispered threats, confused questions, and finally, towering silence.

"Come on," I say to Thomas. "The basement . . . That's where they die."

Then I am racing downstairs, careful to avoid the ghosts of my parents, soon to be made ghosts again when the bullets shred them like tissue. I wonder how many times this can happen; if I come back tomorrow will the whole thing reset like some computer game I have the inability to save?

I'll find out tomorrow, I think. *And tomorrow and tomorrow and –*

"– Stop beating yourself up," Thomas yells after me, leaning over the balustrade. "There's nothing you can do about it now. It *happened*. You're only punishing yourself, and for what? Nothing!"

I am no longer listening.

The basement is dark as a cave or a hole or a longing. I can feel the presence of Grandpa Saul and, oddly, others; many others. It is as if the darkness is packed with people – not quite people and not quite touching, but packed nevertheless. A draught like someone's breath prickles the back of my neck, spinning me like a top, and I see first one face then a whole crowd of faces, men, women, young, old, leaning in, leaning out of the gloom.

"I don't want to see this. Grandpa, take it back. Someone . . . please."

The room is moving.

Unseen wheels spin along an unseen track.

The air, too: shifting. Sucked into gasping mouths.

In this breathing, shifting dark, I squeeze Darth Vader in my hand, finding comfort and strength in his familiar shape.

I know Grandpa wasn't fond of the toy, but sometimes he saw things that weren't really there. Like ghosts. Or the bad in everything.

The bedsprings squeal and the room comes to a shivering halt. My eyes follow Grandpa through the gloom as he shuffles over to the bed to retrieve something from beneath his pillow. Moments later, the deafening sound of a gunshot ricochets off the walls and fills the entire basement. I duck instinctively, anticipating the bullet that shattered part of my skull. Underneath my bandage, bone starts to itch.

I rise to my feet again, ready to flee the basement. But the door opens and into the light spilling down the stairs enter the ghosts of my father and mother. Before I can reconcile Then with Now and warn them of what is about to happen, two further shots are fired.

The first enters the screaming mouth on my father's T-shirt, puncturing his chest and one of his lungs.

The second carries the short delay of indecision, but finds my mother's neck regardless, severing the carotid artery. A doctor provided this detail to me the day after I regained consciousness. Now, I watch the wound spray crimson as the strength rapidly leaves her legs. She falls, beating most of her own blood to the floor.

Seconds later, my father collapses on top of her.

I turn slowly to my grandfather, who looks at the gun with an expression of shock and horror and disbelief; similar to mine, I expect. A moment passes. During it, he and the gun appear to confer psychically on what they should do next. Finally, he mutters, *It should have ended with me.* Repeating it to himself, he steps over the two bodies slumped in the doorway and staggers upstairs.

It should have ended with me . . . It should have ended . . .

Thomas steps into the doorway, seemingly oblivious to whom he just passed on the stairs to get here and the ghostly bodies piled at his feet. He spreads his arms wide in appeal. *What are you doing?*

I hurry to him, mindful to not look down.

"Come on," I tell him. "Grandpa's heading upstairs to kill me."

Posters cover the walls of my old room. Marvel heroes, The Lord of the Rings, Star Wars. Tableaus of Good versus Evil. Standing in the middle of this is an old man, stooped as if by some invisible weight on his shoulders, holding in his loose grip a smoking gun.

I can't tell which side he belongs to anymore.

But I realise something: *I* am responsible for this not him, because this would not be happening if the shot he is about to fire had done its job. If I had not survived.

My bed lies empty. It is empty because I am here, alive, standing in the doorway, with Thomas behind me and peering in. The ghost – or memory – of the bullet, of the weeks I spent in hospital and the darkness that found me there in a brightly-lit ward is enough to make me hesitate before moving any farther into the room.

When I am alongside him, Grandpa Saul suddenly looks away from the bed to where I am standing. For a moment I feel his eyes connect with mine. A chill shudders through me.

The bullet . . . the bullet comes next.

He lowers his eyes to look at what I am holding in my hand. The Darth Vader figure. I watch as Grandpa's pupils swell to twice their usual size. In response? I have no time to decide, because the hand holding the gun rises suddenly through the air – through my hand holding Vader – and brings the weapon around to point at the bed, empty now but not empty then.

He weeps as he mumbles the words, *Forgive me, Joshua, but . . . the line –*

He fires the gun.

Pain flares inside my skull. My fingers spasm and drop Vader to the floor. He bounces and comes to rest under the bed. I can smell the burnt powder in the air.

Weeping uncontrollably, Grandpa Saul staggers from the bedroom onto the landing outside.

There is another gunshot, and his body tumbles loudly down the stairs.

The echoes fade and silence falls over the house.

It is a heavy silence.

Full of tears.

I survived four days in Birkenau. Longer than most.

I never spoke again to that boy from the train, Saul, who had by my reckoning saved my life on two separate occasions, but I saw him, glimpses of him anyway, crossing the camp on the way to his new job.

He was chosen to join the Special Works Unit, or Sonderkom-mandos; *perhaps because of his size.*

I was forced to dig trenches. Back-breaking labour. Many men with weakened hearts simply gave up, falling right where they stood. Some were taken away; some – if the trench was being dug with the intention of refilling it the next day (before digging it again) – were left in the hard, winter soil to draw flies while the rest of us dug around their bodies.

Some prisoners were made lieutenants or kapos. They super-vised fellow prisoners in exchange for small privileges from the Germans. I will call this one dirt. No capital 'd'.

Late afternoon, dirt stood on the lip of the trench and regarded me from a height for several long, uncomfortable minutes.

Finally, he said, "You there. Yes, you. What is your age?"

Being a Jew and a prisoner like me, I did not think it necessary to lie to him.

"Fourteen," I answered.

He walked away. I thought that was the end of it.

Seconds later, dirt returned with a German officer, trailing him like a dog. The officer grabbed me roughly around the bicep and dragged me out of the trench.

"Come with me, Mister Su-su-seventeen."

I was frogmarched away, to a group of prisoners corralled outside a nearby barracks. I was sent sprawling amongst them. The guards laughed.

I turned onto my back to watch the officer walk away, and finally recognised him as the one from the platform who had asked my age. He said a few words to dirt, motioned for something to be brought over, then handed him a hunk of bread. I realised two things: the first was that I'd been made part of some trade-off; the second was that I was going to die. Today. Now. I did not even know the date.

They pulled me onto my feet, cuffed me around the head for sport, then led all of us to our end.

Sore and stumbling, I glanced back for one last scathing look at the mongrel who had betrayed me. I saw him, pushing another prisoner toward my shovel, which stood, still upright in the earth.

I never again spoke to the boy, Saul, or got the chance to tell him my name, but I saw him, once, crossing the wastes of the camp like some beaten angel, and then again, often, after the end.

As we lay – and stood, some of us, propped against the cold stone walls – inside the gas chambers, the Germans sent in the Sonderkommandos to remove and dispose of our bodies.

Saul came to me and carried mine out into the open air. The sky looked beautiful and frightening, as things that are out of reach so often are.

Saul looked at me, tears filling his eyes.

I wanted to thank him but I had neither the air nor the working lungs with which to begin the process. So, I made a silent vow instead, to my saviour and friend, to never leave his side until I was able, somehow, to say those words.

Breakfast with the Weissmann's is different.

Different bad and different good.

Bad because mom and dad and grandpa aren't here. Good because things don't seem so awkward anymore. Not since I went back to the old house yesterday.

I feel like a book has been closed. Closed on a story that wasn't really mine in the first place. It was Grandpa Saul's story, and I know now that he didn't want to do what he did. But it wasn't exactly an accident either.

More important, I think, *it was something inside him and not me that caused it. Something that got twisted.*

"It's okay that I'm okay," I say to the table. "Isn't it?"

I notice that Mr Weissmann has some cereal milk on his chin. I wonder if he's mad about something; maybe about me going back to the old place. He didn't seem angry last night when I got back, but then you never know with parents – especially foster ones, who aren't even the real kind.

He reaches across the table and pats my hand.

"Yes," he says. "Yes. It's okay."

I blink. Sip my orange juice. Which, it turns out, is possibly the best that I have ever tasted. I make a mental note to ask Mr Weissmann – Alan – later what kind of oranges go into making it. I want to know. I want to know because he said it's okay to be okay.

"What do you want to do today?" he asks after we're finished eating our breakfast. "It's the weekend and you've been cooped up inside that hospital for so long I figure we need to do something fun. What do you say?"

From the other side of the table, Thomas nods his head rapidly in agreement.

Maybe the book isn't quite closed yet. "Can we go to the

funfair, maybe?" I ask, nervously.

Mr Weissmann – Alan – claps his hands together.

"There's no maybe to it, Joshua. We're going!"

"And Thomas is coming too, right?"

"Thomas?" he says. "Sure. If Thomas wants to come, he can come."

A clear day. The sun is out. The spring weather isn't all that hot but it's comfortable if not welcoming. The year seems slow to get out of bed, stretch, put on its clothes before summer arrives. In the car, my stomach does flips long before I step on any of the rides. I feel as if I am standing on top of a tall tower with a beautiful view spread out all in front of me, but when I look down I see a thin glass floor under my feet. And there's a crack in the glass. Close one eye, look at it a certain way, certain angle, yes, I think I see it.

DREAMLAND. Where Dreams Are Free.

Words above the funfair gate. I can't help but think there ought to be a question mark at the end. In fact, my life feels like a giant question mark at the moment. A crack in the shape of a question mark.

After a few minutes inside I am struck by how quiet the place is; how bare it all seems. Everywhere, row upon row of light bulbs that are not only unlit but seem empty, incapable *of* light. Everywhere, litter blown in gusts across the ground so that it seems to creep when you are not looking. Everywhere, rides going through the motions with mostly empty seats.

It occurs to me that this is the kind of day that Grandpa would have appreciated here. He'd wanted to keep his distance from everything and everyone. He would have been able to see the fair without actually seeing it come alive. Even the calliope music sounds more subdued than usual, as though pacing itself for long, empty days and nights ahead. Which causes me to wonder, *Will the summer ever return to this place?*

Thomas gives me no time to answer as he appears at my side, takes my hand, and drags me at a run over to the rollercoaster.

Over to the helter skelter.

To the hurricane.

And it begins to dawn on me that even with no crowds, even with the lights out and the bulbs empty, this can still be a fun place to be. It's about what you give to the funfair not the other way around.

A couple of hours later, we find ourselves with no rides left but the last: the ghost train.

Excited, I climb into the front wagon and wave for Thomas to join me.

He shakes his head.

I wave again, harder. *Come on.*

Another shake of his head. *I can't.*

"What's wrong?" I ask. "We're going home after this. Get on."

His eyes fix themselves on mine, shining with blue fire. "You're going to make it," he says. "You're younger than he was and not quite broken. You still have the ability to dream. You gave me my voice back!"

"What are you talking about?" I ask, but his words feel like a cold hand caressing the back of my neck. As soothing as they sound, I want to scream.

"You're not broken, Joshua."

The motor sputters into life.

"Wait," I tell him. "Wait! You're going to be here, right? When the ride ends and I come out the other side, you're . . ."

The wagon begins to move, a slow, jerking motion along the track.

The mouth of the tunnel, black curtain obscuring what lies beyond, looms closer and closer.

Thomas keeps pace with the train until the curtain blocks him from my sight. Even so, his voice manages to find me edging through the dark on my own.

Thank you, it says.

GARY McMAHON

ONLY BLEEDING

There was fire in the sky.

I looked out of the window, across the fields at the back of my house, and saw the red glow hanging above the distant warehouses. I hoped it wasn't a sign of another riot, or criminal damage. I was sick of hearing about people destroying the areas where they lived. This wasn't protest, it was self-harm.

Turning away from the window, I glanced at the bed, and at Sarah lying there under the thin duvet. Her blonde hair was a tangled mess. She was sweating. Her small, pale hands were resting on top of the cover.

I walked across to the bed, knelt down at her side, and kissed her on the damp forehead. She moaned in her sleep and I backed away, shuffling on my knees, not wanting to wake her. Standing, I left the room. When I closed the door, I paused there, out on the landing, wishing that she would be well again.

Downstairs, I felt restless. Television could not hold my attention, I was cautious of using alcohol as a crutch, and the house seemed simultaneously too small and too large. I put on my overcoat and went outside. The street was dark. The streetlight closest to out house was broken – it had stopped working weeks ago and still the council had not sent anyone to carry out the repairs.

I started to walk in the opposite direction to the fire I'd seen reflected against the sky. No destination in mind: I simply wanted to keep moving until my restless energy was all used up. I passed the derelict pub with its steel-shuttered doors and windows, the three repossessed houses at the end of the street, and turned the corner.

To my left there was a line of trees, their thin branches scratching against the sky. They seemed restless in the chilly night, as if trying to uproot and join me on my walk. The darkness above them was big and dark and almost starless. On my right there was a row of shops, each one closed for the night. One or two of them had gone out of business and were protected by steel anti-vandal devices that resembled oversized shark cages.

Up ahead of me I could make out someone sitting in the road. This seemed unusual, even in the rough neighbourhood where I lived, so I slowed my pace and became wary. I thought it must be a vagrant, or perhaps a drunk who had stopped for a rest.

A pizza delivery moped approached from behind the figure, and when it got close the driver simply steered around the person in the road, not even sparing a glance as his vehicle wobbled slightly. The moped gained speed and was gone within seconds; I could hear its monotone engine receding into the night.

Jesus, I thought. *Is this what we've become? Are we so uncaring that we'd leave someone sitting in the road like that?*

As I neared the figure, I realised it was a child – a small boy. He was sitting in the middle of the road, staring down at the ground. Unlike the moped driver, I could not just steer around him. I had to try and help.

About twenty yards from the boy, I stopped walking. He was wearing a baseball cap that was too big for his head and a waterproof sports jacket. But underneath the modern outer layer he had on some kind of costume, perhaps Victorian in style. Something that looked like the kind of thing a Dickensian street urchin might wear. The long brown coat was too tight for even his emaciated frame and its hem hung down below his waterproof jacket. His chunky little boots with their thick soles looked like a primitive type of corrective footwear.

"Are you okay?"

He didn't answer; didn't move.

"Hello . . . Are you hurt?"

Still there was nothing.

"Listen, I don't mean you any harm. I'm friendly – yeah?"

Suddenly he looked up. His face was small and pale but he looked angry.

"Hi." I held out my hands in a placatory gesture. "Look . . . I won't hurt you. I just want to know if you're okay."

He nodded.

"You sure?"

He nodded again.

"Can I help you? I mean, do you need me to call someone?" I started to reach into my pocket for my mobile phone.

"Stop," he whispered. I could barely hear him. But for some reason I did what he said without even thinking about it. "Are you hungry?"

Puzzled, I took a step forward. "I don't . . . .sorry? What did you say?" I looked around. There was nobody else in the vicinity. It crossed my mind that this might be some weird, convoluted prelude to a mugging.

"Are you hungry?" He smiled, and the anger faded from his features.

"I haven't thought about it . . . probably, yes." I'd decided to humour him. He might not be right in the head. Perhaps he'd gone AWOL from a local hospital.

"Here." He stood in one smooth motion, as if pulled upright by strings. Raising his arms at either side of his body, he opened his hands. A straight razor dropped onto the road. Even in the darkness, I could see that he was bleeding. "Everybody's hungry. You're all so fucking hungry, all the time."

"Shit . . ." I ran to him, grabbed him without thinking. "What happened?"

"Hush," he said, softly, and his voice was nothing like that of a child. "Feed." In a movement that was too quick for me to stop, he pressed one of his bloody wrists against my face, my cheek, my open lips. I tried to pull away, but his other hand was gripping my neck and he was strong, so very strong. I went down onto my knees, forced there by his sheer strength, and the syrupy blood crawled down my throat.

It tasted good. The blood. To my absolute horror, it tasted wonderful. Like warm honey, or an ice-cold drink on a hot day; like fish and chips eaten straight out of the newspaper wrapping, or a tall glass of beer.

When I opened my eyes the boy was gone. My lips were warm with blood. I wiped them and got to my feet, stumbled back along the street to my house and locked the door behind me.

Sarah was in a bad way that night and all the next day. I was unable to leave the house. She slept most of the time, but whenever she woke up she coughed up a horrible slimy substance into the bucket I kept beside the bed and suffered painful bouts of diarrhoea. I had to keep changing the sheets. She was ashamed, but I tried my best to reassure her. To love her.

"Just leave me, Mike," she said, more than once. "Walk away and leave me. Or dump me at the hospital gates. They'll have to take me in."

Fighting back the tears, I held her against me, appalled by her frailness and the way her bones felt like sticks wrapped in old damp sheets. She was dying and there was nothing I could do. There was nothing anyone could do. We'd brought her back home to fade out. None of the treatments had worked. She was slipping away.

That night, as I sat downstairs in the dark drinking whisky and wishing that I could do something to take away her pain, I found myself thinking about the boy I'd found in the road the night before. I'd been too busy that day to give him any serious thought, but now I had no choice. I remembered how cold his hands had been, and how easily he'd overpowered me; the long Victorian coat under his jacket; his strange commanding voice.

Was he a ghost? I didn't even know what that meant; didn't believe in the supernatural. But the boy had been something other than entirely human. I knew that. I could not deny the evidence of my senses.

I finished my drink and left the house, retracing my route from the previous night. The boy was not there. The road was empty. As I turned away, feeling oddly bereft, I caught sight of something at the edge of the trees. He was standing there, hands in the pockets of his dirty brown trousers, and watching me.

"Are you still hungry?"

I nodded.

"Then come," he said, turning away and strolling into the trees. "Come and take some more."

I followed him between the trees and to a small hollow down by the narrow river. He sat down on the ground, took out the straight razor, and slashed the blade across the palms of his hands. This time the moon and the streetlights made it easy to see; his blood was not red but black. It ran slowly and thickly, like crude oil.

"Feed," he said, and his eyes were black, too. His mouth was a toothless hole in that tiny white face beneath the too-large baseball cap. For a moment, I thought he looked half-finished, like a badly-constructed doll.

I sat down opposite him and bent to his open palm, lapping at the blood like a cat or a dog. It tasted good, but not quite as wonderful as before. This time the effect was not as intense. Like a drug, it was always better the first time and you could spent a life-time chasing down but never repeating that first experience.

Afterwards, I sat with my eyes shut. He sang to me; a soft, slow lament, something like a sailor's shanty but in a language I did not recognise. Yet I knew exactly what he was singing about: loss, forced austerity; the slow decay of a society that had once been rich and dissolute but was now poverty-stricken and falling apart at the edges. Somehow the act of drinking from him made it hurt less. With his dark blood in my mouth, I could break free.

We could be free.

"Can you help me?"

He kept singing.

"Please . . . help me. I don't want her to die."

The singing stopped. "I can always help you, but at a price. Nothing lasts forever. All I can offer you is a little more time."

I grabbed his ice-cold hand. "That's enough. It has to be."

He nodded. We stood and walked back to my house. At the door, he paused and waited for me to do or say something.

"What's wrong?"

He laughed; a small, dry sound at the back of his throat. "Don't you know?"

"I'm sorry . . ."

"You have to invite me in."

"Please," I said. "Come inside."

We went upstairs, moving slowly, with a sense of ritual that only became apparent to me after the fact. At the bedroom door, I turned to him and he smiled. His face looked like a tiny skull in the gloom of the landing.

Sarah was sleeping so deeply that she was barely even breathing. The room stank of shit and vomit. The bucket at the bedside was half full and some of the contents had slopped over the side and onto the carpet.

"Sorry about the mess," I said.

The boy took my hand. A chill passed through me. I could feel his emptiness like a cold breeze.

"Where are you from? Who are you?" My voice was raw.

He turned to me, his face a blank, an open-ended statement. "I'm from all over. I don't have a name, or if I do it's long forgotten."

He went to the bed and climbed up onto the mattress, straddling Sarah. He removed his sports jacket and rolled up the sleeves of his curious little frock coat. Then he took out the straight razor and cut into the thin, white meat of his forearms. Thick black blood bubbled to the surface, hung in rubbery strings, and then dripped onto Sarah's face. In her sleep, she began to lick the blood from her lips. After several minutes of this, the boy seemed to lose strength and climbed down off the bed.

"It's done," he said, and then he went over to the corner, sat down, and lowered his head between his knees.

I went to Sarah. She was still sleeping, but her breathing was easier. Some of the colour had returned to her face. Whatever the boy had done, it had worked. She looked better – healthier – than she had done in God knew how long. But I wanted more; I needed her to gain more strength.

I went over to the boy but he was sleeping, too. I shook him but he didn't wake up. Without thinking about what I was doing, I dragged him across the floor to the bed. He seemed weaker now, as if the bloodletting had drained some of his strength. I went through his pockets and emptied them. A battered pocket watch, a small, dusty diary with nothing written inside, an ivory-handled straight razor.

To my eternal shame, I opened the razor and started to cut. I cut into his arms, his face, his throat, and pushed him onto Sarah. She reached out and embraced him, clutching his body tightly against her. The boy began to twitch, then to convulse. He bucked against her, but Sarah held on, drinking him dry.

I turned away, unable to look at what I had done. The sounds were enough. Those horrible sounds of her feeding.

When she was finished, I carried what was left of the boy downstairs and set him tenderly, almost reverentially down on the sofa. He was nothing but an empty skin. No bones, no internal organs; just a sack of flesh, emptied.

Nothing lasts forever, the boy had said. But maybe forever is too much; perhaps all we ever need is a tiny bit longer, a fraction more time to try and set things straight But the problem is, we want that little bit more time and time again, until it becomes to seem like a form of forever.

Sarah's newfound strength lasted two weeks, and then she once again began to dim. The colour left her cheeks, her skin turned sallow, and her eyes took on a dullness that scared me so much I could not look directly into them.

There was not much to say, but we talked long into the night. I wanted her to feel close to me.

"We took too much in one go," I said, holding her hand as I lay down beside her on the bed. My nose was filled with the hot stench of her sickness but my stomach no longer turned at the smell. "We should have rationed it, made it last longer."

"I know. But don't we always? It's our greatest weakness as a species. We always take too much; destroy the very things that can sustain us." She squeezed my hand, but weakly. "Why should this be any different?"

I began to weep.

"Don't cry for me," she said. "Not any more."

Wiping my eyes on the pillow, I turned and grabbed the straight razor from the bedside table. The blade shone, catching stray light through the window from a passing car.

"What are you doing?"

"It's worth a try," I said, and pressed the sharp edge of the blade against my wrist.

Through the window, I saw the dull red haze of fire in the sky. I had no idea if it were real or simply the beginning of some kind of vision. Over in the corner of the room, something stirred. A dark patch, a shadow: the sad, cold ghost of a ghost who had once bled for us.

R.B. RUSSELL

NIGHT PORTER

Marianne had no choice but to take the position of night porter at the St. Denis Hotel; it was either that or have her job-seeker's allowance cut because she had already turned down too many other offers of work. She tried to tell herself that if she didn't think too much about the unsociable hours it really wasn't such a bad situation. Her shifts were from ten in the evening to seven in the morning, six days a week, and she reasoned that for several hours each day, especially those towards the end of her shift, she would be left alone to read; nobody would be looking over her shoulder.

Reading was what Marianne liked to do. Most of the jobs she had been offered would have reduced the time she could spend with her nose in a book (as her mother always said). Working as a night porter was a compromise she was willing to attempt, even if the manager, Mr. Lane, had been very uncertain about hiring a woman for the job. His fears appeared to be justified during her very first shift; at three in the morning a group of eight men, all drunk, tried to return to two rooms that had been booked for four people, and they became abusive when Marianne refused to let them all stay. She had been told by Mr. Lane, to use her initiative, but she had also been warned not to do anything to put herself, or other guests, in danger. Marianne told the drunks that she would telephone for permission to let them in, but, instead, she called the police. As the local station was just around the corner in Dern Street, the incident was cleared up surprisingly quickly. Quite where the men were taken away to didn't concern her; everything was in order once more.

On her second night Marianne booked an elderly couple into a double room just after midnight, only to have the woman appear an hour later to report that her husband had died. It was a heart attack, apparently, and entirely natural, but it still shook Marianne.

And on her third night working at the St. Denis, a guest set light to their bedding at two in the morning. More damage was caused by the Fire Brigade than by the fire itself, and evacuating the other guests caused chaos. Marianne stayed on after her shift to help to clean up, and for the following week there seemed to be no end to the work required to set everything straight again. She had to admit to herself that she had certain obsessive-compulsive tendencies; she hated disorganization and mess.

Marianne couldn't help wondering what might happen next, having called out the emergency services three times in her first three nights, but after those incidents everything seemed to go quiet. For the following few weeks the guests were all well-behaved and there were no dramas. A number of odd characters passed through the hotel, but after a while she failed to notice or even remember the more eccentric guests; they became simply names that she would enter into the register, faces she would never see again. The job was a compromise, but one that she could live with because every night she managed to find several uninterrupted hours to read. The only time she had to put her book down was when, once an hour, she was expected to walk up and down the corridors, on the three floors, just to make sure that everything was in order. She dutifully padded around the small hotel seeing nothing untoward, and hearing, at worst, the muted sounds of sexual activity, loud snoring, or the television playing quietly in the room of an insomniac. She would return to the book she had left at the front desk, and would continue to read, undisturbed, for another fifty-five minutes, until she would have to walk around the corridors once again.

And then, two months into her job, at about half past one in the morning, while she was reading a Ruth Rendell novel, a large and expensive silver Mercedes pulled into the small car park in front of the hotel. A woman got out of the front of the vehicle and helped a young man from one of the back doors. She almost carried him across the car park and into the reception.

"A room for the night," said the woman, who was rather too well-presented in her sharply-pressed grey trouser suit, and too perfectly groomed for that time of the morning. Marianne had noticed that all of their usual guests would look rather uncared-for by the early hours.

"Just the one bed," the woman added. "My friend is rather tired and a little emotional. He won't be able to go home until the morning."

"Don't you think he ought to go to a hospital?" asked Marianne. There was nothing obviously wrong with him, but he appeared to be confused. He was not necessarily drunk, but it struck Marianne that he might be on drugs. He also looked a great deal younger than his companion, which seemed odd. His "supporter" had to be in her fifties, if not older.

"No, he's fine," said the woman. "Nothing that a decent night's sleep won't cure. How much is a room?"

"£60, with breakfast."

"I really do just want to go to bed," said the young man suddenly. "I feel a little wobbly on my feet."

"Look, here's a nice round £100 in cash," said the woman. "I'll happily pay the extra because there's a chance he might sleep in tomorrow and I don't want any fuss if he does. He'll miss breakfast, I'm sure, but he's bound to wake up and clear out before anyone needs to clean the room."

Marianne wanted to say no, sensing trouble, but didn't feel confident enough to turn them away.

"Is there a problem?" asked the woman.

"No, that will be fine," replied Marianne, deciding that the risk was worth taking. However, she insisted on seeing identification for the guest, and from the woman who was paying.

Marianne told Miss Fisher that she could take Mr. Charles up to 34. It was the room that Mr. Lane said should be used by guests who looked likely to make any kind of disturbance. It was the only bedroom in the hotel without any immediate neighbours, and was one of the few that had not been recently refurbished. The young man was helped up the stairs by his unlikely companion, and Marianne resolved that she would give them only a couple of minutes before going to check that nothing untoward was taking place. In her mind she uncomfortably played out scenarios involving Rohypnol and rape, but just as she was about to go up, Miss Fisher came back downstairs. Marianne was assured that Mr. Charles was fine, and the woman left.

Marianne returned to her Ruth Rendell novel, but found it hard to concentrate. She wondered whether she hadn't read too much modern detective fiction. Miss Fisher and her friend had worried Marianne, but she couldn't really explain why. She remembered that the extra £40 in the till needed to be either accounted for or taken as a tip, and in the end she decided to have it for herself. She had earned it in those two minutes when she had worried what might be happening in room 34.

The incident of the "tired and emotional" guest and her "friend" vaguely troubled Marianne all day. When she arrived at work the following evening, she asked the manager:

"Was everything alright after last night?"

"Fine. Any reason it shouldn't be?"

"A young man was brought in by a friend and he seemed the worse for wear . . . I nearly said 'no', but in the end I put him in room 34."

"I've not heard of any problems."

And so began an ordinary, uneventful evening. Marianne was steadily busy until one o'clock but there had been nothing demanding to attend to; in between guests coming and going she had tidied up the reception area and the office. Once it was quiet she returned to her Ruth Rendell paperback and the rest of her shift slipped by without her really noticing it.

Marianne had the following night off work. She kept to her usual routine, going to bed at seven in the morning, and getting up again at two in the afternoon. Over the past few months she had become increasingly frustrated by living with her mother, and had considered moving out. She was finally earning some money and could probably pay rent for a room somewhere, or even a small flat. However, now that her hours didn't coincide so frequently with her mother's, she was more content with the present arrangement.

She read during the afternoon, and went out just before her mother returned from work. Marianne had an hour to browse in a local bookshop before it closed, and finding a Henning Mankell paperback she hadn't read before, she decided to treat herself to dinner in a local pub. A regular wage was still a novelty, and it felt wrong to pay for a meal when her mother would have been happy to cook for her. However, it felt good to be out, and she started to read her book as she waited for her food, and then as she ate.

Marianne was interrupted just as she was finishing her meal; some old school friends had arrived to celebrate a birthday, and she stayed drinking with them until after closing time. Before she had taken her job as night porter she would have declined the invitation to go on to a club, but she was still wide awake, and they spent the rest of the evening in The Milky Way on Mill Street. Marianne would have liked to have found somebody to take home, and once again regretted not having a place of her own. However, relationships were going to be even harder to find now that she kept the hours she did.

At work the next night it was very quiet, with very few guests booked into the hotel, and all of them back quietly in their rooms by eleven, which was how Marianne liked it. She tidied up the reception area and wiped down the tables and the insides of the windows. It had turned cold and there were occasional snow-flurries outside, which seemed to keep people off the streets. When everything was tidy, Marianne sat at the counter and continued reading her Henning Mankell paperback.

She had walked the corridors twice that evening, and was back at the reception desk with her book when she happened to look up, and stare out of the glazed front door. She was wondering whether the settled snow really amounted to even a centimetre, when the Mercedes drove into the car park. She recognized it as the expensive silver model that had brought Mr. Charles as an overnight guest only the week before. Once again, the older woman got out of the driving seat and helped somebody else out of the car. As had happened the previous week, she had to support this second person as they made their way to the front door.

"Miss Fisher," said Marianne in her most neutral, professional voice.

"Good evening. You were on the desk last week, weren't you?"

"Yes, when you paid for a room for Mr. Charles."

"That's right, and I can't believe that I'm in a similar situation tonight . . . My friend's name is Fitzpatrick. He's had a very, very long day. I made the same mistake as with Mr. Charles of taking him out to a restaurant rather than bringing him straight here . . . He really will be no trouble."

"I would rather not book him in, not in this state."

"But you let my other friend stay."

"I did, but I shouldn't have done."

"Was he any trouble?"

"No."

"Well, then. Mr. Fitzpatrick is just the same; tired and a little drunk."

Marianne could not make up her mind what to do. During her

job interview Mr. Lane had put various awkward scenarios before Marianne and he had obviously been pleased by her common-sense replies. This wasn't as clear-cut a situation as any she had been asked about, though, and she hesitated.

Miss Fisher had to prompt her again for a decision.

"Room 34 is available," Marianne agreed reluctantly. "That will be £60. I will need to see identification, as before."

"Of course."

Miss Fisher smiled, but Marianne did not feel able to trust the woman. She recognized her own prejudice against this self-confident older woman, with her heavy make-up and expensive clothes. And she hated herself for agreeing to do as the woman asked. While Miss Fisher took Mr. Fitzpatrick up to his room, Marianne went to put the cash in the till and found that she had, again, been paid £100 in notes. This time she put the difference into the charity box.

As before, Miss Fisher was back down again in less than a couple of minutes. Once the Mercedes had driven away Marianne went upstairs and stood outside the door of number 34, listening, but she could not hear a sound. The young man was probably asleep, or trying to get to sleep, but this time Marianne knocked. She had decided that she would have to be honest and say that she was concerned; worried because he had looked so ill. It might get her into trouble, disturbing a guest, but her conscience insisted that she had to take the risk.

There was no answer. Marianne knocked once more. It was still strangely quiet, so she went down to the office and made a new electronic card key. After knocking again at the door of room 34 and still receiving no reply, she unlocked it and walked inside.

Marianne was immediately hit by an icy cold. Her first thought was that Fisher had left the window open to help the young man sober up, but in the streetlight that flooded into the room Marianne could see the window was closed. The room was empty. Nor was Fitzpatrick in the *en suite* bathroom.

Marianne checked the window, wondering if the young man

had climbed out of it, but it was firmly locked from the inside. Anyway, there was quite a drop to the street below, and down on the pavement there were no footprints in the snow.

Fitzpatrick couldn't have passed Marianne on the stairs, and the lift hadn't been used. The disconcerted night porter went back down and looked at the security tapes in the office. They showed that the young man had not come back through the lobby at any time; he had simply disappeared.

She couldn't decide what to do. She considered calling the police, but where was the evidence of foul play? The guest was free to leave whenever and however he chose to, and the fact that she had not seen him go could always have been her mistake.

While she tried to decide what to do, Marianne made sure that her note of the name and address of Miss Stephanie Fisher was recorded legibly, and as an afterthought she made a separate note for herself. She told herself that she was being unreasonably over-careful, but in the office she played back the digital recording from the security camera in the car park and took down the registration number of the S(s)ilver Mercedes. Just to be sure, she copied the file containing the footage from the front desk camera into a new folder on the computer; she did not want it to be erased after a couple of days.

Marianne found it impossible to get back to her Henning Mankell book. It suddenly grated on her that the novel was set in Sweden during a heat-wave, while in Britain it was snowing. She was also annoyed to discover that she had previously been reading the Mankell books "out of sequence". But the cause of her discontentment wasn't really the book.

"I don't know," said Mr. Lane simply. "I asked the cleaner and she doesn't remember having had to do anything in room 34 for weeks. To be honest, I'm not going to worry. Your Miss Fisher has paid the bills and nobody's done anything wrong. Although we can't think of an explanation for a disappearing guest, that doesn't mean there isn't one."

"If she comes in again, wanting a room for another young man, I'll refuse to book them in. And I'll call the police."

"If you really think there's something illegal going on, by all means tell them to try another hotel."

And that is exactly what Marianne suggested when Miss Fisher arrived the following week. Once more it was a young man she brought with her. They had all been the same kind of pretty-boy that annoyed her; she preferred her men a little more, well, masculine. They had all been under the influence of drink or drugs, and Marianne had read enough crime novels to be able to imagine all manner of reasons for Fisher dumping them at the hotel. They could well have been robbed or abused. Prostitution was possible. The only part of the whole story that Marianne did not understand was how the previous guest had managed to disappear from his room, and why.

"Which hotel do you suggest?" Miss Fisher asked, pleasantly enough.

It was three in the morning and, although it wasn't snowing this time, it was bitterly cold outside. The man was even younger than the previous two, perhaps even younger than Marianne herself. She was uncomfortable when she realized that she actually felt something maternal or protective towards him, and Marianne asked herself if turning him away was the best thing for his safety. If she booked him in, then at least she would make sure that this time she kept a close eye on him. She would put him into a different room from where the only other way out would be though a window into an inner courtyard.

"Room 18," she said. "I'll have to come up with you."

"There really is no need," said Fisher. "I can take Mr. Evans up to his room."

"I need to reset the lock on the door," Marianne lied. "It will only take a second."

All three of them went up to the room with Marianne leading the way. She opened the door with her master keycard and explained, as nonchalantly as she could, that it would now be reset.

She then made sure that Fisher's key worked and she handed it over to her. The woman took the young man inside and Marianne used her master key to go into the room opposite, which she knew to be empty.

She watched through the squint in the door, and when the Fisher left Marianne waited for her to walk down the corridor before she came out. She listened to the woman going down the stairs, and although she couldn't hear the woman crossing the hall past the unmanned reception desk, she felt the slight change in pressure as the front door opened and closed.

Marianne risked getting into a great deal of trouble, but, nevertheless, she opened the door to room 18 with her master key and walked in.

"Please excuse me," she said, immediately noticing how cold it was in the darkened room. "I do apologize, but I . . ."

Her first reaction had been to look towards the window again, to see if it was open, which it wasn't. But her attention was immediately taken by the young man standing just inside the brightly-lit bathroom. He was wearing only a tee-shirt and his hands were tied to the door handle with what looked like a dirty strip of some white material. He was obviously distressed; he was gagged and the look in his eyes was at first wild, but then suddenly hopeful, pleading. Then he looked from Marianne to somebody else who was inside the bathroom with him.

Suddenly that person pushed past the terrified young man. The first thing that struck Marianne was that the man who appeared was really very, very old. He had a long face and his wrinkles were deep, like the cracks in dried earth. He was also completely bald. He was dressed in a brown suit that, even back-lit from the bathroom and almost entirely in silhouette, appeared dirty and stained. In one hand he carried a hotel towel, and in the other he had a huge hypodermic syringe that looked like it was made of corroded brass.

"You shouldn't be here," he said with a low, quiet but insistent voice.

"I'm the night porter," said Marianne, without thinking.

"I know, Night Porter," the man said. "Can we agree that you have seen nothing here? Would you like to leave and never think about this again? It would be for the best."

Marianne reasoned that she could be out of the room and downstairs, phoning for the police, long before the old man caught up with her. But the young man was staring at her, trying to scream at her to stay and help him.

"No," said Marianne, shaking, still considering running. "*You* can leave."

"I will, when I've finished."

And the man was across the room with an unbelievable speed and agility. Instinctively Marianne flung the door open to run out and it crashed into him.

That should have given Marianne enough time, but as she reached the stairs she could already hear the man coming down the corridor towards her. Marianne vaulted over the banisters between the two sections of the dog-leg stair and managed to get her footing right as she landed. She took another leap into the reception area and ran across to the desk. She immediately picked up the telephone and hit nine three times before looking up.

The man was already standing by her as they both heard the distant, tiny voice asking which emergency service was required.

"Police," said Marianne, upset by how shaky and thin her voice sounded. How had the man appeared so quickly beside her? What did he intend to do with the syringe he was holding?

But the old man just smiled at Marianne, and walked away, backwards. Although he appeared quite calm, and the movement was effortless, the man seemed to move too quick; he was at the stairs and climbing them backwards, too soon, before he should have done . . .

"The St. Denis Hotel," Marianne added into the mouthpiece of the phone. "A guest is in danger, room 18 . . ."

She put the receiver down on the counter and unwillingly returned to the foot of the stairs. She looked up, but the old man was gone; he would already be in the corridor. Marianne followed reluctantly, and when she saw that the first floor corridor was empty, she made herself walk along to the door of room 18.

She hesitated before going back inside, but room 18 was now empty; both the old man and the young man had gone. It took a great deal of courage for Marianne to look around the door into the bathroom, and she wasn't sure if she really felt any relief in finding nobody there. The only signs that there had ever been anybody in room 18 were the horrible piece of material still attached to the door handle, the towel on the floor, and the state of the sink. There were dark marks on the white porcelain, as though somebody had been washing something very black and oily in it.

The police took seriously the call from Marianne. The security tapes clearly showed Miss Fisher and the young Mr. Evans, leaving the silver Mercedes and entering the hotel lobby. Fisher was traced through the number plate and questioned, but Marianne was told that she could have nothing to do with the disappearance of Evans. Traffic cameras clearly showed her driving away as soon as she had left the hotel. Evans had apparently been acting as Miss Fisher's "escort" that night, quite legitimately.

The old man with the bald head didn't appear on the security tapes at all. There was only a partial shot of Marianne herself at the telephone calling the police; unfortunately, the cameras were angled too far towards the front door to show the whole reception desk.

Marianne was given a couple of weeks off work, paid, by Mr. Lane. It was very good of him, thought Marianne, who felt bad taking the money when she didn't intend going back. How could she return after what had happened? The idea of being alone in the hotel at night was unimaginable. Well, not quite alone; there would be guests, of course, locked away in their rooms. But who else might be behind the closed bedroom doors? The old, bald man?

Marianne continued to keep the hours that she had done when

working at the St. Denis. She didn't admit to her mother that anything had happened at the hotel; instead she would go to The Milky Way until five in the morning, and then walk around the streets, sobering up in the cold dawn until she could go home after seven. She would still go to bed at the same time, although she would now be getting up at more like four in the afternoon.

Not that she could sleep; Miss Fisher and the old man insisted on invading her thoughts as he lay awake in bed, threatening to enter her dreams if she dared to lose consciousness.

Marianne had never been a regular anywhere before, but The Milky Way made it easy for her. She knew one of the barmen who worked there during the week, and at the weekends her old school friends would turn up. It was dark and full of alcoves where she could hide away and nurse a drink for hours if she had to. However, she soon got to know several other regulars, including a middle-aged man called Anthony, who she was becoming quite attached to. Anthony was an insomniac, and, distressingly, probably an alcoholic. Marianne worried that she might end up the same as him, but she enjoyed his company, and he seemed to tolerate hers. Marianne knew that she could not keep up the lifestyle indefinitely, not least because the St. Denis Hotel stopped her pay after two weeks, and the little money she had saved was already dwindling. She was convinced that her mother would find out what had happened, as Mr. Lane telephoned every week to ask after Marianne, leaving messages on the answer-phone. (Luckily, Marianne had always managed to intercept and erase them.) The hotel manager was trying to make it easy for her, Marianne knew that. She also knew that at some point she would have to re-apply to the benefits agency, and Lane could easily tell them that she had just walked out of the job. Then there wouldn't be any money coming in for at least a month.

It was three weeks later, perhaps four (Marianne had lost some sense of time), when she saw Miss Fisher walk into The Milky Way. It was a weeknight, and not at all crowded. Having bought drinks at the bar, Fisher sat at a table at the back. With her was yet another young man.

Marianne had been talking to Anthony. At some point in their friendship she had told him about the hotel and Fisher. She now pointed the woman out to him.

"Ask her," he said, and because Marianne had finished her fourth glass of wine, and felt safe in such a public place, she did so.

"The police have already interviewed me," Fisher insisted, uncomfortable at having Marianne confronting her across the table.

"I know, and they could *prove* nothing," said Marianne.

"Because there's nothing to prove! You gave them a description of the man they need to talk to."

"It's too much of a coincidence," Marianne dismissed the reply. "You're in league with the bald old man."

"I really don't know him. Look, I'm here for a quiet drink with my friend . . ."

"Another one of your escorts?" She turned to the young man, who looked confused at the sudden appearance of Marianne and her accusations.

"I hope she's paying you well?" Marianne asked. "I don't know what services she'll ask of you, but if she tries taking you back to a hotel afterwards, don't let her. There'll be an old man with rusty hypodermic waiting for you."

"Please, Miss . . . Night Porter," said Fisher. "Please leave us alone. Otherwise I'll have to call the management."

"And tell them what? I'm a regular here, don't you know?"

"I like to have company of an evening. I'll take a companion to a restaurant, or a bar, or sometimes a club like this. When my young friend is tired I drop him off at a hotel with a couple of hundred pounds in his pocket to thank him."

"And that's when they meet your bald friend . . ."

The young man had been looking increasingly uncomfortable, and Marianne watched in amusement as Fisher opened up her purse, handed him some notes, and told him that he could go.

"I hope you're feeling happy with yourself," said Fisher, as the young man walked away.

"If I've saved his life, yes!"

"And how, exactly, have you done that?"

"By saving him from you, and the old man who disposes of your 'escorts' for you."

"And how does he dispose of them?"

"I don't know," said Marianne. "Perhaps he injects them with something to dissolve them . . . so all that's left is an oily, fatty mess in the sink!"

Fisher laughed, to which Marianne took exception. She hadn't realized how drunk she was, or how tired. She realized that she had voiced a private fantasy that really was too fanciful. She decided to leave Fisher and the scene of her minor triumph, resolving to walk away without looking back. She made her way back to Anthony and apologized to him, saying that she was going home. She was depressed that he simply said goodnight and let her go. She looked back at him on her way out, and he was heading for the bar.

As she was leaving, Marianne went in to the ladies'. She sat on the toilet and replayed the scene with Fisher in her head, confused, unable to decide if she had made any sense. As Marianne walked out of the cubicle she heard the main door open and Miss Fisher walked in.

"I have nothing to hide, Night Porter," said the woman.

"You drug your young victims," said Marianne, wondering why she was continuing to be confrontational when all she wanted to do was leave.

"No, I don't drug them. I buy them a decent meal and they usually end up drinking too much."

"It's called prostitution."

"No, they only act as company. Nothing sexual happens."

"No?" asked Marianne. She was relieved to have been able to get past the woman, and was now close to the door, able to leave.

"Night Porter, how I envy you," said Fisher. "And the young

men I pay to keep me company. I admire your youth, your vitality, your innocence . . ."

"Bullshit."

"You could help me meet young men. There would be something in it for you . . ."

Fisher had come forward, almost without the younger woman noticing, but Marianne pushed her away. Suddenly there was a flurry of arms and legs as Fisher slipped backwards on the wet floor, and, when she fell, there was a horrible sound as her head hit the dirty cracked tiles. The woman didn't move, and immediately an almost black liquid started to flow from out under her head. In the dim, ineffectual light it took a few moments before Marianne realised what it was. But she didn't have time to find out how badly Fisher might be hurt because she was frozen by a blast of cold air. A cubicle door had opened. She had thought they were alone, and she was confused to see that it was the cubicle she had, herself, just come out of.

Suddenly there was the old, bald man with the deep wrinkles. He looked at Marianne, then at Miss Fisher, and he smiled.

"I'll finish her off for you," he said. "In a few moments there will be nothing."

"I don't want to know," said Marianne, backing away.

"Good, good. Then we can agree that you have seen nothing here. Leave and never think about this again."

"But why help me?" asked Marianne, although her voice was so quiet she hardly knew whether she had articulated her thoughts.

"Why?" asked the old man. "I was always there to tidy up for you before. And I'll be there when you need me again."

LISA TUTTLE

SOMETHING SINISTER IN SUNLIGHT

Another sunny day in L.A. It was getting him down – the weather, along with everything else. There was something sinister in sunlight. Not so much in England, when the weak, gentle sun made a special appearance, but day after day, unrelieved by clouds or rain, it struck Anson as unnatural. He found it just as perversely oppressive as the regulation smiles and bonhomie of store clerks and waiters. "Have a nice day, now!" It made him homesick, nostalgic for sullen youths with bad teeth, too proud to pretend they *enjoyed* being your server, while he missed the soft grey skies and sodden ground.

He'd created a whole little *schtick* about it – made Harry laugh when he'd skyped him – but it had fallen flat when he'd tried it out at a poolside party yesterday. Americans: they didn't take offense; they just didn't *get* it. The English sense of humour. British comedy was supposed to be big in the States just now, so maybe it was *him*. He wanted to prove his versatility, show another side to his character, and it didn't work. Producers, directors, audiences wanted just one thing from him, the same performance again and again. Maybe it was the best he could do. Who was he to say they were wrong?

He thought of his last conversation with his agent.

"So you're saying I should be grateful for *whatever* I'm offered?"

"Of course not, Anson. But those last two – they weren't bad parts – and not inconsiderable."

"They were the *same* part. Serial killer. Sinister, high-functioning sociopathic murderer."

"Well, you're *very good* at that. And you bring something to –"

"To an underwritten, clichéd part? I should bloody well hope so. Jay, it's depressing. Why can't I do something else?"

Jay had been silent for a worryingly long time. Afraid his agent was trying to come up with a new, more palatable formulation of the bitter truth, he had jumped in first.

"Look. I'm not saying I have to be the *lead*. I don't mind being the villain. I just want to do something different – something that is not just another replay of Cassius Fucking Crittenden."

It had been his first role in a major Hollywood motion picture – fourteen years ago. It was maybe a little strange to cast an English actor as a serial killer from the backwoods of Kentucky, but everybody knew the Brits were good at playing evil, and Anson thought he did a passable, if eccentric, job with his hillbilly accent. How much his performance contributed to the decision to transport the character of Cassius Crittenden into a new TV series, who could say, but Anson was offered the role. At the time, it had seemed like his big breakthrough, but in recent years he had come to feel it had been not just the high point, but also the end of his career.

Originally, the villain was slated to die at the end of the first season. But his character was too popular; so, in the second season it was revealed that the serial killer had survived his apparent immolation in a burning car, and he returned to taunt the detective hero.

In retrospect, Anson felt he should have walked away after the first season. As a character, Cassius had always been fond of masks and disguises, and the circumstances of his 'death' meant it would have been easy enough to use burns, scarring and plastic surgery as an explanation for the appearance of a different actor. But to walk away from a sure thing, from regular work – extremely well-paid – to return to the insecurity of the acting life was not in his character. And so, even though he'd never liked Los Angeles, he had stayed – for six years.

Six years on the series, and then it ended. It had been a relief to get back home, wonderful to have the freedom to do whatever he wanted. For a little while there had been plenty of offers; he could take his pick. He didn't have to go back to L.A. There were films, a role in a David Hare play, a TV series set in the 1960s, in which he played a hard-bitten yet soft-hearted journalist, and a string of smaller parts, which grew smaller and less frequent as the years went by.

Somehow, nothing else he did ever attracted the same attention. They were like a succession of wrong turns, each one leading him down a one-way street in a further wrong direction. Until finally it seemed he had never done anything noteworthy or memorable except play the continuing role of a psychotic killer on a popular American TV series. The roles he was offered became depressingly similar.

This trip to California, urged by his agent, now seemed to him the worst wrong turn of all, the final nail in the coffin of his career. If he was remembered at all, it was as Cassius Crittenden, and that memory fatally coloured the perception of every casting director, every producer, every show-runner . . . they could not imagine him, Anson Barker, successfully filling any other role. Didn't these people understand about *acting*? Or . . . was he kidding himself? Maybe he just wasn't any good.

Self-doubt, self-pity, all the personal fears came out when he was alone at night, like roaches through the floorboards and invisible cracks in the walls of the borrowed apartment.

He wished he was home, where he didn't have to cope with the eight-hour time difference before he could talk to Harry – where he could be in Harry's arms, not just looking at him on a screen – where he could call up some of his mates to meet for a drink, or just drop in to a pub or a cafe, one of the places where he was known – and *not* as the actor who used to be Cassius Crittenden.

He wished he had never come. But now that he was here, he had to see it through. A few more days, one last meeting, and then he'd put it all behind him, go back to London, find something else to do.

Making an effort to shake off his depression, he went out for a late breakfast at the Blu Jam Cafe. It had become a comforting habit – just a ten-minute drive, and French toast to die for.

It was crowded – closer to lunchtime than breakfast, he realized – and the waiter had just told him there'd be a half-hour wait, then paused and said, "Unless you're joining . . . her?"

Anson had not noticed the woman giving him a wave from her corner table, and once his attention had been drawn to her, he did not recognize her. But it was instantly more appealing than either going away or hanging around on the sidewalk for half an hour, so he agreed.

She was mid-thirties, he guessed, with sharp, not unattractive features, bright blue eyes, glossy, wavy auburn hair. She wore a bright blue blazer over a white shirt – something about the ensemble said 'estate agent' to him, although insurance or low-level finance seemed equally possible. She was vaguely familiar, but he still couldn't place her.

"You don't remember me, do you, Anson?"

"Sadly, no – but I shan't forget you again, I promise."

She stretched out her hand. "Elissa Condé. We met at Jack and Aura's party?"

"Of course. You're an architect."

She smiled so tightly it seemed more a grimace. "Good to know I'm not *utterly* forgettable."

He remembered her profession because *Harry* was an architect

– and because he hadn't quite believed her. The other thing he remembered about her – now, and too late – was that she'd given off a crafty, vaguely stalkerish vibe; pretending to have no idea who he was, and asking none of the questions people normally asked when you said you were an actor. But she knew who he was, all right, he had seen it in her eyes, and she hadn't wanted him to know she knew. She wanted him to think their meeting was purely accidental – *like this one* – when in fact she had engineered it for her own purposes.

He felt a prickle of excitement. This woman might be dangerous . . . but he wasn't afraid. What could she do to him? She wanted something, and she thought he didn't know, whereas in fact he had the edge – he didn't *know*, but neither was he fooled. And it might be interesting to find out what she was up to.

He ordered the crunchy French toast and coffee; she asked for organic granola with soya milk, and a pot of green tea.

When the waiter had gone, Anson treated Elissa to a kindly, avuncular gaze. "I'm sorry I had to abandon you so abruptly at the party. It must have seemed very rude. But I wasn't there to enjoy myself – it was all business. But now, here we are! We can make up for our missed opportunity. What would you like to talk about?"

She seemed a bit taken aback by this approach. "Oh, I don't know . . . what do you think of L.A.?"

"The traffic is even worse than it was when I lived here. *Not* my favourite place, I have to say. I'm looking forward to going home next week."

She looked worried. "Where's home?"

"London." He drummed his fingers on the table. "What about you? Native Angelino?"

"Pretty much, yeah."

"And you like it."

"Sure. It's OK. I mean, I don't really know, because I've never lived anywhere else."

"Travel much?"

"Some. But I hate flying."

"Sing it, sister! But what can you do? If you want to go any-where . . ."

"I drive. It takes longer, but not always, when you consider the time you save hanging around in airports."

"That wouldn't work for me."

She looked at him blankly. "Why not?"

"London, remember? Can't drive across the sea."

"Oh, right. I wasn't thinking . . ."

"You've never been abroad?"

"I've been to Mexico."

"OK. Did you like it?

"Cozumel was pretty nice, but really, I wouldn't go again. It was my boyfriend's idea – my boyfriend at the time. I'm not with anybody now. But I mean . . . why go to Mexico, when you can get the same stuff here? The restaurants here are better. And for scenery – I'd rather go to Taos, or Monterrey."

He was baffled by her. Conversation was hard work, and she seemed strangely incurious about him – about everything, really. Or else she was keeping a really tight grip on her emotions, fearful of giving away her secret. What *was* her secret? That she was ob-sessed by him, in love with him, imagined they were soul-mates . . . or, more drearily, she'd written a script, had an idea for a series, thought he could get her an acting job? Well, she'd have to tell him eventually. To his own surprise, he was actually curious. Instead of being bored, he found himself touched by a deep, unexpressed sadness in her. The dreariness of her imagination somehow put his own worries into perspective.

Finally, television entered the conversation. Elissa became more natural, and openly enthusiastic, as she talked about her favourite shows, one of which, it came as no surprise, was the one Anson and Harry had taken to calling 'That Which Shall Not Be Named.' Yet still she said nothing that could be taken as an admission that she knew Anson had played the part of Cassius Crittenden – not even when she invited him to her house for dinner.

"You *have* to. Come on, don't try to wriggle out of it. You've already said you're not doing anything on Friday, and you're fed-up with take-outs. Blu Jam is closed in the evenings, and even if it wasn't, man cannot live by French toast alone."

That startled a laugh out of him; she was nothing like as dull as she'd seemed at first. Yet the prospect of spending an entire evening alone in her company made him uneasy.

"You said you liked Italian food. Well, let me tell you, I make The. Best. Lasagne. *Ever*. And there's somebody I want you to meet. Somebody you *have* to meet. You'll thank me for it."

"Really? Who is this paragon?"

"You have to come and find out."

He wagged a reproving finger. "You had better not be trying to match-make. I'm a happily married man."

She went pale, and he realized he had genuinely shocked her. "You're *not!*"

"Well, no, not really." He gave her a somewhat puzzled smile. "You're right. Same-sex marriage isn't legal *quite* yet, and I must admit Harry and I didn't sign up to a civil partnership, but we're quite the devoted couple, even so. Been together three years and six months. I'm not looking for anyone else."

"You *can't* be gay."

He put his napkin on the table, too cross and weary with her stupidity to respond.

"*Cassius* isn't gay!" It was a cry from the heart.

He had to laugh, although he wasn't amused. "No, no, *Cassius* isn't gay – nor is he English – nor *real*. It is called *acting*."

She began nodding her head rapidly, like a tic. "Of course. I hadn't thought . . ."

"Clearly not."

She gave him an anguished look. "I'm sorry. I didn't mean anything – I wasn't trying to – I'm sorry if I offended you. I was just so surprised, because, well . . . Cassius! He's so real to me, I forgot. It's just hard for me to remember, talking to *you* . . . that . . . even though you *look* like him, you're not . . . not the same."

"I know," he said, trying to be kind. But he didn't know how *anyone* – except the very youngest, most ignorant, mentally-challenged and obsessive fan – could confuse the player with the part. And especially when it was a case of an educated, urbane Englishman who had played the part of a crafty, hillbilly monster, years ago. And if she really thought he was *anything* like Cassius, what on earth was she thinking, to invite him to dinner?

"It's very flattering, truly, to think I created a character that seems so real and matters so much to you, but . . ." Light flashed, searingly, off the blade of a butter knife; he blinked and rubbed his temples, feeling the faint, insidious throbbing of an incipient migraine. "But . . . I have often thought fans, rather than seeking out actors they *think* they admire, should take advice from the Wizard of Oz – what were his words? 'Pay no attention to the man behind the curtain!'"

"Oh, no! I don't agree *at all*. It was such a thrill to meet you! Such a *privilege!* I hope I haven't offended you. I could just *shoot* myself, honestly, what an idiot, so stupid. I don't have anything against gays – I'm not *like* that – it was just such a shock, to think of *Cassius* as . . . as . . . I mean, you agree, don't you, that Cassius is *not* homosexual?"

It seemed to Anson that the fictional serial killer was driven by a lust for killing, not for what a normal person would categorize as sex, and that defining them by the gender of their victims was hardly significant, but he had no desire to argue the case with Elissa.

"You can claim him for heterosexuality – it doesn't make him normal."

"Oh, Anson!" She gazed at him reproachfully. "I'm not saying gay sex is abnormal! But Cassius is attracted to women. He doesn't have sex with men, only women."

"Before he *kills* them."

She smiled. "But he didn't kill *every* woman he slept with." A major plot point had Cassius falling in love with a woman called Melinda Valentine, and then, after one night of passion, having to renounce her, as he struggled against his conflicting urges, to kill her, or to keep her safe. In the end, that love proved to be his weakness, as he was finally captured – his death was seen by fans as self-willed, a deliberate sacrifice to save the only woman he had ever truly loved. It was all a load of tosh; pernicious tosh, Anson sometimes thought, for it made no sense at all, morally or psychologically, and it had allowed the villain, a degraded, psychopathic monster, to become a romantic anti-hero in the eyes of many.

"Of course. Melinda Valentine. Amazing what the *right woman* can do." Anson spoke automatically, his thoughts preoccupied by the tension building in his head, and the spot like an after-image in his visual field (he called it 'the solar flare'). He wondered if he could get home in time to ward off the worst of the migraine with a couple of tablets and two hours lying perfectly still in the dark. "I'm sorry about this, but I'm afraid I have to run."

"That's all right – as long as you've forgiven my stupidity, and you're still coming on Friday? Great! Seven o'clock? Here, my address and phone number. Give me a call if you need directions."

The rental car had sat-nav, so Anson easily found Elissa's house, although it was much farther away than he'd expected, more than an hour's drive. Since he'd met her in a local cafe, he'd thought she lived in the neighbourhood.

But even at a quarter to eight, he was the first to arrive. He felt a flare of suspicion, as Elissa, bare-legged in a dark-blue slip-dress under a grey cashmere cardigan, led him into her candle-lit living-room, Tom Waits' gravelly voice from the speakers, the air redolent of a herby tomato sauce and melted cheese, but empty except for the two of them. He felt better when he saw the glass-topped table had been set with three places.

"I was about to apologize for being late, but I see your other friend isn't here yet."

She shrugged, smiling. "Never mind. He'll be welcome whenever he turns up."

She took away the bottle of wine he'd brought, and returned from the kitchen bearing two large glasses of red.

"Cheers."

They clinked glasses. He took a sip. It was not as good as the bottle he'd brought, but it was nice. Thinking of the long drive back, he resolved to be abstemious. Just the one.

Elissa sat down on the couch and patted the cushion beside her. When he sat down she moved, shifting her legs so that her short skirt rode up, revealing her thighs, and his mouth dried at what he saw there. Inked in shades of grey was a portrait of Anson's face as he'd looked portraying Cassius Crittenden.

That was the moment when he should have leapt up and run screaming from the room.

Without the benefit of hindsight, he took a big gulp of wine, repressed his natural horror, and said, "I hope that's not permanent."

"Why?"

"For *your* sake, dear. Hasn't it occurred to you what a *turn-off* it would be for anyone . . . anyone you cared to take to bed?"

She wet her lips, staring into his eyes. "Anyone . . . except Cassius."

"*Especially* Cassius. Unless you think he's an absolute monster of narcissism."

Her eyes widened in alarm. "No, of course not. I thought it would be like . . . well, I didn't think. It's not a real tattoo." She scrambled to her feet and hurried out of the room.

He heard another door open and shut, and then the sound of running water. And that was his second chance – as he thought later – to make his escape, while that crazy woman was busy scrubbing Cassius' visage from her inner thigh. But he wasn't afraid, and he was hungry, the smells from the kitchen making his mouth water, and the wine she had poured for him tasting more delicious with every sip.

When Elissa emerged from the bathroom she was flushed and slightly bedraggled looking, her left thigh red and moist from its scrubbing. She'd taken off the cardigan, and the slight, sleeveless dress, dampened with splashed water and her exertions, clung to her body. She didn't seem to be wearing anything else, and it looked more than ever like an undergarment, not meant for public view.

Anson jumped up, remembering his last film, set in the thirties, when gentlemen rose when a lady entered the room. He didn't want her to snuggle up close, or reveal any other hidden secrets. Now that her arms were bared he saw she had a tattoo, maybe a heart, red and black, just below her shoulder on her right arm.

"Perhaps you should give your friend a ring," he said. "Find out what's keeping him. I hate to think of your delicious lasagne drying to dust while we wait."

She stared for a moment as if not understanding, and then said flatly, "You're right, we may as well eat now."

"But your friend?"

"He'll come when he comes."

She brought out the lasagne and a bowl of green salad, and re-filled his glass before he could stop her.

"I wonder . . . could I possibly trouble you for a glass of water?"

She giggled.

"I'm sorry?"

"I'm sorry. I shouldn't laugh, but . . . you sound so *different*."

He guessed he'd been exaggeratedly, hyper-English – some Americans brought it out in him, especially when he'd been drink-ing. He looked again at his glass, to see how much he'd had, but of course he couldn't tell, since she'd refilled it. Unnervingly, despite his resolve not to touch it, it looked not as full as a moment ago.

She brought him a glass of sparkling water, and he gulped down half of it immediately.

"Is the lasagne too salty?"

"No, it's delicious. Quite possibly, as you claimed, The. Best. Lasagne. *Ever.*"

Light flashed off the rim of a glass, like a solar flare. He shut his eyes.

"Are you all right?"

"Yes. No. I get these headaches. I'll be fine. It's just the light."

But he wasn't all right; he could barely stand. He didn't understand how it could have come on so suddenly; it was never like this. Was he about to pass out? Surely he hadn't had that much to drink.

He didn't want to go into her bedroom, but that's where she led him, into the blessed darkness, and he collapsed onto the bed with a groan.

"Please, leave me."

"Can't I do something?"

"Just leave."

When he woke up, or came to, sun was shining through a gap in the curtains and he could hear birds cheeping monotonously outside. He had a dull, throbbing headache, but it was not a migraine. He was naked and alone in an unmade bed that reeked of sweat and sex – unmistakable.

The last time he'd had sex with a woman – more than ten years ago – drugs had been involved, but *that* had been consensual, and he could remember it still today. Not like the events of last night.

She must have put something in his wine.

He groaned and shut his eyes, thinking of her reaction to *his* reaction to the painted face on her thigh, remembering how she had emerged from the bathroom, moist and pink, scrubbed clean . . . for him.

Why? Was it a fan's scalp-hunting . . . or something more sinister? Did she want his baby? *Christ!*

Ignoring the pounding in his head, he rolled out of bed, stumbled to the bathroom, vomited, then showered, attacking himself energetically with a flannel and shower gel until every last snail-trail of her touch had been eradicated.

Afterwards he prowled quickly and edgily through the house. It was obvious that she'd cleared out, knowing how angry he would be, but she might have left him a note. The dishes from last night's dinner were still on the table, the food congealing on two plates, the third place setting pristine. Of course, there never had been a second guest invited.

He felt a lust for revenge, considered doing something destructive while he had the chance: smashing the glassware, breaking the TV, cutting up her clothes, pissing on the carpet . . . but he could imagine too well how that could backfire. She might accuse *him* of rape; might even get him convicted of *her* crime. Nobody would believe what had *really* happened; he could hardly imagine it himself.

At last he left, stopping along the way in a neighbourhood he didn't know for breakfast at a fast-food outlet. He would never return to Blu Jam; he would change his habits for the few remaining days he'd be in this city. Although he had to go back to the apartment for his things, he decided to move into a hotel. At the thought that she might have discovered his address, might be waiting for him there, he went hot and cold, fury and horror combining in a toxic brew.

But there was no one in the apartment, which appeared unchanged from when he had left it the previous evening. Nevertheless, he began to pack as soon as he had changed his clothes, and it was then, as he checked the pockets of his jacket before putting it away, that he found Elissa's note.

My darling

You're reading this, so things did not work out as I wished. I knew the risk and chose to take it. I did it for you. I like to think that if we'd had more time together you would have come to love me as I love you. But since that didn't happen, take it as my gift. No regrets. I set you free. Now go and live your life as it was meant. Think of me kindly, if you can. The next woman

He began to shake and tears of sheer rage blurred his vision before he could read to the end. He crumpled the note in his fist and tried to control his breathing. The bitch, the crazy, reactionary, intolerant, ignorant, vicious, mad bitch – how dare she? Dope him and force him to have sex with her, stupidly convinced it would set him free. And yet, although he couldn't remember it, something had gone wrong; it wasn't the happy experience she'd imagined, and she could only try to salvage her fantasy by running away, leaving this silly, deluded note.

He tore it to shreds. He would have burned them, but for the lack of matches.

It was nearly three o'clock in L.A. which meant it was 23:00 hours – eleven o'clock at night – in London; time for his regularly scheduled Skype with Harry. He washed his face and composed himself. Much as he longed for the comfort of his lover's understanding, it was too strange and complicated a story to share now, when the distance of half a world still separated them. Better to wait until they were together, when he'd come to terms with what had happened, and knew how to tell the story.

Harry, sitting at the breakfast bar with his laptop open, his mug with the London skyline close at hand, the unkillable spider plant visible over his left shoulder, the print of wild horses on the wall behind him – the cosy familiarity of it all, softened by lamplight, might have made him cry, if only Harry's beloved face had not worn such a grim, unwelcoming expression.

"All right, let's hear it; make it good."

"What?"

"Your explanation. Your *apology*, Anson, for that fuckwitted, demented phone call this morning."

"This morning?"

"You're going to pretend you don't remember? I *thought* you were drunk, but really, that takes the biscuit. Time for the twelve steps if you're having *blackouts* now . . ."

Pain lanced through his temples; he put his hands on top of his head to keep it from splitting open. "Somebody drugged me. Put something in my drink. I can't remember calling – when did I call you? What did I say?"

Alarm warred with anger in his lover's face. "Seriously? Christ! Are you all right?"

"I'll tell you all about it – after I'm home. When did I call?"

"About nine – well after midnight your time – I was on my way out the door. You were doing a kind of Woody Harrelson *shtick* – it didn't make a lot of sense, to be honest. I don't really remember what you said, but I thought it was a shitty way of breaking up with me, if –"

"No!"

"Well, you seemed set on staying in California. Expressed your love for the golden state. I thought – reading between the lines – you'd been offered a part, open-ended, starting immediately, and you were too nervous to tell me honestly that you weren't coming back, so you'd got drunk and let this backwoodsman break it to me."

"Nobody's offered me anything. I've got a meeting on Monday, but even if he promises me the lead in *Die Hard: The Musical* I'm flying out of here the next day. I can't wait to get home. I miss you."

"You look like shit."

"I love you too."

"Migraine?"

Anson realized he was kneading his temples and squinting against a non-existent light. "Yeah. Quite a lot, recently. It's the sun, I think."

"Well, stay out of it. Go lie down. Take care of yourself, all right?"

Anson didn't lie down after talking to Harry, even though his head was pounding. He took his tablets with a glass of water, and finished packing, eager to get away to the anonymity of a hotel room. Maybe he'd try the airport, where he could feel he was already on his way home.

The sun was low but still lancing painful beams of light off every reflective surface; each car in the small parking lot became an aggressor, and he all but closed his eyes as he shuffled towards his rental.

Opening the lid of the trunk immediately cut off those painfully distracting shafts and blades of light, and he opened his eyes wide, shocked by what he saw inside.

The woman's body had been carefully placed, lying curled on one side. She wore only the dark blue slip of a dress, arms and legs bare. There was no blood visible, and the distortions and discolouration of her dead face was hidden by the same sweep of hair that covered the damage done to her neck. It was the way Cassius Crittenden always dealt with his victims; after sex, while they lay relaxed and unsuspecting beside him, he strangled the woman with a tie or a belt, then he washed and dressed her before laying her down, curled up so she looked at first glance as if she'd merely fallen asleep.

His eyes were drawn to the tattoo on her upper arm; the tattoo he had glimpsed on Elissa's bare arm the previous evening. It was a dark red love-heart, with lacy scalloped edges, and the initials M.V. in the centre. He had seen it before, but not on this woman. He'd known it previously as a fake tattoo, created to adorn the arm of the actress who played Melinda Valentine to his Cassius Crittenden.

He heard the voice of Cassius as if it came from outside himself; knew it was impossible, but the drawling voice of an imaginary American psychopath was the last thing he heard in his final moments of knowing himself to be an English actor called Anson Barker.

"Who did she think she was? Who did she think *I* was? Sorry, darlin', but you didn't know *what* you were messin' with, and now you've paid the price."

SIMON KURT UNSWORTH

PRIVATE AMBULANCE

Eᴌɪsᴇ ᴅʀᴏᴠᴇ ᴀ private ambulance.

Unlike most ambulances, this one was dressed in a monotone, sombre grey, had no sirens or flashing lights, and the patients it carried were beyond treatment or help or hope of recovery. There was no need for rush, no pressure on Elise to arrive at her destination quickly, there was simply smooth movement of the world rolling past the windows and the knowledge that in the vehicle's chill rear, her passengers rode in silence. She never turned the radio on when she drove, despite the fact that the ambulance's cab was separate from the back section, feeling somehow that it would be disrespectful during these final journeys. Elise gave the dead serenity and grace wherever she could, quietness after life's noise.

These night-time rides were the ones that she enjoyed the most; there was little traffic, especially out here where the buildings had given way to farmland and the ground rose to hills, and she could drive without effort or concentration, letting her mind reach out into the sky and land around her and find shapes and scents and sounds that, she thought, few other people ever felt or smelled or heard. Old man Tunstall's funeral parlour was out in one of the villages, serving the isolated communities scattered throughout the farmlands. Actually, they maybe weren't isolated communities, Elise thought, but one huge community stretched thin and laid across the hills and valleys and fields like a net, hundreds of individual strands twisting around each other in links that stretched from farmhouse to terraced street to barn and back to farmhouse. Few people escaped the area, once arrived, not for any length of time; Tunstall had once told her that most of his business was what he called "in-house", people from the area dying at home and being buried in the land that had sustained them. It was only occasionally that Elise was called on to take a body from the hospital in the city to Tunstall's, and the runs were always at night.

Outside, the ground was dusted with frost and occasional banks of snow. It had been bitterly cold these last few weeks, the earth hardening, becoming frigid, and Elise drove slowly, letting the vehicle's weight give it grip on the iced surface. The roads glistened in the dying moonlight and, around her, the fields drowsed under a caul of ice and the journey was all that mattered, this last journey between the places of life and the places of death.

Elise carried only one traveller that night. "He killed himself," the morgue attendant had told her in a voice somewhere between glee and horrified awe, "and we don't know who he is!" The man had apparently walked to the banks of the river that wound down from the hills, passing through the town on its way to the sea, stripped, knelt down on the ridged and furled mud at the bitter water's edge and frozen to death. His clothes were in a bag next to Elsie now, neatly folded, the top of the bag rolled and held down with tape.

"He was frozen solid," the morgue attendant had said, "and we had to defrost him like a piece of chicken!" Elsie had met people like the attendant before, people for whom the mechanics of death were the most fascinating part of the journey, for whom the biology of things was the most important. There had been the paramedic who had told her, voice rich with undisguised fascination, about the suicide who had jumped from a tall building and landed on the ground at an odd angle. Their head, said the paramedic, had connected hard with a kerbstone and cracked open and their brain had burst free and slithered, almost intact, across the road "like a big pink snail"; he had asked her out for a drink after telling her this. She had refused, politely, and taken the suicide's body into her private ambulance to begin its next stage of the procession into the ground. For Elise, death wasn't a moment; rather, it was a string of moments, a set of markers that led from life to burial or cremation, to earth or fire, and she saw herself as a companion and guide to these, the most significant of journeys.

The rear of the ambulance shifted slightly as she went round a corner, the wheels slipping over ice, and she slowed.

The dead man was being delivered to Tunstall's Funeral Home simply because Tunstall had a council contract to deal with the unidentified dead; there were spaces in the graveyards out here. In the cities, space for the departed was rapidly being filled and the real estate of passing on carried heavy costs that council couldn't pay, so people like Elise's passenger were sent out, to where populations were lower and the grounds cheaper.

The rear of the vehicle shifted again. There was a noise as it shifted, a gentle knocking.

Elise slowed again, dropping smoothly through the gears, letting the engine quieten. There was another thud from behind her, and a slight shiver ran through the vehicle. Had she run over something in the road? A rock or branch, maybe an animal? She glanced in her wing mirror but the road behind her, painted in fragile moonlight, was clear. She let her speed creep back up, happy that all was well. Elise took the dead man on.

Another thud, another slight shiver. Movement. In the rear of the vehicle.

Elise's first thought was that something had come loose back there, one of the straps holding the man's coffin possibly, that it was flapping, but no; the thud had been too loud and the shiver too heavy to be caused by a simple loose strap. Perhaps the coffin itself was moving, slipping on its base and banging against the vehicle's wall when she went around corners?

Another corner, slower now, but no accompanying shift or thud, the road straightening, letting the ambulance speed up and then a definite bang from the rear. Elsie started, the tyres shimmying across the surface of the frozen road before she grasped the wheel and brought the vehicle back into line. The bag of belongings next to her fell from the seat into the footwell with a rustle of plastic and sound that was almost organic, like an owl opening its wings and stretching. Making sure the road was straight ahead for a while, Elise turned and tried to peer in through the small observation window between the cab and the refrigerated rear section. The glass was dark, throwing back a reflection of her face, eyes inked pools below her pale forehead.

She turned back to the road, lifting her foot from the accelerator and taking the vehicle gently left, in towards the roadside. When it came to a halt, she put the ambulance in neutral and unclipped her seatbelt, turning properly to the observation slit. Cupping her hands around her eyes, she peered into the blackness that travelled at her back. It was almost absolute, a gloom that was broken only vaguely by pale edges and shapes.

Something moved loosely in the dark and then the engine of the ambulance abruptly cut out.

Elise jerked back from the glass. What had that been? She twisted back around and turned the key, starting the vehicle again. The engine sputtered for a moment, caught and slipped, caught again and grumbled to full life. She opened the driver's side door and stepped out, leaving it open so that the cab lights fell across the road. There were no other lights out here, no streetlamps, no cars or trucks barrelling along the road, just the stars above her and the moon dipping low as the night came to its end. She made her way to the rear of the ambulance, reached out and took hold of the handles, felt the cold bite of chill metal against her fingers and palms, felt rather than heard something bump behind the doors, and then swung them open.

Everything was in its place. The coffin and its inhabitant were still on the lower ledge of on the right side, where she had placed them, and the straps around the wooden box were still tight and fastened. She climbed in, crouching and pulling on the padded nylon cables; there was no give in them. She looked around, seeing nothing that shouldn't be there, nothing loose that would have explained the movement or the sounds. Experimentally, she placed her hands on the end of the coffin and pushed, wondering if the noises had been caused by it moving up and down rather than swinging sideways, but the casket remained still. Something inside it, then? No, she had watched as the dead man had been placed inside, the padding arranged around him to prevent precisely the kind of movement she was wondering about.

There was nothing on the other ledges, three of them, that could have moved. The rear of Elise's ambulance was, as ever, neat and clean and a fitting cradle for the dead on these, the last of their courses.

The engine, then, or something mechanical underneath the vehicle. She would simply have to drive carefully and hope she made it to Tunstall's, then make a judgement there about whether it was safe to drive back. She returned to the front of the ambulance and climbed in, shivering in the warmth. With the door shut and the belt back across her chest and securely clipped she pulled away, keeping her speed low. The road was rising now, curling around one of the fells. It would fall and rise several more times before she reached Tunstall's, she knew, and wondered if the ambulance would make it. She dug her phone from her pocket and checked it; a good charge but not much signal.

Another curve in the road and this time something *definitely* moved in the rear of the ambulance, banging hard against the side and setting the vehicle rocking outwards on its axles before it fell back to stability, distorting the vehicle's balance for a moment. This time, the bang had been accompanied by a noise that might have been a sheet tearing or something flapping, a long low noise only just audible of the sound of the engine. Her foot jerked on the accelerator, sending the ambulance lurching forward and onto the other side of the road before she could bring herself and it back under control, return them to the right side of the centre line and to a better speed.

Before Elise could do anything else there was another bump, this time even harder, jolting the vehicle and making the wheel twitch in her hands, and long, drawn out noise like something dragging across metal from somewhere behind her. The dead man's bag of belongings slithered across the foot-well, the top pulling open and spilling the contents out. There were jeans and a dirty brown coat, pieces of paper covered in writing, and feathers. They must have been in the pockets of the jacket, dozens and dozens of them, *hundreds* of them, small and large, black and white and brown, speckled and plain, floating out in drifts. The smell of them, of the clothes, was rich and earthy, grimy with sweat and death and cold. One of the feathers settled on Elise's hand and she shook it off violently, not liking the greasy feel of it.

Another bang, another moment where the ambulance belonged not to Elise but to itself, another correction and control regained and still they were travelling on, Elise wanting to get to Tunstall's now, to get out of the ambulance and into light and company. Feathers drifted around the cab, dancing and spinning, as she pressed down on the accelerator, urging the vehicle to gather up the road and loose it out behind them, now sure that the problem wasn't the ambulance or its engine but whoever was in the ambulance's rear, *whatever* was in the ambulance's rear.

She risked a glimpse behind her. As she turned, there was a long cracking noise and the unmistakeable sound of wood splintering and something falling, the vibration of it rattling through the floor, heavy against her feet. There was a dash of pale movement in the slit, a pallid shape that rose behind the pane and then fell again, not a hand or a face but something indefinable, as though it was wrapped in linen or muslin.

The engine cut out as Elise jerked back from the glass, reaching out to turn the key even though she was still coasting forward, gears in neutral and nothing, nothing, no reaction from the ambulance except to slow and slow, inertia and the slope bringing it to a halt soon, too soon. The internal lights clicked off with a sound like a gunshot, the dashboard's glimmer suddenly extinguished. She put the handbrake on, ignoring the increasingly loud, repeating sound of flapping behind her, not looking at the glass, not looking at whatever might be peering through at her, turning the key again and again trying to start the vehicle. And then the thing with the head like a dog seated next to her turned and drew back lips from teeth that were huge and which were the colour of old, tarnished ivory. She shrieked and jerked back from it, fumbling for the handle and opening the door and falling out into the road a single frenzied jumble of flail and cry. Her shoulder struck the gritted concrete and an off-colour bolt of pain leapt through her upper body and she cried out again, helpless.

A series of taps and shudders ran through the vehicle, tiny vibrations that she could hardly see, visible only as a shiver against the distant night. Feathers, more feathers than she had ever seen before, more than could have possibly been in the bag, drifted out after her, curling and circling in thick clouds, floating upwards instead of down, rising on breezes Elise could not feel. There was another bang, this from the centre of the ambulance, as though something had struck the partition between the space of the dead and the space of the living, then the long drawn-out groan of something opening and the unmistakeable sound of coins falling into a dish or cup.

For a moment Elise had the terrible sense of having offended something vast and old and she screamed, a wordless apology wrenching out of her. In the now-dark cab of the ambulance, the dog-headed thing shook its head and grinned and held its arms out, and from all around her she heard the sound of beating wings.

PRIYA SHARMA

THE RISING TIDE

Everything's wide at Newgale; the beach, the sky, but it's water that draws me. The sea goes on for miles.

The rising tide comes in, chasing and baiting. I scream at it, but it doesn't help. I still feel dead. The crash of the waves swallows up the sound.

I wander. Further up the beach are surfers who look as sleek as seals, dressed in neoprene as they brave the breakers. How free they must feel.

A figure walks towards me. A girl, with a dog that turns in circles around her. The animal crouches, belly to the ground, waiting for her to hurl the ball she's carrying. When she does the dog's off like a shot, making ripples and splashes on the water glistening on the sand.

Closer, and I see the girl more clearly. The sight of her shocks me to a stop. Her black hair streams out behind her in the wind. The girl's mouthing something. I think it's my name. Her dog bounds up to me, sniffing and licking, keen to be acquainted.

"Get down, you brute." She catches the dog's collar and hauls him back. "I'm so sorry."

I try to speak but my throat is tight. I'm choking on emotions that I can't swallow.

"Jessica?" The word comes out, faint and strangled.

It's not Jessica. There's no way it could be her. Not here. Not now. This isn't a teenager but a woman with straight, brunette hair, not Jessica's lively black curls.

"Are you okay?" The woman puts the dog on its leash. "Can I do anything to help you?"

I shake my head, tear stricken and mute. She lingers for a moment, looking awkward and uncertain, and I have to turn my back on her to make her go away.

"Have a seat."

My GP ushered me in. Pictures of children that I presumed were hers hung over her desk. There was the overwhelming odour of air freshener as if she'd sprayed away her last patient.

I explained why I'd come. She passed me a box of tissues when I started to cry.

"It sounds like a terrible situation for everyone." Her vague tone made me think that, having listened to my tale, she'd already apportioned blame. "What's your mood like?"

She asked me the standard questions relating to my malady; poor sleep, inability to eat, mounting anxiety and loss of pleasure.

"Any thoughts of suicide?" She clutched the string of bright beads around her neck.

"No," I lied.

I'd thought about getting on a train and running away. I'd thought about throwing myself under one.

"Could you fill this in for me?" It was a formal depression questionnaire. The modern NHS requires that everything be quantified, even misery.

She totted up my score.

"Right, I think we should start antidepressants." She was brisk. The use of 'we' gave the process an illusion of democracy.

"Yes."

"Citalopram, twenty milligrams a day," she said.

Citalopram, a drug to keep my serotonin circulating. To bathe my brain in this happy chemical and make me well again. Or functional, at least.

"Do you need to see a counsellor?"

I shake my head.

"I'll write you a sick note."

"I can't go off sick."

"Nonsense. You're not well enough to work."

"I can manage."

"It's not just about you." She uncapped her pen. "It's about patient safety too. You need a clear head."

Patient safety. That stung, as it revealed what she, and everyone else, must have really thought of me.

Arosfa's the name of the hut that stands on the top of Treffgarne hill, near Lion's Rock, within sight of a cluster of houses and church that comprise the village.

Arosfa. An apt name given by my father. It means 'remain here'. That's all I want. To stay here and never have to face the world again. It's all I have left of Dad. We'd come here at weekends. He'd shrug off his overalls and roam as if set free. We'd walk and talk all day. I'd go with Dad while he went about his real vocation; a cleansing or a healing ritual.

Now Arosfa's windows are dirty and the floor unswept. Dad would be upset to see it so neglected.

When I get back from Newgale, the door's ajar. I stand, listening, sure that I'd locked it before I left. There are no signs that it's been forced. I push the door open. No one's there but I have the feeling of being only seconds too late to see who was standing there.

Nothing. Nothing but the stained and faded curtains, made in exchange for Dad's shingle cure, which hang in the window. Dad's empty whisky bottles, thick with dust, line the shelves. Each one was payment for a divination or a charm. His books are swollen with damp but look undisturbed. Piles of my clothes are left where I dropped them. Dirty cups and plates are all over the place. I should clean up.

Then I see the wet patches that stain the floorboards, making them darker. Footprints. Not the outline of shoes but heels and toes, fainter along the arches where the curve lifts away. I put my foot alongside them. The intruder's feet are smaller than mine.

My mobile's flashing at me. I've got a missed call.

"Cariad? It's Tom." There's a pause. There's a hard edge to his voice, like he's daring me to be furious at him for his defiance. "I know you said not to call but we need to talk. About the girl. About us."

The last thing I want to do is talk.

"Let me know you're okay, even if you don't want to see me."

More silence.

"Let me help you. You don't have to go through this alone." His anger rises. "The thing is, I love you. And I think you love me."

I wish he'd said it before Jessica. I wish I'd said it back. Not just because I'm too ashamed to face him now but because depression's a dark hole where no light goes. Your dearest wish becomes as inconsequential as crumbs.

I don't deserve Tom.

"Cariad, please . . ."

I turn off the phone, cutting him off mid-sentence.

I had met Tom on the first day of my new job in the Casualty department of Bronglais General Hospital, Aberystwyth. It was a new speciality to me, a new hospital and a new town. My orientation session had been curtailed after half an hour due to the department being busier than normal so I had no idea where anything was or who to ask for what. The staff were a hard, sardonic lot.

"Maria, would you mind looking at this x-ray?" I asked. Dr Maria Callaghan, registrar, was our supervisor. "This bloke hurt his shoulder. I'm not sure if there's a hairline break of his . . ."

"Posterior or anterior?"

"Sorry?"

"What did they teach you at medical school? The force of injury," she enunciated each word, "was it posteriorly or anteriorly?"

"Oh, anterior. Head on tackle."

She slapped the film onto a light box.

"No fracture. No dislocation."

Then she walked off.

I could feel the blotchy flush breaking out on my chest and face, the redness a beacon of upset, anger or embarrassment.

"Hey, don't let her get to you. I'm Ellen." Her badge said Nurse Practitioner. "Or, don't let her see when she does. If you need help, come and ask me."

If Maria was bad, the paramedics were worse. It takes a certain sort to survive the forefront of the frontline.

"We need you in our ambulance, now." A paramedic stopped me in the corridor. "I can't tell whether this guy's dead or not."

He ran out to his domain, parked in the ambulance bay. I followed thinking how badly hurt is this man, that they're not bringing him inside? Were they expecting me to perform heroics, such as a chest drain or tracheostomy?

We got into the back of the ambulance.

"What do you think, love? Will he make it?" The paramedic roared with laughter.

The man on the trolley stared at me with a blank eye. The other side of his head was a nebulous hole full of crushed eye, shards of skull and macerated brain.

The door opened and a second paramedic addressed us.

"Piss off, Glynn. Let her alone."

I should've told Glynn to piss off myself but my mouth was too dry. Not that I was squeamish but it was surreal. I'd never seen a human head so decimated.

Glynn got out, still giggling, and the other man climbed in and closed the door.

"Sorry about him. I'm Tom." I must have looked particularly stupid because he asked if I knew how to verify a death. "I mean, you might as well do it now that you're here."

I nodded. Of course I did, but before Casualty I'd worked on a ward for the elderly where death occurred in bed or on the toilet.

"What happened to him?"

"Tyre blew out and he hit a tree at high speed. Poor lad didn't stand a chance."

Tom was tall. He stood back, not crowding me like Glynn had.

I checked the body, a pointless exercise to formalise the obvious. No heartbeat, no breath sounds, no pain response, the lone pupil fixed and dilated. Rest in peace.

"What's the C stand for Dr Evans?" Tom asked when I handed the form back to him.

"Cariad." Meaning darling, dearest.

"And are you?"

"What?"

"Beloved."

I scowled at him. It was only later that I realised he was flirting with me.

I reinforce Arosfa's door with bolts from a shop in Haverford-west. When I wake the next morning the light's mean and thin, unable to reach the corners of the room. The crows caw from the trees.

I get up and brush my teeth at the sink, not bothering to clear it of dirty dishes. I use bottled water as what's coming from the tap is brackish. I should get the electricity reconnected. It would be better than camping lanterns and torches.

I sit outside on the stone bench, wearing a jumper and coat over my pyjamas. The foil strip crackles as I pop out an antidepressant. I wonder what Dad would say about it as I swallow the pill.

Physician, heal thyself.

I remember lying on the camp bed in the dark. I was sixteen. Across Arosfa there was silence instead of Dad's breathing from the depth of dreaming. I looked at my watch. The luminous hands told me it was two in the morning.

"Dad?"

He was outside. There was no light pollution to nullify the night and hide the stars.

"Why are you up, Cariad?" Dad took off his jacket and put it around me. He took a slug from his bottle of whisky. "Are you okay, chick?"

"Yes."

He touched the curve of my cheek where there was a bruise.

"Are you going to tell me then?"

"You've heard it all already."

"Yes, I've heard it from everyone. Just not you. Cariad, you're not one for scrapping. What made you go at that girl like that?"

"I hate her."

"I don't recall bringing you up to hate people. It's bad to wish ill on others. The universe will send it back to you, ten fold."

I scowled.

"What did she say to get you so riled?"

"She said . . ." I struggled to say it. "She said that you were a piss artist that sold crap and empty promises."

"I've had worse said about me." I shot an angry look at him as he laughed. "I'm sorry." He nudged me. "Think about it. She didn't say that, Cariad. Emily Appleton's never had an original thought in her life. That's her dad talking. We've always agreed to ignore stuff like this. Why did you get so upset?"

"I just did."

He took a deep breath. I'd never spoken to him in that tone before.

"Cariad," he said slowly, "I think that you got so upset because you think she's right." Dad was wily. "It's okay, you know. Don't cry. This is how life works. You've got to find your own way."

"I'm not rejecting you." I wiped my face.

"When did you get so wise?" He laughed. "Will you promise me something?"

"What?"

"Keep a door open here, for possibilities." He tapped my forehead. "Don't close your mind to the idea that beneath what we know there's a whole world that we can only guess at. There are things in life that we know that we don't understand. The real danger is the stuff in the blind spot that we don't even know exists."

"That's a riddle."

"It's the long way of saying that what you don't know about is what bites you in the butt."

"Sorry to keep you waiting."

I'd been seeing my GP for four months. I felt like she was sick of me. Or maybe I was sick of her. Or sick of still feeling the same.

"How are you?"

She was an expert in communication, having had special training. She knew exactly how to tell me that she didn't have much time without saying it aloud. Her gaze kept darting to her computer screen.

"Improved." I cut things short, knowing it was what she wanted to hear.

"Are you less tearful than last time?"

"Yes." That was true. I'd gone beyond crying.

"Are you sleeping?"

I nodded. I slept through afternoons, having spent the night lying awake. Two in the morning was the hardest time. The drowning hour where misery was at its deepest.

"Any idea when the inquest will be?"

"Not yet."

The thought was terrifying. I didn't want to face the family's anger and the Coroner's inquisition.

"Cariad," her face softened, "I'm not trying to rush you back to work but the longer you're off, the harder going back will be. When do you think you'll be ready to get back in the saddle?"

This from a woman who looked like she'd never fallen off the horse.

"Soon. Just not yet. I need a bit more time."

Before I hadn't wanted time off. Now I couldn't face going back.

"What will you do with yourself?"

"I'll go to my Dad's." I didn't mention that Dad was dead.

"Where's that?"

"Near Haverfordwest."

I wanted to be away. To leave Aberystwyth and drive along the blue of Cardigan Bay, past the painted houses of Aberaeron. I knew I was nearly at the Landsker line and home when I reached the Preseli Hills, whose blue stone made the inexplicable two hundred and fifty mile journey to the Salisbury Plain for the building of Stonehenge. The beautiful Preselis, whose hollows fill up with sun by day and at night the mist pours itself onto the road.

My GP's nails were bare but elegantly shaped, at the end of tapered fingers. I looked at her hands as she signed the sick note because I couldn't bear to look her in the face.

I sat beside Maria at the workstation, both of us writing in patients' records. She broke the silence. "You get upset easily, don't you Cariad?"

Any opportunity to undermine me.

"Do I?"

I tried not to sound defensive but I was strung out from self-doubt, stretched thin as an onion skin by the line of patients that never seemed to lessen. Sometimes I felt there was a whole wave of them about to crash down on me. Their fear made me fraught, as did their anger at being kept waiting. Waiting to be seen, waiting for test results, waiting for another doctor to come when a senior's opinion was needed.

"Yes, you should watch that," Maria continued. "Being too emotional is how you make mistakes. And you'll do no good trying to be everyone's friend. The nurses all tell me how caring you are, which is all very well, but it's only part of the job."

There was me, thinking it was the very essence of our vocation.

"Cariad, I'm not saying this to be hurtful. I'm trying to be supportive." Like all good bullies she knew how to couch her comments so as to avoid reprisal.

"Hello, my beauties." Glynn tapped the desk, the oily rag of a man eager for attention. "Which one of you is taking me out later?"

Tom hung back. We shared a smile that contained all that had passed between us. When I looked away, Maria was staring at me, unhappy with what she'd seen.

The cliffs at Newgale are covered in sporadic patches of gorse, some of it bearing yellow blooms. When gorse goes out of flower, love goes out of fashion. Another piece of Dad's wisdom. The cliff face is spotted with pink thrift and white sea campion. The rock itself is layers of different coloured stripes, marking time's strata. This is what we are. Layers of history, one event laid down upon another. We are less consequential than sediment.

The tide has carved out caves. We imagine that we can do what stone can't; that we can hold back the rising tide and remain whole and unaffected. So much for my grandiose plans of helping people. I can't even help myself.

I squat in one of the caves. It smells of rocks and salt. I've come armed with one of Dad's empty whisky bottles. I half fill it with pebbles and then say her name over and over, Jessica, Jessica, into the bottle's mouth. I pray her in and then screw the cap on. I'm not sure if I've recalled it as Dad taught me. This was his legacy, this knowledge that's so at odds with everything else about me. I wish I'd listened more when Dad talked.

The match flares in the cave's cold shade and I hold a candle in the flame, letting wax drip around the bottle top to seal it.

I'll contain Jessica this way. I wade out into the cold water. The tide dragging at my thighs threatens to drag me down. I've not got a good throwing arm but I cast the bottle out as far as I can. It lands with a splash and then it's gone.

I'd been working at Bronglais General for five months when I first met Jessica.

Saturdays were the worst. Inebriated brawlers and the hopeless attempting suicide were heaped upon victims of heart attacks and strokes. They threatened to overwhelm me. No matter how much I studied, I never knew enough. No matter how hard I worked, I couldn't keep up.

The girl in the cubicle was wrapped in a blanket. Her dark curls were stiff with brine. The woman that fussed over her was striking too. Like the girl, she had a beaked nose and black eyes but her hair was unruly and streaked with grey. She was taller, scrawnier, and her long black coat flapped around her as she moved.

"Hello Jessica." I read her name from the casualty card. "I'm Dr Evans. Are you Jessica's mum?"

The tall woman nodded. She hovered over me in a mix of anxiety and threat that I read as 'Look after my girl'.

"What happened to you, Jessica?"

"I nearly drowned."

"How?"

"My dog went into the water. We were on the beach." She smiled, rueful. "I went in after him and we got caught in a big wave."

"She was lucky," her mother's mouth became a thin line. "A group of lads were body boarding and one of them was close enough to reach her."

"How long were you in the water?"

"I don't know. It felt like forever."

"I'll bet. Did you black out at all?"

"No."

"Good. You must've been terrified."

Her mother started to cry. I envied Jessica that maternal love.

"I'm okay, Mum. Don't fuss."

I checked Jessica's chart. Her pulse and blood pressure were normal and she wasn't hypothermic.

"Come on, Jessica. Let's check you out."

She looked at me with admiring shyness, hesitating as if she wanted to say something. I paused, encouraging her to speak.

"I'm going into lower sixth in September. I want to study Medicine when I finish."

"Then we might work together one day. What do you think about that?"

I put my stethoscope to Jessica's chest and listened to the steady *lub-dub* of her heart as her atria and ventricles contracted in turn. Her lungs inflated normally, a healthy pair of bellows.

"Everything seems fine," I said. "How's the dog?"

"Damn the dog," her mother spat. "Leave the bloody thing to drown next time."

"He swam to shore in the end. Mum's friend took him to the vet."

The curtain twitched.

"Excuse me." Ellen pulled me from the cubicle. "Maria wants everyone in the resus bay now. There's been a pile up."

"One second," I told Ellen and went back in. "Sorry about that. Your chest x-ray is normal, Jessica. I think you're okay to go home. If you feel short of breath or get chest pains, a cough or fever, then we need to see you again."

I remember thinking, at that moment, that I'd hit my stride. My confidence was growing. I was finally playing my part.

"Are you sure?" her mother asked. "The vet's keeping the dog in for observation."

To which I replied, "Don't worry, Jessica will be fine."

Painful thoughts. They gnaw.

Everything's magnified by the unflinching lens of two am, my every defect, fuck up and misstep that obliterates any modest successes.

Then, of course, there's the one act that negates everything. Even when I close my eyes, it's there.

I get up, sliding from my sleeping bag. When I put my feet down, they land in a cold puddle on the floor. I'll check that the roof's sound in the morning. Not that it matters. Damp permeates everything. It's in the walls. It's gathered on the window. Everything smells dank.

When I go outside the night's murky. A gusty wind makes the low mist twist and swirl around me. It softens and blurs the lights of the houses. I need to pee but can't bear the idea of going to the *ty-dach*, the little house. The toilet drops into the neglected septic tank that's now rank. I don't want to be alone in there. Ivy has insinuated itself through the wall panels and crept up the inside. I walk out into the middle of the field instead.

Wet grass brushes my legs as I squat and relieve myself. Steam rises. A chill goes up my back which makes me feel exposed. There's a dense fog, blowing in fast over the hill. I'm vulnerable, unable to run and overcome by the idea that I'm going to die out here, knickers around my ankles, urine running down my leg.

I glance over my shoulder, wondering at the fullness of my bladder. The fog eddies and whirls in the wind, making shapes too fleeting for me to focus on.

My stream slows to a trickle. I hear something behind me, higher pitched than the hoot of an owl. I look back again, pulling up my pyjama bottoms. A black shadow is in the fog's depths. Something's coming out of the night.

It's taking shape, pulling itself together from pieces of darkness. It looks like a long legged figure with straggly hair. A raven of a woman. Her long coat flaps around her. She's covering the ground between us in great strides.

It's the *Gwrach-y-Rhibyn*. The Hag in the Mist. She's a death omen.

I run. As I near Arosfa I hear a shriek and I stumble. My mistake is looking back. The hag's in flight, her coat transformed into great wings. I try and scramble to my feet but my trembling legs collapse and because of this she passes over me with a shrill scream of frustration that her clawed hands are empty.

She's circling but it's enough time for me to get to Arosfa. I slam the door behind me, lock it and throw the bolts. The hag hits the door with a thud. I upturn the table and put it against the door and then sit on the opposite side of the room. I can hear a strange fluttering sound, as if she's hovering outside.

How long the night is. The wind picks up, rattling the roof. The hag taunts me. Just when I think she's gone, there's a sudden slapping sound against the door or one of the walls, followed by a flap, flap, flap as she prowls around Arosfa, trying to get in. I drag the bed to the centre of the room and sit with my legs drawn up and my arms wrapped around them.

Around dawn the wind drops and everything's quiet. I think the hag's gone. I doze off for an hour and then wake with puffy, swollen eyes. I pull the curtains and the clarity of the morning light mocks me, as does the torn black bin liner lying on Arosfa's step when I open the door.

Jessica was rushed in the night after I saw her. Glynn pushed the trolley. Tom worked on her as they went.

"Bleep the crash team. Now."

Jessica's skin was white, her lips cyanosis blue. The rhythms of resuscitation failed to rouse her. I stood trembling instead of piling in and helping. I couldn't even muster the basic primer for survival. The ABC of airway, breathing and circulation.

Her mother stood by, her gangly limbs impotent as they hung by her side. We looked at one another.

"What's happened to Jessica?"

"She said she couldn't breathe. By the time the ambulance arrived, she'd collapsed."

More doctors and nurses ran in, answering the call. Ellen pulled the curtain across the bay so that Jessica's mother wouldn't have to witness the indignities required to save a life.

"We need to help Jessica now," Ellen spoke to her mum. "Go

with Jamie and he'll get you a cup of tea. I'll come and get you when there's news."

"I want to stay."

"Let them help her." Jamie put an arm around her, gentle and insistent. He was the best member of staff at calming relatives and breaking bad news. "We'll only be around the corner when she needs you."

There were enough people with Jessica, I told myself. I'd just be in the way.

Maria found me later, in the staff toilets. She stood beside me as I washed my hands, removing smudged mascara with her little finger. She watched me in the mirror.

"You saw her yesterday, didn't you?" She didn't need to explain who she was talking about.

"Yes. How is she?"

"It doesn't look good. She went into the sea, right?"

"She was fine yesterday. Her chest x-ray was normal. I don't understand."

"Secondary drowning." She uncapped her lipstick and applied the coral bullet to her mouth. It was as though she was suddenly talking under water. I had to concentrate on the movements of her lips. I must've looked blank because she started to explain. "The surfactant that keeps the lungs open gets stripped off the lungs by sea water. Drowning follows within twenty-four hours."

Maria didn't need to tell me. I'd read about it, briefly. Without surfactant, her lungs had collapsed and she'd starved of oxygen. So Jessica had drowned on dry land.

"What were her blood gases like?" Maria tied her hair up in a knot. "That's the crucial bit."

Blood gases. A special measurement to check the gas profile in the blood. As soon as she said it I knew the yawning truth was that I hadn't done it. I didn't know I should have. Like my dad said, the most dangerous kind of ignorance isn't what we know that we don't know but what we have no inkling of.

Which is a long way of saying that what you don't know about is what bites you in the butt.

I wake from fitful sleep with a start. It's dark. The mattress is sodden with water that's level with the bed. I turn on my camping lantern but it doesn't reveal where the water's coming in.

This isn't a leak. It's pouring down all four walls, flooding in faster than it can drain out.

I wade through the water that's up to my thighs, lighting the lanterns as I go. I unlock the door but the top bolt won't budge. It looks clogged up with decades of rust, not shiny and clean as it had been when fitted only a few days ago. I get down, soaking myself, trying to force the bottom bolt but this is stuck too. I shoulder the door in frustration but all I get for my efforts is a jarring pain from shoulder to elbow.

I try and smash the window over the sink with a chair but it's reinforced with wire mesh. Sodden, I haul myself up onto the narrow draining board which creaks under my weight. I try and kick the glass out, not caring about my bare feet, without success.

Stop. Be calm. I find my mobile by the bed but it's too wet to summon help. What else? Preserve the light, move the lanterns to higher places to keep them dry. My waterproof torch is in my bag. I put its loop around my wrist.

The empty kettle floats. Plastic beakers and melamine plates bob past me. I'm flotsam and jetsam too. The room's filling up fast. I have to tread water.

Outside there's a frenzied barking. I shout, a waterlogged sound, hoping some nocturnal dog walker will hear me, but no.

The lanterns are submerged one by one. They glow momentarily making a ball of watery light, then they flicker and go out. Darkness magnifies the water's sound, the rush that's filling Arosfa up.

I turn on the torch. The white arc swings about, illuminating choppy water and the pale face in the corner.

Water's treacherous. It's brought Jessica to me. She's been baptised and now she's reborn. Her hair's plastered to her scalp. Her lips are dusky, her skin translucent and mottled from being submerged too long. Her neck and shoulders are bare. She glows, as if lit from within. Jessica opens her mouth and pebbles fall out. The bottle that I cast into the sea floats between us. The bottle top has been smashed off. Red wax still clings to the broken bottle's neck.

Jessica dips beneath the surface.

Fear's energising. I scream and thrash. Water slops into my mouth, drowning my shout. I taste brine, brine up here on Treffgarne hill.

There's churning, as if deep, vast undercurrents are about to pull me down. I feel a sharp tug at my pyjama leg. I kick out. Then Jessica yanks me down. I lose the torch in a panic. The beam of shrinking light descends.

Jessica's hand is clamped around my ankle as we follow the light into the depths. I might as well be out at open sea. Just when I think my chest will explode, she lets me go. I break the surface as if catapulted up, gasping and coughing. Waves buffet me about.

It's not mercy on Jessica's part. She's toying with me. This time I can feel her full weight, both arms around my calves like a clinging child. For someone so slight she's like a plummeting anchor taking me to the ocean floor.

This time we go further into the inky water. It doesn't make sense; we're too deep to be within Arosfa. It must be oxygen deprivation making me disorientated. I start to panic and struggle even more, desperate to inhale, even if it's just saltwater.

Jessica grants me another reprieve. Air has never seemed so sweet. I surface with aching lungs but all I can manage are shallow breaths. Not that there's much air left, only a few inches between the water level and the roof. I have to tip my head back to keep my mouth and nose clear.

It's not over though. Jessica comes up in front of me. I take a deep breath and tip my head so that I can keep her in sight. Her eyes are empty, like everything's been poured out of her. Her arms slide around me, like a lover's, her legs twine about mine. She's a dead weight. We sink like a stone.

The sea is vast. I'm weary of the struggle. I want to give in but the fear is physiological, my cells fighting to save themselves. The pain is surprising.

Then it comes. I have to gasp. I'm stunned as cold water floods my lungs, freezing me from within. Bubbles escape from my nose and mouth. Stars explode at the periphery of my vision.

Jessica releases me, which makes me sad because it's now that I want someone to hold me. I drift.

Being lost brings me a contrary clarity. My life returns to me. Mum, when she was still alive. It was dusk and I was in the garden of the cottage at Molleston, watching her as she stood at the sink. She looked up and saw me, giving me a broad smile.

I remember the afternoon sun sliding around a classroom. The algebraic symbols scrawled on the board finally rearranged themselves from a jumble into something I understood. In that moment I had the joy of intuition, of a knowledge as complex as my father's, and it thrilled me because it was mine.

I remember kissing Tom in a darkened room that was washed by the light of a mute television. Kissing him until my mouth felt bruised and swollen.

And Jessica's sweet, trusting smile.

The last bubbles escape into blackness.

Down at Newgale beach the sea is wide and the tide carries on rising.

STEPHEN LAWS

THE SLISTA

Y OU MUST BE gud, says Svival. You must be gud, or The Slista
will come get you.

Svival has been a-telling us about The Slista long as we can
member. It is the only thing what we are fright about. No thing
other has us a-fright. Not the hair-things I done found called rats
now, which can bite and go scratcsh but taste good. Not the all
kinds Big Noyse that go past window of our under-the-ground
place in the Big Howse. Not the sky thunders, not nothing else. But
The Slista – this is the big scare thing.

Svival told us long tyme that we are all safe here in the underground place where no one go. No one no we here – the five of
us. We are the famly – me, and my name is Critch (which now I
can rite when I been looking at story-book brung down once by
Svival). Then there is Kate, who is next down from me. Then Morris, he boy. Then Declin and True. One time there was six – but
Kenny come out of Kate very little small and he not good with
noyses. No noyse be made when peepuls come. That is why we
be safe all tyme. So Svival, he come down from up the-stare-place
very a-noyed and Kenny not make noyse no more and we not need
rats for long tyme. Svival say – no noyse, or peepuls here and tell

The Slista. It come home and taken all us away to Bad Place away from under-ground place. So, shhhhhhh.

We all have the Big Love here in dark. We all brothers (that is word in book) and sisters (that is also word in book). We strong but all different. Kate has fingers gud for tear-up. Morris, he fast and move no hearing noyses. Declin, eyes that see thru and tell all. True, go on up-wall to (ceiling) – that word from book. True, teeth long and sharp for byting. Me, all kinds things. But me Big One and love and keep all.

Then one day, Svival come down say listen. We listen, and there are noyses coming up with his voyce. Wet noyses. His two eyes wet and I say Svival, what is rong? He sit bump on wood stare and say You all must listen. We listen, and he say I am going sleep and no wake lyke Kenny. Morris make wet eyes, but Svival say no, no, no and no! I have been telling many tymes that all sleep long tyme but go Happy Place, isn't that right? Morris make eyes dry, and we say yes Svival we always reddy for long sleep and not being sad becoz you said. Svival nod and say yes, yes, you must let me go to Long Tyme Sleeping Place and you must all leave the Big Love in the Downstares Dark. Go out and find different Big Love in the Downstares Dark. There are lots of them. One will be waiting some-wheres for you. So you will find it.

Why asks True? Why Svival, if you go to Long Tyme Sleeping Place we no stay in the Big Love here? Becoz, says Svival – and you must not be feared – I must go to Long Tyme Sleeping Place very soon and The Slista will come.

Now we are a-fright, but Svival say No! Do not be a-fright! The Slista will come in the Big Car (You member Big Car what you seen thru little looking-place?) We say yes, Svival – we member Big Car. Well, say Svival – he come in Big Car and find me in Long Tyme Sleeping Place and he say Good, now I will eat Svival and take away Big Howse. But you will be gone-way to diffrint place and he will not be finding any of Svival's Lovelies.

How can The Slista be doing these things, we ask? Svival say The Slista come from Big Place called Offis or Offises, with Magic

Papers that have Magic Words that can take happy places and happy peepuls lyke us away frever.

We all ask – What must we do, Svival? Be gone away, be gone away, says Svival. And member all things I been telling you since little tymes. Look after you and yous all. Pro-tect and keep the Big Love.   These are the Rules of Svival, he says.

And then he is gone to Long Tyme Sleeping Place there on the wood stare. And at same tyme, with no tyme for the wet eyes, True says listen there is noyse of the Big Car out-side. We go run little looking place and yes there is Big Car. Do not be a-fright I say when Man in Black Cloth-rap stuff get out Big Car and come with skware bag. But I am a-fright insyde, becoz this is The Slista and skware bag will have Magic Papers and Magic Words. But also and but – I am Big One for love and keep all and I am now new Svival becoz old Svival is now gone to Long Tyme Sleeping Place. So I must be the Big Up.

Morris, I say, be fast and go to the up-the-stare place and be make no noyse. Declin, I say, go all-so and open the Ding-Dong Door when go Ding-Dong, then hide up on hi place. True, I say, you go other too – and up on up-wall (ceiling) for to wait. When Ding-Dong Door go Ding-Dong – I will be speaking with Svival voice and I will say: Cum in wy doanchoo? (Lyke we heer befor lots of tymes). My Svival voice better coz is rumbler than other Lovelies. Kate, I say, be reddy with fingers. True, I say, also to be reddy with the byting.   We go and we are been reddy.

Ding-Dong says the Ding-Dong Door.

So now we are been going away from the Old Big Love under-the-ground Old Place and – just lyke the old Svival sayed – we are finding the New Big Love under-the-ground New Place and we are reddy to come into it. When the peepuls who are in the up-the-stares don't see, me and the Lovelies will come into it and be new Happy.

They are wanting me to keep old name Critch, but I say oh no, oh no, I will be now the new Svival not the old Critch. Becoz that is the job of the oldest to do, and they say oh all-ryte, yes then are glad. But I am gud in-side because they love me as the Old Critch and will love me as the new Svival.

Svival was kind to us and I will be kind to them. This is the Laws of Svival, member?

I will be kind and we will be warm and happy and hirt ennyone what will want harm us. We will eat nyce things all tyme. Nycer and nycer things. And when Long Sleep will come for me then Kate will be new Svival after me – and we will be going on. I lyke thinking when I go Long Tyme Sleeping Place, they will be eet of me and I will be of them hear in bodees and of them in Long Tyme Sleeping Place also.

Happy lyke when we eet Old Svival.

But not Happy lyke when we eet The Slista.

He not tasting nyce.

Not nyce, at all.

REECE SHEARSMITH

DOG

I HAVE NEVER LIKED dogs. I find them dirty and stupid and totally worthless. I don't understand the mind of anyone that has a dog. How can you possibly find time to care for it? Let it stink out your home? Walk alongside it, scooping up its hot shit off the pavement and grass? "Let's go for a lovely walk . . . oh, don't forget the little plastic bag to scoop up the endless shit that this creature is going to squeeze out along the way." Never mind about the piss. It can piss anywhere it likes. I know that you are thinking that I sound unreasonable. People are very protective of these idiot creatures. I find it bizarre. They are of no value. I have no time for dog owners and their beasts.

I suppose, as an introduction that might be called "setting out my stall", I must at this point explain my position. I am not so deluded to recognise that my views at first may sound extreme; but I must insist that you hear me out. As you will see – it all comes to bear.

From the age of about 11, summer holidays were spent with my grandparents. I would be taken on day trips to the seaside and the stately homes of the North of England. It was a curiously pious way to spend the long stretch between the summer and autumn terms of school. I found nothing odd about it, apart from, of course, the pervading sadness that sullied most of the enforced merriment. Sadness because in the time before I was fostered off to my grandparents I'd had my own two functioning parents and a super little brother who I loved very much. My brother's name was Elliot. I knew him for ten years before he was killed and both my parents went mad with the grief of it. You're probably thinking you have cottoned on to the gist of my tragic tale, and have leapt to the conclusion that my brother was killed by a dog. A dog attack. Mauled and bitten. But that is not what happened. Little Elliot was killed by a dog, yes – but it was ultimately far worse than had he simply been savaged by one. Elliot died of toxocariasis, the disease that hides in dog shit, blinding those that fall foul to it. Thus my brother went blind first. And being blind after having had sight is a hell that I would not wish upon anyone. Except dog owners. For it was dog owners on a day out without, I presume, a little plastic bag about them, that sealed my brother's fate. Elliot was blinded by the disease that lives in dog faeces, and two years after he lost his sight, he was struck down and killed, having wandered sight-lessly into the path of a van delivering cakes . The detail of the cake van is slightly absurd I know, but to mention "Mr Kipling only seems to make it worse.

I heard the accident first. I was in the garden with my parents. Then a screech and a thud. The sound of my brother's death. I re-member hoping selfishly, as time seemed to slow down and swim around me, that it wasn't Elliot. Not for his sake, but for mine. I would be in such trouble if he had been hurt when he was now so much my responsibility. I had been his eyes since the dog shit took his away. It's odd, but up until his actual death, the guilt had always been "Who let him touch the dog shit?", "How did he end up with it in his eyes?" After this – his actual death – there could be no ambiguity about who was to blame. It was me. Ironically enough all because I took my eyes off him. When we ran outside the driver was already out of the van and trying to pull Elliot out from under the front wheels. I remember how upsetting it was to see the man tugging on his limp arms. Even then I thought it was probably wrong to be pulling on him like that, but I think the man was in shock. He was shouting that he hadn't seen him and "There was no time to stop", and even more curiously, "I'm not from round here". The rest is as horrible as you might expect. Rushing and screaming and crying and misery. I hope you didn't think this was going to be anything but nasty. There is no way of wrapping these events up nicely.

So as you can see, my childhood was ruined by a dog. It can be traced back. It is, unfortunately, that simple. The story – if I am actually even telling one (I'm not so sure that I am) – doesn't end there. My brother and his death was one thing. But my revenge – my revenge on the lady that owned the dog, the original dog that blinded my brother – that is another thing.

It must read as unusual, I suppose, to wait so long over such a matter. I can imagine hastier people, once they had a lightning rod singled out for their rage and injustice, just kind of getting on with it. But not me. I waited. Initially I had to, as it wasn't clear, as I have already stated, "Who let him touch the dog shit". It was months of nights alone with my brother, sat in the dark with him, to be at one with him, that I coaxed out of him the exact moment that he came into contact with the disease toxocariasis. We were able to whittle it down – over many months of talking – to an incident in our local park. Strangely enough, now without his sight, Elliot became almost bat-like with his hearing, and his sense of smell was also heightened. Doesn't really do it for me, as far as a trade of the senses. All you really need to be able to do is see. Take smell away if you must. But in this instance, the curious amplification of Elliot's other senses helped us triangulate and hone in on the day he fell in the excrement. The smell overwhelmed him to recall it. I could almost smell it myself. But alongside this was the voice of the owner – a woman, with a shrill high-pitched rather condescending tone – that Elliot was able to recall and ultimately, crucially, recognise again. Elliot remembered the woman berating him more than the dog. "Shuffling around in it like that – you've made an awful mess!" As though Elliot himself were responsible for shitting in the park.

It is an awful feeling when, having done nothing wrong, you start to feel like you are being painted as the "baddie". I began to feel like that after we killed the first dog. Yes, I know I didn't mention it earlier, but it took time to find the right woman and dog responsible. We did in fact get through several until before we uncovered Mrs Lovelever. It was quite fortunate in a way, as quite by accident (and I suppose you could call them "accidents") we were able to hone what we were doing, until we were quite skillful at it. Bear in mind, it was all me really, as Elliot was of little help. He could hardly be used as a "look out". Basically we would sit in the park or I would orchestrate walking alongside dog walkers (after our talks I had narrowed it down to older ladies) and invariably because of his white stick they would always strike up conversation with us. It is insult to injury that the blind are so instantly pitiable. I knew people that would cry just at the sight of Elliot. A small boy, smelling his way through the world, when he should be out climbing trees, playing football or cycling down country lanes. It was a combination of all that AND the tragic wearing of the blacked-out spectacles that left him looking so sad. I always found them so final. The curtain is down. Nothing to see here. No point in pretending that any light will ever get through. All boarded up. After getting the ladies chatting I would ask them about their dog as a way of getting them to talk at length (and they always would) so that Elliot with his bat-like hearing could have a good listen and decide if we were, in fact, in the company of our target. It would never take very long for Elliot to dismiss ones that were definite "no's". It was harder when he wasn't sure. The signal for a "no" was Elliot would give a cough. If he wasn't sure he would remain silent. It used to frighten me when he stayed quiet. My heart would race in the minutes that passed, as it would become more and more possible that we had finally found the person responsible. Sometimes the women would ask Elliot if he wanted to stroke their dog. It was always a queasy moment. We decided that it was always best to say yes. It made the women feel good, like they were giving Elliot purpose for a few seconds. "His miserable life isn't all that miserable today, he touched my dog for thirty seconds and it licked him." Pathetic.

The first time it happened, that Elliot thought we had the right woman, I nearly passed out in fear. My heart was pounding anyway because he hadn't dismissed her with a cough. I think he was unnerved too and he let her say her goodbyes and leave before gasping, "I think that's her." I needed it confirmed immediately.

"Are you sure?"

"I think so. Yes."

When it came to the next step, it felt very much like passing through a door into something you knew would change your life forever. People in normal life don't do what we were doing. Spending, in fact, a LOT of time doing. It was obsessional, but it felt in check because I recognised it was obsessional. When a woman was a distance away, we would wait for her to be separated from her dog (this was before they had those long ball throwers with what looks like an ice cream scoop at the end), so we relied on sticks or balls thrown by hand that would send the dogs running off into the woodland that surrounded the park. Of course it didn't always happen so smoothly. Some never let their dog off the lead, so they were reluctantly abandoned. But it was quite an easy task to get the dog once it was in the woods and simply take it home with us via a footpath through the trees. The owners would be left calling for their mutt from the edge of the green, not realising at that point they were never going to see it again.

Now then. Killing a dog. You won't want to hear this. We did it in the shed, and not always when my parents were out. I don't know why. It did occur to us that there might be noise and barking etc. but I think we felt untouchable. I could always imagine a scenario of being caught, but equally imagine being able to explain it all away. The first one we killed was hard because it was the first one. In actual fact, it should have been easy as it was a very little dog;

one of those that look more like a rat. It never ceases to amaze me
that people spend any time on these creatures, putting red bows on
their heads and stuff. Anyway. Elliot stood in the corner panting;
the dog was running round in circles. I think it was excited because
it was in a new place. It took some courage to even decide how I
was going to kill it, and it was made worse by having to narrate
everything every step of the way for Elliot's benefit. It made it all
very firm and real. I think it might have stayed more in my head,
not having to say it all out loud, if you know what I mean. I pulled
down a hammer, hanging from two nails on the shelf, and braced
myself.

"What have you got? What have you got?" hissed Elliot.
The first strike: I missed it and hit the floor. The dog barked and
growled at my act of aggression. After that point it occurred to
me I might end up bitten, so I quickly thought of something. I
grabbed a hessian garden waste bag that was crumpled up in the
corner and threw it over the dog. It got out from under it quickly
enough, and it took several goes to get it covered and then stand
on the bag either side of the dog, pinning it tight to the ground
underneath. But I did it. It was then much easier to hit the bulge
in the middle of my legs without feeling nearly half so sickened. It
squeaked on the first hit, then kind of whistled, then stopped altogether after about twenty smacks with the hammer. I don't know
why but I started counting the blows out loud, like it was an important part of the process. As if there was a correct number I had
to get to. I suppose I stopped at twenty because it was a round
number. Elliot said, "Is it dead? What does it look like?" and it
was in his asking what it looked like that all remorse or sadness
or upset for what I had just done, completely and utterly disappeared. Fuck this stupid cunt dog. My brother was blind because
of it. It deserved to die. I lifted up the sack. At first I couldn't pull it
away from the mess underneath. I had hit so hard in places that the
material was pushed in and out of the dog and it was mangled. I
stopped bothering in the end and folded the whole thing in on itself
and took it to a bin in the park. I just walked along casually, with

Elliot of course, and put the whole lot in the rubbish like it was nothing.

The realisation that there were flaws in our plan came very quickly. On our way home from the park, after the first killing, we passed a woman talking to a sandy-coloured Labrador and Elliot whispered to me, "Oh God, I think that's her." And thus it began. A spate of dog killings. Each one satisfying in the moment,, but lasting only as long as it took to walk past another possible candidate. Curiously, I never got annoyed about it. Elliot was blind, how was he supposed to know? Ultimately we realised this was going to be a little bit trial and error. Once that was understood, it was actually – and I don't mean for this to sound ghoulish – quite fun. Aside from the fact they were all mistakes in regard to them being the wrong dogs, in our eyes (ha) they weren't – because they were still dogs. We had moved beyond our own feeble search for justice, and our punishment had become far more encompassing. This was about the eradication of a much bigger problem. And so it followed that we began experimenting with different ways to kill dogs. I remember one spate of killings that were purely about how quickly and succinctly it could be done. Finding that "sweet spot" that, with one blow, would kill it instantly. (I had read they kill pigs this way) I never managed it with one, but I think I did do it in three once. Anyway. We once tried to drown one, but it didn't work, it kept getting out and splashed and thrashed most of the water away. And a paddling pool is not the best receptacle to drown an angry dog in fighting for its life. We needed a tin bath really.

Other methods included cutting all the legs off first, then finally the head. This could only be attempted with the more ratty dogs as I previously stated. We tried injecting one using an old icing sugar pipe. Didn't really work. Annoyed, I think we blow torched it with an old aerosol can. Stank the shed out though.

I can't remember when we decided that we had been getting it all wrong and it was the owners of the dogs who were actually to blame and not the dogs themselves. (The irony of this part is that some of you will be less appalled at our killing of the old women than the killing of their stupid fucking dogs.)

I do know when it was, actually: we were sat watching That's Life with Mum and Dad. Cyril had just done a funny limerick, and there was one of the many awkward segues into something more serious from Esther, when she turned her attention (yet again) to some child abuse or other, as was often the way. It was always shocking, but made worse because only moments before we had seen one of the team burst into song at a garden centre and grab a passer-by and made her join in. What I got from this report, which was about cruelty to animals, was that people who owned the animals seemed to be getting the blame. What I didn't get from the report was any pang of guilt that I had been cruel to animals. It never even occurred to me. It just made me shift focus from the animals to the people.

The first old woman (Elliot assured me she was the one) was very sweet really, and accompanied us back to our house without any fuss. I told her that poor, blind Elliot wasn't feeling very well and would she mind seeing that we got home alright. As I have said, people go a little bit weird around blind people – silly really since they are the one set of people that can't see how you are (or are not) behaving, but she readily said of course she would help. Her dog was big. I was secretly pleased we were going to kill her and not it. I wouldn't have known where to begin, but as we walked along I thought, she would easily fit into two rubbish bags. We got to our house and I told her, if she wouldn't mind, to put her dog in the shed, just out of the way, as our mum was allergic. She said of course and once she was in there I grabbed the dog hammer (did I mention it became known as the dog hammer?) and smacked her on the head with it. She was puzzled at first and sort of bent double. This gave me a nice pop at the back of her head which I hit with the claw part and wrenched free, pulling off part of her scalp and a bit of skull, I thought. Anyway, she was easy and it all went well. The annoying part was the "get rid", which took ages as despite being little, she was still bigger than what I'd been used to. I don't remember how many more we killed. I think probably about eleven or twelve. They all merge into one when I think back. There's the odd funny detail: one of them, I remember, her false teeth flew out when I hit her head. I was laughing and Elliot was saying, "What? What's funny about it?" It was ages before I could tell him, I was laughing so much. Another one tried, quite quickly after the first blow, to grab me; she was quite strong. I hit her again and then, as she burbled on the floor, I cut her feet off with a saw. I chopped them off with her shoes still on, but I concede it was done in spite because she had actually managed to scratch me. (I told my mum that I must have done it playing. She didn't care.) I don't know why I did this, but because a lot of them were old, they nearly all wore glasses and so I began keeping them. I had about eight pairs when we finally met Mrs Lovelever.

I knew it was going to be different when, as usual, we sidled up to her and I got her talking. Her dog was a collie dog, which I hated. When she spoke the dog ran off and she shouted in a clipped Barbara Woodhouse voice for it to come back. Elliot went white. I saw the colour drain from his face. I felt sick. He didn't need to say or do any more. I knew this really was her. And that dog – that actual Lassie lookalike dog – was the cause of Elliot being blind. We both stood there for a moment and then I managed to get things back on track. I quickly used Elliot looking awful to ask if she would mind taking us home. At first, because I presumed she was a horrible cow, she might not agree to it, but once again the blind card worked and she came back with us.

It was a long walk home. I wanted to have time to talk to Elliot. I wanted to ask him how he wanted me to do it. Did he have a preference? What had he particularly enjoyed the sound of? As it was, we got home and I did the usual thing of getting her to go to the shed. Elliot stood in the garden, almost too afraid to come in. His new role – since we had just been killing the owners – was to take hold of the dogs on their leads; get them out of the way whilst I did the deed. But he just stood there.

"Come on, Mandy. Inside!"

The old woman barked her order but the dog ran off. Elliot stumbled after it, out of the garden. I told Mrs Lovelever he would bring Mandy back. It occurred to me, once we were standing in the shed, that Mrs Lovelever hadn't recognised the new blind version of Elliot. I couldn't help myself.

"You don't remember my brother, do you?" I said.

"Who?" she said.

"My brother. Elliot. The blind boy we walked home with."

She looked confused and it made me feel incredibly angry. She didn't even have the decency to remember the incident.

"He got your dog's shit on him and he went blind because of it."

It was then that she started trying to leave the shed. I was annoyed that Elliot wasn't there to see it, but of course he wouldn't see it. I grabbed a screwdriver and stabbed her with it. She tumbled back and held the stab wound. After that she couldn't speak. She tried to but all that came out was a kind of low gurgling. It was odd out of an old woman's mouth. I finished her off quite quickly. It was not at all as I had imagined, but it is different when you go through the door. I had learnt that. It's never as you imagine. I think there had simply been too much build up. It was like Christmas or birthdays. It was just over and done and that was that. I killed the dog as well of course. THE dog. I strangled it with wire. When I emerged from that stinking shed, dragging the dead dog on a wire behind me, my mother and father were standing there. There was no sign of Elliot.

They looked at me in disbelief, appalled, I presumed, at the sight of the dead dog. I thought: wait until you see inside the shed!

"Where's Elliot?" I said. That was when we heard it. Screech and thud. The sound of my brother's death. He had run out into the road chasing the very dog that had blinded him in the first place, and was knocked down dead by a Mr Kipling van. Big cherry bakewells pictured on the side.

Both Mrs Lovelever and her dog Mandy survived. I suppose

because an ambulance was called they managed to save her. My brother – not so lucky. I went into a home as I was considered "troubled". I never needed to admit to the other murders of either the dogs or the owners. I just said we wanted revenge and had targeted Mrs Lovelever. It was a "one off". My grandparents looked after me when my parents couldn't bear to look at me anymore. Which I thought fair enough. The day trips they said were to "normalise" me.

It was a long time ago now. I still don't like dogs. It was only recently they told me I never had a brother called Elliot. But that can't be right. I still have his stick and glasses.

REMEMBERING GRAHAM JOYCE

(1954–2014)

2014 brought a devastating blow to the genre. Graham Joyce, one of the greatest storytellers of our age, succumbed to lymphatic cancer. Luckily for us his words remain, what words! If you haven't yet, please seek out his novels which include *The Silent Land*, *The Tooth Fairy* and *Some Kind of Fairy Tale*. These are beautiful books written by a much-loved and missed author.

As tribute, I offer you Graham's 'Under the Pylon', a short story that was originally published in Nicholas Royle's *Darklands 2* (1992). I am honoured that Sue Joyce, Graham's wife, is introducing this mysterious and haunting tale.

JOHNNY MAINS

THIS STORY IS about the magic and mystery surrounding the Indian rope trick, a feat which was advertised in the theatres and music halls of the Victorian period but which apparently was never performed. It was also very much inspired by a pocket of land behind the house where Graham grew up. The gardens of the neighbouring houses all back on to it. Why it wasn't incorporated into these gardens I don't know. Maybe the builder had hoped to squeeze a few more properties onto it at a later date or perhaps it was because it is dominated by a towering electricity pylon.

This patch of scrubby ground served as a playground for the kids from the surrounding houses. It was the venue for impromptu football games, communal bonfire nights and the building of dens. Graham spent happy times there with his friends but was always aware of the menacing presence of the pylon, particularly on rainy days when the cables would buzz and hum.

Another interesting element to this place was the presence of the retired barge people who lived in the house next to the pylon. Graham often talked to the old bargee who built fantastic fully working miniature barges. The legend was that an official from the Coventry museum had heard about these and had tried to buy one but the old man had refused. The family felt that they were looked down on by the neighbours and Graham's dad being the kind soul he is did his best to include them by buying some of the crafts they made (I still have one of their crocheted blankets) and even had their daughter as Godmother to one of Graham's brothers.

For most of us these experiences would be nothing more than pleasant childhood memories but Graham as always was able to see the magic which existed just below the surface and concocted from these elements this wonderful story of magic and menace.

SUE JOYCE

GRAHAM JOYCE

UNDER THE PYLON

Aᶠᵀᵉᴿ ˢᶜᴴᴼᴼᴸ ᴼᴿ during the long summer holidays we used to meet down by the electricity pylon. Though we never went there when the weather was wet because obviously there was no cover. Apart from that the wet power lines would vibrate and hum and throb and it would be . . . well, I'm not saying I was scared but it would give you a bad feeling.

Wet or dry, we'd all been told not to play under the pylon. Our folks had lectured us time and again to keep away; and an Electricity Board disc fixed about nine feet up on the thing spelled out DANGER in red and white lettering. Two lightning shocks either side of the word set it in zigzag speech marks.

'Danger!'

I imagined the voice of the pylon would sound like a robot's speech-box from a science-fiction film, because that's what the pylon looked like, a colossal robot. Four skeletal steel legs straddled the ground, tapering up to a pointed head nudging the clouds. The struts bearing the massive power cables reached over like arms, adding a note of severity and anthropomorphism to the thing. Like someone standing with their hands on their hips. The power cables themselves drooped slightly until picked up by the next giant robot in the field beyond, and then to the next. Marching into the infinite distance, an army of obstinate robots.

But the pylon was situated on a large patch of waste ground between the houses, and when it came down to it, there was nowhere else for us kids to go. It was a green and overgrown little escape-hatch from suburbia. It smelled of wild grass and giant stalks of cow parsley, and of nettles and foxgloves and dumped house-bricks. You could bash down a section to make a lair hidden from everything but the butterflies. Anyway, it wasn't the danger of electricity giving rise to any nervousness under the pylon. It was something else. Old Mrs Nantwich called it a shadow.

Joy Astley was eleven, and already wearing lipstick and make-up you could have peeled off like a mask. Her parents had big mouths and were always bawling. 'The Nantwiches,' she said airily, 'could only afford to buy this house because it's under the pylon. No one wants a house under the pylon.'

'Why not?' said Clive Mann. It was all he ever said. Clive had a metal brace across his teeth. He was odd; he stared at things.

'Because you don't,' said Joy, 'that's why.'

Tania Brown was in my class at school (she used to pronounce her name 'Tarnia' because of the sunshine jokes) and she agreed with Joy. Kev Duffy burped and said, 'Crap!' It was Kev's word for the month. He would use it repeatedly up until the end of August. Joy just looked at Kev and wiggled her head from side to side, as if that somehow dealt with his remark.

The Nantwiches Joy was being so snobbish about were retired barge people. Why anyone would want to rub two pennies together I've never understood, but they were always described as looking as though they couldn't accomplish this dubious feat; and then in the same breath people would always add 'yet they're the people who have got it'.

I doubted it somehow. They'd lived a hard life transporting coal on the barges, and it showed. Their faces had more channels and ruts than the waterways of the Grand Union.

'They're illiterate,' Joy always pointed out whenever they were mentioned. And then she'd add, 'Can't read or write.'

The Nantwiches' house did indeed stand under the shadow of the giant pylon. Mr Nantwich was one of those old guys with a red face and white hair, forever forking over the earth in his backyard. Their garden backed up to the pylon. A creosoted wooden fence closed off one side of the square defined by the structure's four legs. One day when I was there alone old Mrs Nantwich had scared me by popping her head over the fence and saying, 'You don't wanna play there.'

Her face looked as old and green and lichen-ridden as a church gate. Fine bristles sprouted from her chin. Her hair was always drawn back under a headscarf and she wore spectacles with plastic frames and lenses like magnifying glasses. They made her eyes huge, swimming.

She threw her head back slowly and pointed her chin towards the top of the pylon. Then she looked at me and did it again. 'There's a shadow orf of it.'

I felt embarrassed as she stared. She was waiting for me to speak, so I said, 'What do you mean?'

Before she answered another head popped alongside her own. It was her daughter Olive. Olive looked as old as her mother. She had wild, iron-grey hair. Her teeth were terribly blackened and crooked. The thing about Olive was she never uttered a word. She hadn't spoken, according to my mother, since a man had 'jumped out at her from behind a bush'. I didn't see how that could make someone dumb for the rest of their life, but then I didn't understand what my mother meant by that deceptively careful phrase either.

'Wasn't me,' said Mrs Nantwich a little fiercely, 'as decided to come 'ere.' And then her head disappeared back behind the fence, leaving Olive to stare beadily at me as if I'd done something wrong. Then her head too popped out of sight.

I looked up at the wires and they seemed to hum with spiteful merriment.

Another day I came across Clive Mann, crouched under the pylon, and listening. At that time, the three sides of the pylon had been closed off. We'd found some rusty corrugated sheeting to lean against one end, and a few lengths of torn curtain to screen off another. The third side, running up to the Nantwiches' creosoted fence, was shielded by an impenetrable jungle of five-foot-high stinging nettles.

It had been raining, and the curtains sagged badly. I ducked through the gap between them to find Clive crouched and staring directly up into the tower of the pylon. He said nothing.

'What are you doing?'

'You can hear,' he said. 'You can hear what they're saying.'

I looked up and listened. The lines always made an eerie hissing after rain, but there was no other sound.

'Hear what?'

'No! The people. On the telephones. Mrs Astley is talking to the landlord of the Dog and Trumpet. He's knocking her off.'

I looked up again and listened. I knew he wasn't joking because Clive had no sense of humour. Like I said, he just stared at things. I was about to protest that the cables were power lines, not telephone wires, when the curtains parted and Joy Astley came in.

'What are you two doing?'

We didn't answer.

'My Dad says these curtains and things have got to come down,' said Joy.

'Why?'

'He says he doesn't like the idea.'

'What's it got to do with him?'

'He thinks,' Joy said, closing her eyes, 'things go on here.'

'You mean he's worried about what his angelic daughter gets up to,' I said.

Joy turned around, flicked up her skirt and wiggled her bottom at us. It was a gesture too familiar to be of any interest. At least that day she was wearing panties.

I had to pass by the Dog and Trumpet as I walked home later

that afternoon. I noticed Mrs Astley going in by the back door, which was odd because the pub was closed in the afternoons. But I thought little of it at the time.

Just as we became accustomed to Joy flashing her bottom at us, we were well inured to the vague parental unease about us playing under the pylon. None of our parents ever defined the exact nature of their anxieties. They would mention things about electricity and generators, but these didn't add up to much more than old Mrs Nantwich's dark mutterings about a shadow. I got my physics and my science all mixed up as usual, and managed to infect the rest of the group with my store of misapprehensions.

'Radiation,' I announced. 'The reason they're scared is because if there was an accidental power surge feedback . . . ' (I was improvising like mad) 'then we'd all get radiated.'

Radiated. It was a great word. Radiated. It got everyone going.

'There was a woman in the newspaper,' said Joy. 'Her microwave oven went wrong and she was radiated. Her bones all turned to jelly.'

Tania could cap that. 'There was one on television. A woman. She gave birth to a cow with two heads. After being radiated'. The girls were always better at horror stories.

Kev Duffy said, 'Crap!' Then he looked up into the pyramid of the tower and said, 'What's the chances of it happening?'

'Eighteen hundred to one,' I said. With that talent for tossing out utterly bogus statistics I should have gone on to become a politician.

Then they were all looking up, and in the silence you could hear the abacus beads whizzing and clacking in their brains.

Joy's parents needn't have worried. Not much went on behind the pylon screens of which they could disapprove. Well, that's not entirely true, since one or two efforts were made seriously to misbehave, but they never amounted to much. Communal cigarettes were sucked down to their filters, bottles of cider were shared round. Clive and I once tried sniffing Airfix but it made us sick as dogs and we were never attracted to the idea again. We once persuaded Joy to take off her clothes for a dare, which she did; but then she immediately put them back on again, so it all seemed a bit pointless and no more erotic than the episode of solvent abuse.

It was the last summer holiday before we were due to be dispatched to what we all called the Big Schools. It all depended on which side of the waste ground you lived. Joy and Kev were to go to President Kennedy, where you didn't have to wear a school uniform; Clive and I were off to Cardinal Wiseman, where you did. It all seemed so unfair. Tania was being sent to some snooty private school where they wore straw hats in the summer. She hated the idea, but her father was what my old man called one of the nobs.

Once, Tania and I were on our own under the pylon. Tania had long blond hair, and was pretty in a willowy sort of way. Her green eyes always seemed wide open with amazement at the things we'd talk about or at what we'd get up to. She spoke quietly in her rather posh accent, and she always seemed desperately grateful that we didn't exclude her from our activities.

Out of the blue she asked me if I'd ever kissed a girl.

'Loads,' I lied. 'Why?'

'I've never kissed anyone. And now I'm going to a girls' school I'll probably never get the chance.'

We sat on an old door elevated from the grass by a few housebricks. I looked away. The seconds thrummed by. I imagined I heard the wires overhead going chock chock chock.

'Would you like to?' she said softly.

'Like to what?'

'To kiss me?'

I shrugged. 'If you want.' My muscles went as stiff as the board on which we perched.

She moved closer, put her head at an angle and closed her eyes. I looked at her thin lips, leaned over and rested my mouth against hers. We stayed like that for some time, stock-still. The power lines overhead vibrated with noisy impatience. Eventually she opened her eyes and pulled back, blinking at me and licking her lips. I realised my hands were clenched to the side of the board as if it had been a magic carpet hurtling across the sky.

So Tania and I were 'going out'. Our kissing improved slightly, and we got a lot of ribbing from the others, but beyond that, nothing had changed. Because I was going out with Tania, Kev Duffy was considered to be 'going out' with Joy, at least nominally; though to be fair to him, he was elected to this position only because Clive was beyond the pale. Kev resented this status as something of an imposition, though he did go along with the occasional bout of simulated kissing. But when Joy appeared one day sporting livid, gash-crimson lipstick and calling him 'darling' at every turn, he got mad and smudged the stuff all round her face with the ball of his hand. The others pretended not to notice, but I could see she was hurt by it.

Another time I'd been reading something about hypnotism, and Joy decided she wanted to be hypnotised. I'd decided I had a talent for this, so I sat her on the grass inside the pylon while the other three watched. I did all that 'you're feeling very relaxed' stuff and she went under easily; too easily. Then I didn't know what to ask her to do. There was no point asking her to take off her clothes, since she hardly needed prompting to do that.

'Get 'er to run around like a 'eadless chicken,' was Kev's inspirational idea.

'Tell 'er to describe life on Jupiter,' Clive said obscurely.

'Ask her to go back to a past life,' said Tania.

That seemed the most intelligent suggestion, so I offered a few cliched phrases and took her back, back into the mists of time. I was about to ask her what she could see when I felt a thrum of energy. It distracted me for a moment, and I looked up into the apex of the pylon. There was nothing to see, but I remembered I'd felt it before. Once, when I'd first kissed Tania.

When I looked back, there were tears streaming down Joy's face. She was trembling and sobbing in silence.

'Bring her out of it,' said Tania.

'Why?' Give protested.

'Yer,' said Kev. 'Better stop it now.'

I couldn't. I did all that finger clicking rubbish and barked various commands. But she just sat there shaking and sobbing. I was terrified. Tania took hold of her hands and, thankfully, after a while Joy just seemed to come out of it on her own. She was none the worse for the experience, and laughed it off; but she wouldn't tell us what she saw.

They all had a go. Kev wouldn't take it seriously, however, and insisted on staggering around like a stage drunk. Clive claimed to have gone under but we all agreed we couldn't tell the difference.

Finally it was Tania's turn. She was afraid, but Joy dared her. Tania made me promise not to make her experience a past life. I'd read enough about hypnotism to know you can't make people do anything they don't already want to do, but convincing folk of that is another thing. Tania had been frightened by what happened to Joy, so I had to swear on my grandmother's soul and hope to be struck by lightning and so on before she'd let me do it.

Tania went under with equal ease, a feat I've never been able to accomplish since.

'What are you going to get her to do?' Joy wanted to know.

'Pretend to ride a bike?' I suggested lamely.

'Crap,' said Kev. 'Tell her she's the sexiest woman in the world and she wants to make mad passionate love to you.'

Naturally Joy thought this was a good idea, so I put it to Tania. She opened her eyes in a way that made me think she'd just been stringing us along. She smiled at me serenely and shook her head. Then there was a thrum of electrical activity from the wires overhead. I looked up and before I knew what was happening, Tania had jumped on me and locked her legs behind my back. I staggered and fell backwards onto the grass. Tania had her tongue halfway down my throat. I'd heard of French kissing, but it had never appealed. Joy and Kev were laughing, cheering her on.

Tania came up for air, and she was making a weird growling from the back of her throat. Then she power-kissed me again.

'This is great!' whooped Kev.

'Hey!' went Clive. 'Hey!'

'Tiger tiger!' shouted Joy.

I was still pinned under Tania's knees when she sat up and stripped off her white T-shirt in one deft move.

'Bloody hell!' Kev couldn't believe it any more than I could. 'This is brilliant!'

'Gerrem off' screamed Joy.

Tania stood up quickly and hooked her thumbs inside the waist of her denims and her panties, slipping them off. Before I'd had time to blink she was naked. She was breathing hard. Then she was fumbling at my jeans.

'Bloody fucking hell!' Joy shouted. 'Bloody fucking hell!'

The lines overhead thrummed again. Tania had twice my strength. I had this crazy idea she was drawing it from the pylon. She had my pants halfway down my legs.

Then everything was interrupted by a high-pitched screaming.

At first I thought it was Tania, but it was coming from behind her. The screaming brought Tania to her senses. It was Olive, the Nantwiches' deranged daughter. Her head had appeared over the fence and she was screaming and pointing at something. What she pointed at was my semi-erect penis; half-erect from Tania's brutal stimulation; half-flaccid from terror at her ferocious strength.

Olive continued to point and shriek. Then she was joined at the fence by Mrs Nantwich. Filthy buggers,' said the old woman. 'Get on with yer! Filthy buggers!'

A third head appeared. Red-faced Mr Nantwich. He was just laughing. 'Look at that!' he shouted. 'Look at that.'

Tania wasn't laughing. She looked at me with disgust. 'Bastard,' she spat, climbing quickly back into her clothes. 'Bastard.'

I ran after her. 'You can't make anyone do what they don't want to,' I tried. She shrugged me off tearfully. I let her go.

'Filthy buggers!' Mrs Nantwich muttered.

'You can't make anyone!' I screamed at her.

'Look at that!' laughed Joe Nantwich.

Olive was still shrieking. The power lines were still throbbing.

Clive was trying to tell me something, but I wasn't listening. 'It wasn't you,' he was saying. He was pointing up at the pylon. 'It were that.'

I never spoke another word to Tania, and she never came near the pylon again. I was terrified the story would get back to my folks I didn't see why exactly, but I had the feeling I'd reap all the blame. But a few days later something happened which overshadowed the entire incident.

And it happened to Clive.

One afternoon he and I had been sharing a bottle of Woodpecker. He'd been listening again.

'Old man Astley's found out.'

'Eh? How do you know?'

He looked up at the overhead wires. 'She's been on the phone to the Dog and Trumpet.'

He was always reporting what he'd 'heard' on the wires. We all knew he was completely cracked, but it was best to ignore him. I changed the subject. I started regaling him with some nonsense I'd heard about a burglar's fingers bitten clean off by an Alsatian, when Clive took it into his head to start climbing the pylon. I didn't think it was a sensible thing to do but it was pointless saying anything.

'Not a good idea, that.'

'Why?'

Climbing the pylon wasn't easy. The inspection ladder didn't start until a height of nine feet – obviously with schoolboys in mind – but that didn't stop Clive. He lifted the door we used as a bench and leaned it against the struts of one of the pylon's legs. Climbing on the struts, he pulled himself to the top of the door, and standing on its top edge he was able to haul himself up to the inspection ladder. He ascended a few rungs and seemed happy to hang there for awhile. I got bored watching him.

It was late afternoon and the sky had gone a dark, a cobalt shade of blue. I finished off the cider, unzipped my trousers and stuck my dick outside the curtains to empty my bladder. A kind of spasm shot through me before I'd finished, stronger even than those I'd felt before. I ignored it. 'So the burglar,' I was telling Clive, 'knew the key was on a string inside the letter box. So when the owners came home they got into the hallway and found,' I finished pissing, zipped up and turned to complete the story. But my words tailed off, 'two fingers still holding the string . . . '

I looked up the inspection ladder to the top of the pylon. I looked at the grey metal struts. I looked everywhere. Clive had vanished.

'Clive?'

I checked all around. Then I went outside. I thought he might have jumped down, or fallen. He wasn't there. I went back inside. Then I went outside again.

Spots of rain started to appear. I looked up at the wires and they seemed to hum contentedly. I waited for a while until the rain came more heavily, and then I went home.

That night while I lay in bed, I heard the telephone ring. I knew what time it was because I could hear the television signature blaring from the lounge. It was the end of the late night news. Then my mother came upstairs. Had I seen Clive? His mother had phoned. She was worried.

The next day I was interviewed by a policewoman. I explained we were playing under the pylon. I turned my back and he'd disappeared. She made a note and left.

A few days later the police were out like blackberries in September. Half the neighbourhood joined in the fine-toothcomb search of the waste ground and the nearby fields. They found nothing. Not a hair from his head.

While the searches went on, I started to have a recurring nightmare. I'd be back under the pylon, pissing and happily talking away to Clive. Only it wasn't urine coming out, it was painful fat blue and white sparks of electricity. I'd turn to Clive in surprise, who would be descending the inspection ladder wearing fluorescent blue overalls, his face out of view. And his entire body would be rippling with eels of electricity, gold sparks arcing wildly. Then slowly his head would begin to rotate towards me and I'd start screaming; but before I ever got to see his awful face I'd wake up.

We stopped playing under the pylon after that. No one had to say anything, we just stopped going there. I did go back once, to satisfy my own curiosity. The screens had been ripped away in the failed search, but the nettles bashed down by the police were already springing up again.

I looked up into the tower of the pylon, and although there was nothing to see, I felt a terrible sense of dread. Then a face appeared over the Nantwich's' fence. It was Olive. She'd seen me looking.

'Gone,' she said. It was the only word lever heard her say. 'Gone.'

Summer came to an end and we went off to our respective schools. I saw Tania once or twice in her straw boater, but she passed me with her nose in the air. Eventually she married a Tory MP. I often wonder if she's happy.

Inevitably Kev and I stopped hanging around together, but not before there was a murder in the district. The landlord of the Dog and Trumpet was stabbed to death. They never found who did it. Joy moved out of the area when her parents split up. She went to live with her mother.

Joy went on to become a rock and roll singer. A star. Well, not a star exactly, but I did once see her on Top of the Pops. She had a kind of trade mark, turning her back on the cameras to wiggle her bottom. I felt pleased for her that she'd managed to put the habit to good use.

Just occasionally I bump into Kev in this pub or that but we never really know what to say to each other. After a while Kev always says, 'Do you remember the time you hypnotised Tania Brown and . . . ' and I always say 'Yes' before he gets to the end of the story. Then we look at the floor for a while until one of us says, 'Anyway, good to see you, all the best.' It's that *anyway* that gets me.

Clive Mann is never mentioned.

Occasionally I make myself walk past the old place. A new group of kids has started playing there, including Kev Duffy's oldest girl. Yesterday as I passed by that way there were no children around because an Electricity Board operative was servicing the pylon. He was halfway up the inspection ladder, and he wore blue overalls exactly like Clive in my dream. It stopped me with a jolt. I had to stare, even though I could sense the man's irritation at being watched.

Then came that singular, familiar thrum of energy. The maintenance man let his arm drop and turned to face me, challenging me to go away. But I was transfixed. Because it was Clive's face I saw in that man's body. He smiled at me, but tiny white sparks of electricity were leaking from his eyes like tears. Then he made to speak, but all I heard or saw was a fizz of electricity arcing across the metal brace on his teeth. Then he was the maintenance man again, meeting my desolate gaze with an expression of contempt.

I left hurriedly, and I resolved, after all, not to pass by the pylon again.

BIOGRAPHIES

STEVEN J DINES' fiction has appeared in numerous publications including *Black Static*, *Not One of Us, Crimewave, Fireside*, and *Interzone*. Originally from Aberdeen, Scotland, he now lives south of the border in Salisbury with his wife and son. He is currently seeking a publisher for his first novel and putting together his debut collection of short stories. www.stevenjdines.com

HELEN GRANT read classics at St. Hugh's College, Oxford, worked in marketing for ten years before beginning a career as an author. She is the author of the novels *The Vanishing of Katharine Linden*, *The Glass Demon*, *Wish Me Dead* and *Silent Saturday*.

CHRISTOPHER HARMAN lives in Preston in the UK and is a librarian. His stories have appeared in various magazines and in the anthologies *Acquainted with the Night*, *Shades of Darkness*, *Strange Tales*, *Unfit for Eden*, *The Ghosts and Scholars Book of Shadows*, *Rustblind* and *Silverbright* and in the Terror Tales series. *The Heaven Tree and Other Stories* is a collection of his stories published by Sarob Press.

ANDREW HOOK is a much published short story writer with a number of works in print. Books to be published in 2015 will include the novel, *Church of Wire*, a short story collection *Human Maps*, and – as editor – the anthology, *punkPunk!* He co-edits the surreal *Fur-Lined Ghettos* magazine. www.andrew-hook.com.

JANE JAKEMAN is Welsh by birth and education. She lives in Oxford with her Egyptologist husband. Jane is an art historian as well as a novelist, and a reviewer for respected publications such as *The Independent* and *The Times Literary Supplement*. Her novels include the 'Lord Ambrose Mysteries'.

GRAHAM JOYCE was the multi award-winning author of numerous short story collections and novels, which include *The Tooth Fairy*, *Smoking Poppy*, *The Facts of Life*, *The Limits of Enchantment*, *The Silent Land*, *Some Kind of Fairy Tale* and *The Year of the Ladybird*. He won the British Fantasy Award six times, and the World Fantasy Award for 'Best Novel' in 2003 for *The Facts of Life*. He also won the O Henry Award. He died in September 2014.

STEPHEN LAWS is a full-time novelist, born in Newcastle upon Tyne. Married, with three children, he lives and works in his birthplace. The author of 11 novels, numerous short stories, (collected in *The Midnight Man*) columnist, reviewer, film-festival interviewer, pianist and recipient of a number of awards, Stephen Laws recently wrote and starred in the short horror movie *The Secret*. stephen-laws.blogspot.co.uk.

ALISON LITTLEWOOD is the author of *A Cold Season*, *Path of Needles* and *The Unquiet House*, all published by Jo Fletcher Books. Her short stories have been picked for *The Best Horror of the Year* and *The Mammoth Book of Best New Horror* anthologies, as well as *The Best British Fantasy 2013* and *The Mammoth Book of Best British Crime 10*. Alison lives in Yorkshire. www.alisonlittlewood.co.uk.

REBECCA LLOYD writes short stories and the occasional novel. Some of her writing has been recognised in literary contests and has been published in anthologies and magazines. In many of her stories, elements of the fantastical are blended into the mundane – as in real life. She is interested in the inventive ways people deal with what life throws at them. She is the author of the novel, *Hal-*

fling and two collections of short stories, *Mercy* and *The View from Endless Street*.

HELEN MARSHALL is an award-winning Canadian author, editor, and doctor of medieval studies. Her poetry and fiction have been published in *The Chiaroscuro*, *Abyss & Apex*, *Lady Churchill's Rosebud Wristlet*, Tor.com and have been reprinted in several Year's Best anthologies. Her debut collection of short stories *Hair Side, Flesh Side* was named one of the top ten books of 2012 by January Magazine. It won the 2013 British Fantasy Award for Best Newcomer and was short-listed for a 2013 Aurora Award by the Canadian Society of Science Fiction and Fantasy. Her second collection, *Gifts for the One Who Comes After*, was released in September, 2014.

GARY MCMAHON is the author of two 'Thomas Usher' novels, *Pretty Little Dead Things* and *Dead Bad Things* and three 'Concrete Grove' novels – *The Concrete Grove*, *Silent Voices* and *Beyond Here Lies Nothing*. He has edited several anthologies, has had many anthology appearances and has several short stories collections to his name. His latest novella is *The Bones of You*.

ALISON MOORE was born in Manchester in 1971. Her short fiction has been published in *Best British Short Stories* anthologies and broadcast on BBC Radio 4 Extra and is collected in *The Pre-War House and Other Stories*. Her first novel, *The Lighthouse*, was shortlisted for the Man Booker Prize 2012 and the National Book Awards 2012 ('New Writer of the Year'), winning the McKitterick Prize 2013. Her second novel, *He Wants*, was published in 2014.

ROSALIE PARKER writes short stories and screenplays as well as co-running independent publishing firm Tartarus Press with R.B. Russell. Before that she worked as an archaeologist. Rosalie won a World Fantasy Award in 2004 for editing Strange Tales. Her collection, *The Old Knowledge and Other Strange Stories* was published by Swan River Press in 2010, and reprinted in 2012. 'In the Garden' was included in *The Mammoth Book of Best New Horror 21*, and subsequent stories have appeared in *Morpheus Tales Rural Horror Special, Supernatural Tales, Faunus, Terror Tales of London and Yorkshire*.

SARA PASCOE is a comedienne, writer and actress who has been performing stand-up since 2007. She co-wrote Channel 4's *Girl Friday*, has starred in Twenty Twelve and it's spiritual follow-up W1A. Sara is also the winner of the 2014 Chortle Breakthrough Award.

JOHN LLEWELLYN PROBERT won the 2013 British Fantasy Award for his novella *The Nine Deaths of Dr Valentine*. Its sequel, *The Hammer of Dr Valentine*, has just been published (both are available from Spectral Press). He is the author of over a hundred published short stories, six novellas and a novel, *The House That Death Built*. His second novel, *Unnatural Acts*, is forthcoming from the same publisher, Atomic Fez. His first short story collection, *The Faculty of Terror*, won the 2006 Children of the Night award for best work of Gothic Fiction. www.johnlprobert.com.

R.B. RUSSELL is a writer and publisher living in the Yorkshire Dales. He runs Tartarus Press with his partner, Rosalie Parker. He has had three short story collections published: *Putting the Pieces in Place*, Ex Occidente Press, 2009, *Literary Remains*, PS Publishing, 2010, and *Leave Your Sleep*, PS Publishing, 2012. Russell has also had published two novellas, *Bloody Baudelaire*, Ex Occidente Press, 2009 and *The Dark Return of Time*, Swan River Press, 2014. A collected edition, *Ghosts*, was published by Swan River Press in 2012.

MARK SAMUELS (born 1967) is the author of five short story collections: *The White Hands and Other Weird Tales* (Tartarus Press 2003), *Black Altars* (Rainfall Books 2003), *Glyphotech & Oth-*

er Macabre Processes (PS Publishing 2008), *The Man who Collected Machen & Other Stories* (Chomu Press 2011) and *Written In Darkness* (Egaeus Press 2014) as well as the short novel *The Face of Twilight* (PS Publishing 2006). His tales have appeared in *The Mammoth Book of Best New Horror*, *Year's Best Fantasy and Horror*, *The Weird*, and *A Mountain Walks*.

PRIYA SHARMA's work has been published by *Interzone*, *Black Static*, *Alt Hist*, *Albedo One* and Tor.com, among others. She has been reprinted in various Best of anthologies, including *Best British Fantasy* 2014. www.priyasharmafiction.wordpress.com.

REECE SHEARSMITH is an actor and writer. He starred in and co-wrote *The League of Gentlemen*, *Psychoville* and *Inside No 9* all for BBC2. He is equally at home on stage, screen or radio. But he is mostly at home at home.

LISA TUTTLE is a multi-award winning author and editor. Her first novel *Windhaven*, written with George R.R. Martin, was an expansion of the novella *The Storms of Windhaven* and received critical acclaim. As editor, Tuttle's *Skin of the Soul: New Horror Stories by Women* is seen by many as a defining anthology in the genre. Other novels include *Familiar Spirit*, *Mad House and The Silver Bough*. Short story collections include *A Nest of Nightmares*, *Stranger in the House* and *Objects in Dreams*.

SIMON KURT UNSWORTH lives in an old farmhouse in the north of England with his wife Rosie and various children and animals. His stories have been published in critically acclaimed and award-winning anthologies, including six volumes of *The Mammoth Book of Best New Horror* and also *The Very Best of Best New Horror*. His first novel, *The Devil's Detective*, came out in March 2015.

CONRAD WILLIAMS is the author of seven novels, four novellas and over 100 short stories, some of which are collected in *Use Once, then Destroy* and *Born with Teeth*. In addition to his International Horror Guild Award for his novel *The Unblemished*, he is a three-time recipient of the British Fantasy Award, including Best Novel for One. His debut anthology, *Gutshot*, was shortlisted at both the British Fantasy and World Fantasy Awards. He is currently working on a series of crime thrillers for Titan Books, writing the script for a major new video game based on one of his own novels, and editing a new anthology called *Dead Letters*.

EPILOGUE

Mention must go to my daughter Marnie who constantly reminds me that nothing is more important than dropping everything to go and play with her dinosaurs. She's right, of course, and if you're ever invited to a Dinosaur Tea Party, you're a very privileged person indeed.

JM

NEW FICTION FROM SALT

ALSO AVAILABLE FROM SALT

ELIZABETH BAINES
Too Many Magpies (978-1-84471-721-7)
The Birth Machine (978-1-907773-02-0)

LESLEY GLAISTER
Little Egypt (978-1-907773-72-3)

ALISON MOORE
The Lighthouse (978-1-907773-17-4)
The Pre-War House and Other Stories (978-1-907773-50-1)
He Wants (978-1-907773-81-5)

ALICE THOMPSON
Justine (978-1-78463-031-7)
The Falconer (978-1-78463-009-6)
The Existential Detective (978-1-78463-011-9)
Burnt Island (978-1-907773-48-8)

MEIKE ZIERVOGEL
Magda (978-1-907773-40-2)
Clara's Daughter (978-1-907773-79-2)

NEW SHORT STORIES FROM SALT

CARYS DAVIES
The Redemption of Galen Pike (978-1907773-71-6)

STELLA DUFFY
*Everything is Moving, Everything is Joined: The Selected
Stories of Stella Duffy* (978-1907773-05-1)

CATHERINE EISNER
*A Bad Case and Other Adventures
of Disturbed Minds* (978-184471-962-4)

MATTHEW LICHT
Justine, Joe and the Zen Garbageman (978-184471-829-0)

KIRSTY LOGAN
The Rental Heart and Other Fairytales (978-1907773-75-4)

PADRIKA TARRANT
Fates of the Animals (978-1907773-58-7)